Works by Charles Tindell

MAC Detective Agency Mysteries

This Angel Has No Wings

This Angel Doesn't Like Chocolate

This Angel's Halo is Crooked

Non-fiction

Seeing Beyond the Wrinkles:
Stories of Ageless Courage, Humor, and Faith

Study Guide (Seeing Beyond the Wrinkles)

The Enduring Human Spirit:
Thought-provoking Stories of Caring for our Elders

This Angel's Halo is Crooked

A MAC Detective Agency Mystery

Charles Tindell

Charles Tindell

HILLIARD HARRIS

HILLIARD HARRIS

P.O. Box 275
Boonsboro, Maryland 21713-0275

This Angel's Halo is Crooked Copyright © 2007
by Charles Tindell

First Edition-August 2007
ISBN 1-59133-233-8
978-1-59133-233-6

Book Design: S. A. Reilly
Cover Illustration © S. A. Reilly
Manufactured/Printed in the United States of America
2007

Dedicated to: The South Side Writers Group

Acknowledgements

I want to thank all those along my journey who have encouraged me in my writing. Writing is solitary in itself, but what is put on paper is the result of my experiences with others over the years. I have been blessed by their insights on life.

Acknowledgement must be made to those whose reading and critiquing of my manuscript proved invaluable. Special thanks are to be given to Jean K. Mattson whose editing has proven to be a life saver. Much thanks also to Linda Wagner for her contribution to the final editing.

A word of appreciation is also expressed to the members of the South Side Writer's Group that meets weekly at the library in Eagan, MN— Betty Bassett, Catherine Borden, Anita Buck, Libby Cantrell, Yvonne Cecchini, Georgia E. Cook, David Fingerman, Barbara Lee Fisher, Gary Hackenmueller, Carolee Jones, Diana Lundell, Laverne McLaughlin, Lisa Rae McMahon, Carole Mannheim, H.L.Montgomery, Maria Murad, Lucille Sukala.

I wish to express my gratitude to my publisher, Stephanie Reilly, and to my editor-in-chief, Shawn Reilly; their continued guidance and encouragement has been greatly appreciated.

Sincere appreciation is expressed to the staff at Panera Bread of Apple Valley, MN . They have been very supportive and generous in their encouragement in my role as their unofficial resident author.

I wish also to thank my wife, Carol, for her support. Thanks also go to my sons, Scott, Andrew, and Robert.

Finally, appreciation is given to my readers. Thank you for your support and encouragement.

Chapter 1

Howie Cummins leaned back in his chair, propped his feet up on his desk, and pondered the ivory-colored envelope in his hands. He had found the envelope that morning. Someone had slipped it under his door. Handwritten with a flair but giving no clue as to gender, it was addressed to *Howie Cummins, MAC Detective Agency*. He was sure it contained a card, but what kind of card? His birthday wasn't for another three months and since it was only the end of September, he didn't think it was a Halloween card (not that he ever got any), and it was too early for a Christmas card. One of his partners, Mick Brunner, was getting married in the last week of October, but Howie had already received that invitation.

"I'm personally delivering this to you," Mick had said as he placed the wedding invitation on Howie's desk two weeks earlier. "Since you're the best man, I want to make sure you remember to put the date on your calendar. Mary and I don't want to be stood up at the altar by you."

"Don't worry. I won't forget."

"Humor us," Adam, his other partner, had said. "Write it down. I'm going to be in the wedding, too, and I don't want to spend my time looking for you."

Now, slowly moving the envelope back and forth under his nose, Howie closed his eyes and sniffed. He caught a faint whiff of something, but wasn't sure if it was perfume or a men's cologne. Whatever it was, though, it smelled expensive.

"Well, here goes nothing," he muttered as he tore open the envelope and pulled out the card. The front of the card showed a grinning calico cat peering into a doghouse. The plump feline reminded him of the Cheshire cat from *Alice's Adventures in Wonderland*. "Now, what's this all about?" Inside the card was a handwritten greeting. *Just keeping in touch.* "What? No signature?" He looked at the back of the card. Nothing. "What's going on?"

He was reexamining the handwriting on the envelope when the downstairs street entrance door banged shut. He cocked his head toward his office door and listened. The two flights of wooden stairs from the street level to his office door creaked with every footstep. Whoever it was, the person came up slowly as though tired and weary, and had stopped at the first landing to rest.

Howie took one last look at the card, put his feet down, and prepared to meet his visitor. He had just placed the card in the desk drawer when the office door opened and Mr. Gaylord Underwood walked in. The lanky, middle-aged man with deep-set, coal-black eyes, pointed chin, and beak-shaped nose quietly closed the door behind him. Wearing a dark-blue suit, starched white shirt, and a nondescript tie, he looked every bit the part of the funeral director that he was.

As soon as Howie saw Underwood, his thoughts flashed back to March of 1964, over three years ago. March twenty-third, to be exact; the day his father died. Underwood had handled the funeral arrangements, giving advice and offering suggestions. Howie had barely turned twenty-four at the time, and having no other close relatives, depended upon Underwood's experience and guidance. It wasn't the first time that Underwood had come into the picture for the Cummins' family. Years earlier, the man had also handled the funeral for Howie's mother.

"Hello, Mr. Underwood." Howie stood up. The troubled look in his visitor's eyes told him that this wasn't going to be a social call.

"Howard, may I have a word with you?" Underwood asked, his voice more solemn than Howie remembered.

"Certainly." Howie preferred not to be called Howard, but didn't make an issue of it. Underwood had called him by his given name from the first time they met. "Have a seat," he said, gesturing to the least worn of the two brown leather chairs in front of his desk.

"Thank you." Underwood slipped into the chair, and, sitting with perfect posture, placed his hands in his lap. He took in his surroundings. "Wasn't this Doc Anderson's place?"

"Yeah." Howie sat back down. "When he retired I moved in shortly after my father died. This room serves as my office." He motioned to the door behind him. "My living quarters are behind that door; there's a kitchen, bedroom, and bathroom. It's a little tight for space, but it serves my purposes."

"Your father would be proud of you opening up this detective agency." Underwood's voice had such a rich golden quality that he could easily have been a radio announcer. "And I understand that your two friends are working for you. I remember meeting them at your father's funeral." He stroked his chin. "It's Adam and Nick, isn't it?"

"Adam and Mick," Howie corrected, but was still impressed by Underwood's memory. "It's Mick Brunner and Adam Trexler; they're only part-time." He thought about adding that he occasionally needed to work a few hours at the soda fountain downstairs at Kass' Drugstore in order to make ends meet whenever the cash flow dried up, but decided not to go into that for now. "Mick's a junior high school teacher and Adam's going to seminary to become a minister."

2

"Is that right?" Underwood nodded his approval. "Well, I'm pleased to hear that those two are doing well, but I'm not really surprised. I remember them as being such considerate young men. The three of you have been friends for a long time, haven't you?"

"Since shop class in seventh grade."

"That's nice." Underwood cleared his throat. "Howard, I need to engage the services of your agency." The thin smile he had worn since he first entered faded. "We have a…a difficult situation at the funeral home." He cleared his throat again. "A body is missing."

"What? Did I hear you right?" Howie disguised his surprise. He wanted to give Underwood the impression that, with a couple years of experience under his belt, he was a seasoned detective and nothing surprised him anymore. "You did say a body, didn't you?"

"Yes." Underwood appeared more relieved now that the purpose of his visit was known. "Three nights ago the deceased, a young woman, was removed from her casket."

"You mean stolen?"

Underwood's left eye began to twitch. Several moments passed before he acknowledged Howie's descriptive word. "I'm sorry, but I never would have thought that I would ever have to use such a word to describe something that happened at my place of business." He rubbed his eye and the twitching stopped. "Her visitation had been earlier that Tuesday evening from five to eight. The family left around eight-fifteen. We locked up at nine. The next morning when we came in—"

"And what time was that?" Howie asked as he took out a notepad and pen.

"Around eight-thirty. Of course we didn't discover that she was missing right away. The service was scheduled for eleven that morning." If Underwood was upset, his voice didn't reveal it. "When we went in around nine to set up the flower arrangements…" He paused as if what he was about to say was beyond belief. "We discovered to our horror that she was gone."

Howie jotted down the times. "So it had to have happened some time between when you left Tuesday night and when you came in the next morning?"

"Yes, that's right."

"Was there any evidence of a break-in?"

The funeral director shifted in his chair. "The back door was found partially opened, but the detectives said that the lock showed no evidence of being tampered with and that whoever took the body apparently saw no need to make sure the door was shut."

"So you did call the police?"

"Certainly. Right away."

"I don't understand, then." Howie put his pen down. "If the police are involved, why are you coming to me?"

"Because the family is quite upset. They are demanding that I do everything in my power to locate their daughter." His eyes reflected a hint of desperation. "They're not satisfied with only the police being involved."

Howie noted the dark lines beneath Underwood's eyes. He wondered how much sleep the man had lost in the past couple days. "This has to be hard on them...and you," he said, feeling sympathy for him.

"Yes, very hard." Underwood's tone signaled that he appreciated the understanding he was being shown. "I told the family that I would hire a private investigator, and that satisfied them for the time being. I came to you because I know you and you've lived on the North Side all your life. I reasoned that you might have some contacts that the police don't have." He hesitated. When he continued, an undercurrent of pleading could be heard in his tone. "You will take the case, won't you?"

"Of course." Howie still felt a debt of gratitude to Underwood for all the help the man had given him during some difficult times in his own life. "Why don't I get some basic information down?" He picked up his pen again, wondering how Mick and Adam would feel about tracking down a corpse. He would soon find out. His partners were coming over in a half hour to see if there were any new cases for them to work on. Up until just a few minutes ago, there hadn't been. "Why don't you begin by telling me the names of the employees who were working that evening?"

Underwood's eyebrows rose. Although he kept his tone even, he could barely get his words out. "Sur...surely, you're not suggesting that this was an inside job?" He leaned forward, placing his hands on the edge of Howie's desk. "The police already questioned my staff. They didn't say anything to me about them being under suspicion. You don't think that—"

"No, no," Howie said softly, trying to calm Underwood. "It's just that I want to talk to them about that evening to see if they noticed anything unusual." He wouldn't, however, rule the employees out as suspects. If he knew the police, they would also be doing background investigations on the staff as well; that was just standard operating procedure. Detective Jim Davidson, his contact at the North Side's Fifth Precinct informed him just last week that the men in blue had their hands full investigating a series of gas station robberies that had occurred in the past several months. That being the case, the cops probably wouldn't be able to devote many man-hours to this type of investigation. Howie jotted down the two names that Underwood gave him, noting that both of the employees had worked at the funeral home for over ten years. "Why do you think someone would want to steal a body?"

"I wish I had an answer for you on that, but I don't." Underwood settled back in his chair; the nervous twitch in his eye had reappeared. "In all my thirty years in the funeral business, I have witnessed some strange things, but never, never anything like this." His eyes narrowed, causing his forehead to furrow. "This is so unspeakably cruel. The poor family is devastated."

"I'm sure they are."

"Howard, you have no idea." Underwood massaged his forehead. "The grandmother fainted, the poor father had a difficult time comforting his hysterical wife, and the minister and myself had our hands full trying to calm the others in attendance. It was a horrible scene, a nightmare come true."

Howie waited until Underwood collected himself before asking his next question. "Would somebody take the body to sell it for medical research?" He recalled reading in the paper last month about someone donating his body to the University of Minnesota.

"That's not very likely," Underwood replied. "There are too many controls on something like that, and it would be impossible without the proper paperwork."

If he had been inquiring about a missing person who was still alive, Howie could have asked a thousand questions. "This body...ah, how many days will it last before it begins to...ah...you know what I mean?"

"Before it decomposes?"

"Yeah."

"You needn't worry about that. Let me assure you that because of the embalming process, the body will hold up for many months." Underwood's thin smile reappeared for a moment. "We pride ourselves in doing a good job."

Howie flipped a page in his notepad. "What was this woman's name?"

"Carole Anne Phillips. Her first and middle names end with e, and there are two l's in her last name." Underwood waited until Howie finished writing. "She was a lovely girl."

"I'm sure she was. How old was she?"

"Twenty-three." Underwood paused. "She died from a heart condition," he added as though it was necessary to explain why a person so young had died. "Her parents told me that she had been diagnosed with it in her late teens." He sighed. "She was so young and had so much to live for."

"That's tough."

"It most certainly is. I see too much of that in my line of work, however. But then to have this happen..." Underwood slowly shook his head, his eyes revealing disbelief. "I still can't understand how anyone could be so insensitive and cruel to do something like this." He looked toward the window and seemed to gaze at nothing in particular. Nearly a minute ticked off the clock before he turned his attention back to Howie. "Would you like her description?"

"That would be helpful." Howie felt strange writing down a description of a dead person. The missing person cases they had had in the past had always concerned people who were still breathing.

"She has dark brown, shoulder-length hair." Underwood glanced at the arm of his chair. "The color is similar to the color of this chair I'm sitting in." His lips formed a gentle smile. "The beautician we hired to do her hair for the funeral just raved about how wonderful her hair was to work with."

Howie looked up from his notepad. He couldn't imagine having a job fixing the hair of a corpse. "Go on," he said.

"She is a little over five feet. If I remember, her weight is approximately

111 pounds." Underwood's voice became clinical-like, reflecting a professionalism that he obviously took pride in. "Other than a small scar on her right ankle and a birthmark on her left shoulder, there are no other distinguishing physical marks." He allowed himself another half smile. "Her skin was flawless. Carole Anne was a very beautiful young woman. Such a tragedy."

"What was she wearing the night she was taken?"

"A light gray skirt and a baby blue angora sweater. Her mother said her daughter loved that sweater." Underwood squeezed the bridge of his nose as though deep in thought. "And oh, yes. She also was wearing a pearl necklace and matching earrings."

"Were the necklace and earrings valuable?"

"No, only in the sense that they were her mother's at one time. It was more sentimental value than anything else."

Howie asked some closing questions, and discussed and agreed upon his fee. He assured Underwood that he and his partners would get on the case immediately, reminding him that they would be talking to the two employees who had worked that evening. "I'll stay in touch with you," he promised.

"Howard, I can't tell you how much this means to me. Thank you." Underwood got up and walked to the door. Before opening it, he stopped and turned. "Whoever did this has to be some kind of monster." He stood there for a moment, and left, quietly shutting the door behind him.

Chapter 2

After Underwood left, Howie wrote himself a note to check with Jim Davidson, his detective friend from the Fifth Precinct, for any leads the police may have come up with on the stolen body. Davidson had proven to be a useful contact ever since Howie and his partners started the detective agency. Howie had first been introduced to the man through a mutual acquaintance over a year ago. Detective Davidson had liked him right from the start. "Call me JD," he said. "All my friends do." He then slapped Howie on the back and said that if he ever had any questions or needed help, to just give him a call. JD had even made a special trip up to the office to meet Adam and Mick. Although Howie's partners liked the idea of having an eighteen-year police veteran to call upon as a backup, Howie was adamant about not using him in that way.

"And why not?" Adam had asked, his tone confrontational.

"Because we can't be running to the cops every time we get stuck on a case," Howie shot back.

"But why can't we just call on him when we get into a real bind?" Adam said, proving to be the more unyielding of his partners on the issue.

"Look, if we did that, what kind of creditability would we have?" Howie put an edge to his voice so his partners knew that he wasn't going to back down, and would play the *boss* card if necessary. "And on top of that," he continued, "it'd get around the North Side that we're nothing but a bunch of amateurs." He slammed his fist on the desk. "And as long as I run this agency, I'm not going to allow that to happen! Have you got that?"

Adam shifted uncomfortably in his chair. The wall clock above the gray filing cabinet marked time. "Yeah, I've got it," he finally said.

Mick, on the other hand, had understood and had come around more to Howie's way of thinking than Adam.

Although Howie didn't want the men in blue looking over his shoulder, he had no qualms about calling JD and pumping him for information. Since Underwood had already contacted the cops, Howie was counting that JD could provide him with the inside scoop on what, if anything, the police investigation had turned up.

Howie reviewed his notes from his conversation with Underwood and put them aside. He opened his desk drawer and took out the unsigned card

7

he had received. He read the greeting again and sniffed the envelope, wondering who could have sent the card. Before he had time to speculate, the downstairs entrance door banged shut. After listening for a moment, he identified the footsteps to be those of his partners. His ability to nearly always identify people by their footsteps was a source of pride. Of course, he couldn't identify first-time visitors, but even then, he could often tell their gender, approximate weight, and sometimes their mood. In less than a minute, the office door opened and Mick and Adam walked in.

Mick stopped to straighten Howie's movie poster of *The Maltese Falcon* starring Humphrey Bogart. The framed poster, Howie's pride and joy, hung on the wall opposite the office door. It was the first thing he wanted people to see when they came in. Once Mick seemed satisfied that the poster was straight, he joined his partners, taking the chair next to Adam.

Howie noted that Adam continued to be quieter and more moody than usual since their last case. That was understandable. His partner had learned a tough lesson about trusting people with that one. With his brooding personality, bedroom eyes, and a shock of dark-brown hair constantly falling over his forehead, Adam could always try modeling if he decided not to become a minister. His slim athletic body and six-foot frame would only enhance his chances of appearing in magazine ads. Howie, however, hoped he'd stay with the agency since he had the makings of a good detective.

"Well, how does it feel to know that you'll soon be a married man?" Howie asked Mick, knowing that Adam would join in the conversation when he was ready.

"It feels great. You should try it."

"I don't think so." Howie's dating life was next to zero. At four inches shy of six feet, baby-blue eyes, a winsome smile, and fairly trim, he considered himself suitable date material. His lack of social life, however, was more due to his commitment to get the detective agency running on its own. "I still can't figure out why you and Mary wanted a wedding just before the snow flies," he said. "Why don't you guys wait like everybody else and go for a June wedding?"

"Because we love the fall and the winter months," Mick replied in his usual upbeat attitude. It took a lot for him to get down in the dumps. Although their first case a year ago had been especially traumatic for him (more so than the other cases they had worked on since then), he seemed his old self again. "We'll take a few days after the wedding, go up north to Duluth, and then take an extended honeymoon during Christmas break and go skiing." He settled back in his chair, stretched out his long legs, and put his hands behind his head, interlocking his fingers to form a cradle in his black curly hair. At 6' 2" and 235 pounds of solid muscle, he needed space to stretch out. "But enough of my wedding plans," he said. "Have you got anything for us yet?"

"As a matter of fact, I picked up a case just before you guys got here."

"That's great." Mick gave a thumbs-up to Adam.

"I just hope this one is a little more normal than what we've had in the past," Adam said, his eyes expressing curiosity.

Mick rested his hands in his lap. "That goes double for me. Do you remember what you told us when you first asked us to come in with you?" he asked Howie.

"Not exactly."

"That detective work would add some excitement to our otherwise dull and boring lives." Mick raised his bushy eyebrows as he stole a sideward glance at Adam. "The past couple of cases have added enough excitement to last me a lifetime." He acknowledged Adam's nod with one of his own. "I think we're both ready for something nice and ordinary, like a missing persons case. We should be able to handle that with no problem."

"You're in luck, then," Howie replied. "Because that's exactly what we have."

"Hey, what do you know? I'm a psychic." Mick gave Adam a playful punch. He was always trying to get his partner to lighten up. "So who's our client?"

"Gaylord Underwood."

"What!" Adam's eyes became alert. "You mean of Underwood Funeral Home up on Broadway and Lyndale?"

Howie nodded and watched as his partners exchanged glances.

"So what's up with Mr. Underwood?" Mick asked, his voice hedging on suspicion.

"Like I said, it's a case of finding a missing person."

"Who's missing?" Adam asked. "Somebody in his family?"

Mick straightened in his chair and folded his arms across his barrel chest. "This isn't a kidnapping, is it?"

"Not technically," Howie replied. Their past couple of cases involved kidnappings that he and his partners would just as soon forget. "It's one of his...ah, clients."

"A client?" Adam said. "What are you talk—" His eyes flashed with recognition. "Are you implying what I think you're implying?" When Howie nodded, Adam slumped back in his chair.

Mick's face registered puzzlement as he glanced from Adam to Howie. "I might be a little dense, but what are you guys talking about?"

"The body of a young woman is missing from the Underwood Funeral Home," Howie said. "It was stolen."

"You're kidding!" Mick exclaimed, his eyes registering disbelief.

"I wish I was. According to Underwood, the deceased was taken some time between nine Tuesday evening and nine the following morning."

"Are the police involved?" Adam asked.

"They are, but Underwood is hiring us because the family is insisting that he do everything he can to get their daughter back." Howie ran his hand through his thick reddish-blonde hair. "I know it's a weird case, but I couldn't say no to the guy."

"You did the right thing as far as I'm concerned," Adam said.

"I'm with Adam," Mick said. "All I can think of is that young woman's poor family. What a crummy thing to deal with."

"So how do you suggest we go about this?" Adam asked.

"For now, just keep our ears open," Howie replied. "You know how talk gets around on Broadway. Maybe we'll hear something that might connect with the case." He thought about Adam's mother. As a waitress at Andy's, a small sandwich shop on Broadway, she often got the inside scoop on everything going on in the North Side. "Why don't you talk to your mom? She may pick up something from one of her customers."

"Yeah, that's a good idea," Mick said. "I bet something like this would be a hot topic of conversation."

Howie checked the wall clock. "Sorry guys, but I have to go to work in fifteen minutes. Tomorrow's Saturday; what do you say we meet in the morning around nine?"

Once his partners had left, Howie straightened out the papers on his desk, took one last look at the unsigned card he had received, and headed downstairs to Kass' Drugstore. He had promised Kass he would work at the soda fountain until nine. After work, he would come back to his office and jot some notes down for a plan of action as to how they would handle the investigation. The first thing they would do would be to interview the two employees who worked that evening, and then talk to the Phillips' family. The case certainly was bizarre and he had an uneasy feeling about it, but he couldn't put his finger on why.

Chapter 3

Howie put aside his uneasy feeling about the Underwood case and channeled his energies into waiting on a steady flow of customers at the soda fountain at the drugstore. As usual, Friday night was busy; teenagers, older couples, and families with young kids all decided it was a good time to stop and have a special treat. The stream of customers finally tapered off and he could at last take a breather after serving countless numbers of sundaes, malts, phosphates, double-decker cones, and banana splits. He didn't mind the job and the extra cash came in handy, but working behind a soda fountain (even if it was only part-time) didn't fit in with his image of being a detective.

"That was quite a rush you had," Kass said, walking up to Howie after having spent most of the evening working the cash register at the front of the store. Hershel Kass, in his mid-fifties, reminded Howie of a beardless Santa Claus. With a ruddy complexion, rotund figure, and infectious laugh, Kass made others feel joyful just to be in his presence. Kass often kidded that, with his bald top encircled by a fringe of thinning brown hair, he could also pass for a monk, albeit a Jewish one. For nearly thirty years he had been doing business on the corner of Third and Broadway. He owned the building that housed the drugstore and the apartment above it where Howie lived. He had been a friend to Howie, Mick, and Adam ever since they had started coming into his establishment as young kids, barely into grade school. "I bet you're tired," he said to Howie.

"A little." Howie leaned against the counter. He glanced at the stack of unwashed dishes sitting next to the sink, hoping that they would magically disappear.

"Don't worry about them," Kass said. "Why don't you take a break and have something to drink. I'll help you do the dishes later."

"I'm not going to argue with you on that." Howie walked around the counter and plopped down on a stool, relieved that the other five stools were empty. He needed a break from dealing with customers.

Kass wiped the counter in front of his tired helper with a towel he had gotten from under the sink. "So, what will you have…a malt, or how about one of my banana splits?"

"A cup of coffee will do just fine, and make sure it's good and strong."

"Coming right up."

Kass had proven to be a good friend to Howie over the years. Howie was especially grateful for what he had done for him when Howie's father died. He and his father had lived in a duplex a couple blocks off Broadway on Emerson Avenue for nearly thirteen years. When Kass learned that Howie needed to move after his father died because he couldn't afford the rent on his own, he sent word through Mick that the two of them should have a little talk.

"Doc Anderson is retiring from his dental practice next month," Kass had said. Anderson's office had been above the drugstore for nearly as long as Kass had been there. "What do you say about me remodeling the space into an apartment for you?"

"That would be great, but I'm not sure if I could afford it. How much are you asking?"

"Don't worry about the rent," Kass had replied, waving off any further inquires about such a minor detail when it came to friendship. "We'll work something out." His eyes twinkled as he broke into a broad smile. "I know," he announced as if the idea had just popped into his head. "You can work for me at the soda fountain a certain number of hours every month and that will help square things."

Later, when Howie revealed that he was planning to start a detective agency, Kass was thrilled. He told Howie that when he and Mick and Adam become famous detectives, he would put their pictures on the wall over the hot fudge dispenser with a sign stating that they had their beginning above his drugstore. "You'll make my place famous."

Howie was staring at that spot on the wall where their pictures would be hung when Kass came back with a cup of steaming coffee.

"Here you go," Kass said as he set the cup of coffee on the counter in front of Howie. "Are you sure you don't want something to eat?"

Howie shook his head; sitting and just relaxing were enough for the moment. The clanging of the cowbell over the entrance door, however, drew his and Kass' attention to the front of the store as Squirrel, a well-known local street bookie, scurried in. Squirrel (nobody knew his given name) scanned the area with pea-size black eyes that darted back and forth. With front teeth too large for his lips to conceal and dark-brown unruly hair always in need of grooming, people joked about him living in a tree and gathering nuts in the fall. Squirrel glanced around, spotted Howie and Kass, and headed toward them. Rapid side-to-side jerking movements of his head made him appear as if he expected something or someone to jump out from behind one of the displays counters.

"Hi, there," Squirrel said to Howie while acknowledging Kass with a nod. "I've been looking for you. You weren't in your office so I came here. You're a hard guy to track down. Hey, you look tired. Too many cases, huh? Chasing too many dames? What have you—?"

"Whoa!" Howie said. "Slow down, will you?" Squirrel's rapid-fire delivery along with a high-pitched voice that sounded like a squeaky wagon wheel made him difficult to understand, let alone listen to. "Don't talk so fast. You're giving me a headache."

"Okay, okay," Squirrel said. "Like I was saying..." His nose began to twitch. "You're a hard guy to track down." The squeaky wagon wheel picked up speed again. "But now that I found you, we need to talk. It's important."

"I'll leave you two alone," Kass said.

"Oh, no," Squirrel said. "You don't have to do that. I ain't got no secrets from you." He hopped on the stool next to Howie. Barely over five feet tall and with his feet dangling high above the floor, he looked like a little kid. "Hey, Kass, I'll lay you three-to-one odds that I can tell you how many banana splits, give or take two, were served here this evening."

Howie offered Kass a knowing smile. Squirrel had the reputation of betting on anything and everything; the fact that he usually won only added to his growing legend. "Are you going to take him on?" Howie asked, noting that Squirrel had glanced at the dirty ice cream dishes sitting by the sink, and no doubt had counted the ones used for banana splits.

"Not me," Kass said. "I've learned my lesson." His eyebrows knitted together as he shook his finger at Squirrel. "The last time we bet, you hoodwinked me."

"How did he do that?" Howie asked.

"He bet me that he could eat three banana splits in under five minutes." An incredulous look appeared on Kass' face as if he still couldn't believe that a guy as skinny as Squirrel could accomplish such a feat. "And he did! I don't know where he put it all."

"It was a piece of cake," Squirrel replied, nonchalantly examining his fingernails. "But Kass, this bet's more in your favor." He blew on his nails a couple of times and buffed them on the front of his checkered sport coat. "I'll even give you four-to-one odds."

Kass glanced at Howie and then back at Squirrel. He opened his mouth, paused, and wagged his finger at the little guy. "No, no...not even at ten-to-one."

"Suit yourself. You had your chance." Squirrel buffed his nails on his jacket again. "But I tell you what I'll do because I'm such a nice guy." He sucked air between his teeth a couple of times. "I'll even be willing to go as high as five-to-one. What do you say? A bet?" Hearing no response, he shrugged and turned his attention to Howie. "I suppose you're wondering why I've looked you up."

Howie took a sip of coffee. "Yeah, it crossed my mind."

"Well, I didn't come in for a malt." Squirrel glanced at Kass. "Sorry, no offense." He turned his attention back to Howie. "You're still a detective, ain't you? You're for hire, ain't you?"

"Yeah. Why?"

"I need your services."

Howie and Kass exchanged puzzled looks. Howie wasn't about to commit to Squirrel until he heard the guy out, and this wasn't the time nor place to do that. Besides, he wanted some time to think through whether he even wanted a bookie for a client. "Come up to my office in an hour and we'll discuss it there."

"Sure enough, sounds cool to me." Squirrel hopped off the stool and winked at Kass. "One last chance to take my dough. Five-to-one odds ain't bad, and I'm giving you them because you're my friend."

"Not today," Kass said.

"Okay, it's your loss. I'll see you in an hour," Squirrel said to Howie and then scampered for the door.

Squirrel's offer to Kass amused Howie. It was well known from one end of Broadway to the other that the guy wouldn't give his own mother five-to-one odds unless he knew he had a sure winner.

"That character will bet on anything," Kass said, his eyes twinkling with amusement. "What do you think he wants to hire you for?"

"I don't know." Howie watched Squirrel go out the front door. "But I'll lay you ten-to-one that it won't be anything routine."

Chapter 4

Shortly after nine Howie finished his duties at the soda fountain, said good night to Kass, and went back to his apartment. He had just walked into the kitchen to look for something to eat when he heard his office door open.

"Anybody home?" a man yelled in a squeaky voice.

"Come on in, Squirrel! I'll be with you in a minute. I'm out in the kitchen." Howie poured himself a cup of coffee; he would eat later. "Do you want some coffee?"

"Naw, that stuff will kill you! Have you got a beer?"

"Don't have any in stock right now."

Squirrel was standing in front of the movie poster when Howie walked back into his office. "I always liked Bogart in that flick," Squirrel said. He pointed to the poster. "That's pretty slick. Where did you get it?"

"From the theater down the street." Howie set his coffee cup on his desk and sat down. "The manager owed me a favor." He watched with amusement how Squirrel's nose twitched as he looked over the rest of the office. Two leather chairs, a hand-me-down couch, a four drawer file (dented), a mahogany desk that needed refinishing, and a brass floor-standing lamp with only two of the three light sockets working wasn't much to check out.

"So this is what a detective's office looks like," Squirrel said. "It ain't bad, but the place could stand some new furniture."

"Why don't you have a chair and we'll get down to business," Howie said. Kass had shared the various rumors about Squirrel's background: that he was abandoned by his parents and grew up hustling on the streets; that his parents are wealthy and have an estate on Lake Minnetonka; that his mother is a hooker and his father is serving a life sentence at Stillwater State Prison. Howie had even heard that Squirrel spent a couple of years in a school for delinquent teenagers in southern Minnesota, and that at age thirteen, he hotwired and stole his first car. The word around Broadway was that although he never admitted to any of these stories, neither did he deny them. Apparently he liked the reputation the rumors brought him.

"Not bad," Squirrel said as he rubbed the arm of the chair he sat in. "It's a little worn, but it's real leather and not that imitation stuff." His eyes darted back and forth, taking in as much as he could. "I bet this was a dentist office before you took it over." He stroked his chin. "In fact, I'm so sure that it was I'll give you three-to-one odds that I'm right. Is it a bet?"

Howie shook his head, picked up his coffee and took a sip.

"Listen, if I lose, I'll just chalk it up to experience and add it to your fee." Squirrel leaned forward to make his pitch. "I'd give you even better odds, but I've got to be honest and tell you that I'm not so sure on this one." His nose twitched as he sucked air through his teeth. "Maybe I should just give you two-to-one odds."

"I don't think so."

"Why not?" Squirrel sounded offended, but Howie sensed it was a ploy. "The bet's in your favor," the little guy argued. "I've never been up here before."

"I'll tell you why I won't take that bet," Howie said. "For one thing, you've been around the North Side long enough to know that Doc Anderson had his practice here." Squirrel started to protest, but Howie cut him off. "And the second thing is that I saw you give my chair the once over. You and I both know that it's a converted dentist chair. Now, it doesn't take much of a brain to put two and two together." Squirrel's sheepish smile told Howie that he had the guy dead-to-rights. "Now, why don't we quit playing games and you just tell me what you're here for?"

Squirrel leaned back in his chair and scratched the side of his face in a slow deliberate motion. "Okay. No more games. It's about my partner, Newt."

"Newt?" Howie took out his notepad. "Does this Newt have a last name?"

"Aldrich. His first name is Newton, but I call him Newt. It's a nickname." Squirrel's button- nose wrinkled. "I know it's different, but he's odd that way."

"So, what about...Newt?"

"He ain't been in his apartment for the past three days, or if he's there, he ain't answering the door or picking up the phone. I tell you, he ain't his normal self; the guy's been acting strange for a couple of weeks."

"What do you mean *strange*?"

"Secretive like." Squirrel became very animated, gesturing with his hands as he talked. "In the past he's always shared everything with me; broads he's dated, the kinds of things he's involved in when he ain't with me. He even told me about what the fortune-teller predicted when she read the tea leaves in his cup. We're partners. We share everything."

"I'm not sure what this has to do with hiring me. If he's acting strange, get him to go see a shrink...or maybe back to that fortune-teller."

"Naw, it's more than that." Squirrel shifted in his chair. "Newt's got some money—my money." He paused, got up, walked over to the door and opened it.

"Are you expecting somebody?" Howie asked.

"Just checking to make sure nobody's out there. You can't be too careful, you know." Squirrel sat back down. "As I was saying...Newt's got my

16

dough…and I'm worried about him."

"You're worried about your partner?" Howie suppressed a smirk. "You don't exactly look too overcome by grief."

"Oh, yeah?" Squirrel thrust his chin out once and then a second time. "Well, I'm the type of guy that keeps his emotions bottled up."

"Don't you know that can kill you faster than coffee?"

Squirrel shrugged. "So we ain't going to live forever. Besides, not showing emotions comes in handy when you're drawing to an inside straight and you ace your card. Do you know what I mean?"

"Do you think your partner is in some kind of danger because of all that money?" Howie asked and then followed up when Squirrel hesitated. "Or are you worried that Newt took a hike and left you high and dry?"

"Are you kidding? He'd never do that to me." Squirrel raked his hand through his hair a couple of times; if he was trying to comb his bush into submission, it didn't work. "Whatever he's involved in is making him weird and I'm worried."

"About your money?"

Squirrel's eyes narrowed as he sucked air through his teeth again. "So I'm human. I care about my dough." He leaned forward. "I care about Newt, too. He's a good guy. We work well together. That's why I want you to find him."

Howie took a sip of coffee, set his cup aside, and drummed his fingers on his desk. "Okay…why don't I get some more information down?"

"So you're taking the case?"

"Yeah." Howie figured that this would be better than looking for a corpse.

Chapter 5

The two men struggled to carry the lifeless body of the young woman down the embankment toward the river; a couple of times they almost dropped her as they navigated the slippery slope.

"She's heavier than she looks," said the one who had hold of her shoulders. Even though the night was cool, sweat poured down his face, stinging his eyes.

The other man, older only by a few years, offered a thin smile. He was well aware that his helper was nervous about doing this, and that pleased him. "Haven't you ever heard of the expression 'dead weight'?"

"Yeah, I...I've heard of it. But how come she's stiff as a board?"

"It's quite simple. A body becomes rigid once it's embalmed."

"How come you know all this stuff?"

"I've had the good fortune of dealing with bodies before and after they had been embalmed." The man took pleasure in seeing the shocked look in the eyes of his helper. When you keep a person in fear, it's easier to control them, he thought.

"Where are we going with her?"

"Under the bridge."

"Why...why there?"

"Be patient. You'll soon find out."

In a few minutes they reached their destination. They laid a blanket out and positioned the unclothed body upon it. The younger man watched as the other man took from his jacket pocket what looked like a black eyeglass case.

"What's that?"

The man opened the case and removed what appeared to be a knife. "This is my prize possession." He held it up. "It's a scalpel. Do you like the pearl handle?"

"Sure, but wha...what are you going to do with that?"

The man offered a twisted smile, and knelt down besides the body. As soon as the younger man realized what was going to be done, he turned aside and tried to concentrate on the hum of the traffic on the bridge above them.

Chapter 6

"Did I hear you right?" Mick asked after he finished his fourth piece of toast, washing it down with what remained of his second glass of milk. Adam, sitting across from him at the table in Howie's kitchen, listened with interest as Mick continued to press the issue. "You did say we now have two cases, didn't you?"

Howie nodded, took a sip of coffee, and leaned against the refrigerator. He had hoped by treating his partners to a Saturday morning breakfast of toast and scrambled eggs that they would be more receptive to the second client he had agreed to take on. The fact that Squirrel's only apparent means of support came from being a bookie might pose more of an ethical dilemma for his partners than himself. Adam, studying to be a minister, would take issue with representing someone who's involved in gambling, and possibly crooked gambling at that. "So I manipulate the odds a little," Squirrel pointed out when Howie had raised that question in anticipation of his partner's objections. "But I don't cheat unless they've got it coming!" Mick, on the other hand, might object to taking Squirrel's case on for a different reason. As a teacher, Mick would argue that having a client of such questionable character could send the wrong signal to his junior high students if they ever found out about it.

If both of his partners objected to their new client, however, Howie had already decided that he would take the case himself. He had ethics, but also had bills to pay. Besides, he found Squirrel to be a likeable kind of rascal.

Adam set his coffee cup down and picked up where Mick had left off. "So, what's this other case all about?"

"There's a client who wants us to find his partner. He—"

"Hold on just a minute," Mick said. "I've got just one little question before you go any further." He glanced over at Adam and winked. "Is this missing partner alive or are we looking for another corpse?"

"No, this person is still breathing." Howie took another sip of his coffee and waited for the inevitable question. Mick asked it.

"So, who's this new client? Anybody we know?"

"Yeah, I think both of you have crossed paths with him." Mick and Adam exchanged glances. "The guy's from the North Side," Howie continued. He walked over and set his coffee cup down on the counter. "It's

Squirrel," he said as he leaned against the counter, arms folded across his chest.

"What!" Adam cried. "That guy's a known bookie."

"Wait a minute," Howie said, irritated at Adam's sometimes self-righteous attitude.

"Wait a minute, nothing!" Adam shot back. "That guy's hustled from one end of Broadway to the other end." He looked at Mick for support. "He even pitches nickels with the shoeshine kids on the street."

"Squirrel isn't going to take us into any shady areas with this case of his, is he?" Mick gently asked in an obvious effort to ease the tension between Howie and Adam, a role he often played.

Adam piped up. "If you ask me, Squirrel's whole life is lived in the shade."

"Hey, Preacher," Mick said, keeping his tone cordial, "you're getting good at painting word pictures."

"Look, Mick! Don't try to soft soap me!"

"I was just trying—"

"I know what you were trying!"

"Let's all settle down," Howie said quietly but in a tone that signaled he had enough. He took his time to pour himself a fresh cup of coffee and then sat down at the table, wondering how he could present Squirrel in a more favorable light. "Let's consider the facts here." He took the saltshaker and placed it in front of his partners. "Number one. Squirrel's partner, a guy by the name of Newt Aldrich, hasn't been seen for three days. And number two…" He slid the pepper shaker next to the salt. "According to Squirrel, Newt's got a great deal of money that belongs to him."

"Is this money he's won in gambling?" Mick asked.

"I didn't ask, but the point is, the guy's missing and Squirrel's worried about him."

Adam rolled his eyes. "Give me a break. If I know Squirrel, he's more concerned about getting his money back than his partner."

Howie shrugged. "I won't argue with you on that, but we need to approach this in a business manner. Think of him as a client who has hired us to find his partner—that's pretty cut and dried. He's not asking us to do anything illegal. And if we find out anything different, we'll drop the case."

"Is that a promise?" Adam asked.

"Hey, just trust me, will you?" Howie saw what he thought to be a softening in Adam's eyes, and he hoped that meant that his partner was coming around to see his point of view. Adam could come across as obstinate in maintaining ethical standards as a detective, but he had a compassion for the plight of people and would compromise up to a certain point. His compassion was one of the strengths he would bring to his future work as a minister. By the same token, however, that same strength could be a detriment in detective work. Mick also cared for people, especially kids, but at this moment, he looked as if he needed further convincing to extend that caring to their new client. "Even a guy like Squirrel deserves the benefit of a doubt, doesn't he?" Howie argued. "His partner could be in real trouble. Who knows what could have happened to him carrying around all that dough? We're in the business of helping people, aren't we?"

"I have to admit that he's got a point there," Adam said.

Mick glanced at Adam and then directed his words to Howie. "Okay, but the first hint that we're slipping into the shade, I'm out of it. I don't want the kids in my classes to get the wrong impression."

"That goes for me, also," Adam said. "Any sign that we're crossing the line, you can count me out."

"I understand." Howie felt better about his partners' agreeing to take on the case, but decided to build one further layer of support for Squirrel. "Listen, I know about the pitching for money with the kids, but I also heard that when one of kid's fathers got laid off work just before Christmas last year, the next day a basket of food was found on their doorstep with an envelope containing a hundred bucks."

"And you're saying it was from Squirrel?" Adam asked in a voice teeming with skepticism.

"That's what I heard, but if you ask him, he'll deny it."

Mick's face became a question mark. "Why would he do that?"

"A reliable source told me Squirrel thinks that such a do-good story like that could ruin his reputation around Broadway."

"That's a laugh," Mick said.

"Look at it this way, then." Howie locked eyes with Mick. "With you getting married next month, any extra money coming in would help, wouldn't it?"

Mick's gaze turned inward for a moment. "Okay, you've made your point, but as long as it's clean money."

"Thanks. I knew I could depend on you." Howie paused. "Say, doesn't Mary have a wedding shower coming up on Tuesday?"

"Yeah. Why?"

"I was just curious to know how the plans are coming for that." He offered a winsome smile. "Do they still play that stupid game where they stand on a chair and drop clothespins into a milk bottle?"

Mick shook his finger at Howie. "You're not fooling me. I know you're changing the subject. You don't have to worry. I said I'd go along on this case." He picked up his fork and playfully pointed it at his boss. "But don't make Squirrel out to be some kind of angel." He waited as if expecting a reply. When none came, he leaned back in his chair and offered a half smile. "And yeah, they still play that clothespin game. And no, I'm not going to be there during the shower."

"How come?" Adam asked.

"Mary said I didn't have to. She just wants me to make an appearance at the end." Mick picked up the salt-and-pepper shakers and handed them to Howie. "So now that we got that settled, why don't you just tell us how you want to handle these two cases?"

"Okay, here's what I've got figured out." Howie took out his notepad and opened it. "Mick, you interview the two employees who were on duty that night at the funeral home. Underwood told me that both of them are working this weekend. So you can see them today or tomorrow." He wrote down the information, tore out the page, and handed it to Mick. "Here are their names."

Mick looked over what Howie had written and slipped the paper in his shirt pocket. "I'll talk to them this afternoon."

"Good." Howie turned to Adam. "Would you go and talk to the family of Carole Anne Phillips?"

"Sure thing."

"And what are you going to do?" Mick asked.

"A couple of things," Howie said. "I'm going to contact JD and see if he can tell me anything about the Phillips' case. After that, I'm going down to a bar on Hennepin Avenue." His partners gave him a quizzical look. "Squirrel told me that his partner has been known to frequent this place," he explained. "Who knows? Maybe I'll get lucky and find the guy having a beer." When he reached for his cup of coffee, he knocked over the saltshaker.

"Oh, oh, now you've done it," Mick said. "You better take some salt and throw it over your shoulder or else we'll have bad luck on these cases."

Howie picked up his cup of coffee, took a sip, and gave his partners a smug smile. "I don't believe in superstitions."

Chapter 7

Mick was thankful that there were only a couple of cars at the Underwood Funeral Home as he pulled into its parking lot. The nearly empty lot meant he wouldn't have to wait until a service or visitation was over. And since it was only a few minutes after four, it would be too early for the staff to be on a supper break. Perfect timing. Howie had given him the names of Leon Sparks and Herb Whitehead to interview.

"Do them separately," Howie had advised. "That way you'll be able to concentrate more on their body language."

"I understand," Mick said, knowing that it was his boss' conviction that you could learn as much or more from body language than from whatever answers you were getting to your questions.

After parking the car, Mick sat for a moment and went over the list of questions he wanted to ask. For sure, he wanted to know if anything out of the ordinary happened that evening. He was also curious about their backgrounds and what each thought of the other. Although Howie didn't bring it up, he might even ask what they thought of their boss, Gaylord Underwood. Satisfied with the questions, he got out and headed toward the front entrance.

The funeral home had been exactly that at one time—a home. When Underwood bought the property, he renovated the large two-story structure into a funeral parlor rather than tearing the house down and starting over again. His plan was to have a place that felt comfortable and gave a feeling of personal warmth when you walked into it. It certainly was that. Mick had experienced that reaction when his grandfather's funeral was held at the place several years ago. The memories of that day were vividly brought back as he opened the door and walked into the parlor/reception area. With matching powder blue couches and lounge chairs, light oak end tables, and burnished brass floor-standing lamps with shades matching the color of the end tables, the ambiance was more of a large living room. From the ten-foot ceilings hung crystal chandeliers that added a touch of elegance to the space. The sweet fragrance of flowers permeated the room as a piano rendition of "Amazing Grace" quietly played in the background.

"Hello, may I help you?"

The deep somber voice came from Mick's right. When he turned, a slightly-built man stood no farther than five feet away. The man looked as though he was wearing an ill-fitted hairpiece; either that or he needed to find a different barber. He appeared to be in his early forties. His dark suit looked in need of a pressing. He offered Mick an anemic smile, but didn't extend his hand.

"I'm looking for Leon Sparks and Herb Whitehead," Mick said.

"I'm Leon Sparks," the man replied. "Herb's out on a call. If you've come for the Carlson visitation, the family isn't scheduled to be here until five."

"That's not why I'm here. My name is Mick Brunner and I work for the MAC Detective Agency on Third and Broadway." Giving the location of the office had been Howie's advice. He always said that when you're interviewing people on the North Side, always tell them where the office is located. "They tend to open up more when they know you're from the area," he added.

"I'd like to ask some questions about the missing body of the young woman, a Miss Carole Anne Phillips," Mick said.

Leon's smile disappeared. "Oh, yes, what a dreadful thing. Why don't you come into the office? We can talk in there."

The office, adjacent to the reception area, was nicely furnished with an oak desk, a couple of high-back chairs, and a small couch tucked away in the corner. Leon invited Mick to have a seat and then took his place behind the desk. He moved a stack of manila folders to one side. "There's getting to be more and more paperwork in this business," he lamented. He leaned forward, interlaced his fingers, and rested his hands on the desk. "Mr. Underwood mentioned that someone from your agency would be talking to us. He said that we should give our full cooperation. I'm certainly ready to do that."

"I appreciate that. Now, Mr. Sparks, if I may ask you some questions."

"Call me Leon, please."

"Sure enough." Mick crossed his legs and spoke in a relaxed tone of voice intended to put the man as ease. "Leon, can you tell me anything about the night of the Phillips' visitation? Did anything seem out of the ordinary?"

"I'm not sure I understand."

"Did anyone spend an unusual amount of time viewing the body? Or did you notice anyone walking around the place, being in any areas they shouldn't be?"

"You mean like casing the place?"

"Exactly."

"Not that I recall." Leon rubbed the side of his cheek. "And as far as anyone spending a lot of time at the casket, the father and mother did, as well as some of the other relatives, but I wouldn't say that was unusual. Carole Anne was the only daughter, and her parents and the rest of the family were still in shock. I'm sure you understand."

"Were you there during that entire evening?"

"Oh, yes. We have to be present. Mr. Underwood wouldn't have it any other way." The smile reappeared on Leon's face.

While Mick acknowledged Leon's smile with an understanding nod, he perceived the smile as more professional than genuine.

"We're here to meet the needs of the family in any way possible," Leon said in a tone that seemed more genuine than his smile.

If Leon was hiding anything, his body language wasn't giving any indication, and he appeared very much at ease. "Then I may assume you were here when the place was locked up?" Mick asked.

"Oh, most certainly."

"Who was the last one to leave the building?"

"The three of us left together. Mr. Underwood closed up the office. I did one last check in the viewing room and made sure that the side door was locked. Herb made sure the front and back doors were secured."

"How long have you and Herb worked together?"

A hint of defensiveness flickered in Leon's eyes. "Nearly ten years."

"Is he pretty reliable?" As soon as Mick asked the question, Leon shifted slightly in his chair momentarily breaking eye contact.

"Is this to be held in confidence?" Leon asked, glancing at the closed office door. "I know that you'll probably share this with your partners, but nobody else, right?"

"Of course."

Leon moved his tongue over his bottom lip. "I want you to understand that I like Herb. We've always worked well together. When I first came here, he showed me the ropes. He answered all my questions, and even took me out to lunch. He's such a kind—"

"Look, Leon." Mick intentionally kept his voice calm, but he made sure that his tone signaled that he wasn't about to waste any more time. "I'm sure he's a nice guy and all that, but just get to the point."

"A couple years back he had kind of a problem."

"And what kind would that be?"

Leon's tongue moved over his lip again and this time his eyes flickered before he spoke. "Herb liked his liquor. He said it relaxed him and got his mind off work." He leaned forward, his eyes searched for understanding. "You know that working with grieving families all the time can be very stressful." He paused as if waiting for validation.

"Go on."

"Anyway, he started showing up at work every now and then with alcohol on his breath. He chewed gum, but I could still smell the liquor." Leon's tongue continued to stroke his lower lip. "Even though I knew about it I didn't tell Underwood. I figured that Herb could still do his job. As far as I was concerned, that was all that mattered. Besides, like I told you, I liked the guy."

"You said a couple of years ago he had the problem. Do you mean to tell me that he's on the wagon now?" Mick waited, but Leon didn't answer, nor was he making eye contact. It was time to stop playing Mr. Nice Detective.

25

"I asked you a question," he said in a tone that he often used when dealing with an uncooperative student in his classroom. "I'd like an answer."

"You won't tell Mr. Underwood, will you?"

"I told you already, this stays with me and my partners."

For several moments, it seemed like Leon wasn't going to say anything. When he did speak, though, the words came rushing out. "Herb's been hitting the bottle again. I think he's got money problems."

"What kind of money problems?"

"He likes to play poker, high stakes." Leon glanced at the door and lowered his voice. "One of the guys I know who plays cards with him tells me that Herb's not a very good card player; he doesn't know when to quit." His eyes widened and he put his hand to his mouth. "Oh, my god! You don't think he had something to do with the missing body, do you? Just because the guy takes a few drinks doesn't mean—"

"At this point, I'm just asking questions," Mick said. "Nobody's a suspect," he added, knowing that as soon as he reported this to his partners, Howie would put Herb Whitehead at the top of the list of suspects. "When do you think Herb will be back?"

"I'm not sure. Sometimes these calls take time. The coroner has to come, and the family usually has a lot of questions. But when he does come back, he's going to have his hands full helping me with a visitation. We're expecting a couple hundred people coming in and out of here in the next three or four hours."

Mick glanced at the wall clock behind Leon. It was nearly four-thirty, just enough time to go home and shower. He and Mary were having dinner at six; she wanted to talk with him about her wedding shower on Tuesday. "I'll stop and talk to him tomorrow afternoon," he said. "He's working tomorrow, isn't he?"

"Yes, should I tell him you're coming?"

"No." Mick didn't want to give Whitehead the chance to suddenly leave town. "I'll stop by unannounced. It's better that way. I wouldn't want him to get nervous."

"You're not going to tell him that I told you about his drinking, are you?" The apprehension and anxiety in Leon's voice matched what his eyes broadcasted. "I promised him I wouldn't tell anybody."

After Mick assured Leon he wouldn't share the contents of their conversation with anyone other than his partners, he asked a few more questions, gave him a business card, and got up to leave. "If you think of anything else about Herb or that night, give us a call. I'll be in touch with you."

As Mick walked to his car, he was pretty sure that they might have gotten their man. The question would be motive. Why would a person do something like that? The thought of anyone stealing a body disgusted and angered him.

Chapter 8

Just as Mick was leaving the Underwood Funeral Home, Howie was walking up to Margo's Watering Hole on Fourteenth and Hennepin. The bar, a seedy brick-faced windowless building just on the fringe of downtown Minneapolis, was wedged between a print shop and a second-hand clothing store. Margo's had the reputation of being the place to be for those who liked to mingle with the more *colorful* characters of society. Weekend nights after ten at Margo's were considered prime time if a person wanted some action. Late Saturday afternoon around five, however, was fine with Howie.

As soon as Howie walked into the place, cigarette smoke mixed with the pungent odor of beer assaulted him. He blinked a couple of times, his eyes adjusting to the dingy lighting. When he was finally able to distinguish individuals and shapes in the bar, he took note of a couple of middle-aged men dressed in jeans and tee shirts sitting in one of the four booths to his right.

The two men in the booth glanced at the newcomer, dismissed him with a sneer, and resumed their animated conversation. Curls of smoke rose like incense from their booth. At the far end of the bar a barrel-chested giant of a man stood behind the counter filling a beer glass with foamy golden liquid. The bartender's thirsty customer, an equally burly giant, wore jeans, a red flannel shirt cut off at the shoulders, and sported a straw cowboy hat. Both of the giants had cigarettes dangling from their mouths. Howie walked up to the bar, sat on a stool, and waited. Although the bartender had served the cowboy and now appeared to be laughing and shooting the breeze with him, it was several minutes before he decided to attend to his new customer.

"So, what's your poison today, a glass of suds?" The bartender, wearing bib overalls and a white tee shirt with a slight tear in one shoulder, had a face that only a mother rhino could love. Behind him, hung on the wall, a sign read *Margo's Watering Hole – Where All the Animals Go.* "We got the best tap beer on Hennepin Avenue. No other joint can even come close to it."

"It's a little early for me," Howie said. "I'll pass on it for now."

The bartender took a drag off his cigarette and snuffed the butt out in a large glass ashtray on the counter. "You a cop?" he asked as he exhaled smoke from the side of his mouth.

"No." Howie took note of the guy in the cowboy hat at the end of the bar looking in their direction and scowling. If the cowboy or one of those two characters in the booth made a threatening move toward him, he would make a quick exit. "What makes you think I'm a cop?" he asked calmly while keeping track of the only three customers in the place.

The bartender snorted. "Because of that sport coat you've got on. Nobody wears something like that in here unless they're a cop." He took a dishtowel from underneath the counter and began wiping the countertop in front of Howie. "And then there's your squeaky clean-cut look. Hell, you don't even look like you could grow peach fuzz. Maybe I should ask for an ID." He continued to wipe the counter. "And I bet you ditched your necktie before you came in."

Howie took a quick glance in the direction of the two guys sitting in the booth. They had stopped talking and were looking his way. Neither appeared too friendly. "Look, I'm Howie Cummins, and I run the MAC Detective Agency over on the North Side." He thought that revealing he was a detective would bring some kind of response. The bartender, however, remained impassive as if it was an everyday occurrence having detectives dropping in. "I'm here to ask some questions about one of your regular customers."

The bartender stopped wiping the counter. "Yeah, and who would that be?"

"Newt Aldrich."

"He ain't in some kind of trouble, is he?"

"If you're asking if he's in trouble with the law, the answer is no." Howie lowered his voice. "A friend of his is concerned. He hasn't seen Newt for several days and he's worried."

"Is that so?" The bartender scratched his chest in a slow up and down motion as though he enjoyed every moment. "Well, I haven't seen him either for nearly a week."

"Is that unusual?"

"You could say that. Old Newt usually pops in on a pretty regular basis—every three or four days."

"Have any of the other bartenders seen him by chance?"

"I'm the only bartender."

"How about Margo, the owner? Maybe she's seen him."

The bartender tossed his towel aside and leaned over the counter, so close that their noses were nearly touching. "I'm Margo," he snarled. When he straightened up, he seemed to have grown six inches.

Howie heard the two men in the booth snicker. The cowboy at the end of the bar tipped his hat back as he looked at Margo and Howie. All three of the men probably hoped that this detective would be Margo's late afternoon floorshow. "You're Margo?" he asked, disguising his surprise.

"That's right," he replied with a sneer. His upper lip curled. "Have you got a problem with my name?"

"Not a bit," Howie replied as coolly as he could. Even in the dim lighting, he could see the gathering storm in the man's eyes. "It's just that, ah, my grandfather's name was Margo and I never thought I would ever meet another man with that name." He paused to give the guy time to buy in on the story. "Grandpa was proud of his name. In fact, I've never told anyone this before..." He glanced around before leaning toward the bartender. "My middle name is Margo. I'm named after my grandfather."

"Is that right?" Margo slapped the counter so hard that it caused the cowboy at the other end to flinch. "Well, I'll be damned."

"Hey, Margo, you better watch your blood pressure," one of the men in the booth yelled. "You ain't as young as you use to be."

"And before you do croak, why don't you bring us another round of that slop you call beer," his friend chimed in.

"I'll be right back," Margo said.

The stale smoky air had given Howie a headache. He was glad that Adam wasn't with him. His partner might have had a problem with his willingness to lie in certain situations. "It's what I call situational lying," he had told Adam on another occasion. "Sometimes you've got to lie to save your butt."

"So what do you want to know about Newt?" Margo asked after he had taken his place again behind the bar.

"Did he come here alone?"

"Yeah, usually, except for the last few times." Margo's tone had softened. "He was with a couple of other guys that I'd never seen before."

"What did these other guys look like?"

Margo rubbed the back of his neck. "One guy was average. You know, average height, average built, average looks. Something like you, but taller. I didn't pay much attention to him. It was the other guy that I noticed."

"What do you mean?" Howie reached for the notepad in the pocket of his shirt, but decided that Margo might not like him taking notes. "Can you describe him?"

"He was taller, about six feet, and had a mop of blonde hair that was tied in a ponytail. He even had blonde eyebrows. Newt and them always sat in the corner booth." Margo scratched his chest again. "Funny thing, every time I walked by them, the conversation died down. Hell, they probably thought I might hear their dirty little secrets." He chuckled. "Let me tell you that working as a bartender, you hear it all. Nothing surprises me anymore."

"What can you tell me about Newt?"

"I don't know. He's a nice guy, sort of quiet, but the last couple of times I saw him, he had changed."

"In what way?"

Margo shrugged. "Hell, I don't know. Just different."

"I'd like to get in touch with him. Do you have any idea where else he might hang out?"

"Nope, but maybe his sister knows."

"Sister? He has a sister?"

"He sure does."

"Would you by any chance know her name?" Howie wondered why Squirrel hadn't said anything about a sister.

When Margo grinned, Howie noticed two gold caps on his back lower teeth. "Her name is Charlotte. Hell, I've even got her phone number." He must have noticed the puzzled expression on Howie's face. "Newt showed me a picture of her one night. She's not that much of a looker but with some better makeup, she'd be okay. Her taste in clothes needs improvement. The outfit she wore in the picture reminded me of something my mother would wear. But what the hell, I thought I'd give her a shot. So I asked him for her phone number and I called her up for a date." He shrugged. "She turned me down flat."

"She didn't know what she was missing out on," Howie said without cracking a smile. "Who knows what women want nowadays?"

"Yeah, there's other fish in the sea."

"Could I get her number?" Howie took out his notepad and pen. "It's important that I get in touch with her."

"Just a minute." Margo walked over to the cash register, punched a key with his forefinger, and the drawer dinged open. He lifted the money drawer, took out a handful of slips of paper, and closed the drawer. When he walked back to Howie he was sorting through the slips. "I got it here someplace...here it is." He handed the slip to Howie.

Howie copied down the number and gave the slip back to Margo along with a business card. "Give me a call if you see or hear from Newt, okay?" After Margo promised that he would call, Howie turned, nodded to the two guys in the booth and left. He was anxious to get back to the office and make a phone call to Newt's sister.

The trip back to the office took less time than Howie thought it would. He tore up the stairs, opened his door, nodded to Bogie, and headed for his desk. In one graceful motion, he sat down, took his notepad out, and flipped to the page on which he had written the telephone number of Newt's sister. He picked up the phone and dialed. After three rings, a woman answered, sounding hesitant as though wondering who would be calling her on a Saturday evening.

"Hi, this is Howie Cummins from the MAC Detective Agency. Am I speaking to Charlotte Aldrich?"

"Yes."

"Miss Aldrich, I'm trying to find your brother, Newt. I—"

"He's not in any trouble, is he?"

"No. It's just that his business partner hasn't seen him for a couple of days and he needs to get in touch with him to finalize some transactions." That was as tactful as Howie could put it. "Have you heard from your brother lately?"

"Not for a couple of weeks." Her voice took on a note of apprehension. "You don't think that something has happened to him, do you?"

"No, I wouldn't worry about that, but it'd be helpful if I or one of my partners could come over and talk to you."

"I don't know if—"

"Please, it would help us a lot just to find out what kind of person your brother is, who his friends are, where he hangs out, his interests and so forth. It would help us in locating him."

"Well...I guess if you put it that way." She paused. "You will call first before you come, won't you?"

"Of course."

After Howie hung up, he went over his notes. There was just something about this case that continued to give him an uneasy feeling.

Chapter 9

"Well, I'm glad you're back," Leon said as Herb walked into the reception area of the funeral home. Leon could smell the alcohol on his co-worker's breath. "We've got quite a few people here already."

"Is the boss around?"

"Underwood's with the family," Leon replied, not fooled by the question. Herb wasn't so much interested in talking to the boss as he was how he could pull his act together before Underwood saw him. "Don't worry, though, I've covered for you."

"Thanks." Herb peeked into the room where the visitation was going on. "Let me go to the can and then I'll be right with you."

"Okay, but hurry up." Leon pulled a package of mints from his suit pocket. "And while you're at it, have one of these."

"I don't like those things."

"I think you'd better start." Leon gave Herb a knowing smile. "It'll help freshen up your breath. Do you know what I mean?"

Herb stared at him for a moment. He took a mint and popped it into his mouth. "Thanks."

"We've had a visitor today. A detective."

Herb's eyes widened. "What did he want?"

"He was asking about that missing body." Leon nodded to an older couple who walked in the front door. After greeting and directing them to where the visitation was being held, he turned his attention back to Herb. "I'll tell you more when the crowd thins, but he's coming back tomorrow to talk to you."

"What did you tell him?"

The entrance door opened and several people came in. Leon lowered his voice. "This isn't the time to talk. I'll give you all the details when we're done here tonight." He paused. "And Herb..."

"Yeah?"

"When you're in the bathroom, straighten your tie and splash some cold water on your face. You look like you belong in one of our caskets."

Chapter 10

Howie had slept in after staying up past midnight. Before heading for the sack he had spent the majority of the time reviewing his notes from visiting with Margo, reflecting upon his telephone conversation with Newt's sister, and going over his annotations on the Phillips' case. Now, after eating a breakfast of warmed-up pepperoni pizza left over from earlier in the week, he made himself a fresh pot of coffee, poured himself a cup, and headed toward his office. His plan was to spend the rest of the day leisurely rereading some of his collector copies of *Police Gazette* and perhaps take in a movie. His unexpected noonday visitor, however, not only changed all of that, but now was also in the process of giving him a headache.

"I sure would like to know what Newt's up to," Squirrel said as he paced back and forth in Howie's office, occasionally stopping to glance out the window as if expecting to see his partner at any minute.

"You're not going to see him go strolling by with a billboard on his back advertising his plans," Howie said. More than likely Newt had already blown Squirrel's wad of cash.

Squirrel paused at the window again, this time opening it. The cool fall breeze sent papers scattering from Howie's desk. Without paying any attention to the mutterings of the person behind him, Squirrel leaned out the window and looked in both directions. "He's got to be out there someplace." He leaned further out. "Newt, I know you're out there!" he yelled. "You're not going to get away with my dough!" He stood there for a full minute, as if expecting a response, and then slammed the window so hard that the windowpane shook.

"Hey, watch it!" Howie cried as he continued to pick up papers.

Squirrel turned to face Howie. "I just know that he's out there walking the streets." His beady eyes sparkled mischievously, and a sly half smile appeared on his face. "I'll lay you five-to-one that he's in trouble." The half smile became a full-fledged grin. "In fact, because I like you, I'll even give you—"

"Sit down, will you?" It was the third time Howie had made that request since Squirrel barged into his office twenty minutes ago. It had taken a good ten minutes to calm the little guy as he chattered incessantly while flailing his arms. One minute, he would be expressing concern over what could have happened to his poor old partner, and the next minute he was cursing Newt up and down for running out on him with the money. It was a litany that he repeated so many times that Howie was mouthing the words even before they were spoken.

And I trusted him...we were partners...the jerk didn't even tell me where he was...I took the guy under my wing...he was like a kid brother to me...I wonder how much of my dough that chump has left...when I see him I'm going to wring his scrawny little neck...

Squirrel's constant chattering and pacing only aggravated Howie's headache and the guy's annoying habit of sucking in air and smacking his lips didn't help. "Sit down and do it now!" Howie demanded. He stood up and pointed to a chair.

Squirrel stopped in mid stride and stared at Howie like he had been caught with three aces up his sleeve.

"And quit smacking your lips! It's driving me up the wall."

"Okay, okay, don't get your dandruff up." Squirrel moved over to the chair, plopped down, and crossed his legs.

"That's better." Howie sat back down. "Now let me get this straight," he said, speaking quietly, hoping that his tone would calm his agitated client. "Newt called and..." At the mention of Newt's name, Squirrel's nose twitched, his eyes popped out, and he started to get up. Howie glared at him and gestured for him to stay put.

"Can I help if I'm fidgety?" Squirrel crossed his arms and although he gave Howie a defiant look, he remained seated. "I have to move around. I've got nervous blood. If I sit too long I feel like I'm locked in a cage."

"If you start pacing again, I'll personally lock you up in a cage." As much as Howie hated to admit it, he enjoyed Squirrel's quirky personality. "Okay, let's go over it again," he said, softening his tone. "Newt called you and told you what?"

Squirrel uncrossed his arms and leaned forward; the fingers of his left hand drummed against the side of the leather chair. "That he would see me in a couple of days. He sounded calm but I knew something was going on."

"Did you ask him if anything was wrong?"

"Sure I did, but he said things were cool. When I asked what he'd been up to, he was vague. Get this—he said he had been busy." Squirrel leaned back in the chair and crossed his arms again.

"Did he mention the money?"

"No."

"And you didn't ask him about it?"

"I was going to, but I was afraid I'd spook him if I did." Squirrel looked like he still hadn't forgiven himself for keeping silent on that issue. "If I would've mentioned the money, he would've hung up on me. I just know it. This way when I see him, I can wring his neck."

"Did he say anything about where's he been staying the past couple of weeks?"

When Squirrel uncrossed his arms and took a deep breath, Howie hoped that it was a sign that he was beginning to relax, but then he heard the tapping of Squirrel's foot against the desk. "I asked him," Squirrel said, "and he told me he's been with somebody."

"A female somebody?"

"Don't he wish." Squirrel ran his fingers through his hair a couple of times in a futile attempt to comb it into submission. "Newt can't score with women like I do."

Howie tried to imagine what type of woman would go out with someone like Squirrel. His own social life lately hadn't been anything to brag about either, though. Mick was always trying to fix him up, but so far nothing had clicked.

"Dames like to hang around me because they know that the best things come wrapped in small packages." Squirrel paused, looked at Howie as if measuring him, and added, "You should know that."

"Do you know anything about this guy that Newt's hanging around with?"

"Only that he was learning some heavy-duty stuff from him."

"Like what?"

"I don't know. He was speaking mumbo jumbo." Squirrel rolled his eyes. "He was yakking about getting in touch with spiritual powers and that he was going to be set free." He shook his head as if he couldn't believe he was talking about his partner. "The poor guy's probably with some Holy Rollers who want to save him from his evil ways. If you ask me, he's hanging around with the wrong crowd. He should've stuck with me. "

Howie suppressed a grin. He closed his notepad and leaned back in his chair. "If you're going to meet with your partner in a couple of days, I guess you won't need our services anymore."

"We'll have to see about that. If Newt doesn't have my dough, you're going to have to tail him to see where he stashed it." Squirrel folded his arms again and leaned back into the chair, a smug smile on his face. "Besides, you can't be all that busy."

"What makes you say that?"

"Because you only have that one other case." When no reply came, Squirrel blew on his fingernails and polished them on the front of his shirt. "Don't play coy with me. You know which one I'm talking about: the body of that young chick missing from the Underwood Funeral Home."

"How did you know about that?" Howie tried to conceal his surprise.

"Hey, you're talking to Squirrel. It's my business to know things around the North Side." He picked at a hangnail. "I have my ways. Besides, I'm laying three-to-two odds that she'll be found by...let's see, it's..." He stroked his chin and glanced at the wall clock. "It's nearly one. Today's Sunday...let's say by Tuesday, no, Wednesday evening." He blew on his fingernails and polished them again on his shirt. "At the latest, Thursday morning. Once I analyze this some more, I may even give better odds."

Howie massaged his temple. "Is there anything you won't bet on?"

"Hey, watch what you're saying!" Squirrel's tone and facial expression indicated that he was offended. "I have my scruples, you know."

"How do you know for certain that the body will be found?" Howie asked, wondering if he even knew what the word *scruples* meant.

"I don't know for sure. That's why I'm not giving greater odds." Squirrel leaned forward. He spoke in a whisper. "You're supposed to keep things between you and your clients quiet, right?"

"That's the way the game is played."

"Okay, so what I'm going to tell you, you'll keep to yourself. Do I have your word?" After Howie nodded again, Squirrel leaned back in his chair and relaxed, the smug look reappearing. "Because I like you, I'm going to let you in on how I operate."

"Lucky me."

"I figure that whoever took the body can't keep it that long. I mean after all, what do you want with a body? It's not exactly worth much on the street." Squirrel paused. "It's sort of used merchandise...in a manner of speaking. Do you know what I mean? Whoever took it probably did it for a joke."

"And who would do something like that?"

"College kids. They're always doing dumb things like that." Squirrel reached into his shirt pocket, took out a package of gum, and offered Howie a piece.

Howie declined the gum. He watched as his client popped in three sticks; the resulting wad causing Squirrel's right jaw to swell to more than double its size.

"That's why I never went to college," Squirrel mumbled between chomps. "My education comes from the streets."

"If they're college kids, what are they going to do with the body?" Howie asked.

"Nothing. They're probably too scared now and want to dump it. I wouldn't be a bit surprised if some morning Underwood comes to open up his place and finds it on the front step."

"You don't really believe that, do you?"

"Naw, the odds of the body showing up on his doorstep would be..." Squirrel pinched his bottom lip. "The odds have got to be at least twenty-to-one against that." His eyebrows shot up. "Hey, that gives me an idea. If I get some of my pals to spread the rumor that that was going to take place...hmmm, I could pick up some fast dough." He snapped his gum. "There are always a few suckers out there who'll believe whatever they hear. They'll get greedy and think they can outfox old Squirrel."

Howie cleared his throat. "Look, we need to draw this to a close."

"Oh, yeah? Why?"

"Because I've got some stuff to attend to."

"Detective kind of stuff?" Squirrel leaned forward, his eyes widening.

"Yeah." Howie stood up, hoping that his visitor would take the hint.

Squirrel got up and walked toward the door, pausing just as he put his hand on the doorknob. "I bet you're meeting with some gorgeous dame, ain't you?"

"You never know." As soon as Squirrel left, Howie walked back to his desk, took out a bottle of aspirins, and headed for the kitchen to get a fresh cup of coffee.

Chapter 11

At five-thirty Sunday afternoon, some four hours after Squirrel left Howie's office, Brian Turner and Peter Fisher, two fourteen-year-old boys, were making their way down the river embankment by the Broadway Bridge. Earlier that summer Brian and Peter had discovered the area under the bridge and decided that it was a perfect spot to get away from the prying eyes of adults. The bridge, less than a half mile from Howie's office, spanned the Mississippi River, and connected north and northeast Minneapolis.

"Hurry up before anyone sees us," Brian said, a skinny kid with tousled blonde hair. "Come on," he urged, holding up the half full bottle of wine as an enticement to his friend who was a good ten feet behind.

"Are you sure your father's not going to miss it?" Peter asked as he struggled to keep his footing on the steep slope.

Brian laughed. "Shit, my old man's too drunk to notice."

"But what if he does ask?"

"I'll just play dumb." Brian waited until Peter caught up. "How about your old lady? Will she miss her smokes?"

"I don't think so." Peter's eyes reflected the uncertainty in his voice. "I swiped them from an open carton. She'll think my father took them."

Brian turned to go, but suddenly stopped. "Duck down!" he whispered.

"What's the matter, cops?"

"No, there's some woman down there and she's naked."

"What's she doing?"

"I don't know." Brian raised his head and peeked at the woman lying on a blanket, her head resting on a pillow. "I can't see her face, but it looks like she's sleeping."

"And she's bare naked?" Peter remained crouched behind his friend.

"Yeah—she doesn't have a stitch of clothing on...not even her panties."

"Maybe she's sunbathing."

"Don't be stupid," Brian said, jabbing Peter with his elbow. "How's she going to get any sun under the bridge?"

Peter sneaked a look over his friend's shoulder. "Let's get closer before she wakes up," he said, his voice cracking with adolescent excitement.

"Just be quiet, then," Brian warned. Neither of them had ever seen a naked woman before except in a magazine that Brian's older brother had shown them. Come Monday, he would really have something to brag about to the other kids at school. His brother could keep his dumb magazines; he was about to see the real thing.

"Do you see anybody else around?" Peter asked. "I bet she—" He tripped over a root nearly falling headfirst. "Sorry."

Brian wondered why the woman hadn't heard his noisy friend.

"Hey!" Peter said as they got closer. "What are those black specks all over her?"

"How should I...oh, shit!" Brian cried as some of the black specks flew away and others landed.

Chapter 12

The detective glanced over at the two teenage boys who stood watching the coroner, his assistant, and two police officers struggle to carry the body bag up the steep embankment. "What time did the kids find the body?" he asked the officer who had first arrived at the scene.

"Around five-thirty," the officer answered. "They didn't realize right away that she was dead. It was only when they decided to move in closer that they sensed that something wasn't right."

"What tipped them off?"

"The flies."

"That would do it." The detective glanced around the area. "What were they doing down here in the first place?"

"Their story is that they just wanted to see how high the water was…that they had never been down here before."

"Sure, and if you buy that, I've got a bridge to sell you."

The officer grinned. "I didn't buy their story, either." His smile faded when he glanced over at the two boys. "But I didn't press them on it. They've been through enough."

"So, how are they doing?"

"They're pretty shaken up. This is going to stay with them for the rest of their lives." He looked in the direction of the teenagers again. "The kid with the blonde hair, his name is Brian, said that he got sick to his stomach when they went in to get a closer look and saw what had been done to her."

"What about the other kid?"

"I guess he just about fainted."

"How did we get notified?"

"One of them flagged down a passing car and yelled to the driver to get the cops. According to the driver, the kid, that was Peter, was just about hysterical."

"I'll talk to them in a few minutes. Is it a positive ID?"

"Oh, yeah. We called the funeral director, a Mr. Gaylord Underwood. He owns a place over on Lyndale and Broadway. From the description at the briefing the other morning, we knew we had his missing body." The officer glanced at the spot where the Phillips woman had been found. "In my book, whoever did this must be some kind of sicko."

"We've got a lot of those kinds running around," the detective replied matter-of-factly.

"Well, I've been a cop for nearly fifteen years and I've never seen anything like this."

Chapter 13

Howie sat in his chair and stared at the telephone on his desk, willing it to ring. An hour earlier, Jim Davidson, his police detective friend, had called.

"Hey, I got something that might interest you," JD began.

"What's that?"

"I just got word that a body was found."

"Where?" Howie got out his notepad.

"Under the bridge on Broadway."

"When?"

"A couple of hours ago."

"Was it the Phillips girl?"

"I don't know, but—just a minute." Howie heard JD yell to someone that he would be right with him. "Like I was saying, I don't know, but I was told it was a young woman in her twenties."

Howie massaged his forehead, hoping to ward off a headache. "You'll let me know if it was her, okay?"

"Sure enough. I'll call you as soon as I find out. Got to go. Hang in there."

The time had passed slowly and Howie thought about calling Underwood but decided to wait until he received confirmation from JD. When the phone rang, he grabbed it before the second ring, almost dropping the receiver.

"MAC Detective Agency…Oh, hello Mr. Underwood."

"Howard, I got a call from the police." Underwood's voice sounded shaky. "They found Carole Anne's body."

"Where?" Howie asked instinctively, but having already made the connection.

"Under the Broadway Bridge. On this side of the river."

"How did the cops find her?"

"What do you mean?"

"Did they get a tip or something?"

"Oh…I don't know. They didn't tell me." Underwood was silent for a moment. "I guess at the time I was too unsettled to think to ask. I can't even imagine who would leave a body in a place like that." The longer he talked, the calmer he sounded, no doubt his professional experience dealing with death coming into play. "The officer who called asked for a description of Carole Anne...apparently they were pretty sure, but they wanted verification."

"What are you going to do now?"

"I'm leaving for the coroner's office in a few minutes. They'll release the body to me once they're done with it."

"Done with it? Done doing what?"

"The officer wouldn't discuss it over the phone. He said that a detective would meet me at the morgue. I called the family to let them know."

"How did they take it?"

"They were relieved, but still very upset that their daughter's body was stolen in the first place." Underwood paused. "The poor grandmother is now under a doctor's care because of this whole experience."

"Sorry to hear that."

"The family wants you to stay on the case, Howard."

"They do?" Howie picked up a pencil off his desk, rolling it back and forth between his thumb and forefinger. "There's not much of a case now that the body's been found."

"On the contrary," Underwood said. "They want you to track down whoever's responsible for this awful thing...and so do I." His tone turned indignant. "Whoever did this terrible deed has to be brought to justice." He let out an audible deep breath, and then spoke in a more subdued tone. "May I inform the family that you'll stay on?"

"Of course."

Howie hung up and leaned back in his chair, tapping the eraser end of the pencil against his chin. Squirrel's prediction that Carole Anne's body would be found within a few days was right on. Either the guy had some kind of sixth sense, or he had something to do with it. That last thought was dismissed as quickly as it came. Squirrel may be a lot of things, but he was no body snatcher. He tossed the pencil on the desk and got up to get himself a fresh cup of coffee. He had just gotten back with his coffee when the phone rang.

"Mac Detect—"

"Who have you been talking to?" JD asked. "I called a few minutes ago and your line was busy."

"Underwood called me."

"Oh, so you know."

"Yeah, but I had a gut feeling that it was the Phillips girl when you first called me." Howie took a sip of coffee. It was strong and hot, just the way he liked it. "Underwood said he was going down to the morgue to meet with some detective."

"Did he say which detective?"

"No."

"It's probably Ryan, then. I heard he got called out earlier." JD paused and Howie heard him say to somebody that the file was on the chief's desk.

A few seconds later he was back on the phone. "I didn't get a chance to call you right away because I got called out on a robbery. Did Underwood mention anything else?"

"No, except the family wants me to stay on the case." Howie was sure that both Adam and Mick would want to see this case through as well. "The officer who called Underwood didn't offer much information." He flipped open his notepad. "How about it, JD? Can you give me anything more?"

JD didn't reply right away. "I can tell you that the body was mutilated."

"What! Are you kidding?"

"I wish I was. The cop I talked to was really pissed. He'd like to spend five minutes with whoever did it."

"How bad was it?"

"Bad enough."

"So tell me."

"Tell you what?"

"Come on, JD, don't play coy with me. How was she mutilated?"

"I've already told you more than I should have."

"Don't give me that line. You know you can trust me."

JD lowered his voice. "Look, I can't be talking about this here. Too many ears around. Do you know what I mean?"

"Can you call me later?"

"We'll see. It depends how tight the chief wants this."

"Look, if you don't, it's just going to make the case a lot tougher for us."

"Talking about cases...you should know that we've been investigating something involving your friend Kass."

"What!" Howie's adrenalin surged. "What's going on with him?"

"He's been receiving letters."

"What kind of letters?"

"The kind signed with a swastika."

Chapter 14

As soon as the phone rang, Howie picked it up, wondering who would be calling him at seven on a Monday morning. "MAC Detective Agency."

"Hey, Howie, this is JD."

"You're up early."

"Listen, I don't have a lot of time, but I've got something more for you on the Phillips girl."

"Wait a minute." Howie took out his notepad and picked up his pen. "Okay, go ahead."

"He carved on her forehead."

"What!"

"Whoever the creep was, he took his time."

"What did he carve?" Several seconds passed. "JD?"

"That's as much as I can give you for now."

"Come on, JD, what else?" Howie waited. "You're not telling me everything."

"I'll call you later."

Before Howie could say another word, there was a click and he was left with a dial tone. He put the phone back on the receiver. He leaned back in his chair, closed his eyes, and wondered what kind of lowlife they were dealing with.

Chapter 15

"I don't understand." Howie set his cup of coffee down and looked at Mick in amazement. His partner had just finished reporting to Adam and him about his visits with Underwood's two employees, Leon Sparks and Herb Whitehead.

"How in the world could Whitehead get the two caskets mixed up?" Adam asked.

"Maybe he was hitting the sauce," Howie said.

Mick nodded. "According to Sparks, he was."

It was early Tuesday evening and Howie and his partners were going over the Carole Anne Phillips' case. His partners were pleased that the body had been recovered, surprised that it was found under the Broadway Bridge, and shocked to the point of outrage when told that her forehead had been carved up.

Now, as Howie had anticipated, both were glad that the case was still theirs to handle, and were determined more than ever to find out who could have done such a horrible thing.

"When did this mix-up about the caskets happen?" Adam asked.

"Earlier this year," Mick said. "It was on a Saturday afternoon and Sparks said that they were pretty busy. In the rush, Whitehead took the wrong casket to the church for the service. Luckily for him, he got there early enough."

Howie glanced at his notes. "And you said that it was the minister who pointed out that they had the wrong body?"

"Yeah, he came up to the casket as they were setting it up for the visitation. He stood there for several moments staring at the body and then asked who it was."

"Really?" Howie stifled a chuckle. He would have loved to witness that whole scene. "I don't mean to make light of this, but you have to see the humor in it, don't you?" He glanced back and forth between his partners before giving Adam a knowing grin. "Can't you just imagine something like that happening to you once you become a preacher?" Upon receiving a silent cold stare in reply, he turned his attention back to Mick. "What happened after the preacher asked his question?"

"Well, when Whitehead told him that the person in the casket was a Mr. Wilshire, the minister got a shocked look and exclaimed, 'But I was supposed to perform a service for a Mr. Larson'." Mick was now trying to suppress a grin. "Sparks said that Whitehead called him in a panic, told him about the mix-up, and pleaded for him to bring the Larson body to the church as soon as possible."

A disgusted look swept across Adam's face. "From how Sparks describes Whitehead, it's hard to believe that he's anything but a screw-up. The guy may be a suspect but I have my doubts about him." He waited while Howie scribbled something in his notepad. "Besides having a drinking problem, Whitehead doesn't sound like he's too bright. He may be involved in some way, but in my opinion he doesn't have the brains to have planned it."

"What do you think?" Howie asked Mick. "You've had a chance to talk to the guy. Does he have the smarts to pull off something like this?"

"I don't know. When I was with him I couldn't smell any liquor on his breath." Mick shifted in his chair, stretching his long legs in front of him. "He seemed to be a pretty normal guy; not real smart, but I'd say of average intelligence. When I asked him about his work and how it was going, he said that it was going fine, and that he had just had his yearly review a couple of weeks ago and received high marks from Underwood."

"That doesn't jibe with how Sparks described him," Howie said. "Do you think that he was stretching the truth about Whitehead's drinking?"

"I don't know, but when I asked Whitehead if there was anything he could tell me about Sparks, he said that the man had recently separated from his wife and that Sparks was pretty broken up about it. Of course, he told me not to say anything to his partner." Mick sat up straight and leaned forward toward Howie. "To tell you the truth, I'm not sure if I believe either one of those characters."

Howie pointed his pen at Mick. "I'll tell you what, then. Why don't you track down Mrs. Sparks and ask a few questions?"

"What do you expect from her?" Adam asked.

"I don't know, maybe nothing. But we have to check out every angle." Howie offered Adam a sly smile. "A divorced woman will usually be very honest about her ex-husband. If he's the type to stretch the truth, we'll find out in a hurry." He turned back to Mick. "Anything else about Whitehead?"

"No, I think I've given you all of it." Mick glanced at his watch. "Guys, I've got to be going soon."

"What's the rush?" Adam asked.

"Mary's expecting me to put in an appearance tonight."

"Oh, that's right," Howie said. "The big wedding shower."

Mick rolled his eyes. "She wants to show me off to some of her girlfriends who haven't met me yet." He shrugged and gave his partners a look of resignation. "I'll put in my time, charm them for a while, and then get the heck out of there."

"Wait a minute." Howie flipped to a new page in his notepad. "Before you leave, there's one other item that you and Adam should know about."

He waited until he had their full attention. "Kass is having some problems."

Adam and Mick glanced at each other. "What kind of problems?" Adam asked as Mick sat down.

"JD told me that Kass has been receiving threatening letters the past couple of months." Howie paused to allow that bit of information to sink in. Adam sat silently, his eyes reflecting concern. Mick's eyes, however, continued to register a question mark. Of his two partners, Adam was quicker to see the darker side of human nature. Mick, on the other hand, always had the tendency to look at the positive side of life and to find the good in people. "The letters are signed with a swastika."

"What!" Mick exclaimed. "Why would he get something like that?" He shook his head as if he still couldn't believe what he was hearing. "The guy's been at that drugstore for thirty years. He's helped countless people in that time. Everybody on the North Side thinks the world of him."

"Apparently not everybody," Howie replied.

"But who would do something like that?"

"I don't know, but we're going to find out."

Adam gnawed at his lip. "It's obviously somebody who hates Jews." The tone in his voice matched the repulsion now seen in his eyes. "How come he's never mentioned the letters to us?"

"You know Kass," Howie said. "He helps everybody with their problems, but keeps his own to himself. He probably assumed that we're too busy to be bothered."

Mick rubbed his knuckles. "We need to talk to him."

"I agree," Adam replied. "Is he working now?"

"Yeah," Howie said. "And as far as I'm concerned, now is as good a time as any." He offered Mick a sympathetic smile. "Look, I know you have to go to the shower. Don't worry, though. We'll fill you in after we talk with Kass."

"Man, I feel I should go with you guys."

Howie shook his head. "Listen, Kass is going to feel guilty enough knowing he's taking our time with this. The guy would really feel bad if you missed out on the shower." He gave his partner a knowing nod. "You go ahead. It'll be all right. Just say hello to Mary for us."

"Okay, but you guys tell Kass that he has my full support."

"We will," Adam assured him.

"If there's anything he wants me to do, just tell him I'll be there for him." Mick glanced at the clock again. "And tell him that we'll find out who's sending him those letters." He stood up to leave. "What a crazy world. I just don't understand why someone would do something like this."

Chapter 16

When the doorbell rang, Mary Wheeler wondered who it could be. All of the invited guests for her wedding shower had arrived a half hour ago and were now getting ready to play party games. After excusing herself from the other girls, she headed for the front door. She glanced at the grandfather clock in the hallway. It was still too early for Mick to arrive. She opened the door to find a freckle-faced young man dressed in a light-blue jacket, dark pants, and a white shirt with a red bow tie.

"Special delivery for a Miss Mary Wheeler," the young man said. A shoebox-sized package wrapped in brown paper was tucked under his left arm.

"I'm Mary Wheeler."

"If you'd just sign for this, I'll be on my way." He handed her a clipboard with the delivery slip attached. "Sign on the bottom line please." He pulled a pen from his shirt pocket and handed it to her without making eye contact.

Mary signed the slip, took the package, thanked the young man, and closed the door. She walked back to her guests, wondering who it could be from since there was no card.

"Is that from Mick?" Mary's friend, Karen, from high school days asked.

"I bet it is," chimed Veronica. "Don't you think so?" she asked Mary.

"I don't know. There's no card with it."

"Well, open it. Maybe the card is inside."

Mary removed the brown wrapping only to discover that the box inside had been wrapped in an elegant silver foil paper with a white bow attached. She smiled. "I still don't see a card, but I suspect it might be from Mick." One of the things she loved about him was his thoughtfulness.

Veronica gently fingered the bow on the package. "Aren't you going to open it?"

"Not right now." Mary set the gift with the others. "I think I'll save it until last. By then Mick should be here."

Karen giggled. "You better hope it's not too personal or else he's going to be mighty embarrassed."

"Ooh, I can hardly wait," Veronica said.

Chapter 17

When Howie and Adam walked into the drugstore, they found Kass standing behind the counter at the soda fountain chatting with a young boy of eight or nine. Elbow on the counter, his chin resting in the palm of his hand, their friend appeared as though he didn't have a care in the world. As soon as he saw the two detectives, he waved them over. They walked past the kid and took stools at the far end of the counter.

"What brings both of you here this evening?" Kass called out, still with his youthful customer at the other end of the counter. His eyes, gleaming with their usual merriment, gave no indication that anything could be wrong in his life.

"Have you got a minute, Kass?" Howie glanced at the kid who was just finishing a dish of chocolate ice cream. "We'd like to talk to you."

"You would, huh?" Kass' eyes shifted between Howie and Adam. He said something to the young boy and walked over. "You two look so serious." Worry lines appeared on his forehead. "You're not having troubles, are you?"

"*We're* not," Adam said.

Howie eyed the kid who now had his nose in a comic book. Although the boy didn't appear to be paying any attention to them, nevertheless, he lowered his voice. "Kass, why didn't you tell us about the letters?"

"Letters?" Kass got a dishtowel and began wiping the counter in front of his two friends. "What letters?"

"Ah, come on, Kass, don't play innocent with us," Adam said. "We've known each other too long."

When the young boy looked in their direction, Howie whispered to Adam not to say anything more. He waved the boy over. The kid hopped off his stool and cautiously approached them. "What's your name?" Howie asked.

"Ronny."

"Well, Ronny, I tell you what. If you leave us alone so we can talk, I'll buy you a comic book."

Ronny's eyebrows shot up and his brown eyes nearly doubled in size. "Really?"

"Yeah, really, but the deal is that you have to leave after you get your comic book. We've got some business to talk over with Kass."

"Sure thing, mister, but it's going to cost you two comic books."

Howie ignored Kass' snigger. "Okay, but then you're out of here." He motioned toward the magazine rack in front. "Go pick out your comics and take off. I'll pay for them when I leave." He watched with satisfaction as the kid scampered away.

"Ronny's quite the little business man, isn't he?" Kass said with a smile.

"That's one way of putting it," Howie muttered as the kid rushed out the front door, carrying the spoils of his extortion. He turned back to Kass. "So tell us about those letters."

"There's not much to tell." Kass reached under the counter and got a couple of glasses. He filled the glasses with ice water and set them in front of Howie and Adam. "Would you boys like something to eat?"

Howie shook his head. "The letters, Kass."

Kass took a deep breath and let it out slowly. "They've been coming every week for the past couple of months." The usual mirth seen in his eyes disappeared as his tone turned somber. "Are you sure you want to hear about this?"

"That's why we're here," Adam said.

"What can I say?" Kass shrugged. "The messages are anti-Semitic. Whoever's sending them is a Jew hater. All of it is garbage."

"Why didn't you tell us about them?" Howie asked.

"I don't know. I guess because I didn't want to bother you." His eyes continued to shift between the two of them. "You boys are busy enough with your detective work. You have more important things to do than be concerned about an old man like me." Howie was about to protest when Kass added, "Besides, I went to the police about it."

Adam glanced sideways at Howie. "Have they come up with anything?" he asked Kass.

"No, but they tell me that they're working on it." Kass paused. "Whoever sends these letters is quite clever."

"What do you mean?" Howie asked.

"There are no fingerprints and they're postmarked from both Minneapolis and Saint Paul. A couple of them have even come from outside the Twin Cities."

Howie picked up his glass of water and took a sip. A customer came into the drugstore, stopped at the magazine rack up front, and began paging through one of the magazines. "What exactly is in these letters?"

"Same old hate talk."

"It sounds like it has happened before," Adam said.

Kass nodded. "Oh, yes. When I first opened up nearly thirty years ago, I received a couple of anonymous phone calls. One day the words *Christ Killer* were painted on the entrance door. I ignored it and nothing more ever came of it." He gazed turned toward the front door as though remembering that day. "I never had any problems until recently." He poured himself a glass of water, took several sips, and sighed. "These letters, though, have a more ominous feel to them. Would you like to see the latest one?"

"Yeah, we would." Howie watched as Kass headed toward a back storeroom that had been converted into an office. "Did he look worried to you?" he asked Adam once Kass had disappeared into his office.

"He sure did. He's trying to sound upbeat, but he's just covering up." Adam took a sip of water. "I've never seen him like this before. What are we going to do?"

"I don't know yet." Howie drummed his fingers on the counter. "But there's no way we're going to stay out of it. Not after all the times he's helped us over the years." The resolve in Adam's eyes indicated that he was with Howie all the way on this. That would be true of Mick as well.

Kass came back a few minutes later and handed Howie a legal-size white envelope. On the front of the envelope was printed, in stylized letters, *To the Jew.* Howie took out the letter and unfolded it as Adam looked on. The printing was the same as on the envelope. *It's time for your kind to get out. Do it quickly or you and your friends won't have anything left.* The Swastika sign was the only signature.

Adam asked to see the letter. "When it refers to your friends...is that a reference to other Jews?" he asked as he handed it back to Kass.

Kass nodded. "That's how I read it."

"That thing is a bunch of crap," Howie said as he watched Kass fold and stuff the letter back into the envelope. "Don't you worry; we're going to do everything we can to help."

"You boys don't have to."

"Oh, yes, we do." Adam's tone was adamant.

Although Howie wasn't sure where the case would lead them, it didn't matter. Kass was a friend and he stuck by his friends. "We'll be in touch. Let us know if you receive any more letters." He and Adam got up to leave.

"Just a minute," Kass said. "Let me write a check for you."

"A check?" Howie glanced at Adam. "What for?"

"Your services."

"Forget it."

Frown lines appeared on Kass' forehead. "But—"

"But nothing," Howie said. "We're not taking your money, and that's final."

Kass sighed. "You boys are too good to me. Thank you." His eyes glistened. "Thank you very much."

"You'd better save your thanks until we come up with some answers on this." Howie had a feeling, however, that the answers wouldn't come easy.

Chapter 18

Mick arrived at Mary's just as she was finishing with the opening of her presents. After being introduced to the other girls, he stood off to one side and looked on as his soon-to-be-bride proceeded to open the last three gifts. The first one she unwrapped contained a rolling pin and a Betty Crocker cookbook.

"Is your future husband going to be using the cookbook?" Bonnie asked.

Mary smiled, took hold of the rolling pin at one end and playfully made a threatening gesture toward Mick. "He'd better if he knows what's good for him."

After the tittering of the group died down, Mick shrugged and held out his hands as though to say *what can I do; she's the boss.*

The next gift contained a lavender negligee. "Ooh," several of the girls said in unison. Mick blushed, being acutely aware of the looks in his direction. He was relieved when Mary set it aside without saying a word. She had blushed as well, though.

"This last one has no tag," Mary said. "But I've a pretty good idea who it's from." She eyed Mick.

"We've all been waiting for this one," a friend said.

"It's going to be hard to top that last gift," another one teased.

"It's not from me," Mick said, but Mary didn't hear him. She had already turned her attention to the package. He watched with interest as she took her time unwrapping it, and, after tossing the paper aside, set the box on her lap.

"Don't make us wait any longer," urged the girl sitting on her left. "We want to know what kind of taste your future husband has."

"I didn't—" Mick's words were drowned out by the voices of Mary's friends urging her to open the box. *It's not my gift* he mouthed, but Mary wasn't looking in his direction. His smile disappeared when, to his horror, he recognized the type of box sitting in her lap. He started moving in her direction, praying that it was just a coincidence.

"Here goes," Mary announced as she lifted the lid off the box. "Oh, my god!" she cried as she leaped up. The box fell to the carpet and its contents tumbled out.

The screams of the other girls echoed in Mick's ears as he stared in revulsion at what lay next to the shoebox.

Chapter 19

Howie stood at his office window and stared at the street below as he reflected on what Kass had said about the letters. He had hoped to discuss Kass' problem further with Adam, but his partner had decided that there was still time that evening to pay a call on Newt's sister, Charlotte.

"Anyway, I need some time to think about what's happening to Kass," Adam had said. Then he added, "We'll talk about it tomorrow when Mick's with us. I'm sure the three of us will come up with something."

A couple of kids running down the sidewalk now broke Howie's concentration. He went back to his desk, sat down, and took his notepad out of his shirt pocket. At the top of a blank page, he wrote *Kass – Hate Letters.* After underlining the words several times, he put his pen down. Who could have sent such terrible letters and why? His head ached with unanswered questions. As he massaged his temples his movie poster caught his eye.

"Okay, Bogie, where do I go from here?" The clock ticked away the minutes as Howie waited for an answer. Finally, he took a deep breath, picked up his pen and began drumming on his notepad. He tried to think of what could be done. By the time his partners came tomorrow morning, he wanted to have several concrete steps that they could take in investigating the case. The only thing he could think of, however, was to contact JD at the police department. After writing Davidson's name down with the hopes of getting a lead from him, he pondered what else could be done. Fifteen minutes went by and he found himself still staring at his only idea. Frustrated, he decided to get a cup of coffee and hopefully jumpstart his brain.

Out in the kitchen, he poured a cup of the reheated coffee left over from that morning. Or was it from two mornings ago? He walked back to his desk, sat down and took a sip, grimacing over the taste of the black liquid. After another sip, he picked up his pen and wrote *Contact Kass' friends.* Howie hoped that one of Kass' friends might know of any possible enemies Kass could have. It was a long shot, but he didn't have any other ideas. Just as he was about to take another sip of coffee, the phone rang.

"MAC Detective Agency."

"Are you going to be in your office?" Mick asked, his voice shaky.

"Yeah. What's wrong?" Commotion could be heard in the background.

"What's going on? Are you still at Mary's?" A woman yelled Mick's name.

"Look, I can't talk now. I'll tell you and Adam all about it when I get there."

"I'll be here, but Adam won't. He went to see Newt's sister."

"Okay, but stay in your office. Don't go anyplace. I've got something to show you. You're not going to believe it."

Chapter 20

After he parked the car, Adam got out and walked across the street to the white-framed duplex where Newt's sister, Charlotte, lived. The daytime temperature had dropped considerably and the chill in the evening air made him wish that he had worn a jacket. He stopped by one of the many huge oak trees lining the street and glanced around, wanting to get the feel of the neighborhood. Though cars were parked on both sides of the street and lights were on in most of the houses, the block seemed quiet. It didn't surprise him that the area was peaceful. In this section of town the law-abiding residents took pride in their neighborhood. These home owners kept their dwellings in good shape and their modest-size lawns and decorative bushes neatly trimmed. Unlike the North Side, the only concerns in this south side neighborhood were to keep your lawn free of dandelions and to make sure your dog didn't bark too late at night.

Adam dug the slip of paper out of his pants pocket and rechecked the address that Howie had given him. According to the street number, Charlotte Aldrich lived on the left side of the duplex. That was good, because the windows on the right side were dark. The muted glow through the drawn front window drapes on Charlotte's side signaled that she was home. When he had called earlier to ask to visit, she had told him she had to run an errand, but would be home when he got there.

He took one final look around and headed up the walk to the front door. Just as he reached out to ring the buzzer, he heard commotion coming from inside the house. At first, he thought it might be the television set, but then a woman screamed. He tried the door, found it unlocked, and cautiously opened it. "Shut up!" he heard a man yell. Adam couldn't make out what the man said next, but the harshness of his tone left no doubt that the woman was in danger. The fight, if it was that, sounded like it was coming from a room on the left beyond the entryway. He hesitated, realizing he had no right to intervene in a quarrel. Howie hadn't said anything about Charlotte being married or having a boyfriend. The woman screamed again, and he didn't hesitate. He rushed down the hallway and into the living room.

A heavyset man with bushy black hair stood over a woman sprawled on the couch, her arms in front of her face. Instinctively, he rushed the guy. At six feet, Adam had a good four inches on the man, and although outweighed by fifty pounds, Adam was confident he could hold his own. The man, though, knocked Adam aside as if he had just brushed aside a pesky mosquito. Adam fell, hitting his forehead on the edge of the coffee table. Bolts of lightning followed by sharp stabbing pains flashed through his consciousness, and for a moment, he thought he might pass out. He lay on the floor for an indeterminate amount of time, his breaths coming in short shallow spurts as he blinked his eyes to regain focus. The first thing he saw was a black bobby pin lying on the beige carpet, not more than a foot away from his nose. By the time he struggled to his feet, the bushy-haired man was gone. The woman lay curled on the couch like a frightened animal, staring at him with fear in her eyes.

"Are you okay?" Adam asked as he touched his forehead. It was tender, but at least it wasn't bleeding. He thought about pursuing the man, but didn't want to leave the woman alone. Besides, he was in no condition to be chasing someone when he felt as though he had just been hit with a sledgehammer. "Are you okay?" he asked again.

"I...I think so." The fear in her eyes faded a bit. "Who...who are you?"

"Adam Trexler." He noticed that her lip was bleeding. "I work for the MAC Detective Agency. I called earlier..." He paused. "You're Charlotte Aldrich, aren't you?"

"Yes," she replied tentatively. The fear in her eyes had disappeared. "Where did you say you were from?"

"The MAC Detective Agency over on the North Side."

A flash of recognition crossed her eyes. "Squirrel hired you, didn't he?" She straightened her dress and ran her hands through her short brown hair a couple of times. "He wants you to locate my brother, doesn't he?"

When Adam nodded, the throbbing pain radiating from his forehead caused him to wince. "Who was that man who was knocking you around?"

"I don't know. I never saw him before tonight."

Adam moved over to the chair across from the couch. "How did he get in?" he asked as he slowly lowered himself into the chair.

Charlotte took a deep breath. "He knocked on my door and when I answered, he said that he had a message from Newton. I, of course, let him in since I've been so worried about my brother." She touched her mouth, felt the blood, reached for a tissue, and gently dabbed at her swollen lip. "The next thing I knew, he was hitting me."

"Do you know why he would do that?"

"No. I wish I did, though." She leaned her head back on the couch and closed her eyes as she breathed deeply in and out.

While Newt's sister rested, he took the opportunity to reflect upon what had just happened. That she appeared so calm after going through such a traumatic experience surprised him.

Charlotte Aldrich's high cheekbones gave her a gaunt appearance. She couldn't be much more than two or three inches over five feet, and probably didn't weigh over a hundred pounds. Her muddy-brown eyes matched her hair. Howie had told him that she was in her mid-to-late twenties and that she worked as a librarian in the Richfield area. Adam didn't like to stereotype people, but she certainly fit the image of a young, but matronly librarian. Perhaps with a different hairstyle and the right kind of makeup (if she even wore makeup), she might be considered reasonably attractive, but her looks certainly weren't the type that invited men to turn their heads as she walked by. He imagined her spending evenings listening to classical music, reading books, drinking herbal tea with a wedge of lemon, and being in bed right after the ten o'clock news. She probably had few dates because men would be intimidated by her intellect.

Charlotte opened her eyes, took another deep breath, and looked over at Adam. "Maybe he's connected with the other man in some way."

"What other man?"

"A man who's been showing up at the library where I work. He has a black mustache and coal-black eyes. He's very creepy looking."

"And how old is this guy would you say?"

"I don't know, maybe in his late thirties or early forties."

"Has he ever approached you?"

"No, but he's always watching me." Charlotte shuddered and wrapped her arms around herself. Her eyes took on an intensity that transformed their color to a richer brown. "Several times I have caught him staring at me. When I do, he quickly turns away and pretends he's reading a newspaper."

Adam wondered if the man could be connected with the disappearance of Charlotte's brother. "How long has this been going on?"

"For a couple of weeks now."

"Do you have any idea of why he would be watching you?"

Charlotte leaned forward. "Being a woman these days can be frightening. You can never be too careful. Even in the suburbs, a library is no longer as safe as you might think. There are too many strange people out there. Don't you agree?"

"Oh, yes. We've met some in the kind of work we do." Adam wasn't sure if the person Charlotte was describing was some kind of pervert who had a thing for librarians, whether she simply had an overactive imagination, or if the man was connected with the heavy-set intruder, or maybe even with Newt. Although he was curious as to what the man with the mustache might be all about, he needed to get to the reason why he had come in the first place. "Can you tell me anything about your brother that would help us in locating him?"

"If I had been asked that a couple of months ago, I could've been able to give you an answer. I would've told you what his likes were, the name of his friends, where he hung out..." Charlotte shook her head, her eyes reflecting a deep sadness.

"What's the matter?"

"Newton has changed so much lately that I wonder if I know him at all."

"Changed? In what way?"

"He used to be so fun loving." A shadow of disapproval came over her. "Then he began to go to bars and hang out with the guys. The bar thing was Squirrel's influence."

"Sounds like you don't like Squirrel."

"It's not that—I just don't approve of his lifestyle. He wasn't being a very good role model for my brother to emulate."

"Did you tell Newt that you disapproved?"

"Of course. Both he and Squirrel knew that." Charlotte placed her hands in her lap, rubbing the top of her hand with the fingers of the other. "But then he got involved with some other people. After he met them, he stopped going to bars and carousing around." Her eyes flickered. "I suppose I should've been thankful for that, but he became so serious and completely lost his sense of humor. He just wasn't the brother I knew." She clasped her hands together. "I can't be sure, but I think the people he met must be part of some kind of religious group."

"Why do you think that?" Adam asked, glad that she didn't know that he was planning to become a minister.

"Because he would mention going to these *prayer meetings* as he called them. That was so unlike him. I mean neither of us had ever been very religious." Charlotte waited as if she expected a comment. When none came, she continued. "When I asked him about the meetings, he would only get this sly smile on his face and then change the subject."

"And you don't know anything about these meetings?"

She shook her head. "All I know is that they were at night…late at night. It didn't make any sense to me at all."

"Do you think these people had something to do with his disappearance?"

"Maybe. I don't know. Everything is so confusing."

The room felt warm to Adam and his head throbbed from the blow he took. "Is there anything else you can tell me about your brother that might be—"

The ringing of the telephone in the next room startled both of them. Charlotte hesitated, letting it ring several times. "Excuse me, but I think I'd better answer that. I'm expecting a phone call from a friend." She got up and left the room.

Adam heard her answer the phone, but after her initial hello, her voice softened so he couldn't hear what she was saying.

While she was gone he glanced around the room, wanting to get a sense of what this woman was all about. Howie always told him that you could discover a lot about a person from their surroundings.

The furnishings in the living room were tasteful but hardly extravagant. A five-foot, dark-oak bookcase filled with books stood against one wall. Atop the bookcase, at both ends, sat two matching vases with red dragons painted on them. Beautifully framed prints of classic paintings adorned two of the walls. He recognized one of the paintings as a Rembrandt only because there was one like it in the library at the seminary. There was no television set in the room, but there was a stereo with a stack of records beside it. He was about to get up and check out the titles in the bookcase when Charlotte walked back into the room.

"I'm sorry. It was just someone from work." She sat down on the couch and crossed her legs, her dangling foot twitching back and forth. "I believe you were about to say something before the phone interrupted us."

"I was just going to ask if there was anything else you could tell me about Newt," Adam replied, wondering why her manner had become curt.

"I'm afraid there's nothing more I can tell you."

"Are you sure?"

"Of course, I'm sure."

Unlike Howie, Adam never felt comfortable pressing people to talk. "Well, I guess I'll be leaving then, unless you'd like me to stay for a while in case that man comes back."

"Thank you, but that won't be necessary."

"I think it might be a good idea for you to call the police and file a report."

"I'll do that."

Adam stood to leave. "I'll be in touch," he said, anxious to get outside where it was cooler and breathe in some fresh air.

Chapter 21

Newt Aldrich needed a smoke in the worst way, but didn't dare light one in *his* presence. He stole a glance at the clock. "Do...do you think it's over?"

"Perhaps." The sympathetic smile *he* offered lacked warmth. "I did tell you that it was necessary, did I not?"

"Ye...yes."

"And you believe me, don't you?"

"Sur...sure." Necessary or not, Newt hated the thought of his sister being slapped around. He hoped Charlotte would understand. But would she? Did he even understand? He wanted to ask why it was necessary, but knew from experience that it would be best not to inquire. The last time he had questioned something, the icy stare he received back sent chills down his spine.

"Don't worry. She won't be hurt. I just wanted to throw a little scare into her." His tone turned threatening. "After all, you wouldn't want her to panic and go to the police, would you?"

Newt shook his head.

"Good, I'm glad you understand." He paused. "Why don't you call her and make sure she understands."

"Whe...when do you think I should call?"

"You can call her now." He rose and walked over to Newt. "I'll leave so that you two can have a nice brother-sister chat." He patted him on the shoulder. "And after you're done talking with your lovely sister, be sure to make that second call."

As soon as he had left, Newt called his sister. "Come on, come on...answer." When the phone was finally picked up, he had to control himself from shouting into the receiver. "Sis, this is Newt. Are you okay?"

"Yes." Charlotte lowered her voice. "Where are you?"

"I can't tell you now. Listen, I'm calling because I know about what happened to you tonight. The guy's gone now, isn't he?"

"Yes, but how did you know he was here?"

"It doesn't matter. Are you sure you're okay, Sis?"

"I'm a little shaken up, but I'll be fine. Don't worry about me."

"Why are you speaking so quietly?"

"Because there's a detective in the living room."

"A detective!" Newt's heart skipped a couple of beats as he shuddered to think how *he* would react to that news. "What's a detective doing there?"

"Squirrel hired him to investigate your disappearance. He just happened to be at the front door when I yelled for help. Lucky for me, he chased the guy away."

"That's good. I'm so thankful that you're okay." Newt fumbled in his shirt pocket for his pack of cigarettes. "What did you tell the detective when he asked about me?"

"That I didn't know where you were."

Newt breathed a sigh of relief. "Look, Sis, don't tell that detective anything more and just get rid of him, okay?"

"Sure, of course."

"And don't tell the police anything about what happened tonight."

"Why?"

"I can't go into that now. You just have to trust me on this."

"Are you in some kind of trouble?"

"I would be if you went to the police."

"I don't understand. What's going—"

"Look, I don't have time to talk now. If you care about me, you'll stay away from the cops. And get rid of that detective."

"Okay, I will."

"Sis, I've got to go." Newt hung up without giving her a chance to reply. It had been a relief to hear her voice, but he was puzzled. For what she had gone through, she sounded quite calm. Maybe she was in a state of shock. She had always been a strong person, but he still worried about her. In a couple of days, if he got the chance, he would check on her.

He picked up the phone again to make the second call. After dialing the number, he lit a cigarette and took a long drag. On the seventh ring a familiar voice answered; organ music played in the background.

"It's Newt. He's ready for number two."

"You shouldn't be calling me here." There was a hesitation. "When does he want it?"

"This Friday."

"What! You've got to be kidding. It's too soon. I can't do it."

"All you have to do is to make sure we can get in. Nobody will suspect you."

"That's easy for you to say."

"Just do it. And remember that he doesn't like to be disappointed." Newt allowed his last remark to sink in. "We'll be there around eleven that night. Make sure the door's unlocked."

Chapter 22

Howie looked up from the magazine he was reading. The downstairs entrance door had slammed shut and the wooden stairs creaked with the weight of the person coming up. By the sound of the thudding of the footsteps, it had to be Mick and he was taking two stairs at a time. Within moments, the office door flew open. In the doorway stood Mick, his breathing coming in shallow spurts, his nostrils flaring.

"Are you okay?" Howie asked. "What in the world happened at—" He caught sight of the shoebox his partner clutched under his right arm. "Oh, damn!" He locked eyes with Mick. "It's Damien again, isn't it?"

Mick walked over, placed the box on Howie's desk, and collapsed into a chair. "That was delivered to Mary's tonight." His voice shook with anger. "She thought it was a surprise shower gift from me."

"Oh, man, I'm sorry. That had to have been awful for her."

"Awful? It was horrible!" Mick clinched his hand into a fist and pounded the arm of his chair. "I can't believe this is happening." He pointed to the shoebox. "Wait until you see what's in that. You'll know immediately it's from him. Nobody else would do something so warped as that." He slammed his fist into the arm of the chair a second time. "I had hoped that we'd never see that creep again."

"You and me both." Howie moved the shoebox to one side, not anxious to open it, but also wanting to let Mick vent his emotions. His partner no doubt was remembering that one night in a cemetery and what Damien had done to him.

"I thought we were finished with him," Mick said, his eyes burning with rage. "I didn't care if I ever saw him again, but now I just want to get my hands around his neck." He looked toward the window and cracked his knuckles.

They had locked horns with Damien in their very first case. A cunning but diabolical adversary, the man had gotten away with murder. Howie recalled the other shoeboxes sent to them and how appalling their contents were. As the wall clock ticked the seconds away, the two of them sat staring at Damien's latest intrusion within their lives. "What's in it?" he finally asked.

"A finger."

"A what?"

"A finger...a human finger!" Mick blew out a puff of air. He shook his head in disgust. "This whole thing is so gruesome. Do you know that it took me forty-five minutes to calm Mary and the other girls down?"

"How are they doing?"

"They're okay for now." Mick buried his face in his hands for a moment as though he was trying to block out the nightmare. "One of Mary's friends will be staying with her tonight. That will help."

Howie had a flashback to the other packages they had received from Damien. The unspeakable contents of those shoeboxes had shocked them. It all began when he and his partners had gotten involved in a case with a woman by the name of Jodelle Hammond. She had hired them under the pretense of finding her cat, implying that her sister had something to do with it. What they didn't know at the time was that the Hammond woman had been mixed up in a group headed by Damien. When she had left the group she took *The Book of Shadows*. As long as Jodelle had the book, her life and the life of her sister were in danger. Damien was the type of egotistical maniac who would destroy anyone who got in his way. He was also the type who would seek revenge, and on that point, it appeared that Howie and his partners were now at the top of his list.

"Did you tell Mary who the package was from?" Howie asked, already guessing the answer.

"You bet I did." Mick clinched his fist again. "And I told her that she got it because it was his sick way of getting to me." He leaned forward, his nostrils flaring again. "We've got to get the police involved."

"Are you sure you want to do that?"

"Yes!" Mick moved to the edge of his seat. "You call JD. I don't want to take any chances now that Mary's tangled up in this mess."

Howie looked at the clock; it was nearly nine. "I'll give him a call the first thing tomorrow morning."

"No!" Mick cried as he pounded his fist on Howie's desk. "That's not going to be good enough. This can't wait until tomorrow. Call him now!"

Mick's outburst took Howie aback for a moment. He had never seen his partner so upset. "Okay, you're right. I wasn't thinking." He picked up the phone and dialed Davidson's number. Although JD always told them that he was willing to help out, Howie preferred to handle their cases by themselves. He didn't want his detective agency to get the reputation of having to run to the cops every time things got rough. "I'm sure he's probably gone by now," he said as the phone continued to ring. He was surprised, however, when his detective friend answered. "Hey, JD, this is Howie. Look, I know it's late, but I need to have you come up to my office."

"Can't it wait until tomorrow?" JD sounded tired. "I was just about ready to go home, open myself a cold brew, and catch the last part of the ballgame."

"You can read the score of the ballgame in tomorrow's paper," Howie said. "I guarantee you're going to forget about baseball once you hear what I have to tell you."

"This better be worth my while."

"It is." Howie glanced at the shoebox. "My partner's fiancée received a human finger in a package earlier this evening."

"What! Did you say what I think you said? A finger?"

"You heard me right."

"Did he report it?"

Howie held his hand over the speaker end of the phone. "He wants to know if you reported it to the cops."

Mick shook his head. "I wanted to keep Mary out of the picture if possible."

"No, he didn't," Howie said. "He brought the package to my office and it's sitting on my desk right now."

"What's it doing in your office?" JD lowered his voice, causing Howie to think that he was keeping his conversation from arousing the attention of his fellow police officers. "Don't you realize that you probably screwed up getting prints? Come on, damn it! You guys should know better than that."

"You don't have to worry about fingerprints with this thing," Howie said, irritated at Davidson's comment.

"And why not?"

"We already know who sent it."

"And who's that?"

"He goes by the name of Damien."

"Damien?" JD didn't say anything for several moments. "Didn't we have some dealings with this guy before?"

"Yeah, my partners and I went head-to-head with him about a year ago. Look, once you get here, I'll explain the whole story to you."

"I'll be there as soon as I can."

Chapter 23

After Adam left Charlotte Aldrich's, he decided to make a quick trip over to the library at the seminary. He needed to pick up a couple of books to finish a paper for a church history class. Once he was done at the library, he would go home and finish the paper.

Tomorrow he would fill Howie in on his visit with Newt's sister. That she seemed to be such a vulnerable person made him want to help her. What also influenced his desire to help was that she appeared to be a loner, and he identified with that. Other than Mick and Howie, he had few friends. Charlotte needed a friend, especially since some guy was stalking her where she worked.

As he turned onto the freeway toward the library, he couldn't shake an uneasy feeling about the car with the one headlight behind him. Although he had noticed the car several blocks earlier, he forgot about it while on the freeway; it was only when he turned onto the Como Avenue exit from Highway 280 that he noted that the car also turned. He stopped at the stop sign and turned right onto Como Avenue. When he slowed to make a left hand turn after having gone a block, he noted that the other car had turned right onto Como Avenue as well. As he waited for oncoming cars before making his turn, a chill went down his back as the car with the one headlight drove past him. He tried to get a glimpse of the driver, but it was too dark to see.

Chapter 24

"Do you want another cup of coffee?" Howie asked.

Mick shook his head. "I don't think so."

"Suit yourself." Mick may have sounded outwardly calmer than when he first arrived, but cracking his knuckles every few minutes told a different story. "Are you sure you don't want any more coffee?" Howie asked.

"Yeah, I'm sure. If I have any more of that stuff, I won't sleep tonight." Mick shot a look toward the wall clock. It had been nearly forty minutes since Howie had called JD. "How long did Davidson say it would take to get here?"

"He didn't say."

"The guy's only fifteen minutes away." Mick got up, walked over to the window, and scanned the street below. "I don't know what's taking him so long."

"He had to finish up some paperwork on a robbery case. Don't worry. He'll be here any minute." Howie stood up and stretched; he needed to settle his partner down. "Do you want anything to eat?"

"I'm not hungry."

"Did you eat supper?"

"No."

"Well, you've got to eat something."

"What have you got?"

"Some liver sausage. I can make you a sandwich, slap some raw onions on it, and top it with mustard. It's good that way."

Mick wrinkled his nose. "Count me out." He came back, sat down, and pointed to the shoebox sitting on Howie's desk. "I'm going to have enough nightmares as it is." The downstairs entrance door slammed and the stairs began to creak. "That must be JD," Mick said.

Howie listened to the footsteps. "It doesn't sound like him."

"Are you sure?"

"Yeah. JD weighs close to two hundred pounds." Howie cocked his ear toward the door. "Whoever is coming up can't weigh more than…I'd say, 130, if that. The footsteps sound familiar, however."

"I don't know how you can tell all of that just by those stairs creaking." Mick got up, moved over to the door, and opened it just as the person reached the top of the stairs.

"Thanks," Squirrel said as he walked in, flashing Mick a toothy grin. He reached into his pocket, pulled out a quarter, and flipped it to his doorman who nearly dropped it. "Keep the change," he said, giving him a wink and a nod.

"What brings you here?" Howie asked as Squirrel strolled over and made himself comfortable in a chair while Mick stood at the door, frowning and staring at the quarter laying in his outstretched hand.

"I was just strolling by, saw the lights on, and thought I'd stop by to see what's cooking." Squirrel pointed to the shoebox on Howie's desk. "Hey, man, it looks like now that you got me as a paying customer, you can afford a new pair of shoes." He reached toward the box. "I've got to see what kind of style you wear. I'll lay you three-to-one that—"

"Don't touch that!" Mick cried as he rushed up and moved the box out of the reach of Squirrel. He tossed the quarter back to its owner before sitting down in the other chair.

"My, my, you're testy." Squirrel flipped the quarter in the air, caught it with a flair, and slipped it into his pocket. "What's the big deal about a pair of shoes?"

"They concern a case we're working on," Howie said.

"Is that so?" Squirrel's nose twitched. "I'll bet you five-to-one that I can tell you the type of guy you're looking for just by the color and style of those shoes."

"I'm sure you can," Howie said.

"Let me take a look then."

"I don't think so."

"Why not? If you can't trust old Squirrel here, who can you trust?"

Howie suppressed a smirk. "I can't show you because of client confidentiality. Isn't that right, Mick?"

Mick nodded.

"Okay, I can dig that. So tell me how far you have gotten on finding Newt." Squirrel crossed his legs and settled back into the chair. "I just want to make sure that I'm getting my money's worth." The corners of his mouth turned slightly upwards and his nose twitched several times. "You know what I mean, don't you?"

"You would be interested in knowing that Adam had a talk with Newt's sister." Howie put an edge to his tone. "How come you didn't tell us that he had a sister?"

Squirrel shrugged. "I didn't think it was that important." He leaned forward, his eyes brimming with curiosity. "So what did she have to say? Does she know where that crook of a brother is hiding out with my money?"

"She didn't have much to say and she doesn't know where he is."

"That's bull." Squirrel scrunched his nose. "Five-to-one she's lying through her teeth."

"We think that may be the case, also."

"So what are you going to do about it?"

"Adam's going back to pay her another visit." Howie thought about mentioning the guy his partner scared off, but decided not to disclose that information. "Can you tell us anything about her?" he asked, wondering how much Squirrel knew about Newt's sister and any possible threats against her.

"I don't know much except that the broad's a book duster."

"A what?"

"A book duster." Squirrel leaned back, blew on his fingernails, and buffed them on the front of his shirt. He glanced over at Howie's partner, but Mick remained passive, apparently not amused by his description. "You know what I mean—a librarian. I only met her once when I picked Newt up where she lived. She's not exactly a hot piece of property. Of course, it was in the evening and I didn't get a real good look at her." The downstairs entrance door slammed, causing Squirrel to jerk his head toward the office door.

"That must be him," Howie said to Mick.

"Who's him?" Squirrel asked, his nose twitching. "Anybody I know?"

"You may." Howie waited for the footsteps to reach the office door. He took note that Squirrel's cocky smile faded when JD walked in.

"Well, if it isn't my old friend Squirrel," JD said in a matter-of-fact tone as though meeting Squirrel was an everyday occurrence.

"Oh...uh, hello, Detective Davidson," Squirrel muttered, giving him but a passing glance.

Davidson greeted Howie and Mick, and turned his attention back to Squirrel. "Don't tell me that you're up here to collect on a bet?" His right eyebrow arched as he turned to Howie. "I'm surprised at you betting with this guy." He gestured toward the street hustler now squirming in his seat. "Don't you know that you can't win with this character?"

"So the two of you know each other?" Howie was amused at how Squirrel's whole demeanor demonstrated that he wished he were someplace else.

"Do we know each other?" JD looked as though he would laugh out loud. "We sure do. We're old buddies." He slapped Squirrel on the shoulder hard enough to make the little guy wince. "Isn't that right?"

Squirrel jerked his head toward Davidson, his eyes turning stormy. "Listen, the two times you booked me, it didn't stick. You didn't have any proof." He got up and offered the police detective his chair. "Go ahead and be my guest."

"You don't have to stand for me."

"I'm not. I was just leaving." Squirrel turned to Howie. "I'll be in touch." He resumed his cocky attitude as he moved past Davidson. "Don't take any wooden nickels, Detective Davidson." For a split second, Howie thought that Squirrel was going to pull out a quarter and flip it to JD.

Once Squirrel was out the door, JD sat down next to Mick. "What was that character doing up here anyway?"

"We're working on a case for him," Mick said.

"You're kidding."

"His partner has turned up missing," Howie said. "He hired us to try and locate him. We've only been on the case for a couple of days."

JD shot Howie a quizzical look. "By any chance is his partner a guy by the name of Newt Aldrich?"

"Yeah, do you know him?"

"Our paths have crossed," JD replied with a half smile. "We've had him down at the station a couple of times, nothing big, just some petty stuff. We haven't heard too much about him lately. I thought maybe that he had left town." He pointed at the shoebox on Howie's desk. "Is that what you called me about?"

Howie nodded. He slid the box toward JD.

"It was delivered to my fiancée's house earlier tonight," Mick said. "She was having a wedding shower. It shook her and her friends up pretty good."

"And you say this guy Damien was behind it?" JD asked.

"No doubt about it," Howie said, having consulted with JD about certain aspects of the Damien case last year. Although JD and Damien never crossed paths, he had warned Howie and his partners that from what they told him about the guy, they were dealing with a dangerous psycho.

If Davidson was sickened when he opened the box, he didn't show it. He had been in police work for eighteen years. Once, over coffee, he had shared with Howie that he had seen more than his share of bodies and body parts. Howie and Mick watched as he tilted the box, causing the finger to thud against the side of the cardboard. Davidson cocked his head to one side and then to the other before setting the box back on the desk. "I'm pretty sure I know where that came from."

"You do?" Mick shifted in his chair away from Howie's desk as though he wanted to have as much distance as possible between himself and the contents of the box.

"I'll have to wait for the lab results, but I'd bet a week's pay that it came from the body we found down under the bridge."

"You mean the Phillips body was missing a finger?" Howie asked.

"Yep, the ring finger of her left hand. It was sliced clean off. Whoever did it used a very sharp instrument." Davidson picked up the box, studied its contents for a minute and set it back down. "I'd say it's a match."

"Oh, man." Mick cracked his knuckles and looked at Howie. "And that creep sent it to Mary. He's trying to play mind games with us again, isn't he?"

"It appears that way." Howie was determined to get as many leads on Damien as he could. The man reveled in exercising control and intimidation over others. No doubt sending the severed finger to Mick's fiancée was Damien's way of announcing he was back. "Look, JD. You said her forehead was carved up. Was there anything unusual about the carving?"

"I could get into a lot of trouble if I told you and it got back to the department." Davidson eyed the two detectives. "It's an ongoing investigation. The chief would have—"

"Come on," Howie said, "you owe me."

"Owe you? For what?"

"I don't know. I'll think of something." Howie paused. "You've got to help us out on this." He gestured toward Mick. "He and Mary are getting married in three weeks. We don't have a lot of time to get this resolved."

"Okay, but keep this to yourselves," JD said. "The letter W was carved into her forehead."

Howie noted that his partner's mouth had dropped open at the disclosure. When Mick moved his hand across his chest, Howie knew why. In their first case, Mick had been kidnapped by Damien and his cohorts, and taken to a cemetery out in the country, about an hour south of the Twin Cities. The next day Damien sent Howie a note with a hand-drawn map of where they could find their partner. He and Adam found Mick tied to a tombstone. What Damien had done to Mick sickened Howie.

"We've got to get Damien before he does anything to Mary," Mick said. "That monster is capable of anything."

JD nodded. "That's why I think you have to be careful on this one. My gut tells me that he's out to settle a score with you guys."

Mick cracked his knuckles. "That goes both ways."

"We're not backing away from him," Howie said. "So any information we can get will be helpful. What do you say that we spend some time comparing notes now?"

"Let's not make it too long." JD glanced at his wristwatch. "I still want to catch the last part of the ball game."

"Okay. Let me begin then by briefly refreshing your memory about Damien and then you can tell us what you know about the case." Howie flipped open his notepad. "Maybe between us we can come up with some leads and nail this guy."

Chapter 25

On a moonless Friday night shortly before midnight, Newt Aldrich parked the station wagon and turned off the headlights. The chill in the air could not prevent beads of perspiration running down his face. He prayed that the two of them wouldn't be there long and that no one would spot them. Damien had insisted that the body be brought to the same bridge and placed in the identical spot where they had left the first body. Newt thought about protesting that it was too dangerous and that there might still be cops snooping around. He kept silent, however. Damien wasn't a person to argue with. Newt had witnessed what happened to others when they tried. In the beginning Damien's power over people had impressed him; now, it just frightened him.

"Help me take her out," Damien said as Newt joined him at the back of the station wagon.

Newt was glad that the body was wrapped in a sheet. He didn't like being around corpses. "She's heavy," he noted, but got no reply as Damien held his end with ease as though he drew his strength from the dead.

"Lay her down for a moment," Damien commanded. "And be gentle about it. We wouldn't want to wake her, would we now?"

"Wha...what's in there?" Newt asked as Damien took a black leather briefcase from the back of the station wagon.

"You'll find out. Be patient."

As they descended down the treacherous slope to the river bank, Newt nearly tripped on roots, and once he almost slipped on loose soil. By the time they arrived at the spot under the bridge, Newt's sweat-soaked shirt stuck to his skin. Damien, however, looked as if he had merely taken a stroll through the park. They set their load down and Newt watched as Damien unwrapped the body. It could have been Newt's imagination, but he thought he caught a whiff of the lingering sweet smell of funeral flowers coming from the corpse. After carefully positioning the young woman on the sheet to make it appear as though she was sleeping on her back, Damien unsnapped the black leather case.

Newt gulped when he saw what Damien took out. "I'll...I'll wait in the car, if that's all right?"

"If you wish," Damien said, a mocking grin upon his face.

As Newt walked away, he could feel Damien's eyes upon him. The thought of those piercing dark eyes caused the hairs on his neck to prickle. Even though the woman was dead, he didn't want to even imagine what Damien was planning to do to her.

Chapter 26

Howie poured himself a second cup of coffee and passed the bag of donuts to his partners. The donuts were his offering for a Saturday mid-morning breakfast meeting. Personally, he could've done without the donuts, but he needed the coffee, the blacker the better. Whenever working on a case, he never slept soundly, especially when there weren't any new leads. And with the Phillips case, what few leads they had had dissolved quickly. Adding to his sleep problems had been JD's visit on Tuesday night informing them about the letter W carved into her forehead. After the police detective left that night, Howie stayed up past midnight trying to figure out what that letter could represent. Although he had a list of a dozen or so possibilities, none of them seemed right, and he was counting on Adam turning up something at the seminary's library later that afternoon.

A couple of times during the week he had gotten up in the middle of the night, made himself a pot of coffee, and moseyed out into his office. He would sit down, lean back, and rest his feet upon his desk. Usually he would just sip his coffee and mentally replay all the facts about the case, but last night, the movie poster of Bogart caught his eye.

"Hey, Bogie, have you got time for a question?"

For you, kid, I've got all the time in the world. What do you need to know?

"When you're working on a case, what do you do when you keep running up against brick walls?"

Yeah, I know what you mean. It happens to all of us. Tough luck sometimes. Stay in the game though. You'll be dealt a better hand.

"I hope so but I wonder if I ever should've gotten into this business in the first place. I could've—what? What did you say?"

I said I don't want to hear you talking crazy like that. Look, let me give it to you straight. Don't be so hard on yourself that you crack under the pressure. You got that?

"I hear you. Don't worry, though, I'm not going to crack."

Good, keep that attitude. I like that. And remember, you're keeping the bad guys in check. Don't let the crooks win.

"So, just keep at it, then, huh?"

That's right, kid. Something will turn up sooner or later. It always does.

Howie nodded and tipped his coffee cup toward Bogie in appreciation for the advice. He set his cup aside, stood up, and walked over to the framed poster. After eyeing it for several moments, he nudged the right side of it up a smidgen. "I wouldn't want you to go crooked on me," he quipped and headed for bed, hoping to get a few hours of shuteye.

The morning had come early. After feeding his partners a quick breakfast in the kitchen, they took their coffee into the office area. "Let's get down to business and review the case," Howie said. It would be a short review, however. The last several days had been quiet. Mick, having no new leads to follow, had spent most of his time with Mary. Adam used the time for researching and writing a paper for school. As for himself, Howie spent time working at the soda fountain. The only positive part of the whole week was that he'd had his office to himself. Squirrel hadn't even dropped in for an update concerning Newt. "Okay, where should we begin?" he asked.

Mick popped the remaining part of his donut in his mouth and washed it down with a couple gulps of coffee. "You're the boss. You tell us."

"What do you say, then, that I start with JD's phone call this morning?" Davidson had phoned him shortly after eight with the news that a second body had been taken from another funeral home on the North Side. When Mick and Adam arrived later that morning, Howie had told them about it immediately. Both, however, said that they preferred to talk about it after breakfast.

"What funeral home did JD say the body was taken from?" Adam asked.

"The one a block past Penn. It's the one with the white pillars in front. The name of it is...ah..." Howie set his coffee down and opened his notepad. "Just a minute...I wrote it down here someplace."

"I think it's called McNeil's," Mick said.

"That's right." Howie found the page and checked what he had written. "The body is that of a twenty-eight-year-old woman, a Mrs. Carolyn Manning. Early this morning, around seven, the body was reported missing, so it had to have been taken some time during the night after the staff went home."

Adam set his coffee cup on Howie's desk. "Did JD tell you if the funeral home was broken into?"

"As he understands it, it wasn't, but he hadn't had time to read the full police report. I guess he's been pretty busy investigating a couple of robbery cases." Howie looked over his notes. After he had received JD's call, he had phoned Gaylord Underwood and asked if he would talk with McNeil's funeral director. Underwood agreed and a half hour later called to share what he had found out. "Underwood said that the woman's husband nearly went into shock when he had learned that his wife's body was missing."

"That news would be tough to take for anybody," Adam noted. "Poor guy."

"They had only been married a year when she died of some kind of blood infection." As Howie continued to share the personal details, he couldn't help but notice the revulsion on Adam's face. On Mick's face, however, there wasn't only revulsion, but also concern. No doubt, his thoughts had turned to Mary.

"Anything else on this?" Adam asked.

"No, but I'm hoping that JD will have more information in the next couple of days. If he does find out anything new, he'll let us know." Howie took a sip of coffee. "Remember, we've got to keep this to ourselves. JD went out on a limb to tell us about this one. He says that I really owe him big time."

Mick cracked his knuckles and looked up, an apologetic expression on his face. "Sorry, guys." He smiled, but it appeared forced. "It's Damien and that package he sent to Mary. That guy is up to his old tricks again and I'm worried about what he's planning." He fingered the buttons on his shirt as though making sure they were buttoned. "If we only knew what he was up to we could do something."

"Well, here's what we do know." Howie raised his forefinger. "Number one: we can be sure that Damien's in town." He raised a second finger. "Number two: he no doubt was involved with stealing the body of Carole Anne Phillips and cutting off her finger."

"And carved that initial into her forehead," Adam added.

Howie nodded. "And number three, he sent that box to Mary."

Mick slammed his fist into his palm. "If I ever get my hands on that man, so help me, I'll kill the—"

"Hey, take it easy." Adam reached over and patted his friend on the shoulder. "I understand how you feel, but don't worry. This time we'll get Damien and make sure he's put away for a long time."

"That'll suit me just fine," Mick said, his voice calmer now. He took a deep breath, blew it out slowly, and fixed his eyes on Howie. "I'm okay now." He rested his hands in his lap. "So what do you think is the significance of that W?"

"I'm not sure." Howie looked over the list of possibilities that he had made and turned to Adam. "Do you think it could stand for witchcraft or wickedness or something like that?"

"It could, but more than likely it's some kind of satanic symbol. If it is, I'm not familiar with it." Adam paused. "I didn't have time this week, but I'll go to the library on Monday and do some research. There's a section on Evil and Demonology. Maybe I'll come up with something that will give us a clue."

"Isn't your library open on Saturday afternoons?" Howie asked.

"Yeah, why?"

"Well, is there any chance that you could go today?"

"I wish I could, but I can't."

"How come?"

"Because I need to spend some time at the library where Newt's sister works and see if I can spot this guy who's been watching her. I called her on Wednesday and talked to her about him." Adam turned his attention to Mick. "She's pretty shook about it and I promised I would get there the first chance I got." His tone turned apologetic. "I should've gotten there before now, and I really want to make it this afternoon. Believe me, if there was any other way…"

"Don't worry, I understand," Mick said.

"Okay, so go ahead and do it." Howie made a notation in his notepad. "The other stuff can wait until Monday. Does she have any idea why this guy's watching her?"

"No, but if he's there today, I'm planning on confronting him." Adam's eyes reflected determination. "Who knows, he may have something to do with Newt's disappearance, or at least maybe he'll provide us with some leads."

Mick leaned toward Adam. "How about going to the library after you're done with that?"

"Sorry, by then I'll have to spend some time preparing for tomorrow morning."

"That's right. I forgot."

"What's going on tomorrow morning?" Howie asked.

"It's Sunday, and I'm going to preach at that church in Long Lake. Remember, I told you about that earlier this week."

"Okay, but why do you have to go out there tonight?"

"I need to practice my sermon and get a feel for the place." Adam turned to Mick. "I promise that I'll go to the school library the first thing Monday morning."

Mick nodded. "Thanks."

"We'll meet for sure tomorrow afternoon," Howie said. "But I think we should also touch base with each other later today. What do you say we get together this evening?"

"That's okay with me," Adam said. "I should have no problem getting back here by eight-thirty at the latest."

"That time is fine with me," Mick said.

Howie closed his notepad and slipped it into his shirt pocket. "Okay, then, that's a done deal."

"Are you two coming out tomorrow?" Adam asked.

Howie hesitated. He hadn't been in a church since his father died. He wasn't sure what he believed anymore. For now, with the detective agency, he had put the whole religious thing on the back burner. "Ah, sure, we'll come. It's at nine-thirty isn't it?"

"No, ten."

"I'll pick you up around nine-thirty," Howie said to Mick.

"That's cutting it pretty close, isn't it?" Adam asked.

"No problem. There shouldn't be much traffic at that time of the morning."

"Do you need directions?"

Howie shook his head. "Once you go through town, you turn right on that first road. Go on that road for a mile or so and you'll run right into the church. It's out in the country all by itself and there's a cemetery across the road from it. Right?"

"That's right."

"What are you going to do this afternoon?" Howie asked Mick.

"Before I get Mary, I thought I'd try and see if I can catch Leon Spark's ex-wife at home. I'm anxious to find out if she has anything that would help us with the case. It shouldn't take too long. After that Mary and I are going out for an early dinner and then she is going to spend the rest of the evening talking with her mother about the wedding plans."

"How's Mary doing?" Adam asked.

"Much better, but receiving that package really unnerved her." Mick shifted in his chair. "I just want to be close in case Damien gets any more funny ideas and tries something else."

"I don't blame you." Howie picked up what was left of his donut and popped it into his mouth, washing it down with lukewarm coffee. "I'm going to wait around for a while and see if JD calls. He promised that if he found out anything new, he'd call me by noon. This afternoon, I'm going to spend some time trying to track down Newt."

"Do you have any leads?" Adam asked.

"Not really. I'm going to try all of the eating establishments in and around the area of Margo's. I figure that if Newt frequented that bar, maybe he ate at one of the restaurants."

"That seems like a long shot," Mick said.

"I know, but who knows what may turn up." Howie picked up his coffee cup, cringed at the grounds covering the bottom like grains of black sand, and put the cup down. "I want to finish this Newt case so that we can fully devote ourselves to Damien."

"Don't forget about those letters that Kass has been receiving," Adam said.

"I haven't forgotten."

"Any new information on that?" Mick asked.

"Nothing. Even JD doesn't have anything new." Howie leaned back in his chair. "Well, we'll see you guys later tonight. Maybe by then something will pop up."

"Something is going to pop up this evening," Mick said.

"What do you mean?"

Mick got up and walked over to the window. "Right now we have blue sky, but according to the weatherman, we're supposed to get a bad storm tonight."

Chapter 27

It was nearly three in the afternoon when Adam walked into the library in south Minneapolis. Charlotte Aldrich, wearing a light-gray cardigan sweater, white blouse, and black skirt stood behind the front checkout counter helping a little boy with reddish-blonde hair sort through a stack of books. At the moment, Newt's sister was so absorbed with the youngster that she wasn't paying any attention to people entering.

Adam walked over to a floor-to-ceiling bookcase some twenty feet away from Charlotte. He randomly took a book from the shelf and began paging through it while occasionally glancing over at her. When Charlotte smiled at something the little boy said, her face took on a radiance, causing it to lose some of its harsher lines. She wasn't attractive, but someone who might be considered pretty. When she was done helping the young boy, she turned her attention to an older gentleman waiting to check out a couple of books. As soon as she had finished with the man, Adam hurried over and stood in front of the checkout counter. Several seconds passed before Charlotte looked up from what she was doing.

"Oh," she said, her eyes widening as soon as she saw who it was standing before her.

"Just act natural." Adam placed his book on the counter. "Pretend I'm asking you some questions about this book." He paused as two teenagers walked by. "We don't want to draw any unnecessary attention to ourselves."

Charlotte regained her composure, picked up the book, and opened it. "I'm just so surprised to see you."

"I told you I'd be here."

"I know, but for some reason I didn't expect you to show up today." Charlotte opened the book, turned it around, and placed her finger in the middle of the page as though pointing something out to Adam. "I thought maybe you'd show up in a couple of weeks." She smiled. "I'm glad you're here, though."

Adam took a library bookmark from a stack on the counter, placed it in the page Charlotte had shown him, and closed the book. "Is he here?"

"I haven't seen him yet."

"Okay. I'm going to sit at one of those tables near the window." Adam waited for a moment as Charlotte looked beyond him in the direction of the tables. "I'll pick one so that we have direct eye contact. You signal me if he comes in."

"How do you want me to do that?" Charlotte asked, her voice revealing a mixture of nervousness and excitement.

"Why don't you, ah…" When he glanced around the library, he took note of an older woman muffling a sneeze. "I tell you what. Rub the side of your nose a couple of times."

"I can do that." She paused. "Should I look in his direction also?"

"No, no. I'll know him from the description you gave me." Just then a middle-aged woman carrying several books came up to the counter and stood next to Adam. The older woman didn't seem to be in a rush and appeared content just eavesdropping on their conversation. "Thank you," Adam said to Charlotte. "You've been very helpful."

"Will there by anything else?"

"No, this will do."

"I hope you'll enjoy the book," Charlotte said.

"I'm sure I will." Adam walked over and sat down at the table, positioning himself so that he had a clear view of Charlotte and the front entrance. He settled in and then was startled when he took note of the title of the book he had pulled from the shelf, *The Devil Rides Outside*.

Chapter 28

As Adam was paging through a book at the library, Mick was ringing the doorbell of a canary-colored, modest-size ranch bungalow in south Minneapolis. Howie had given him the address of Louise Sparks, Leon's ex-wife. "Go see her, will you?" he said. "The woman just might have some useful information."

Mick was about to ring the bell for a second time when the door slowly opened to reveal a very attractive woman wearing a short lavender skirt and silk white blouse, both of which accentuated her curves. Her auburn hair looked as if she had just returned from a beauty salon.

"Hello there," she said in a voice sounding as smooth as silk. If the woman had any apprehension of a stranger at her door, it wasn't evident in her amber eyes. "May I help you?"

"I hope so. My name is Mick Brunner. I work for the MAC Detective Agency over on the North Side."

"A detective?" she cooed. "And what do you want with me?" She looked beyond Mick as though expecting to see someone else.

"Are you Louise Sparks?"

"Yes."

"I'd like to talk to you about your ex-husband, Leon."

"Oh, and what has he done?" Louise arched her right eyebrow in such a deliberate manner Mick wondered if she had ever been an actress. She leaned against the doorframe and folded her arms; a seductive smile revealed teeth as white as sunlight reflecting from freshly fallen snow. "Is he in some kind of trouble again?"

"He hasn't done anything wrong that I know of."

"Then why are you here?"

"We're investigating a case at the place where he works."

"You mean something happened at the funeral home?" Her eyes betrayed her apparent amusement.

"Yes, ma'am. A body was stolen from the home nearly two weeks ago and we've been asked to check into the case."

"Really?" Louise showed no surprise or shock at what she had just been told. "Was it in the paper?"

Mick nodded.

"Is that so? I guess I must've passed it over somehow."

"Well, it wasn't front page news." Mick wondered how long she and her husband had been divorced and if they kept in contact with one another. "I wonder if I could ask you a few questions."

"Where did you say you were from?"

"The MAC Detective Agency." Mick couldn't shake the feeling that she already knew where he was from and was just playing with him.

"And who hired you?"

"Sorry, but that's confidential."

"Who is it, Mother?" The voice came from behind her.

Louise turned her head toward the voice. "It's just some detective who's asking questions about your father."

Mick couldn't see who the voice belonged to, but it sounded like that of a young boy. Leon hadn't mentioned anything about having a son. Mick felt awkward standing at the front door and was afraid that he might not get past it. Howie had repeatedly reminded him and Adam that one of the cardinal rules of detective work was to always try and get invited into a person's living quarters. Their boss maintained that you not only get more answers that way, because people feel more comfortable and secure on their own turf, but you can also get insights into their character. "It's the kinds of things they surround themselves with that provide clues about their interests and who they are," Howie had said, adding, "All good detectives learn to look for such things."

"May I come in?" Mick gave her his best smile, being acutely aware that he wasn't as charming as Howie could be in these situations. "Please, it really won't take very long."

"Yes, of course. It's rude of me to not have invited you in." Louise stepped aside and gestured for her visitor to enter. As he passed her, he caught a whiff of her perfume. He couldn't place it, but it smelled expensive. "I hope you don't mind an untidy house," she said as she closed the door behind him.

Mick was led into the living room. A young boy of not more than nine or ten years old with blonde curly hair sat on the couch. "Why don't you sit here," Louise said, pointing to a cushioned high-back chair near the couch. When she joined her son, he moved closer to her. His ocean-blue eyes expressed apprehension. Mick glanced around, but didn't see anything in particular that gave clues to her character. The only apparent clutter was an assortment of magazines spread on the coffee table.

"May I get you something to drink? Coffee or water or..."

"No, that's fine," Mick said, aware that the young boy was watching him. "Hi, what's your name?" he asked the boy.

The youngster looked at his mother. After she nodded, he replied quietly, "Bradley," and then snuggled closer to her.

"What is it you wish to know?" Louise asked.

"Well, ma'am, anything you'd like to tell me about your hus—I'm sorry, your ex-husband. When I mentioned his name, you asked if he was in trouble again." Mick paused. "What did you mean by that?"

"Is he a suspect in what you're investigating?" Louise asked, her tone revealing curiosity more than anything else.

Mick shot a brief look toward the boy. "Not at this moment, but in order to conduct our investigation we may ask some questions that might imply we think a person is a suspect. We don't draw any conclusions until we have all the facts."

"Okay, so ask your questions."

"Thank you." Mick wished that Leon's son wasn't in the room. He wanted to suggest that it might be better if Bradley didn't hear the conversation, but couldn't think of a way of doing that without having the boy draw the conclusion that his father must be under suspicion. "Was Leon a good worker? I mean, did he go to work every day?"

"My ex-husband would never think of missing a day of work," Louise replied with a note of sarcasm. "He spent more time at that place than he did at home." She put her arm around her son. "That's one of the reasons we're not together anymore."

"Oh, I'm not asking you to go into the reasons for your, ah…situation."

Louise kissed her son on the forehead. "Don't worry about Bradley. He knows all the reasons for the divorce and why his father no longer lives with us." She gave him a squeeze. "Don't you, Sweetie?"

Bradley nodded.

Something about the boy troubled Mick. He had been a teacher long enough to know when kids were hiding problems and bottling their emotions, especially fear. Initially, he had thought that Bradley was afraid of him, but that wasn't it. If he could only spend a few minutes alone with the kid, maybe he would get some answers. He cleared his throat a couple of times and forced a cough. "On second thought, if it's not too much of a problem, I think I could use a cup of coffee."

"It won't take but a minute." Louise got up and straightened out the front of her skirt. She moved with the grace and elegance of a model. "Bradley, why don't you stay here and keep Mr. Brunner company?"

After Louise left, Mick turned his attention to Bradley. The kid sat quietly, hands in lap, his eyes downcast. "What grade are you in?"

"Fourth," came the timid reply, his eyes glued on his blue jeans.

"So, do you like school?"

"It's okay."

"And what's your favorite subject?" Mick asked, determined to get the young boy to open up before the mother returned.

Bradley's eyes shifted to meet Mick's. "Are you really a detective?"

Mick nodded.

The kid looked in the direction of the kitchen, and lowered his voice. "Does that mean people hire you to protect them?"

"Sometimes. Why do you—"

"Here's your coffee," Louise said as she came back into the room. "I hope you don't mind if it's black. I forgot to ask if you took cream or sugar."

"This is fine. Thank you."

For the next half hour, much to Mick's frustration, he and Louise talked only in general terms about Leon. Although he had asked her several times to explain what she had meant when she initially mentioned Leon having been in trouble before, each time she deflected his inquiries. It was almost as if she wanted to leave a cloud of suspicion hanging over her ex-husband. She offered nothing, however, that proved incriminating against Leon or would have been useful in their investigation of him. During the whole time Bradley sat quietly on the couch next to his mother, only occasionally glancing at Mick. When Mick got up to leave, he couldn't help but wonder whom the kid wanted protection from and why.

Chapter 29

Adam remained at the library for most of the afternoon. He had received no signal from Charlotte, however, that the man who had been stalking her had come in. It was nearly five when he decided to leave. He got up, stretched, and then waited until Charlotte was alone at the front desk before approaching her.

"I guess it wasn't his day to show up," Adam said.

Charlotte glanced around as though still expecting to spot the man. "I'm so sorry that you had to spend all this time here for nothing."

"It wasn't for nothing. I read the paper and caught up on reading some magazines." He placed the book he had picked from the shelf when he first came in on the counter. "I don't know what that's about, but I didn't feel like reading it."

"I don't blame you." Charlotte quickly moved the book aside. "Thank you for being here."

"No problem." Adam took one final look around the library. "I'll be in touch."

"What if he…"

"Don't worry. If the guy shows up, give me a call." Adam wrote his name and phone number on a scrap of paper and handed it to her.

"I certainly appreciate what you're doing for me," Charlotte said, clutching the paper in her hand.

"Remember, give me a call if you have to," Adam said. He left to go to his car.

The overcast sky smelled of rain, and thunderclouds were approaching from the far west. Adam checked his watch. There was still time to stop home and get a quick bite to eat before heading to the church. His plans were to be at the church by seven, practice his sermon, and go through the service a couple of times. If everything went well, he would be back at Howie's office by eight-thirty. As he walked to his car, the rumblings of distant thunder warned of the approaching storm.

Chapter 30

Damien finished with his last customer at ten minutes of six, having charmed the older woman with gratuitous compliments while giving her a perm. She had been so taken by the charismatic male stylist that she gave him a five-dollar tip.

"Thank you," he said as he bowed and then kissed her hand. *You old fool.* After leaving the shop, he swung by his living quarters, a modest one-bedroom apartment in southeast Minneapolis. Although wearied by a full day of styling the hair of middle-aged women, he looked forward to his plans for the evening. He walked into the kitchen, opened the refrigerator, and took the shoebox out. After examining its contents, he wrapped the box in brown wrapping paper, and for a final touch, added a red bow. He placed the package on the table and picked up the phone to dial his contact. It rang several times.

"It's me. I'll meet you by that empty lot on upper Broadway. We'll take one car from there."

"Do you think he'll still be there?"

"Oh, yes." Damien's tone took on a note of arrogance. "I know him well. He's very predictable."

"Ah..."

"What is it now?"

"Ah...do you know that it's going to rain?"

"So?"

"I mean it's going to storm."

"Don't worry about a little rain," Damien said mockingly. "Didn't your mother ever tell you that you're not made of sugar?" He glanced at the package on the kitchen table. "Besides, the storm will provide an appropriate backdrop to what I have planned."

After Damien hung up, he picked up the package and left. When he stepped outside into the heavy air, the sky had darkened and lightning flashed in the distance. He slid into his car, placed the shoebox on the seat next to him, and turned on the ignition. As he pulled away from the curb, he began to whistle *Get Me to the Church on Time.*

Chapter 31

Flashes of lightning illuminated the darkened sanctuary. Grotesque figures momentarily danced on back walls, rows of pews, and carpeted aisles. The pie-shaped worship area seated nearly 350; ten-foot-high by five-feet-wide connecting glass panels served as walls on both sides, making the space seem even more expansive. Rain, driven by the howling wind, pounded the wooden roof and glass partitions. Peals of thunder occasionally rattled the building.

Adam had only switched on the pulpit light, not wanting to waste electricity by turning on all the lights in the sanctuary. In addition to the pulpit light, a soft glow came from exit signs at the four doors at the back of the sanctuary and from the exit signs above each of the two doors along both sides of the chancel. One other light provided illumination: the spotlight directed at the large wooden cross. The cross, suspended by wires from the vaulted ceiling, appeared to float in mid-air above the chancel area. The spotlight on the cross provided just enough light for Adam to distinguish the first five rows of pews; beyond that, the pews faded into the darkness.

Whenever lightning flashed, the resulting illumination in the worship space reminded him of a strobe light or the flash of a camera. And after each flash, it took several seconds for his eyes to readapt to the darkened sanctuary. As the storm grew in intensity, what few lights were on began to flicker, causing Adam concern that at any moment he might be plunged into total darkness.

"I'd better get busy and concentrate," Adam muttered to himself as he prepared to go through his sermon a third time. It seemed eerie to be speaking to an empty sanctuary, but it was a good trial run for tomorrow morning when he would be facing a church full of people waiting to hear, and perhaps pass judgment on, his sermon.

A crack of thunder violently shook the glass partitions. Adam looked to see if lightning had struck one of the many trees outside. He stared for quite some time trying to catch a glimpse during the flashes of lightning, but saw nothing that would suggest that a tree or anything else had been hit. After taking a deep breath, he refocused on his sermon notes, and cleared his throat to begin again.

"Have you ever wondered whether God gets tired of watching over His creation?" His voice echoed throughout the empty sanctuary. "Do you think God ever needs to sleep? I would like to suggest that—" A noise startled him. It sounded as though it came from the back of the sanctuary. A door closing? He wasn't sure. He held his breath as he waited, squinting into the darkness. The rain, wind, and thunder provided the only sounds. When a flash of lightning lit the sanctuary, he quickly scanned the space, wondering if somebody had come in. Perhaps a member of the congregation had come to check on him. Although he saw no one, a shiver crept down his back.

"Come on, pull yourself together," he muttered as he wiped perspiration off his brow. He wet his lips the best he could; his mouth and tongue felt dry as sand. As much as he tried to comfort himself with the thought that he was in a house of God, he couldn't help but be affected by how unnerving such a space could be at night, especially during a storm. One of his seminary professors once told a story in class about a little boy who refused to enter a church because he was convinced that there were spooks inside the place. When his mother said that was nonsense and asked where he had got such a notion, the little boy replied, "From the minister. I heard him talking about some ghost being in the church." Adam had chuckled at the story at the time, but now being alone in a dark empty building while a driving rainstorm raged outside, he could sympathize with that little kid.

Adam glanced at his watch; it was nearly eight. It seemed like midnight, though. He briefly thought about calling Howie and telling him that he might not get to the office by eight-thirty. Rather than waste time looking for a phone, however, he decided to quickly go through his message once more, gather up his stuff, and head out. A clap of thunder rattled the glass partitions so hard that he thought they might shatter. "Settle down," he told himself as he wiped his brow. He took a couple of deep breaths, wet his lips, and began his sermon again.

"What time did Adam say he would be here?" Mick asked as he shifted in his chair and glanced at the wall clock.

"Eight-thirty," Howie replied. It was the second time in the past fifteen minutes that his partner had asked about the time. The office lights flickered as lightning flashed outside and a crack of thunder shook the window pane.

Mick rubbed his knuckles. Worry lines appeared at the corner of his eyes. "The storm isn't letting up."

Howie glanced at the rain pelting the window. "It'll probably slow Adam up a bit."

"You think so?"

"Yeah, traffic always moves at a snail's pace during a storm. Don't worry, though, he'll be here." Howie was concerned, however. Adam was the type of guy who always tried to be punctual. If he wasn't there by the time he said he would be arriving, he would call and let you know why he would be late. The clock read eight-fifteen and Howie hoped to hear the telephone ring, or the entrance door at the bottom of the stairs slam shut any second.

"Are you going to try and see if you can talk to that Sparks kid?" Howie asked. Mick had filled him in on his visit with Leon's ex-wife, and he was also curious about the boy.

"I'd like to. He sure seemed afraid of someone." Mick had a genuine concern for young people; it was one of the reasons why he was so popular with his students at school. He liked being a detective, but he had told Howie that he would never leave teaching. "It's pretty unusual for a kid to want to hire a detective to protect himself."

"Yeah, they usually can take care of themselves." Howie had been hired by a kid named Joey nearly a year ago. Joey didn't need any protection from anyone, but he wanted Howie to find his lost cat. The disappearance of the kid's cat had tied in with their investigation of a kidnapping and potential human sacrifice, and had provided an unexpected twist in the case. "Maybe Bradley just wants protection from some bully at school. You're a teacher; you see how those big kids like to pick on the smaller ones."

"I don't think that was Bradley's problem."

"Are you sure?"

"Pretty sure. By the look in his eyes, it had to be something else." Mick cracked his knuckles. "He was afraid of someone, and it wasn't another kid."

Howie didn't think the Sparks kid had anything to do with the case, but knew the kid's problems, whatever they were, troubled his partner. "Do you think his mother would allow you to talk to him alone?"

Mick shook his head. "I don't think so. She seemed to be very protective."

"So what are you going to do?"

"I'm not sure yet."

"Why don't you go back and talk to her?"

"I considered that, but I think she'd just give me the run around again." Mick settled back in his chair and crossed his arms. "You know, it's funny. Even though she didn't give me much of anything to suspect her ex-husband of doing, I can't shake the feeling that she might have been protecting him for some reason."

Howie picked up a pencil and began tapping it on his desk. His partner was bringing up a new and interesting twist. "What makes you think that?"

"I can't say for sure. I wish I could." Mick shrugged and then blew out a puff of air. "All I know is that she made me more suspicious of her husband than before."

"The Bible says that God journeys with us along all of the pathways in life we take. If that is true…" Another flash of lightning filled the sanctuary as Adam rehearsed his message for a third and final time. Out of the corner of his eye he caught a movement in the back of the sanctuary.

"Hello, can I help you?" he called out, still wondering if a church member had stopped by for some reason. As he waited for a reply, he consciously gnawed at his lip. "Is anybody there?" he called out again. He leaned over the pulpit and strained his eyes to penetrate the darkness. Thunder rumbled and wind-driven rain beat against the windows. He wiped his palms on his pants, and tried to swallow, but couldn't. He peered into the darkness once more, wondering if his imagination was getting the best of him. Another flash of lightning. This time there was no mistake about what he saw. A man was moving in his direction. The lightning flashed again, illuminating a second man coming from the other side. Adam opened his mouth to ask them to identify themselves, but the words stuck in his throat.

Mick rose from his chair and walked over to the window; he stood for quite some time staring at the street below. "I have an uneasy feeling about Adam," he said as he instinctively shielded his eyes from a flash of lightning. "I can't—" A crash of thunder shook the window causing him to step back. "I can't explain the feeling, but it's not positive." He turned and faced Howie. "If he's not here soon, I vote that we go out to that church and find him. What do you say?"

"I'm with you." Howie couldn't blame Mick for being uneasy. His partner had been jumpy ever since that package arrived at Mary's. Damien wasn't the type of guy you fooled with; he was cunning and smart, and most of all, dangerous. The guy wouldn't stop at anything to achieve his goals; he had proven that in the past. "It's a little past eight-thirty now. What do you say we wait for another twenty minutes?"

"Why don't we make that ten minutes?" Mick said.

"Okay, and if he doesn't show up or call by then, we'll take a drive out there."

Mick looked out the window. "I sure wish this storm would let up. It looks wicked out there."

Adam turned off the pulpit light and ducked behind the pulpit. He wondered if he should stay where he was. If he did, he could see the men once they got up to the front pews. A crash of thunder shook the windows. Moments later the spotlight shining on the cross went out. At first, he thought lightning had struck nearby and caused a power outage, but the exit lights were still on. Without the spotlight, the sanctuary was in nearly total darkness. He crouched and began moving down the chancel steps toward the front pews. Once he got to those first pews, he would slide under them and the others until he reached the back. If he couldn't see in this darkness, neither could his two visitors. His plan was simple. With them coming down toward him, he would start moving toward the entrance door. If he didn't make a sound, he just might get to those doors without being detected. He wiped the sweat running down his brow, and began moving toward the front pew.

Lightning lit up the sanctuary just as he was about to crawl under the first pew. He didn't see the two intruders and he hoped that they didn't spot him. Another flash of lightning. He saw the man's shoes and legs first. The man was no more than ten feet away. Adam stood and waited for the guy to come at him. Where's the other one? He sensed someone behind him. Before he had a chance to turn, something struck him on the head. Lightning flashed as he slipped into a deep black hole.

Chapter 32

Eight twenty-seven on a chilly, rainy Saturday night and Detective Jim Davidson didn't want to be there. He had arrived on the scene, parked his unmarked car behind a squad, and sat for several minutes hoping that the storm would let up. The call to his desk had come in twenty minutes earlier from one of the officers who found the body. The officer, a rookie by the name of Torgenson, spoke so rapidly that Davidson had to tell him to slow down.

"I was just riding by," Torgenson said, sounding as though he could hyperventilate at any moment. "I decided to check the area out."

"And why was that?"

"Because of the sergeant."

Davidson shuffled some papers on his desk, reports that he would finish on Monday. "And what about the sergeant?" he asked, realizing that Torgenson wasn't going to explain further.

"At the briefing the other night he filled us in on the Phillips' case. You know about that case, don't you, Detective?"

"Yeah, Officer Torgenson, I know all about it." Davidson settled back in his chair and stared at a fly crawling across the ceiling "Go on," he said as he leaned forward.

"Well, the sergeant told us to be on the lookout for any suspicious activity around the Broadway Bridge."

"And did you see any?"

"Any what, sir?"

Davidson rolled his eyes. "Did you see any suspicious activity?" he asked as he waved good night to another detective who was lucky enough to be going home.

"No, sir."

Davidson massaged his forehead. Rookie cops were at the bottom of his list. "Then what made you stop?"

"I just had this hunch."

"Well, good for you, Torgenson." Davidson didn't care if the rookie caught the sarcasm in his voice. He glanced at the clock. "Just hang tight. I'll be there in a little while."

Davidson now turned off his windshield wipers and stared at the rain cascading down his windshield. A flash of lightning followed by a crack of thunder indicated that the storm had no intentions of abating at any time in the near future. "Oh, shit. Might as well do it, she's not going to let up," he muttered, wishing he had an umbrella, but knowing that his peers would never let him hear the end of it if he was ever seen using one. Cops were funny that way. He got out, turned the collar up on his trench coat, and ran toward an older, heavy-set officer in a yellow raincoat waving a flashlight at him.

"It's best to go down this way, Detective," the officer said, using the flashlight to point to a section of the slope that looked somewhat manageable to navigate.

"Thanks." Davidson proceeded to inch his way down. The rain beat against his face. He cursed himself for being stupid enough to go out on such a night, regretting not having let some other detective handle this one. A couple of times he nearly slipped on the steep slope. By the time he got to the bottom, grass and mud covered his newly-polished shoes, and his rain-soaked pant legs stuck to his skin.

"Are you okay, Detective?"

"You must be Torgenson," Davidson said to the officer who had come running out from under the protection of the bridge to meet him.

A surprised look came over the officer's boyish face. "How did you know that it was me?"

"Just a lucky guess." Davidson didn't have the heart to tell him that he had *rookie* written all over him. Besides, a seasoned officer would have stayed dry under the bridge and let the detective come to him. "Where's the body?"

"Under the bridge by one of the support pillars," Torgenson replied and then had to catch up as Davidson rushed past him. "Sorry to have you come out in weather like this," he said, his words bouncing from his mouth as he ran along-side the fast-moving detective. "But I thought that you would want to see this. I wouldn't have called you if I didn't think it was important."

"Don't worry about it." All Davidson wanted to do was to get under the bridge and out of the driving rain. Once he got to the cover of the bridge, he wiped the water from his face and then brushed his hand through his crew cut a couple of times.

A black plastic sheet covered the body. Two officers, both of whom he had worked with before, were off to one side talking quietly. The rumbling of a truck along with the sounds of other bridge traffic could be heard coming from overhead. The smell of dead fish, probably carp, permeated the air. Davidson acknowledged the two officers and then asked Torgenson to lift the sheet. The rookie immediately bent over and pulled the sheet back, exposing the upper portion of the woman's body. If it weren't for her waxen appearance, one might have supposed that the young woman was asleep.

Davidson sneezed once and then again. The thought that he was going to come down with something made him irritable. "You told me you had something to show me," he said to Torgenson.

"Yes, sir."

"Well, what is it? I haven't got all night."

Torgenson face twisted as though he was in agony. "It's..."

"It's what?" Out of the corner of his eye, Davidson could see that the two other officers were watching. They were both veterans and no doubt were enjoying the interplay between him and the rookie.

"She..." Torgenson gulped. "She doesn't..."

Davidson pushed Torgenson aside and ripped back the sheet.

"Sorry, Detective. I...I—"

"Forget it and just stay out of my way!" Davidson squatted for a closer examination. Whoever had done this had to be sick in the head. "Is it a positive ID?" he asked, noting that Torgenson's face was the same color as the corpse.

"Yes, sir. We contacted the funeral director, a Mr...." The rookie officer fumbled in his shirt pocket and pulled out a slip of paper. "Here it is. A Mr. Lyle McNeil. His description of the body taken from his funeral home matches this one."

"He's not coming down here, is he?" Davidson asked as he slowly stood up, wincing at the ache he felt in his right knee, an old high school football injury.

"No, sir, I knew that you wouldn't want that." Torgenson's tone indicated that he was determined to show the seasoned detective that he could handle police work. "I told him that he should meet us at the morgue. I'm supposed to call him when we're done here."

Davidson was anxious to get home, have a long hot shower, and settle down in front of the TV with a cold beer. There was no way he was going down to the morgue; he'd let the rookie spend the rest of the night down at the body motel. "This won't take long," he muttered.

"What was that, Detective?"

"Nothing." Davidson was already convinced that this body and the Phillips case were connected. He glanced up at the bottom of the bridge and looked around the immediate area. Everything was dry for a ten-foot radius. After reaching down and feeling her hair, he announced his findings. "Her body was taken down here before it started raining. My guess it was sometime late last night, probably after midnight."

"You mean Friday night?"

"Yeah, since this is Saturday night," Davidson said, wondering if he would have to spell it out for him.

Torgenson looked at the body and then back to Davidson. "That's great police work, Detective. How did you determine that?"

"Just feel her hair, will you? It's dry as a bone." Davidson sneezed again; this time he felt chilled. Instead of a cold beer, he would fix himself a hot toddy, maybe two or three. "When did it start raining tonight?"

"I think around six or so."

"So that means that whoever brought her down didn't do it before that;

there would've been too many cars driving by. They certainly didn't do it yesterday in broad daylight, so it had to have been sometime during Friday night."

Torgenson's eyes lit up with a question. "But how do you know the body hadn't been down here longer than that?"

Davidson closed his eyes for a moment, wondering if Torgenson would ever make it past his probation period. "Because the rats would've gotten to her by now."

Chapter 33

Mick jumped up from his chair and moved over to the window. He stood looking out at the pouring rain as lightning flashed and thunder rumbled through the skies.

"Any sign of it letting up?" Howie asked as he sat at his desk, paging through his *Police Gazette* magazine.

"Not a bit."

A crash of thunder shook the window pane. Howie closed his magazine and leaned back in his chair. "When I was little, I was afraid of storms...especially the thunder. I used to cover my ears with my hands." He paused, waiting to see if Mick would comment, but his partner continued to stare out the window.

"I remember my mother telling me not to be afraid. She said that whenever it thundered, it only meant that the angels in heaven were bowling."

Mick turned around. "What do you say that we go?" He rubbed his knuckles. "I don't want to wait any longer."

Howie took note of the time: eight forty-five. Adam should have been here by now or at least, called. "Okay. I'll drive. My car's out in front. I'll leave him a note just in case he shows up." He tore a page from his notepad. *Adam – Worried about you. Mick and I took a drive out to the church. Stay here! We'll be back shortly. Howie.* On the way out, he taped the note to the office door.

"Oh, man!" Mick exclaimed as he opened the downstairs entrance door and wind-driven rain hit him in the face. "Is your car unlocked?" He eyed Howie's car parked across the street.

"No, but it won't take long to unlock it. Come on, we'll make a dash for it." Howie took off with Mick right behind him. Mick raced around to the passenger's side as Howie unlocked the driver's side door, jumped in, and quickly unlocked his partner's door.

Mick hopped in. He wiped his brow with the sleeve of his jacket. "How long will it take to get out to that church?"

Howie started the car and pulled away from the curb. "Adam said forty-five minutes but we'll make it in less than thirty."

Chapter 34

"Are we going to leave him like that?" Willard asked.

"What do you think?" Damien's eyes flashed with contempt. "That we're going to take him home with us?" He wondered who was dumber, Willard or the other fool. Neither of them had impressed him, but Willard and Roscoe were warm bodies and they were willing to do whatever he told them to do. He would keep them around until he no longer had any use for them.

"Willard was just asking," Roscoe said in defense of his friend. "There's no need to get mad, is there?"

Damien glared at Roscoe. "Why do you think I had you two tie him up?"

Roscoe and Willard glanced at the unconscious detective and traded sheepish grins.

Imbeciles Damien thought to himself. He had told them to prop Adam up against the front of the three-sided oak pulpit.

"Stretch his arms behind him and secure his wrists with the rope," he had instructed. He waited as Roscoe tied the rope around Adam's left wrist and yanked the detective's arm back.

"Here you go." Roscoe tossed the rope to his partner. Willard pulled Adam's other arm back as far as he could and wrapped the rope around the detective's wrist several times.

"Excellent," Damien said. "Now wrap the rope around the pulpit several times so that our *friend* stays in a sitting position. I want him to be comfortable. After all, the poor man may be in for a long night."

"How did we do?" Roscoe asked after he secured the last knot.

Damien knelt on one knee and examined their work. "It's passable," he announced as he stood up.

"Hey, all right!" Roscoe turned to Willard who was standing quietly to one side, but looking just as eager to receive a word of praise. "We done good!" Roscoe announced and gave his partner a triumphant slap on the back.

A stern look from Damien put an end to their celebration, however. He turned his attention to Adam. "How symbolic."

"I don't get it." A puzzled look swept over Willard's face. "What do you mean, symbolic?"

"Just look at him," Damien said. "A future minister *tied* to his pulpit. He must be very dedicated, don't you think?" He curled his lips into a sneer. "I want his partners to find him just as he is; do you understand that?" Without waiting for their reply, he crouched down to do a final check, placing his hand under Adam's chin and lifting his head so he could see his face. "My poor little detective friend...you're still out cold, aren't you? Or are you asleep because the sermon is too boring?"

Willard snickered. He pointed to his cohort. "Old Roscoe here smacked him a good one. He's going to have one nasty headache when he wakes up."

Damien straightened, walked over to the altar, and picked up the shoebox he had placed there earlier. It had pleased him when both Willard and Roscoe grimaced at the sight of the box, having shown them its contents earlier. Willard had just looked away, but Roscoe gagged when he had seen what the box contained.

"What are you going to do with that?" Roscoe asked, stepping back as Damien walked past him.

Damien placed the box in front of Adam. Once he had positioned it just right, he stepped back. "Perfect," he announced. "And that lighting from the cross adds just enough to make the scene...surreal." On his orders, the spotlight for the cross had been switched on again. He was pleased with his arrangement, but scolded himself for not having brought a camera.

"Don't you think we better get going?" Willard asked

Damien whipped around and glowered at the intrusion. "Don't you ever tell me what I should be doing!" His voice thundered throughout the sanctuary.

"Sorry, I only—"

"Silence!" Damien turned his back on the fools and slowly took in his surroundings. When he spoke again, he did so in a whisper oozing with mocking reverence. "Don't you have any respect for this space? After all, we are in the household of God." He almost laughed out loud when Willard, wide-eyed, looked around and nodded. *You fool!* Damien turned his attention to Roscoe who in return offered a weak smile, but swallowed it under the cold glare he received. *Both of you are fools, but my fools.* He glanced at his watch. "Yes, it is time to go," he announced, satisfied that he had shown that he alone was in control. "I'm sure his partners will soon be here."

As the three of them walked toward the exit door, Damien stopped. "I'll meet you in the car. There's one more thing that needs to be done." He looked toward the altar and pictured what he was about to do. "Oh, my dear Adam, that will certainly add the final touch to a perfect evening, don't you agree? Now, if I only had that camera."

Chapter 35

"Are we almost there?" Mick asked, cracking his knuckles.

"Just a few more minutes," Howie said. He and his partner had just reached the outskirts of the town of Long Lake. Luck had been with them; traffic had been light. It had only taken them a little more than twenty minutes once they had left the North Side.

Mick cracked his knuckles again. He looked toward the sky. The rain had nearly stopped and the storm had moved on.

Howie slowed the car to five miles above the speed limit. He had made good time coming out, but small-town cops had a habit of handing out speeding tickets for their Saturday night entertainment.

"Do you remember how to get to the church?" Mick asked.

"Yeah, don't worry." It was the second time Mick had asked him that question since they left the office. "I told you that I've been there before." Although Howie felt just as anxious as Mick appeared, he kept his tone calm in order to show that he was in control of the situation. "It's the first turn to the right after the main intersection," he said, hoping that his memory was correct. Mick didn't need to know that it had been two years since he had driven past the church and that had been in the daytime. If it wasn't the right turnoff, they would be losing precious time, but he wasn't about to stop and ask for directions.

"Sorry about asking again," Mick said. "I'm just concerned about Adam." He rolled down his window a crack allowing the cool night air to rush in. Thunder and flashes of lightning could be heard and seen in the distance. The storm was heading eastward, away from them.

Other than a mini-market, the windows of the other stores lining the block-long business district of Long Lake were darkened. "There's our turn up ahead," Howie said as he drove through an intersection where two gas stations sat kiddy-corner from each other. One had already closed for the night; the other looked like it was getting ready to close. Within moments, he turned onto a county blacktop road that disappeared into the darkened countryside.

"Maybe you should slow down a bit," Mick cautioned.

The road curved and dipped, but Howie ignored Mick's advice. If this was the wrong road, however, he would have to backtrack. Fortunately and to his relief, within moments the church came into view about a hundred yards ahead. "There it is!" he announced.

Mick pointed to a lone vehicle in the parking lot. "And there's Adam's car."

Howie's gut tightened. He was hoping that the car wouldn't be there, that Adam was back in the office having a cup of coffee and waiting for them to return.

"I don't like it," Mick said as they approached the gravel parking lot. "There aren't any lights on in the church."

Howie turned into the lot and pulled up along-side Adam's car. They jumped out, quickly checked to make sure that their partner's car was empty, and headed toward the main entrance of the church.

"How are we going to get in?" Mick asked.

"Let's hope it's open." The door was open, but not in the way Howie had expected. A hymnal had been used as a doorstop to prevent the door from fully closing. "What's going on here?" he muttered.

"I don't think Adam would've done that, do you?" Mick whispered.

Howie shook his head.

Mick glanced around. "Something's not right here."

"Come on, we're going in." Howie opened the door. He and his partner moved through the vestibule and opened the glass doors leading into the narthex.

"Do you see any light switches?" Mick asked.

"Let's wait a minute." For several moments they stood unmoving and listening, but hearing only the sounds of their own breathing. Howie noted a faint source of light coming through the crack of the doors leading into the sanctuary. "Let's check the worship area." They moved cautiously toward the sanctuary doors, opened one of the doors, and slipped in.

"Up by the pulpit!" Howie cried.

"Adam!" Mick took off running down the aisle.

Chapter 36

"How much longer are we going to wait here?" Willard drummed his fingers on the steering wheel.

Roscoe's voice from the backseat echoed his friend's concern. "Yeah, I think we should go."

"We'll stay until I say we leave!" Damien's tone indicated that the subject wasn't open to any further discussion. After he had added the final touch to Adam's *arrangement*, he had rejoined Willard and Roscoe waiting in the narthex.

They had parked down the road from the church, having the good fortune of finding a spot where they could pull off onto a level grassy area partially hidden from the church by two evergreen trees.

"We could still be spotted here," Willard had complained.

"But that's the excitement of the game," Damien replied.

"Game?" Roscoe said. "What game?"

"A game of cat and mouse." Damien kept his eyes on the church. "It's the nature of a cat to play with its prey before the kill."

When Damien saw the car pull into the church's parking lot, he assumed it had to be Mick and Howie. The parking lot's one lamp pole provided enough light for him to recognize that it was indeed his inept adversaries. He watched as they checked Adam's car and proceeded toward the church's main entrance.

"You should have made them pick the lock like Roscoe did." Willard shifted in his seat so he could look at his friend in the back. "You sure do have a knack for picking locks."

"It was a piece of cake."

Willard turned and faced Damien. "Why did you leave that book in the doorway?"

Damien arched an eyebrow. "I like to think of it as my calling card."

"I don't get it."

"It's no concern to me that you do," Damien said. "But they will understand." He stroked his chin. "Perhaps I should have left them a note." His mouth formed into a crooked smile at the thought of Howie finding a note. "Yes, that would have been nice...like...frosting on the cake."

"They're in," Willard said.

Damien closed his eyes and visualized Howie and Mick nervously trying to find their way in the darkness, and no doubt, fearful of what they might find. "You may start the car now," he said to Willard. As they pulled away, he imagined the shocked expressions on their faces when they found their partner. The thought of it gave him a delicious pleasure. An even greater shock would be when they opened the little present he had left behind. "I trust that they'll like my gift," he said softly to himself.

Willard shot a look at Damien. "What did you say?"

"Just drive."

"Are we done for tonight?" Roscoe asked.

"Not quite," Damien said. "We still have one more thing to do before the morning comes."

Chapter 37

By the time Howie joined his partner at the front of the sanctuary, Mick had already taken the tape off Adam's mouth and was working at untying the rope that bound his wrists. Adam was groggy, but conscious. As Howie worked at untying one wrist, Mick struggled to untie the other. "Are you okay?" Howie asked Adam.

"Wha…what are you doing here?"

"We came to find you. How're you doing?"

"O…okay…I guess." Adam's speech was slow and his words garbled, but he could be understood. He ran his tongue over his lips and winced as his partners continued to work at freeing him. A puzzled expression swept over his face as he first looked at Mick and then at Howie. "How…how did you know to come out?"

"Since you didn't show up at the office, we decided to come looking for you."

Adam looked around. "Where did you put it?" he asked Mick.

"What's he talking about?" Howie asked.

"Just a minute. I'll get it." Mick reached behind him and placed a shoebox-size package on the floor in front of the three of them. The package, wrapped in brown wrapping paper and tied with twine, had a red bow attached to the center. No other markings were on the package. "That was sitting right in front of him. I had to move it. I couldn't stand to look at it."

Mick didn't have to tell Howie who had left it; the package had Damien's handwriting all over it. "We'll get to that later," Howie said, being in no mood to open it now. "Let's get him untied." He continued to work at the knots binding Adam's right wrist.

"There you go, buddy," Mick said, having loosened the knot enough to have Adam slip his left hand free.

With his one hand free, there was now enough slack on the rope for Adam to move his other arm. He groaned as he brought his arms forward, moving them back and forth in front of him.

"Did you see who hit you?" Mick asked

"No, but I saw the other guy."

Howie finally untied the knots and took the rope off Adam's other wrist.

"Was it Damien?" he asked.

"No." Adam touched the back of his head where he had been hit and then massaged his arms for several moments. "The guy was short and stocky. He might have had dark curly hair, but I'm not sure."

"Anything else about him?"

"Not that I can recall. I only saw him for a second when the lightning flashed." Adam groaned again as he moved his arms from side to side in front of his body. He made an effort to stand.

Mick reached out for him. "Want some help?"

Adam nodded. With Mick on one side and Howie on the other, they got him to his feet. "Hang on for a second," he said. "I feel a little woozy."

"Do you want to sit back down again?" Mick asked.

"Yeah, but not here."

With Adam's arms around their shoulders, Mick and Howie helped their partner to the front pew. The three of them hadn't been sitting more than a few moments when Mick pointed to the chancel altar against the wall. "Look at that!" The silver altar cross had been turned upside down; it leaned against the brick wall, base up, at a forty-five degree angle.

"Damien!" Adam uttered the name as though he was cursing. "He knows that it's a sacrilege having the cross positioned that way." He made a move to get up, but sat back down. "Go set it upright, okay?"

"I'll do it." Howie walked up into the chancel area. He wiped his hands on his pants, took hold of the cross, and set it right side up on the altar. On the way back to his partners, he stopped by the package. "We'd better see what's in this thing."

"Don't open it," Adam pleaded. "Whatever is in it doesn't belong here."

"I agree," Mick said.

To Howie, it didn't make any difference where the package was opened, but he didn't push the issue. He wasn't nearly as religious as either of his partners; this being one of the few times he'd been inside a church since his father died. "Okay, we'll take it back to the office and open it there." He scanned the area. "Do you guys see anything else out of place?"

"I don't," Adam said.

Mick stood and looked around. "Neither do I."

"Okay, let's go." When Howie picked up the shoebox, a sense of foreboding swept over him when whatever was inside the package slid to one side with a dull thud.

Chapter 38

Damien opened his eyes as he felt the car slowing down. "Stop at the next gas station," he ordered Willard as they entered the Minneapolis city limits.

"And find one quick, will you?" Roscoe called from the backseat. "I've got to take a leak real bad."

"There's a Texaco up ahead," Willard said. Within moments, he turned right and pulled up to a gas pump. No sooner had he turned off the ignition than Roscoe jumped out and headed toward the station.

A tall, lanky, friendly-looking young man emerged from the garage area and ambled over to the driver's side. "Good evening, sirs. What will it be tonight?" he asked after Willard rolled down the window.

"Fill her up."

"Do you want the oil checked?"

"No!" Damien snarled from the passenger's seat. He disliked the cheerfulness of the young man and was pleased when his smile flickered at the brusque reply.

While the attendant pumped the gas, Roscoe came back and got into the backseat. "I feel like a new man," he chimed. "Now, I'm hungry."

"So am I," Willard said. "Do you think we can stop someplace and get a bite to eat?" he asked Damien.

"I'll think about it," Damien replied, anxious to be done with these two imbeciles. He had been with them long enough. The thought of eating a meal with them disgusted him. *The fools probably wouldn't know which fork to use.* After they finished their next project tonight, he would have Willard drive him to his car. If the two of them still felt like eating, they could go fill their stomachs. He would have a glass of white wine while he listened to Mozart and celebrated the evening.

After the attendant finished pumping the gas, he began wiping the front windshield. At one point he looked through the glass at Damien and offered a smile; perhaps it was his way of making a customer feel good. Damien, however, narrowed his eyes and glared. The attendant's smile flickered again but remained fixed. The young man quickly finished his task and came around to Willard's window. He bent down to look into the car, glancing at Roscoe in the backseat. "Anything else?"

Again, it was Damien who spoke. "Tell him that we have need of a gas can and to have it filled with gas."

For some reason the attendant thought Damien's remark was funny and he snickered. "What's the matter...are you guys expecting to run out of gas?" Roscoe and Willard began chuckling, but when Damien scowled at them, they stopped. The twinkle in the young man's eyes faded. "I'll get one and be right back."

"What are we going to do with the extra gas?" Willard asked Damien.

"When you have a need to know, I'll tell you."

Roscoe leaned forward and touched Damien on the shoulder. "How late are we going to be tonight, anyway?"

Damien whipped around. "Don't...ever...touch me again! Do you understand?"

Roscoe cowered back into his seat. He, along with Damien and Willard, watched in silence as the attendant approached the car.

"Here's the gas can and it's filled." The attendant avoided looking at Damien. "Where do you want it?"

Willard looked to Damien for guidance.

"Put it in the backseat. And then pay the man."

"How much?" Willard asked the attendant.

"With the gas can and eight-and-a-half gallons of gas, and that's including the gallon I put in the can, it comes to $3.26."

"Give him a five and tell him to keep the change," Damien said as he leaned over and smiled coldly at the attendant. The young man took the money from Willard and gave Damien a nervous smile. "Thanks."

Once they were back on the road, Damien closed his eyes and leaned back.

Chapter 39

Howie set the shoebox on his desk, eased into his chair, and, along with Mick and Adam, stared at Damien's unwelcome package as the wall clock ticked away the minutes. The sounds of an occasional car driving by on the side street below drifted up. Adam, still angry at how Damien had desecrated the church, shifted in his chair. Every now and then Mick cracked his knuckles. Somewhere in the distance a police siren wailed.

"Well, who wants to open it?" Mick finally asked, his eyes shifting between Howie and Adam. Although initiating the invitation, he crossed his arms and kept his hands tucked out of sight.

Adam shook his head. "I'm not going to do it." He touched the back of his head, gently rubbing the spot where he had been slugged. If his head hurt from the blow he took, he kept it to himself. "You open it," he said to Howie.

Howie's eyes shifted from the package to Adam and back to the package. He had brought the shoebox from the church out to the car, and when they had gotten back to the North Side, he had carried it up to his office. Neither of his partners had wanted to touch it. He didn't blame them. Damien's sick mind was capable of just about anything. At first, he thought it might be another severed finger, but as soon as he had lifted the package, he realized it was too heavy for just a finger, or even several fingers. What Damien had put in the box could be anyone's guess. Nearly a year ago, the guy had sent them packages containing things that had horrified them at the time. But that was a year ago. With the severed finger that Mary received, he had upped the ante.

"Go ahead and do it," Adam urged Howie. "The sooner you do it, the sooner I can go home and get some rest for tomorrow morning."

Mick reached over and touched Adam on the shoulder. "Are you sure you still want to preach tomorrow?"

"No, I'm not sure, but with the minister out of town I don't have any other choice." Adam stared at the package. "We can't let Damien win this game. When we get him this time, he's got to be put away for good."

"I'm with you on that," Mick said. "The guy shouldn't be out on the streets with normal people." He cracked his knuckles. "We've just got to get him...we've got to!"

"Don't worry, we will." Howie opened his desk drawer, got a pair of scissors, and cut the strands of twine on the shoebox. After ripping off the red bow and crushing it in his hand, he tore off the brown wrapping paper, tossing all of it into the wastepaper basket by his desk. "Okay, here goes," he announced as he exchanged glances with his partners, and slowly lifted the lid. Mick and Adam leaned forward to view the contents.

Mick jerked back into his chair. "Oh, man, no!" he cried. "What kind of person is he anyway?"

"We know what kind of a person he is," Adam replied, grimacing, but not taking his eyes off the contents of the box.

Howie felt sick to his stomach. Two hands, severed at the wrist, palms and fingers together, were bound with twine. The pungent odor of formaldehyde reminded him of when he had dissected a frog in high school biology class. No doubt, the formaldehyde kept the hands from losing their pasty, pale-gray coloring.

"What's that madman up to?" Mick asked. Without waiting for an answer, he got up from his chair, walked over to the window and opened it. With his hands gripping the windowsill, he leaned out as far as he could to breathe in the cool evening air. When he turned back toward his partners, he looked as grim as an undertaker. "Man, this is crazy. I just don't understand it."

"Understand what?" Howie asked.

"Why cut the hands off of someone and tie them together like that?" Mick raked his hand through his hair and massaged the back of his neck. "Is that his sick way of telling us that our hands are tied or something?"

"Hey!" Howie sat up straight. "You might have something there."

"I don't think it's that," Adam said grimly.

"What then?" Mick snapped. He looked away for a moment. "Sorry, I didn't mean to snap at you. This whole thing is getting to me."

"Who can blame you?" Adam said. "We're all on edge with this." He pointed to the shoebox. "Come, take another look and I'll explain what I think he's telling us."

"I don't know if I want to."

"Come on, it'll be all right," Adam said. "You'll want to see what I'm getting at." He paused. "Do it for Mary's sake; remember Damien's got her also involved in this."

Mick turned to the window and inhaled another breath of fresh air. He closed the window and moved back to the desk, but didn't take a seat. It took him nearly a minute before he looked into the box again.

"Okay, here's what I figure." Adam stood up and pointed to the hands. "See how they're bound, palms together? I think he did it that way to make them appear as praying hands."

"What!" Mick's eyes revealed his shock. "Why would he do that?"

"Because he meant this for me. He knows I plan to become a minister."

Howie trusted Adam's insight. His partner had an uncanny intuitiveness where it came to Damien, which was no surprise since Adam still had emotional scars from their last encounter with him. "If that package was for you, what about that other package that was sent to Mary?" he asked. "We know that the severed finger came from the Phillips woman. So what was the W carved on her forehead all about?"

"Maybe it wasn't a W."

Mick grabbed Adam's arm. "What are you talking about?" he cried. "Of course, it was a W."

"Not necessarily." Adam sat back down. "It depends how you view it."

"I think I know what you're getting at." Howie took out his notepad and printed a large *W* on a blank page. "The letter I see is a W." He pushed the notepad toward Mick. "What do you see?"

"It's an—" Mick's mouth dropped open. "An M!"

"Exactly." Howie turned to Adam to see if he was tracking with his thoughts. A nod told him he was. "We all assumed it was a W because that's what JD told us it was." He closed his notepad and slipped it into his shirt pocket. "But we should've known better when it comes to dealing with Damien. When he carved that letter into her forehead, he wasn't carving a W, but an upside-down M."

"And that's one of Damien's trademarks, isn't it?" Mick said. "Just like the upside-down cross we found at the church earlier."

Adam spoke up. "That package was sent to Mary because Damien figured we would eventually learn about the letter carved on the body. He knew that the police wouldn't figure it out, but he assumed we would." He paused as though allowing time for his partners to absorb the impact of what he was saying. "He's manipulating us like pawns on a chess board. This whole thing is his way of telling us that he's back and hasn't forgotten us."

"Not only that," Howie said, having had time to put more pieces of the puzzle together, "but the finger in the box..." He looked at Mick. "JD told me that it was the ring finger." He kept his tone even. "And since you are getting married in a few weeks, he was sending you a message through Mary."

"You mean the M stood for Mary?" Within a split second, Mick's expression changed from puzzlement to anger. "Why that..." He slammed his fist into his palm.

"Mick, it wasn't meant for Mary," Adam said. "It was for you."

"Me?"

"That's right," Howie said. "And the package sent to Adam was Damien's next step. With Adam going to be a preacher, the praying hands are an obvious connection." He took out his notepad again and flipped to the page where he had drawn the letter W. On the top of the page he printed *MAC*. The MAC Detective Agency had been named after the three of them. MAC was an acronym; M stood for Mick, A for Adam, and C stood for Cummins. He underlined the first two letters in the acronym. "I'm pretty sure that when the police find the body from where these hands came from, they are going to find the letter A carved on the body."

"And that leaves one person left," Adam said.

Howie nodded as he underlined the letter C, stared at it for several moments, and underlined it again. He printed the letter *D* under the acronym MAC, slowly drew a circle around the D, and reinforced the circle by going over it again and again, pressing so hard that the lead in his pencil broke. Mick's voice broke into his consciousness. He looked up to see a puzzled but concerned expression on his partner's face. "What did you say?" he asked Mick.

"I said that you better call JD. With that creep on the loose, we need to get the cops involved."

The image of Damien's arrogant smirk flashed through Howie's mind. JD would be more than willing to help to put the guy away. What he wasn't sure of, however, was his own willingness to admit that he needed help. "Maybe we should wait a bit."

"No!" Mick shot back, the veins in his neck bulging. He paused as though embarrassed by his outburst. "I'm not taking any chances of anything happening to Mary," he said in a more controlled voice.

"He's right," Adam said. "We don't know what Damien is going to do next and we don't want to take any unnecessary risks. If it was just the three of us, that's one thing, but now he has involved Mary in his sick game." He turned to Mick. "We're not going to let anything happen to her."

Howie drummed his fingers on the desk. His partners were right. They had been lucky up until now. Damien had dealt only with *dead* bodies. The guy, however, was capable of going to the next level. He had proven that the last time they had dealt with him. He stared at the phone on his desk. If he called JD, he was admitting that he couldn't handle the case. One glance at the determined look in Mick's eyes, however, told him that his partner would give him no choice. He reached over and put his hand on the telephone receiver, well aware that his partners were watching and waiting. The ticking of the wall clock reverberated in his head.

It was Mick who broke the silence. "Look, calling JD doesn't mean that we're giving up because we think we're in over our heads; we just need to consult with him on a few things." He sat but leaned forward; his tone and mannerisms were those of a teacher trying to get across an important point. "Think of it this way—it's like me going to another teacher and asking his advice on how to handle an unruly student." He paused and offered a sympathetic smile. "And just because I may have to seek some help from time to time doesn't mean that I'm not a good teacher."

Howie tighten his grip on the phone, waited for several seconds, picked it up and dialed Davidson's number. On the fourth ring an unfamiliar voice answered. "Is Detective Davidson in?" he asked.

"Nope. He's gone home for the night. Can somebody else help you?"

"No, that's okay. I'll call him tomorrow." Howie hung up, opened his notepad and flipped to the last page where he had JD's home number. "I'm calling him at home," he explained. After dialing, Howie waited, counting the number of rings...six...seven...eight. Just as he thought that no one would answer, Davidson picked up the phone.

"Hi, JD. Howie Cummins here."

"What's up?" Davidson sounded congested.

"My partners and I need to talk to you."

"What about?"

"I'd rather not discuss it over the phone."

"Can't it wait until tomorrow?"

"No. You need to come over to my office tonight." Howie waited for a reply, but only heard JD sneeze a couple of times.

"What's so damned urgent?" JD finally asked, sounding irritated.

"The initial on the Phillips woman wasn't a W."

"What?"

"It wasn't a W carved on her forehead."

"What the hell was it then?"

"I'll tell you when you get here." Howie waited for a response.

"Are you sure it wasn't a W?" JD finally asked.

"Positive. No doubt about it." Howie glanced at the shoebox. "And there's something else. There's a shoebox sitting on my desk containing a pair of hands that were severed from someone, probably a woman."

"Where did you get them?"

"I'll have all the answers for you when you get here." After Howie hung up, he turned to his partners. "He'll be over in fifteen minutes."

Chapter 40

Twenty minutes after Howie called JD, the downstairs entrance door slammed shut, and the stairs began to creak. Howie flipped open his notepad to where he had jotted down the details about what had happened earlier that evening at the church. JD would only want to hear the short version so he could go home and have that long hot shower that he was just about to take when Howie had called. Davidson would get the abbreviated version all right, but he wasn't leaving until they got what they wanted from him.

"Do you think that's Davidson?" Mick asked as the person continued to slowly trudge up the steps.

"Oh, yeah, it's him all right." Howie cocked his head toward the door. "And it sounds like he's dragging."

"I don't doubt it," Adam said. "Didn't you say the poor guy sounded like he was on death's doorstep?"

"Yeah, but he's tough." Howie suppressed a smirk. One night several years ago Davidson was set upon by three thugs. Apparently, the three men thought Davidson an easy target for a mugging. After a furious struggle, two of his attackers lay on the ground, unconscious. The third would-be mugger ran away. In the melee, the police detective received a nasty cut above his right eye, and had broken the bones in his hand when he cold-cocked the second guy. "JD will be okay," Howie added. "We won't keep him too long."

Adam stood up, stretched his arms toward the ceiling, and yawned before settling back down in his chair.

"How's the headache doing?" Howie asked, having given Adam some aspirins when they got back to the office.

"It's okay." Adam rested his head back against the chair, closed his eyes, and breathed in deeply. "I'll stay to see what JD has to say, but then I've got to get home to get some rest. Tomorrow morning is going to be here before I know it."

"So, you're still going to preach?" Howie asked.

Before Adam could reply, the office door opened and Detective Jim Davidson walked in, his gait slower than usual. With watery eyes and a nose that could give Rudolph competition, JD looked like a man who should've stayed home, taken that hot shower, and gone straight to bed. The detective gave Howie's movie poster a passing glance and took a place by the window, sitting on the sill. Mick offered him his chair, but he declined. "This better be worth my while coming out tonight," he said to Howie. His normally gravelly voice sounded as though it was on the verge of becoming hoarse.

"I'll leave that for you to judge." Howie slid the shoebox across his desk toward the detective as Mick and Adam looked on.

"Fancy box," JD quipped. "They're in there?"

Howie nodded.

"Okay, let's have a look-see." Davidson moved over to the desk. Without removing the lid, he examined the shoebox.

"I've already checked for anything that could give us a clue as to where that came from," Howie said. "There's nothing."

Davidson continued to scrutinize the shoebox as if he hadn't heard Howie. After several more minutes, he lifted the cover with both hands and set it aside. If he was taken aback by the contents or the smell of formaldehyde, he gave no indication. He studied the severed hands, slowly rotating the box so he could view them from different angles.

Howie watched his friend with admiration. Even though Davidson wasn't feeling well, the man always gave full attention to whatever was before him. The guy had the reputation of being the top police detective on the North Side and one of the best in the Twin City area. Over the years, detectives from both Minneapolis and St. Paul had consulted him on a number of cases. "So, what do you think?" he asked as Davidson continued his examination.

"Any note come with this?"

"Nope."

"Is there—" Davidson muffled a sneeze and cleared his throat. Howie offered him a box of tissues, but he waved it off, digging a wrinkled handkerchief out of his back pocket. "I shouldn't have gone out in that damn storm tonight." He gently wiped his nose, sniffed a couple of times, and stuffed the handkerchief back into his pocket. "Is there any significance in them being tied together like that?" he asked.

"Go ahead, Adam," Howie said. "You tell him."

Adam sat for a moment before getting up and moving next to Davidson. He spoke to the detective without looking at the shoebox. "I'm pretty sure that they were tied that way to make them appear as if the person was praying."

"They were given to him," Mick said as he gestured toward Adam.

"Is that right?" Davidson asked.

Adam nodded, his jaw muscles tightening.

"Hmmm. Interesting." Davidson moved back to the window. Instead of sitting on the sill again, he leaned against the wall and watched as Adam placed the cover on the shoebox and sat down. JD sneezed, pulled out his handkerchief, and wiped his nose. His gray-blue eyes appeared even paler than when he had first come into the office.

Howie considered offering his sick friend some hot tea, but the seasoned detective would simply scoff at it unless there was a shot of bourbon to go with it. "Hell, forget the tea," he would say. JD was out of luck, however; he had tea, but no bourbon. It wasn't that he was a teetotaler as much as it was that he just hadn't taken time to restock.

Davidson stuffed the handkerchief back into his pocket and focused his watery eyes on Adam. "Okay, tell me what happened," he said as he squeezed the bridge of his nose, shutting his eyes for a second. "And just give me the essentials, will you?"

"That won't be a problem because there's not much to tell." Adam shifted in his chair so he faced JD. "Earlier tonight, I was—"

"And what time would that be?"

"Around seven or so."

"Okay, go on."

"I was at this church in Long Lake, that's a little town west of—"

"I know where it is." Davidson's tone reflected impatience. "What were you doing out there?"

"Getting ready for tomorrow morning."

The detective raised an eyebrow, but said nothing.

"I'm doing the Sunday services at a church," Adam explained.

"That's right. You're the one who's going to be a preacher. Go on."

"I was in the sanctuary and I didn't have the lights on except for the light at the pulpit. There was a spotlight on the cross, but it was still pretty dark in there. From the pulpit, I couldn't see much past the fifth pew." Adam's eyes darkened as though he was reliving the experience. "When the lightning flashed outside, I caught a glimpse of this guy standing in the back of the church. He startled me."

"I bet he did." Davidson folded his arms in front of his chest. "And what time would you say that was?"

"Eight thirty-five."

"That's pretty exact. Are you sure of that?"

"Oh, yes, because I looked at my watch."

"What did you do after you saw this guy?"

"I called out, asking who he was, but he didn't respond." Adam shifted in his chair. "When the lightning flashed again, I caught a glimpse of another guy."

"Two guys, huh? Can you describe either one of them?"

"Not really." Adam gnawed at his lip. "All I know is that the one guy was short and stocky. I think he had dark curly hair."

"And the—" JD shot a glance at Mick.

"Sorry," Mick said. He rubbed his knuckles and put his hands to his side. "Cracking my knuckles is a bad habit."

Davidson turned his attention back to Adam. "And the other guy?"

Adam shook his head. "I really couldn't tell you. He could have been taller than his partner, but I'm not sure."

"Had you ever seen these guys before?"

"Never."

"Did either one of them say anything to you?"

"Not a word."

When Adam shifted in his chair again, Howie wondered if JD's pinpoint questioning was making his partner uneasy. The seasoned police detective had a reputation for being one of the toughest interrogators on the force. His tone always had an unsettling edge that made those whom he was interviewing nervous. Howie was captivated by getting a firsthand look at how Davidson conducted his questioning. He could imagine JD's tone even edgier if he had been interviewing someone suspected of committing a crime.

"Okay, so what happened next?" Davidson asked.

"Since it was pretty dark in the church, I decided that I'd try to slip out without being noticed. But it didn't work." Adam's eyes narrowed. "One guy confronted me. He wasn't more than five or six feet away." He glanced sideways at Howie. "I was prepared to fight, but somebody hit me from behind."

Davidson took out his handkerchief and wiped his nose again. "I assume he conked you on the head. How hard?"

"Hard enough to knock him out," Mick said.

"Yeah, the next thing I knew is that I was tied to the pulpit and…" Adam gestured to the shoebox on the desk. "That thing was sitting in front of me. Other than that, there's not much I remember. Before long, my partners here showed up." He turned toward Mick. "What time did you say that you and Howie got there?"

"Around nine-fifteen or so."

Davidson shifted his attention to Howie. "How did you guys happen to go out there?" he asked, his voice sounding raspier.

"We were all going to meet in my office earlier this evening. When Adam didn't show up, we got worried and decided to go check on him."

"Lucky for him you did."

"We know who was behind it," Howie said.

Davidson rubbed his eyes and blinked a couple of times. "Well, that's going to make my investigation easier. Who was it? Anybody I know?"

"Yeah." Howie leaned forward. "Damien."

"That guy, huh?" Davidson shifted his body. "So he's up to his old tricks again. How—" The coughing began without warning, coming from deep within his chest. "Damn cold!" he muttered once the coughing subsided. "So tell me," he asked Howie. "How does this tie in with the Phillips woman?"

"Like I told you on the phone, it wasn't a W."

"Okay, so what was it? Some kind of satanic symbol?"

"No, it was a letter."

"What the hell are you talking about? You just said it wasn't a W."

Howie folded his hands on the desk. It was time to do some dealing with

JD to get the information he wanted from him. It wouldn't be easy, but he had to try. "It wasn't a W. It was an M. That's why we wanted to talk to you. We thought we could compare notes."

"Compare notes? On what?"

"On the body those hands came from," Howie replied in a sharp tone. "We've given you something. Now we want to know what you found on the body."

"Wait a minute. Before we start comparing anything..." Davidson glanced around, taking time to make eye contact with each of the three detectives. "How can you guys be so positive that it was an M and not a W?"

Mick nudged Adam. "You explain. You know more about this stuff than we do."

Adam turned toward Davidson. "In Satanism, things are written upside-down or backwards."

"And what's that supposed to mean?"

"It shows defiance of established religious beliefs."

"The altar cross at the church where we found Adam had been turned upside down," Howie said. "You thought the letter was a W, but it was an upside-down M."

"Well, I'll be damned."

"Damien needs to be put away for a long time," Mick said. "The guy's out to break us." He began rubbing his knuckles. "The package that creep sent to my fiancée was his opening shot." He cracked his knuckles, rubbed them again, and moved his hands to his sides.

"Okay, JD," Howie said. "Tell us what you know."

"About what?"

"Did you find any letters carved on the body?"

Davidson's face remained impassive. "That's an ongoing investigation. It's police policy not to discuss it outside the department."

"Come on!" Howie snapped, raising his voice. "Don't give us that policy crap! We've given you information. We're willing to cooperate. If you want us to continue to work together, you're going to have to give us a little."

The detective stared at the shoebox for several moments. He flicked something from the corner of his eye. "Okay, but this is off the record." He hesitated as if debating whether he should go on. "There was a letter carved on her body."

"It was the letter A, wasn't it?" Mick said.

A flicker of surprise passed through Davidson's eyes. "That's right." His tone remained calm, almost casual. "How did you know that?"

Adam leaned forward in his chair. "And it was probably carved on her forehead or..." He glanced at Mick. "Maybe on her chest."

The sound of a car with a faulty muffler drifted up from the street below. Davidson looked out the window for a second. Once the car passed, only the ticking of the wall clock filled the void.

Howie studied JD's face. The detective knew the horrible details of what

116

Damien had done to Mick in that country cemetery. Even though the incident had happened a year ago, he was no doubt making the connection with Adam's comment about the letter possibly being carved on the woman's chest. If this had been a poker game, it would have been anybody's guess as to what Davidson held in his hand. "Come on, JD, we're waiting. The sooner you tell us, the sooner you can get home to your hot shower."

"It was on her forehead." Davidson folded his arms across his chest. "So tell me, what message is Damien trying to get across?"

"That he's out to get us for busting up his group last year," Mick cried, his voice cracking with emotion.

"So you think that he's going to make another move?"

"We know he is," Howie said. Tired of looking at the shoebox, he placed it on the floor. "Those letters, M and A, are the first two letters in MAC, the acronym for our detective agency."

"I see." Davidson looked at Mick and then at Adam before turning his attention back to Howie. "That leaves you." He paused, took out his handkerchief and wiped his nose. "Do you want police protection?"

"What!"

"I can send a couple of the boys over to cover your backside for a few days."

"Are you kidding?" Howie shot back, angry that JD would even suggest anything like that. "How would that look?" He picked up a pencil and felt like breaking it in two. "Who would want to hire a detective who can't handle his own cases, who's scared off and runs to the police everytime the going gets a little rough?"

"Howie, it's not like that," Adam offered.

"And it's not going to be like that!" Howie cried. He turned to JD. "Look, we'll cooperate with you and *you* alone, but this is still my..." He shot a look at his partners. "It's still our case and we're going to follow through on it. The cops can work their end and we'll work ours, but there's no meeting in the middle. Is that clear?" He didn't wait for an answer. "I don't need any cop holding my hand. Not today. Not tomorrow. Not ever!" He tossed the pencil aside and leaned back in his chair, his breathing coming hard and fast.

For the first time since arriving, Davidson offered a half smile. He met the eyes of each of the detectives and then scanned the office, only pausing at Howie's movie poster. "Okay, if that's the way you want it. I'll play along, but only as long as you keep me informed."

"And whatever we tell you stays with you?"

"Yeah. Of course."

Howie leaned forward. "And we have your word on that?"

"Damn right, you have my word on it!" Davidson shot back, obviously ticked that his integrity was being questioned. His eyes focused on Adam. "Now, why don't you give me the name and address of that church?"

"Why do you want that?" Howie asked.

"So I can get the hell out of here and go home where I should have been all along." JD sneezed as if to drive home his point. "I'll send someone out to the church to check for finger- prints. Maybe we'll get lucky and come up with something."

"There's no need to go out there," Howie said. "We'll save your boys a trip because we're not filing any police report." His eyes shifted toward Adam. He was counting that his partner would back him even though they hadn't discussed it. "Isn't that right?"

Adam shot a glance at Mick; his partner shrugged as a look of resignation swept over him. "Howie's right," he finally said. "I'm not filing any report."

Davidson frowned. "What in hell is that going to prove?" he asked, his voice becoming even raspier.

As far as Howie was concerned, keeping JD informed and filing a police report weren't the same. "Look, if we file a report, it'll open the case up to too many eyes."

"No, it—"

"Oh, yes it will, and you know it." Howie locked eyes with the detective. "I trust you, but not some of those other clowns down at the precinct." He intentionally changed his tone, hoping a more reasonable one would soften his friend. "Listen, if we did that, we'd be playing right into Damien's hands. He wins at his game, and we'll never see him again." He didn't believe for one minute that Damien would disappear, but counted on JD's burning desire to rid the streets of as many bad guys as he could. You can't nab the bad guys, however, if they aren't around. And JD would be the first to admit that. Howie pressed his argument. "Besides, your guys aren't going to find anything out there anyway. If I know Damien, he had those two thugs wearing gloves."

"Were they?" Mick asked Adam.

"I don't know…they could have been."

Davidson walked over and stood in front of Howie's desk. He placed his hands on the desk and leaned over toward Howie. His once watery eyes had turned to ice. "I'll let you get by with this little game of yours this time, but no more." He jabbed his finger at Howie. "I'm going to send some of my boys out there and I don't give a damn what you think. This is still a police investigation." Once he had made his point, he stepped closer to Adam and looked at his head. "Nasty bump you got there. I'd be angry as hell if somebody did that to me. Are you sure you don't want to file?"

"For what? Running into a door?"

"Suit yourself. Now give me the name and address of that church so I get the hell out of here."

Adam looked at Howie.

"Go ahead," Howie said, knowing that he had pushed JD to the limit.

After Davidson got his information, he relaxed his tone. "I don't know about you three." He shook his head. "You solve a couple of cases, and you think you're…" He glanced at the Bogart poster. "Detective work isn't what you see in the movies."

"We're not doing so badly," Howie retorted.

"I'll give you that," Davidson replied. "But you still have a ways to go. You say Damien's playing mind games with you. Hell, that's probably true, but we all know that he's capable of doing more than that." He paused as if to let his warning sink in. "I'll be in touch." He reached down and picked up the shoebox from off the floor. "If you don't mind, I'll take this with me. Or do you have a problem with that, too?"

"Not a bit." Howie cocked his head. "What are you going to say about it?"

"I'll make out a report explaining everything...that I took your statements, but you didn't want to file a report." Davidson turned to Adam. "Are you sure you don't want to change your mind?"

Adam glanced at Howie before replying. "I'm sure."

"If you have a change of heart, give me a call." Davidson walked toward the door, stopping at the movie poster. "Bogie, take care of these three, would you? They're not quite in your league yet." He turned toward them, winked, and then headed out the door.

Within moments of JD leaving, Mick confronted Howie, his voice reflecting both exasperation and a hint of anger. "JD's right. You know what Damien is capable of. Why didn't you take him up on his offer of protection?"

Howie's eyes narrowed, his words were clipped and to the point. "I'll tell you the same thing I told him. We can handle it on our own."

"But—"

"No buts about it! Now leave it be, will you?" Howie tried to control his emotions, not wanting to take his frustrations out on Mick, but as far as this decision was concerned, it wasn't up for a vote. He seldom exerted his authority as the boss, but on this he wasn't about to back down. "If you don't care to be on this case, I'm sure something else will turn up that would be more suitable for you to handle."

"Come on, guys," Adam pleaded. "We can't do this to each other. This is exactly what Damien wants."

Howie's eyes turned toward Adam for a moment. His partner was right. The thought of Damien smirking at their bickering was sobering. "Look, Mick, I'm...I'm sorry I jumped on you, but this case is important to me. I let Damien slip away once. I'm not about to do it again."

For the next several minutes, nobody said a word. Adam looked stunned; his face reflected the shock he no doubt felt about the flare-up he had just witnessed between his partners. It was usually Howie and him going at each other with Mick being the mediator.

Mick rubbed his hand slowly across his chest a couple of times as he sat staring at the letter opener on the desk. "I disagree with you on one thing," he finally said as he met Howie's eyes. "You didn't let Damien slip away. *We* did." The muscles in his jaw tightened. "And we're not going to allow that to happen again."

"You're right—we're not," Howie replied, relieved that the flare-up between Mick and him had ended.

"I'm going home and get some rest," Adam said as he stood up. "Are you guys still coming tomorrow?"

"Of course we are." Mick looked at Howie. "Right?"

Although Howie nodded, he would really rather have relaxed tomorrow morning by lounging around, having coffee, and catching up on his reading. He could have even slept in since he had no time for religion and God stuff. He'd had enough of that when he was a kid. And as far as he was concerned, all that God business ended when his mother died so young. Besides, all the prayers in the world wouldn't help them catch Damien. God could afford to talk about love and forgiveness, but Howie couldn't, not as long as Damien was loose. He would go, however, but only to support Adam.

Adam started for the door. "See you guys tomorrow, then."

"Wait for me." Mick stood up. "I'll walk down with you. We're finished here, aren't we?" After Howie nodded, Mick joined Adam at the door. Just before he closed it, he turned to Howie. "You'll pick you up tomorrow morning around nine-thirty. Right?"

"Right...and Mick?"

"Yeah?"

"Don't worry, we'll get him."

Chapter 41

After his partners left, Howie rested his head against the back of his chair and closed his eyes. It was nearly midnight and he was exhausted. Damien was on his mind, however, and that wasn't good if he hoped to get any sleep.

He leaned forward and opened the bottom right-hand drawer of his desk and took out a copy of *Police Gazette*. He would go to bed and read until he fell asleep. If he was lucky, it would only take a few pages. Just as he stood and was about to head to his bedroom, the downstairs entrance door slammed shut. He frowned and reluctantly plopped back down to await his late night visitor.

The footsteps sounded vaguely familiar, but he was too tired to make any guesses as to whom they might belong to. Could it be that one of his partners had come back for some reason? Perhaps it was JD. Or maybe some gorgeous blonde. That would be nice. Certainly better than taking a magazine to bed. He set his reading material aside, rested his head against the back of his chair, and closed his eyes again as he waited.

Whoever was coming had now reached the top of the stairs. Howie looked up just as his office door opened. He rolled his eyes and sighed with a renewed sense of weariness. The only blonde he would be seeing tonight would be in his dreams. "Squirrel, what are you doing here at this hour?"

"I would've come earlier but I knew you had a cop up here." Squirrel's nose twitched as he walked over and made himself comfortable in a chair. "Your light was still on so I figured you were up." The little guy settled back in the chair and crossed his legs. His nose twitched again as he glanced around. "Did you know that I can smell a cop a mile away?"

Howie leaned forward, clasped his hands together, and rested them on the desk. "What do you want?"

Squirrel fiddled with the top button of his shirt. "Cops make me nervous." He picked at his teeth with his fingernail for a second. "They have a way about them that—"

"Squirrel!" Howie's sharp tone caused his visitor to flinch. "Just tell me what you want, okay?"

"I need to talk to you."

"Do you realize what time it is?" Howie looked at the wall clock. "Can't this wait until tomorrow?"

"Oh, no! Not this," Squirrel said, his eyes darting back and forth. "You're going to want to hear this. You can bet money on that." He scooted to the edge of his chair. "In fact, I'll bet you six-to-one that—"

"Just tell me and let's get this over with." Howie dug out his notepad. "And make it short, will you? I'm tired."

"Newt called me."

"He did?" Howie's adrenalin kicked in. "When?"

"This morning." Squirrel scratched his chin. "And let me tell you, the guy sounded spooked. Something's wrong. I can feel it. It's in my blood. I know about these things. Something's going on. He—"

"Slow down, will you, Squirrel?"

Squirrel sucked air through his teeth as though that would slow him down. It didn't. "Like I was saying, Old Newt sounded scared, more scared than I've ever heard him before."

"Scared? Of what? Of who?"

"He didn't tell me that." Squirrel crossed his legs and ran his fingers up and down the buttons of his shirt. "But get this. He tells me that I'm supposed to watch over his sister if anything happens to him. And let me tell you, that isn't going to be easy. That dame doesn't like me."

"Okay. Let me see if I got this straight." Howie squeezed the bridge of his nose and let out a puff of air. "Newt called this morning and asked you to take care of his sister if something happened to him. And he sounded scared. Is that right?"

Squirrel scratched underneath his chin and nodded.

"But he didn't tell you why or who he was afraid of?"

"That's right."

"You've got to level with me." Squirrel's fidgeting was giving Howie a headache. "Could there be someone else after that money he supposedly took from you?"

Squirrel's nose scrunched and his eyes widened. "*Supposedly*, my foot!" he cried. He uncrossed his legs and crossed them again. "That crook's got my money!" He began fiddling with his shirt buttons again. "I'm not lying to you! Why would I—"

"Hold it, cool down. Let's not get off on the wrong track." Howie massaged his forehead, reminding himself that Squirrel was a paying client. He needed to take some aspirins before he went to bed. "Do you know of anyone who could be after the money your partner...ah, took from you?"

"I wish I did." Squirrel folded his arms; his beady-black eyes zeroed in on Howie. "And you have my word on that. I wouldn't lie to you. Cross my heart. You can spit on my grandmother's grave if I'm lying."

"Give me a break," Howie said. "When it comes to hard, cold cash, you'd lie to your own mother."

Squirrel stared at the detective for a moment before his lips curled into a sly smile. "I'd only lie to her if it was more than a hundred bucks." He brought his right hand up to his mouth, blew on his fingernails, and made a show of buffing them on his shirt. "I've got my principles, you know."

"I'm sure you do." Howie checked the notes he had previously made on the case. "I've asked you this before, but did Newt ever give any indication of who he might be hanging around with?"

"He didn't drop any names, if that's what you mean."

"Okay, no names were mentioned." Howie drummed his fingers on the desk. "How about what part of town they were from, or what kind of work they did, or the kind of cars they drove, or where they hung out?" He flipped to a blank page in his notepad. "Did he ever mention any of those things, or anything else that might be helpful in this investigation?"

"Let me think." Squirrel sucked air through his teeth while continuing to twitch his nose. He ran his hand through his hair a couple of times in a fruitless effort to bring it under control. "Hey, I remember now. He mentioned something about this one guy he was hanging around with a lot."

"What about him?"

"The guy's got a ponytail."

"A ponytail?"

"Yeah. Newt said the guy was blonde and had this ponytail." Squirrel made a face like he was sucking on a lemon. "You would never catch me having one of those things." He scratched his ear for a moment. "But he never mentioned his name."

"Okay, at least that's something." Howie jotted a few notes down and looked up. "Anything else?"

"Nope, that's it. Newt was pretty close-mouthed about this guy." Squirrel leaned forward. "So what are you going to do?"

Howie checked the time. Twelve-fifteen. He closed his notepad and put his pen down. "Right now, nothing."

"Nothing!" Squirrel cried. "What's going to happen to my mon—to poor Newt?"

"I think *poor Newt* will survive the night." Howie took a deep breath and slowly exhaled. He wouldn't need to do any reading to get to sleep after this conversation. "You haven't given me much to go on."

"Hey, I've given you all I know," Squirrel shot back. "You're the detective. So start detecting." He blew on his nails and buffed them again on his shirt. "That's what I'm paying you for."

"Listen, you little…" Howie bit his lip. He liked Squirrel, but the guy could get on his nerves. He softened his tone. "I tell you what I'm going to do. One of my partners will pay Newt's sister a visit again. Maybe if we tell her that you've talked to him and he sounded scared, she'd be a little more cooperative."

"Ask her about the guy with the ponytail."

"I will."

"Are you going to do it the first thing in the morning?"

"No."

"Why not?"

"Because I'm going to church," Howie blurted out and then wished he hadn't.

"Church!" Squirrel's eyes doubled in size and his mouth dropped open. "Did I hear you right?" He smirked. "You did say church?"

"Yeah. I did." Howie stood and pointed to the door. "Now why don't you go home or wherever else you go at this time of night?"

"But—"

"But nothing!" Howie snapped. "Look. I'm beat and I want to get to bed. I'll be in touch with you when I hear something."

Squirrel got up and walked to the door. Before opening it, he turned toward Howie. "Man, I would've laid ten-to-one odds that you weren't the bible-thumping type."

"Well, you never know about some people," Howie said. Squirrel was still shaking his head in disbelief when he left. As soon as Howie heard the downstairs entrance door slam shut, he turned off the light and headed to bed.

Chapter 42

Howie awoke with a start. He lay in bed for a moment to gather his senses before using the sheet to wipe the perspiration off his face. Several more seconds past before he rolled over and looked at the clock. Nearly one-fifteen: less than an hour since Squirrel had left. He wiped his brow again and thought about his dream. It had taken place in a huge cathedral with a vaulted ceiling and stained glass windows. Adam and Mick, along with Squirrel, sat in the front pew, their faces grim. Kass was also there, so was JD.

In the pulpit, wearing a black hooded robe, stood Damien. With a sneer on his lips, his piercing eyes looked down upon those gathered. From a gold chain around his neck hung an upside-down cross. He slowly raised his hand and gestured with a crooked finger, pointing to an open bronze casket resting on a dark-oak platform in front. People filed by the coffin. *Poor man, he was just starting his career as a detective...I heard he couldn't handle his cases without help from the police...I doubt if his two partners will carry on...*

Howie wiped his brow again and turned over on his stomach. He closed his eyes, hoping to get back to sleep, but tossed and turned for the next several minutes. Just as he was thinking about whether to get up and get something to eat, he heard sirens in the distance. He turned over, closed his eyes again, but quickly opened them as the sirens came closer. When the wailing grew even louder, he sat up and swung his feet over the edge of the bed. He would grab something to eat from the frig and head back to bed. He hoped that by the time he slipped under the covers the sirens would be long gone and he could fall asleep in peace. He sat, listening. The shrill of the sirens now was very close; maybe in the next block.

"What's going on?" The sirens sounded as though they had halted in his kitchen. He jumped up, hurried into the kitchen and looked out the window. On the street below two police cars sat, motors running, their red lights flashing. Two hook-and-ladder trucks could also be seen, and another car with the words *Fire Chief* on the door. Firemen ran toward the front of the drugstore while police officers directed traffic. One cop, motioning and yelling at drivers who had slowed to view the action, waved his arm like a windmill in an effort to get the gawkers to move on. A small but growing crowd had already formed across the street. In the distance, another siren could be heard.

Howie couldn't see any flames. The sound of breaking glass, however, jarred him into action. He ran to his bedroom, threw on some clothes, and headed for the front door while still buttoning his shirt. Within seconds he was down the stairs and out the street entrance door, running nearly head on into a burley six-foot fireman in full gear.

"Anybody else up there?" the fireman asked.

"No, what's going on?"

"Just a little fire. Nothing serious." The fireman spoke with professional calmness. "I just wanted to make sure that the building was evacuated," he said. Then he added, "Don't worry. It's just standard procedure."

Howie headed toward the front of the drugstore, his heart pounding. Flames licked the entrance door as the smell of smoke hit his nostrils. He caught a whiff of another odor as well. A fireman, handling a hose, was already directing its spray toward the door. Within moments, the flames were doused. A third fire truck arrived but left after one of the cops talked to its driver.

"Are you okay?" The familiar voice of Adam, his partner, came from Howie's right.

"Yeah, I'm...I'm doing all right." Howie glanced at Kass' charred front door and the broken windows on either side. "I couldn't believe it when I saw what was going on."

"I know what you mean." Adam moved aside as a fireman rushed past him. "When I saw those fire trucks and all the commotion on your corner, I thought your building was going up in flames."

Howie watched as two firemen rolled up the hose while another inspected the charred area.

"That door's going to have to be replaced," Adam said.

"Yeah, too bad," Howie said. "But at least it doesn't look like the fire got inside."

Adam stepped closer to get a better look, but was ordered by one of the firemen to stay back because of the broken glass. He rejoined his partner. "How could a front door catch fire?"

"It's easy with gasoline."

"What!" Adam said, stunned by his partner's revelation. "You mean it was deliberately set?" He scanned the blackened entrance. "Who would do such a thing to Kass?"

"I don't know. Maybe the same guy who's been sending him those hate letters." Howie dug his fingernails into his palms. The adrenalin rush of the fire had been replaced by anger. "And whoever he is, we're going to get him."

Before Adam could reply, a police officer approached them. "Which one of you lives in the apartment above this drugstore?"

"That's me," Howie said.

The officer took out a small notepad from his shirt pocket. "Can I have your name for my report?"

"Sure. Howie Cummins."

After the officer asked Howie how his last name was spelled, he wrote it in his notepad. "Did you see how this might have started?"

"No, I was in bed." Howie noted that the crowd across the street had begun to dissipate. "I didn't even know there was a problem until I heard the sirens stop in front. I got up and looked out my kitchen window."

The officer cracked a half smile. "I bet that jump-started you."

"You bet it did. When I saw those fire trucks I got dressed and down here as soon as I could." He looked on as the officer wrote down his statement. "When I got here, I smelled more than smoke, though."

"Oh yeah? What else?"

"Gasoline." Howie paused, waiting for a reaction, but none came. "This was deliberately set, wasn't it?"

"It's still under investigation," the officer replied without looking up.

Howie cleared his throat. "Look, my partners and I run a detective agency. I think you'd be safe in sharing that bit of information with us."

The officer looked up, glanced at Adam, and went back to writing in his notepad.

"I'm one of his partners," Adam said. "I just live down the block in the apartments above the dime store." The officer continued to write without looking up. "We're long time friends of the man who owns this drugstore. He'll probably ask our help in finding out who did this." He turned to Howie. "Tell him about our connection with JD."

At the mention of JD, the officer stopped writing. "Are you talking about Detective Jim Davidson?"

"Yeah." Howie hoped that they had made the kind of connection that would gain the officer's trust. "We're good friends. He's worked with us on a couple of cases. JD was up to our office earlier this evening."

"And what's the name of your agency?"

"MAC Detective Agency," Howie said, expecting to see an acknowledgement of name recognition.

"Never heard of it. How long have you been around?"

"For about a year. My office is upstairs." Howie dug through his pockets. "I'd give you one of our business cards, but I don't have one on me." He turned to Adam, but his partner indicated that he didn't have any either. "I could go get one if you'd like," Howie said.

"Don't bother." The officer put his notepad away. "If you and JD are friends, that's good enough for me."

"So, was it deliberately set?" Howie asked, feeling assured that they now had the officer in their confidence. "And don't worry. Whatever you tell us is off the record."

"We didn't find any gas cans." The officer looked toward another police officer who was busy talking to a couple of firemen. "But the fire chief is quite positive this was arson." He glanced toward the front entrance as one of the firemen swept up broken glass. "And you're right about the gasoline. I smelled it also."

"Are there any witnesses to this?" Adam asked.

"Not a one." The officer pointed to Howie. "I was hoping your partner here might have seen something."

A car pulled to the curb across the street and Kass got out. As soon as he saw his young friends, he rushed over to them. "Are you okay?" he asked Howie as he quickly surveyed the damage to the front of his drugstore. In spite of the damage to his building, he appeared and sounded surprisingly calm. "You didn't get hurt, did you?"

"I'm doing okay, but your entrance isn't and you got some smoke and water damage inside."

"Don't worry about that. I've lived a long enough life to know that there are worse things than this." Kass reached out and placed his hand on Howie's shoulder. "Doors and windows can be replaced, friends cannot."

"And who are you?" the officer asked.

"Hershel Kass."

"He's the owner of the drugstore," Adam said.

Kass turned to the officer. "Can you tell me what happened?"

"That wasn't much of a fire," Willard said, his tone signaling disappointment.

"Yeah, we could've done it up real good," Roscoe added from the backseat. "Hell, we could've done some serious damage."

Damien sat silently observing the scene on the corner of Kass' Drugstore. After they had set the fire, he had instructed Willard to park on the side street a block away in a spot where they could view the events unfold.

"Isn't that the guy we tied up at the church?" Roscoe asked.

"It sure as hell is," Willard said with a sneer. "But who are those other two guys talking to the cop?"

"The older gentleman owns the drugstore," Damien said, thoroughly enjoying the scene.

"And who's the short guy?" Willard asked.

"Howie Cummins."

"Who's he?"

"A detective. He lives in the apartment above the drugstore." Damien's lips curled into a smile. "I do hope they appreciate the trouble I went through to bring them together at such a late hour."

"We could've put that detective guy out of business for good," Roscoe said. "How come you didn't want the whole building to go up?"

"Yeah," Willard said. "We could've had one hell of a bonfire."

"Let's just say that this was a playful swat." Damien smiled to himself when he noticed the puzzled glance Willard and Roscoe exchanged. *Fools. They have no understanding of how a cat likes to play with its prey.*

Chapter 43

Howie took a sip of coffee, set his cup down, and sat staring at the black liquid as though in a trance. He yawned, placed his elbow on the desk, and supported his head in the cradle formed by his hand. Although it was nearly one on a bright, clear Sunday afternoon, his body whispered that it needed sleep. To hit the sack for a quick snooze, however, was out of the question. Kass and Adam would be coming any minute. He closed his eyes to rest them, but his head slipped from his hand, and he was jerked awake. He massaged his face for several moments, stood up, stretched, and slumped back into the chair. Although his coffee was lukewarm he gulped the rest of it and set the cup aside.

He and Adam had helped Kass clean up the mess from the early morning fire. They'd swept up the glass inside the store, mopped up the water, and tossed the damaged merchandise. Adam, needing to get a few hours sleep so he would be awake enough to do the church services, had left after they boarded up the broken windows. The entrance door, though charred, still locked and thankfully didn't need to be replaced that night.

"What do you say that we get together and talk about all this," Howie had asked as Kass took one last look around the area.

"Are you sure you want to get involved?"

"What do you think?" Howie wasn't about to take no for an answer. "If it was the other way around, you'd be the first in line to offer help."

"But—"

"No buts, Kass. It's a done deal."

"Okay, okay, I know enough not to argue with you when you use that tone." Kass smiled knowingly. "So what time do you want to get together?"

"Why don't you come up to the office around one or so? I'll ask Adam when I see him at church. I'm sure he'll want to be there."

"How about Mick?"

"I don't think he'll be able to make it. He and Mary still have a few things to do for their upcoming wedding."

"You boys are too nice to me." Kass placed his hand on Howie's shoulder, gently patting it. He kept his hand on his shoulder for a moment, and then dropped it and looked away.

"Something else you want to tell me?"

"I suppose I should, huh?"

"What is it, Kass?"

"You boys are so busy already."

"Come on, out with it."

Kass sighed. "I received another one of those letters."

"When?"

"Earlier tonight."

"Did you bring it?"

"No. I left on the kitchen table."

"What did it say?"

"I don't know. I didn't open it."

"What? Why not?"

"Because I thought it would be just like all the others. I didn't feel like reading that kind of stuff before going to bed." Kass shrugged. When he continued, he did so in an apologetic tone. "I suppose I should have brought it, but when the police officer called me about the fire, my only thought was to get here as fast as I could to make sure you were okay. I was so worried about you."

"Thanks, I appreciate your concern."

"Do you want me to go home and get the letter?"

"No, but bring it tomorrow. Okay?"

Howie didn't crawl into bed until sometime after four that morning, and even then, the adrenalin kept him going for another forty-five minutes. Curiosity about the latest letter didn't help either.

Chapter 44

Howie had just come back into his office from pouring himself another cup of coffee when his door opened and Adam walked in. "Do you want some coffee?"

Adam shook his head.

"Are you hungry?" His partner had come directly from the church in Long Lake and probably hadn't had a chance to eat. "I can fix you a sandwich."

"No, I'm too tired to eat." Adam eased into a chair. "Doing worship services are more exhausting than I realized." He looked over at the clock. "What time is Kass coming?"

"One o'clock." Howie took a sip of coffee. "He should be here any minute."

"Wake me when he gets here...okay?" Adam rested his head on the back of the chair and closed his eyes.

For the next twenty minutes Howie sipped coffee and paged through a magazine. Nearly one-thirty on a Sunday afternoon and he could hit the sack and sleep straight through to Monday morning. He yawned and set his magazine aside when he found himself rereading the same sentence. "Kass is probably still getting things organized in the drugstore," he said, needing to have conversation to prevent from dozing off. He drummed his fingers on the desk. "I said Kass is—"

"I heard you." Adam opened his eyes and breathed deeply while stretching his arms toward the ceiling. "Kass can be thankful that there wasn't a lot of damage." He straightened in his chair, blinking his eyes a couple of times as though waking from a deep sleep.

Howie picked up his coffee cup, wrinkled his nose at the residue of soggy black coffee grounds, and set the cup down. "If there had been any more damage, he probably would've had to close the place for a while."

"Yeah, but he wouldn't know what to do if he couldn't come into work." Adam stood up, stretched again, and walked over to the window. He glanced at the street below before turning and sitting on the windowsill, his arms folded across his chest. "He's just lucky that someone was able to come out on a Sunday to replace that door and those windows."

"I agree. And if I know Kass, he'll be open for business before the afternoon is over."

Adam brushed back a shock of hair that had fallen over his forehead. "That drugstore is his whole life. He'd be lost without it."

"I'm sure whoever started that fire knew that." Howie stood and picked up his cup. He paused for a moment and sat back down. Three cups of reheated coffee was enough. "How's your head doing?" he asked, adding with a slight smirk, "Are you going to live?"

"Yeah, I think so."

"It didn't seem to affect your preaching this morning." Howie had gone with Mick to the first service. He had considered telling his partner that he was too tired to go. "Do you want a couple of aspirins?"

"No. I took some before I went to bed last night, and took some more after I got home from the fire." Adam moved over to his chair and plopped down, his legs sprawled out in front of him. "So what are we going to talk about with Kass? Do you have any ideas about who torched his place?"

"Not yet, but we might have a clue."

"What do you mean?"

"He received another one of those letters."

"What?" Adam frowned. "When?"

"Yesterday, probably early in the evening." Howie couldn't remember if Kass had mentioned a time.

"What did it say?"

"I don't know. He never opened it."

"He didn't?" Adam straightened in his chair and leaned forward, his eyes flickering with questions. "Why not?"

"He figured it was just like the others." Howie leaned back. His body ached from lack of sleep. "I don't really blame the guy. If this letter is like the other ones he received, it wouldn't be exactly relaxing bedtime reading. We'll get a chance to see it, though. He's bringing it with him." He leaned forward. "I have a hunch it has something to do with the fire."

"Do you think so?"

"Oh, yeah. It's too much of a coincidence, receiving another letter and then having his place torched."

Worry lines appeared on Adam's face. "Do you think Kass is scared?"

"He doesn't appear to be, and I don't think he's putting on an act. He was more concerned about me than anything else." Howie recalled how calm Kass appeared when he surveyed the damage done to his drugstore. "You know him...nothing seems to bother the guy." He picked up a pencil and rolled it between his thumb and forefinger. "Do you remember that time when he was robbed and beaten?"

"I sure do. That happened when we were seniors in high school." Adam's gaze turned inward for several moments. "And I remember him coming home from the hospital on a Monday and going back to work on Tuesday."

"The guy's a survivor," Howie said. "And get this. He told me that he hoped he wasn't being too much trouble by coming to us."

"You're kidding."

"I wish I was. You know Kass. He doesn't like bothering *his boys* with something like this when we have so many other more important cases to handle."

"What did you say to that?"

"What do you think I said?" Howie let the pencil drop onto his desk. "I told him that he was just as important as any of our other cases."

"Good for you." Adam leaned his head back against the chair. The clock ticked away several minutes before he spoke. "Is Mick going to be here?"

"No. He needed to spend some time with Mary this afternoon. It has something to do with their wedding. I told him that I'd fill him in."

"I'm sure they have lots of last minute things to do for their big day; it's not that far away now."

"When is their wedding again?"

Adam shot Howie an incredulous look. "It's two weeks from this coming Saturday. Being the best man, you should know that."

"I've got it written down someplace. I wouldn't have forgotten." Howie cocked his head when he heard the downstairs entrance door slam. The heavy, slow footsteps trudging up the stairs told him who it was. "Here comes Kass now."

Adam waited until the footsteps reached nearly to the top of the stairs and then got up from his chair, walked to the door, and opened it just as Kass got there. "Come on in, we've been waiting for you."

"Sorry to keep you boys waiting so long, but the fellow who was replacing my door needed some last minute instructions." The dark circles around his eyes didn't diminish the twinkle within them. "I also fixed him an extra-special banana split as a thank-you for coming out on a Sunday."

"Why don't you guys sit down?" Howie waited for Kass and Adam to get comfortable. "Did you bring the note?"

Kass reached inside his suit jacket and pulled out a white legal-size envelope. "This was taped to the windshield of my car."

"Wasn't your car in the garage?" Adam asked.

"No, my garage is too full of junk." Kass shrugged, offering a sheepish smile. "I'm planning to clean it before winter comes."

Howie took out his notepad. "When did you find the note?"

"Just before I got ready for bed I decided to go out to my car to make sure it was locked. Sometimes I forget."

"What time was that?"

"Around ten." Kass leaned over and handed the envelope to Howie. "The envelope was the same as the others, so I knew what it was right away. That's why I didn't read it." His eyes turned serious. "I read it this morning, though. If I would've read it last night, maybe…" He shook his head and sighed.

"You had no way of knowing," Howie said.

Kass shrugged. "Read it out loud so Adam can hear it also."

Howie examined the envelope. No markings of any kind. He opened it and took out a folded sheet of typing paper. The stylized printing appeared similar to the other letters Kass had shown them.

cass,

> Take this as another warning – you and your kind
> do not belong here. As far as to what you will soon
> discover, consider it as nothing when compared to
> what will happen next if you don't heed these words.
> And don't think about seeking help from your inept
> friends, because they obviously need help themselves.

"Is it signed?" Adam asked.

"No." Howie handed the note to his partner who glanced over it and returned it to Kass.

"I'm not going to allow whoever is sending these awful letters control my life," Kass said, setting his jaw to show his determination.

"What do you suppose that crack about your friends was all about?" Howie asked. "Who do you think they're talking about?"

"I don't know. I wish I did." Kass tugged at his ear. A thoughtful expression enveloped his face. "That part has been puzzling to me." He ran his hand back across his bald head as he reread the note. "I've given it a lot of thought, but I come up with nothing."

"You have lots of friends on the North Side," Adam pointed out.

"Oh, yes. I've been very blessed in that way." Kass scowled. "And it greatly offends me that someone would have the audacity to make such slanderous remarks about any of my friends." He slowly blew out a puff of air. "But I'm sure that it's just another way of someone trying to demean me."

"Could I see that note again?" Howie took the note and scanned it. "Do you mind if I copy this down?"

"Of course not. You do whatever you need to do with it." While Howie wrote in his notepad, Kass continued. "I support you and Adam and Mick. You boys are good detectives. Maybe you'll discover something in it that I don't see."

Howie looked over what he had printed and compared it with the original to make sure he had copied it word for word, printing the letters as they appeared on the note. He handed the note back to Kass. "Are you going to the police with this one also?"

"Oh, yes, I'll give them this one, just like I've given them all the others." Kass' eyes twinkled, causing the dark circles around them to fade a bit. "Pretty soon they'll be able to make a book from all of them." He folded the note, put it back in the envelope, and slipped the envelope into his inside jacket pocket. A hint of a smile crossed his face. "Did you notice that my name was even misspelled this time?"

Adam looked to Howie. "What's he talking about?"

"Whoever wrote that note spelled Kass with a small letter c." Howie flipped to a blank page in his notepad. "Did they spell your name with c or k in the other notes?"

"Always with a small letter k."

"Why the c this time?" Adam asked.

Kass shrugged. "I don't know. Maybe in their own sick mind it was their way of degrading me." He put his hand to his breast and felt the envelope through his coat. "Maybe they're telling me that my name means nothing and that they can do anything they want with it."

"You might be onto something with that," Adam said. "Everything I've read about what happened to the Jews was designed to make them feel less than human; they did all kinds of terrible things to humiliate them."

"Yes, I have a couple of relatives who could speak to that first hand, poor souls." Kass' eyes reflected the sadness in his voice and for an instant he appeared older than his fifty-five years. "I'm so sorry that this is happening." He turned his attention to Howie. "I'm glad that your apartment wasn't damaged, but most of all, I'm glad that you're okay."

"Thanks, but it's you I'm worried about. I think whoever did this is going to try something again."

"He's right," Adam said. He reached over and touched Kass on the arm. "And you've got to be extra careful."

Kass patted Adam's hand and gave him a warm smile. "Don't worry, I will be. I've learned to survive over the years."

"We don't want anything happening to you," Adam said. "Maybe..." He started slowly as though being deliberately careful in his choice of words. "Maybe you should consider staying away from the drugstore...at least until the police can get a handle on this whole thing."

Howie nodded. "That's a good idea," he said to his partner and turned his attention back to Kass. "Adam's right. You could take a little vacation. For all the hours you've put in over the years, no one would deny that you certainly deserve one."

"I'm not running away!" Kass cried as he slapped the arm of his chair. Red blotches appeared on his cheeks and the cords in his neck bulged. "I can't and I won't do that! Not now! Not ever! They're not going to run me out!"

"No one is saying that you're running away," Howie said, taken aback by the intensity of Kass' reaction.

"Maybe nobody is saying that, but they would think that. And even if they didn't, I would feel as if I were running away."

Adam cleared his throat. He appeared to be just as shocked as Howie at Kass' outburst. "But it may be for your own safety."

Kass shook his head. "I'm not going to be scared away. I could never live with myself if I did that." The words he spoke sounded like he may have spoken them at another time in another place. "Whoever they are, let them come. I know their kind. I can deal with them. My people have always dealt with their kind." He took a deep breath, leaned back in his chair, and crossed his arms in front of his chest. His eyes flashed with resolve. "That's all I've got to say. As far as I'm concerned, the matter is closed."

In the silence that followed, Howie sat astounded. He had never heard Kass get so worked up about anything other than being enthusiastic about his drugstore, and, of course, their detective agency. Howie understood Kass' feelings, however. Kass wasn't going to run away from this just like Howie wasn't going to run from Damien.

"Just remember, you're not in this alone," Adam said. "I'm here to help." He gave Howie a sideward glance. "We're all here to help."

"Thank you," Kass said, his voice calmer. "You boys have been so good to me over the years. How can I ever repay you?"

"Repay us?" Howie said. "Come on, it's gone more the other way. You've helped us out more times than I can count. And if it wasn't for you, I could never have started this detective agency."

"You have always been there for us," Adam added. "If anything, we're the ones who are doing the repaying." Kass looked like he was about to say something, but was cut off as Adam continued. "This is only a small down payment on what we owe you. And if Mick was here, he would be saying the same thing."

Kass smiled. "Like I told you before, helping you was done for selfish reasons."

"How so?" Howie asked, already knowing the answer.

"It's simple." Kass' smile broadened as he stuck out his chest. "Once you boys become famous by catching the bad guys, I can tell everybody it all started above my drugstore. My little place will become a tourist attraction. I'll get rich and retire early."

Howie closed his notepad. "We'll try and do our part in making your future dreams come true, but in the meantime, you go to the police with that note."

"I will...I will."

"And make sure Detective Davidson is aware of it."

"Of course."

Howie slipped his notepad into his shirt pocket. "And one more thing."

"What's that?"

"Don't forget you also promised that when we became famous that you would put up our pictures above the hot fudge dispenser."

Kass laughed so hard that tears came to his eyes, but Howie wasn't sure if the tears just came because of the laughter.

Chapter 45

For the past forty-five minutes Mick and his fiancée, Mary, had been going over some of the last minute details concerning their upcoming wedding. She, however, had done most of the talking. Because other things were on his mind, he had to work at listening and focusing on the wedding plans. It was important for her to have him there to get his input on some of the decisions that still had to be made, but he would rather have been with his partners. He couldn't help but wonder what was in that note that Kass was probably sharing with Howie and Adam at that very moment. Also, the whereabouts of Damien and what he could possibly be planning next was something that was always part of his consciousness.

In the comfort and security of her parents' living room, Mary appeared to be at ease as they chatted on the couch. "That about does it," she said while looking over a sheet of paper she had written a list of items for them to talk about. "Can you think of anything else?"

"I don't think so." Mick sneaked a look at the clock and wondered if the meeting with Kass and his partners was still going on. "It looks like you've got the wedding plans pretty well organized." With time being divided between his teaching job and the cases he and his partners were working on, he felt stretched at both ends. Although he looked forward to the wedding, he would be glad when all the hoopla was over. It wasn't the strain and stress of wedding planning that bothered him, however. Ever since Mary had received that package, he had been tense and uneasy. Although he hated to admit it, Damien was overshadowing the wedding. With nearly three weeks before the big event, he was worried about what Damien could be planning. From personal experience, he knew that the guy was capable of anything. The very thought that Damien was in the area again caused him a number of sleepless nights. And when he did sleep, his dreams often involved Damien doing something awful to Mary. Although Mick had not said anything to her, he was scared. Not for himself, but for her.

"Do you think you need to remind him?" Mary asked.

"What? Remind who?"

Mary playfully shook her finger at him. "You haven't heard anything I said in the last few minutes, have you?"

"Sorry. Remind who, now?"

"Do you need to remind Howie of the time for the rehearsal?" Mary smiled. "You know how he can be."

"He'll remember." Mick reached out and stroked Mary's cheek. "How are you doing with everything?"

"I think I'm doing fine." She put her list away. "I'm just pleased that you're willing to sit down with me and go over these things." Her smile gave no indication of what she had been through at her wedding shower. Her inner strength was one of the things that attracted him to her right from the very beginning. "I have some friends whose fiancés told them to take care of everything and they'd show up for the wedding."

"You know me better than that." Mick cleared his throat, hoping that what he was about to suggest wouldn't upset her too much.

"You're doing that again," Mary said.

"Doing what?"

"Cracking your knuckles." Mary had known him long enough to know what that meant. "Something's troubling you, isn't it?"

"When I asked you how you were doing, I wasn't really talking about the wedding plans." Mick cleared his throat again. He could see that certain look in her eyes that signaled that she already suspected what he was going to say. "I was talking about that package you received the other day."

"Oh, I see." Mary took hold of his hand. "I had a feeling that you were going to bring that up."

"Sorry."

"Don't be sorry. It's okay." Mary rubbed the top of his hand, massaging his knuckles. "I can't tell you that it didn't scare me, because it did, and I'm still frightened." She squeezed his hand. "I would feel so much better if you guys caught this Damien person before we got married."

"So would I." Mick broke eye contact.

"What is it? What's bothering you?"

"Nothing." He looked at her. "What makes you think that something's bothering me?"

Mary's eyes reflected the tenderness of her smile. "We have been together since our senior year in high school. Don't you think I know when something is bothering you?" When he didn't reply, she offered, "It's about Damien, isn't it?"

Mick put his other hand on top of hers. "Look, I've been thinking. What would you say if we..."

"If we what?"

"If we...ah...just elope."

Mary's face registered disbelief. "Mick Brunner, how can you even suggest such a thing after all the planning we have done?"

"I was just—"

"I'm not going to allow that man to spoil our wedding!" Mary replied firmly. She softened her tone. "If we run off and get married, he wins by controlling our lives, and that memory would be with us for the rest of our days. Do you want that?"

Mick shook his head. "I know you're right. I'm just concerned about you."

"That's one of the reasons why I love you." Mary leaned over and kissed him. "And do you want to know something else?"

"What?"

"When I'm holding your hand, you can't crack your knuckles."

Mick squeezed her hand. "I love you."

"And I love you." She reached up and gently stroked his hair. "Listen, with you and Adam and Howie there at the wedding, everything will be just fine. Just wait and see. It'll be a day to remember and cherish."

Chapter 46

Mick sat with his long legs stretched out to the side of Howie's desk and rested his head on the back of the chair. He had arrived at the office shortly before five. The dark circles around his eyes gave him the appearance of a man who hadn't slept for a week. "Are you working tonight?" he asked.

Howie nodded. "Yeah, I told Kass I'd help out for a couple of hours. Friday nights can get busy." It had been nearly a week since the fire and Howie had asked Mick and Adam to meet at his office at five. He thought it would be good to touch base again to see if his partners had come up with anything on the cases they were working on. Each day they had met and each day they racked their brains trying to think of new leads. "Adam called from school just before you got here."

"What did he say?"

"That he had nothing to report on either the fire or Squirrel's partner." Although frustrated about the lack of leads, Howie was determined not to show it. His partners didn't need to see his discouragement; it wouldn't be good for morale. "It seems like nobody on the North Side knows about either one...either that, or they're not talking."

"Is Adam still coming up?"

"No, he still had some research to do in the library for some paper." Howie took out his notepad and set it on his desk, hoping that Mick would have something for them. "I told him not to bother and that we'd probably see him tomorrow."

"Well, I struck out also." Mick's tone reflected the somber mood he had arrived with. "It looks like all of our leads have dried up."

"That's not surprising since we didn't have that many to begin with." Howie picked up a pencil and rolled it back and forth between his thumb and forefinger. "Something will turn up. It's bound to."

"The way our luck is running, I wouldn't bet on it."

Howie tossed the pencil aside and flipped the pages in his notepad, scanning all of the names that had been crossed off. In the past five days, he and his partners had talked with a number of people that Kass considered being close, or relatively close, friends. The idea was to gather as many leads as possible from these people with regard to whom they thought could be likely suspects. They were looking for persons who may have had some reason to dislike Kass enough to send him those hate notes or to set his drugstore on fire. It was a time-consuming job tracking the people down. Even with dividing the list of names between the three of them, Mick and Adam had each talked with over fifteen people. Because Howie had more time, he had interviewed close to thirty-five people. "There's nothing new here," he announced as he closed his notepad and slipped it back into his shirt pocket.

"That's just great," Mick said with a note of disgust. "All we seem to be doing is spinning our wheels." He slid his hands back and forth on the arms of his chair.

"Don't worry. Something will turn up. Don't you think?" When no response came, Howie studied his partner's face. "Okay, let's get it out on the table."

"What are you talking about?"

"You."

"Me?"

"Yeah, you." Howie kept his tone even, but was determined to get some answers. "What's eating you?" He pointed his finger at his partner. "And don't tell me nothing because I know you better than that."

Mick got up, moved over by the window, and stood staring out. After a while, he turned, sat down on the windowsill, folded his arms, and drew in a deep breath, letting it out slowly. "It's the wedding."

"What about it?"

"I told Mary that I thought we should elope."

"Is that so?" Howie put on his poker face to conceal his surprise. This was so unlike Mick. For the past year all the guy talked about was how great the wedding and reception was going to be and how happy he was to have Howie and Adam in the wedding. Besides that, Mick was the first in his family to be married and had told them that all his relatives were looking forward to it, especially to the dance afterwards. "Why would you want to elope?"

"I...ah..." Mick's eyes shifted downward. He wrung his hands and cracked his knuckles as he looked around the room, avoiding eye contact. Several minutes passed before he turned his attention back to Howie. "I hate to admit this, but it's Damien I'm..."

"Scared of?"

Mick locked eyes with Howie. For quite some time, he stood staring without speaking. "I...I guess I am." He cracked his knuckles, and, realizing what he had done, folded his arms, tucking his hands in under them. "We all know what that creep is capable of doing." When he closed his eyes for a moment, Howie wondered if he was trying to block out the past and what Damien had done to him in that cemetery. "If anything ever happened to Mary, I don't know what I would do..." The muscles in his jaw tightened. "Except kill the guy when I got my hands on him."

It took Howie a good minute to absorb the powerful waves of emotion coming from his friend. As long as he had known Mick, the man had never used his strength to harm anyone. If there was ever a gentle giant, his partner was it. He got up, walked over to Mick, and put his hand on his shoulder, patting it a couple of times in a gesture to show that he understood what he was feeling. "Look, we've handled Damien once before, we can do it again, and this time we'll get him. Keep the wedding and reception plans. If you don't, that's playing right into his hands. You don't want him controlling your life like that."

"You know, that's what Mary said."

"Well, what do you know...good for her." From the first time when Howie met Mary, he sensed there was something special about her. An attractive and popular girl in high school, she had impressed Howie by her intelligence, common sense, and, most of all, her genuineness. Initially, he had been concerned that when Mick finally got up the courage to ask her out for a date at the beginning of their senior year, she would turn him down. It was to her credit that she didn't. Over the years, she had proven to be good for Mick. When Mick, against the wishes of his father, decided not to play college football, she stood by him and encouraged him to attend the teacher's college he had been considering. "You have to live your own life," she had told him. Howie couldn't have been any happier for the two of them when they announced that they were getting married. A strong and brave woman, it didn't surprise him that Mary had refused to be intimidated by Damien. "So does that mean I'm still going to have the opportunity of being the best man?" Howie asked after he sat back down at his desk.

Mick's face broke into a smile. "You bet you are. It's worth having the wedding just to see you dressed in a tux." He gave Howie a questioning look. "You do remember when the rehearsal is and what time you're supposed to be there, don't you?"

"Are you kidding?" Howie padded his shirt pocket. "I've got it written down in my notepad. And don't worry about the wedding," he said, sensing that Mick seemed to be more relaxed. "We won't let anything happen."

"Can I ask a favor?"

"Of course."

"Promise me you won't get angry?"

At first, Howie thought that his friend was joking, but the look in his eyes told him that Mick was serious. "Go ahead. I'm listening."

"Would you ask JD to be there at the wedding...you know, as a little added insurance?" Mick swallowed hard. "Would you do that?"

Howie drummed his fingers on his desk as he focused on his coffee cup. His partners knew that he didn't like getting the police involved, even if it was JD, because it looked like they couldn't handle their own cases. He always told them that in order to establish a reputation, they couldn't go running to the cops every time things got tough.

"Come on, Howie," Mick pleaded. "It would ease my worries. And JD said we can call on him anytime. It's not like we can't do our jobs." The clock ticked away the seconds as he waited for a response.

"Okay," Howie finally said. "JD would like to get Damien behind bars just as much as we would." He offered a warm smile, wanting to put his partner at ease. "Besides, he likes weddings. He's been married twice."

"That would be great with him being there." The worry lines in Mick's face disappeared as he breathed a sigh of relief. "Thanks. I just know Mary will feel so much better about it…and so will I."

"You tell her for me that it's going to be a great wedding." Howie gave Mick a reassuring nod. "Just think, two weeks from tonight, it'll be all over with and you'll have wonderful memories to take into your old age."

Mick cleared his throat. "Ah…Howie."

"What?"

"Since you're the best man, I think you ought to know." Mick offered up a weak smile. "The wedding is two weeks from tomorrow. Two weeks from tonight is the rehearsal."

"Minor detail. I would've remembered," Howie said. "At any rate, with me there directing the show as best man, it'll be an experience you and Mary will long remember."

"Is that a promise?"

"Hey, you're talking to the best man. Would I lie to you?"

Chapter 47

While Howie served malts, banana splits, and cherry phosphates at the soda fountain to the Friday evening crowd at Kass' Drugstore, Damien was taking care of his last customer at the House of Beauty Salon in Edina near the Southdale Shopping Center. His wealthy customer, a heavy-set woman in her late fifties who wore too much makeup and smelled like she had bathed in perfume, had requested a hairstyle that would compliment her *youthful* personality.

"There you are, Mrs. Gardner, have a look." Damien slowly swung her chair around so that the silly old fool could view herself in the mirror on the wall. He gave her a few moments to admire his work. She, like the others at the salon, knew him as Damon. "I promised that it would make you look ten years younger, but I was wrong—it's more like fifteen years."

"Oh, Damon, you flatter me so." Mrs. Gardner turned her head from side to side admiring her hair in the mirror. "If I didn't know you, I might think you were telling me a little fib."

Damien smiled, bowed, and touched his hand to his lips for a brief moment. "Mrs. Gardner, may the rest of my nights be without slumber if from these lips would flow an untruth to such a lovely creature as the one who sits before me."

The object of his flattery tittered. "Oh, you are so poetic. I could sit here and listen to you all night." Her well-endowed chest rose and fell as she sighed like a lovesick teenager. "But my Herbert is expecting me. I really must go."

"And I'm sorry to see you leave," Damien said, sick of looking at the woman. The only way her looks could be improved would be if she took up permanent residence in a dark cave. "Our time together has flown by and it has been such a pleasant experience."

Mrs. Garner looked at herself again in the mirror, obviously pleased with the results. "Thank you, Damon. You do such splendid work. The girls at the bridge club will be so envious, but..." She wagged her pinky finger at him. "I want you all to myself. Do you hear me?"

Damien suppressed a smirk as he considered that old Herbert must have had the misfortune of having a curse placed on him to have married such an obnoxious creature. "Please, allow me." He helped her up from the chair.

"You're so sweet," she said, giving his hand a squeeze. "Just add this to my account." She reached for her purse, opened it, and took out a twenty dollar bill. "And this, my dearest, is for you."

"Why, thank you, Mrs. Gardner. Your generosity overwhelms me." *And is only surpassed by how lacking you are in beauty.*

"I shall see you in two weeks." She took another look at herself in the mirror. "By then I think I'll be ready for a touch-up." She fluttered her false eyelashes. "I have to keep my Herbert happy, you know."

He'd be happier if he suddenly went blind. "And I shall look forward to your return," Damien said and saw her to the door. "Would you like for me to escort you to your car?"

"Oh, how gallant of you. Thank you, my dear, but I'll be all right." Mrs. Gardner leaned over and planted a kiss on his cheek. "I'll see you in two weeks," she cooed.

Damien locked the door after she left, glad that he was done for the day. He had grown weary of shoveling out compliments to women who, in any other circumstances, he wouldn't have given the time of day. As soon as Mrs. Gardner was out of sight, he reached up and rubbed off her kiss with the back of his hand. After turning the lights off to the main area, he headed for the back room, expecting that his invitation had been accepted and that his *guest* would be there by now. When he walked into the back room, he was delighted to see that Newt Aldrich and Leon Sparks were waiting. It pleased him to see the nervous fear in Leon's eyes.

"Here he is," Newt said. "I brought him just like you told me."

"Why did you send for me?" Leon asked, a definite note of irritability in his voice. "What's so all important that you had to see me tonight? You knew I was scheduled to work. It was just lucky I could get someone to cover for me."

Damien walked over to the sink, ran the hot water, washed his hands with soap, and scrubbed the area where Mrs. Gardner had kissed him. Only after he had dried his hands and face, and had spent several moments admiring himself in the mirror, did he turn around. "I have need of your services again. That's why I sent for you."

"What do you mean?"

"You know exactly what I mean."

Leon's eyes widened. "Hey, look. I've gotten you two already," he cried. "I...I just can't do it. It's not possible."

"My, my, you certainly do get upset easily." Damien motioned to Newt. "Get a chair for our guest here. He seems a little unsteady on his feet." He turned his attention back to Leon. "I do hope you're not feeling ill."

"I'm not sick!" Leon snapped. His nostrils flared. Veins in his temple bulged. "And I don't need to sit down."

"Sit down!" Damien commanded as Newt pulled up the chair in back of Leon and then rushed over and stood behind Damien as though he didn't want to be anywhere near the object of his leader's wrath. Damien's eyes turned icy as he pointed his finger at Leon. "And don't you ever...*ever* use that tone of voice with me again. Do you understand?"

"I was just—"

"Do you understand?" Damien roared.

Leon gulped and nodded.

"Now, sit!"

"I..." Leon nervously glanced behind him at the high-back wooden chair. He stood defiant, his eyes locked upon Damien's unflinching gaze. His defiance, however, lasted but a moment as he broke off eye contact. "Okay, I'll...I'll sit, but I still can't do what you're asking. I've already done more than I should. You're going to have to find someone else to do your dirty work."

"I'm sorry to hear that, but I'm sure something can be worked out. I hope that you're not under the impression that I'm unreasonable. That would hurt my feelings and I'm a very sensitive person." Damien turned to Newt. "Do you think I'm unreasonable?"

Newt's eyes widened and he gulped as though caught off guard being asked a question. "Ah...ah...no."

"Did you hear that?" Damien asked Leon. "Newt doesn't think I'm unreasonable. I'm sure we can come to some kind of compromise. If you need more time, just tell me how much you need. I'm flexible...to an extent."

"It's not a matter of time." Leon acted as if he was going to get up but Damien motioned for him to stay put. "Look, what you're asking me to do is impossible. There are already too many questions being asked by the cops. Arranging for that last body was risky enough."

Damien folded his arms and stood unmoving for several moments without speaking. "You don't seem to understand," he finally said in a quiet, unnerving tone. "It is the basic economic principle of supply and demand. Didn't you learn that in school? I have a need and you...you have the pleasure of fulfilling my demand." His eyes narrowed. His mouth twisted into a sneer. "You wouldn't want to displease me, would you?"

"I've...I've told you already. I...I just can't do it."

"Yes, you've told me that." Damien paused. "But, I believe that I just may have the ideal solution. Excuse me for a moment." He walked over to a desk, unlocked the right-hand drawer with a key he got from his pocket, and took out a small black case, the size that eyeglasses would fit into. He came back to where Leon was sitting. "Get me a chair," he said to Newt.

"Which one?"

"The high-back one with the armrests sitting in the corner. It matches the one our guest is sitting in." Newt quickly brought the chair and then stepped aside. Damien moved the chair closer to Leon until they were sitting not more than two feet apart. "Newt, come out from behind me; it makes me nervous." He gave Newt a knowing smile, receiving a pre-arranged nod in reply. "Go stand behind our guest here so I can see both of you."

Chapter 48

"You know what I want, don't you?"

"I sure do," Howie said to Clifford, a man in his early seventies, who had taken a seat on the end stool. "It'll be coming right up." The elderly gentleman, a regular Friday evening customer, always came in after nine, always ordered a chocolate sundae with extra whipped cream, nuts, and two red cherries, and always sat on the same stool.

After serving his only customer, Howie went to the opposite end of the counter and began refilling the straw dispenser. All evening he had been on watch for anyone who may have had something to do with starting the fire, but no one acted suspicious. It had been a long shot, but there was always the slim chance of a person returning to the scene of the crime. He had read someplace that arsonists liked to visit the results of their handiwork.

Once he had filled the straw dispenser, Howie's mind turned to the note that Kass had received the night of the fire. Something about the note bothered him. He took a napkin and wrote out *cass*, wondering what could be the significance of the person misspelling Kass' name. "Why did they spell it with c instead of k?"

"What did you say?" Clifford called out from the other end of the counter.

"I was just muttering out loud to myself," Howie said. "It was nothing." He slipped the napkin into his pocket.

Clifford chuckled. "That happens to me a lot." He wiped chocolate off his chin and slowly got off the stool. "Just wait until you start answering yourself." He chuckled again and waved good-bye. "See you next Friday."

"Okay."

"Do you want me to leave the money on the counter or pay up front?"

"Pay up front."

"Your tip's under the dish."

"Thanks."

"And say hello to my old friend Kass." Clifford pushed a napkin toward Howie. "Make sure he gets this."

"I will." Howie walked over and picked up the napkin, slipping Clifford's quarter tip into his pocket. The old guy had drawn a sketch of a sundae topped with a mountain of what appeared to be whipped cream. The chocolate sundae lover had simply signed it with a capital C. He placed Clifford's note next to the straw dispenser with the intention of giving it to Kass when he saw him later. Apparently Clifford felt that Kass would know whom the note was from just by the drawing and his initial.

Howie cleared and wiped the counter, and turned his thoughts to the other note Kass had received. He took out the notepad he always carried with him and flipped to the page where he had copied the words.

cass, Take this as another warning – you and your kind do not belong here. As far as to what you will soon discover, consider it as nothing when compared to what will happen next if you don't heed these words. And don't think about seeking help from your inept friends, because they need help themselves.

"Why did they spell Kass with a small letter c?" Howie muttered. "It has got to stand for something. What though?" He glanced at Clifford's note, deciding he should put it by the front cash register to make sure Kass would see it. When he picked up the napkin, however, his attention was drawn again to how Clifford had just signed it with a C. He placed the two napkins side by side, studying them for several moments. *Maybe that's it. Maybe the c stands for one of Kass' friends. But who? Let's see, besides old Clifford, there's Charlie who owns the hardware store across the street. And then there's that tall, skinny lady at the bakery who's constantly flirting with Kass; her name is Corrine or Carolyn.* He scratched his head for a moment. *There's Carol who works at the bar down the street.* None of the people he had thought of thus far, however, were likely suspects. He drummed his fingers on the counter. *Who else has—* A shock wave surged through him. He stared at the *c* as though the letter had just shouted out the answer.

148

Chapter 49

Damien waited until Newt had taken a position standing behind Leon. "Good. That's so much better. Now I can see both of you." He turned his attention back to Leon. "Let's see, where was I?" He stroked his chin as though deep in thought. "Oh, yes, I remember now. I was just about to say that perhaps I could persuade you to change your mind."

"I'm not changing my mind." Leon kept glancing at the small black case Damien cradled in his lap.

"Did you hear that, Newt? Our guest says that he doesn't think I can persuade him to have a change of heart." A sneer formed on Damien's lips. His slender fingers caressed the case. "I certainly do love challenges, but Leon, this must not be your lucky day because I sincerely believe I can sway you."

"Look, I—"

"Let me finish!" Damien ordered, his eyes growing in intensity. "You see, Leon," he began, his tone softening, "I've been told that I have been blessed with the gift of being able to influence people in very creative ways." In a slow, deliberate manner, he opened the case, concealing its contents from his guest. "Are you sure you won't reconsider?"

"I'm not doing it."

"You know I am a very reasonable man, but it troubles me when someone says no to me. I feel...rejected." Damien paused. "Newt, tell me, have you ever felt rejected?"

"Ah...yes."

"And did you feel good about it?"

"Oh, no."

"Leon, do you see how rejection can hurt a person? One can say, in a manner of speaking, that rejection just cuts to the quick; it can be quite painful." Damien's tongue slid across his lips. He smiled and removed a pearl-handled knife from the case. He held the knife up for everyone to see, turning it in his hand, making sure its steel blade reflected the light from the ceiling fixtures. "This is a surgeon's scalpel, and, I might add, a very expensive one. It's a collector's item. Very nice. I believe it was made in the 1920's." The light reflecting off the blade danced upon Leon's face. "It has come in handy so many times. I'd be lost without it. Wouldn't I, Newt?"

Newt nodded. Apprehension flashed through his eyes as he stole a look at Leon.

"It was very useful at my last place of employment." Damien slowly stroked the blade across his palm. "Did you know that I once worked at a funeral home?"

Leon swallowed hard. Beads of sweat broke out on his forehead. "I'm leaving." He started to get up but at Damien's command, Newt grabbed him from behind as Damien swiftly put the scalpel to the man's throat. As soon as Leon felt the blade, he stopped struggling.

"Now, Leon, where are your manners?" Damien chided. "Didn't your mother teach you anything? We haven't finished our discussion. Don't be so rude." He pressed the blade against Leon's throat just enough to break the skin. "I wouldn't move if I were you because with a simple flick of my wrist, the main artery in your neck could be severed. You wouldn't want that, and neither would I because it would be very messy. And that would be most unfortunate because I just purchased this silk shirt." He paused. "Do you like my shirt?" When Leon didn't reply, he pressed harder until a trickle of blood ran down his neck. "I believe I asked you a question and you didn't answer." He looked at Newt. "Did you hear him answer?" Newt shook his head. His breathing came so rapidly that, for a moment, Damien thought his assistant was hyperventilating. "Newt didn't hear your answer either. Hmmm, perhaps you didn't hear me." He applied more pressure on the knife when Leon began to struggle. "I've told you that I wouldn't do that if I were you." Once Leon stopped resisting, he continued. "Now, as I was asking you...do you like my shirt?"

"Ye...yes."

"Good, I thought you would." Damien glanced at Newt, nodded, and spoke to Leon. "Newt is going to release you and I want you to rest your arms on the arms of the chair. After he releases you, he's going to tie your arms down." He was pleased to see the terror in Leon's eyes. "Don't worry, I just want to make sure you don't get up and leave while we're having our discussion because that would be very rude." His eyes went to Newt. "Wouldn't that be rude?" Without waiting for a reply, he turned his attention back to Leon. "If you cooperate, I promise you that I'll put my scalpel away."

"Wh...why are you doing this?"

"I'll explain in a few minutes. Now, remember when Newt releases you, I still have the scalpel pressing against your artery, so please—don't try anything foolish." Damien peered deep into Leon's eyes as though reaching into the very depths of his soul. When he spoke, his silky voice sounded like the purring of a cat. "I can see what you're thinking. You should know by now that you can't keep anything from me." He asked Newt. "Do you know what our guest here is thinking?"

"I have no idea," Newt replied quickly. His tone of voice and body language were suggestive of someone who wasn't comfortable where he was and wished he could be someplace, *anyplace* else.

Damien continued to peer into Leon's eyes. "Newt may not know, but I do, don't I? You're thinking that once he releases your arms, you could get lucky and land a punch, and make a break for it. I suppose there is that possibility of catching me off guard, but I rather doubt it. And even if you did..." He paused, his mouth forming a twisted smile. "I still would have enough time to slice your neck quite deeply. Have you ever witnessed an artery spewing blood?" He paused as though expecting an answer. "It's spectacular, like...like a volcano erupting. And I'm afraid you'd bleed to death before you even got to the car. So, Leon, I would advise you not to try anything foolish. Do I make myself clear?"

"Ye...yes."

Damien motioned to Newt to release his grip. "I believe there are some extension cords in the bottom of that gray cabinet in the corner. And while you're there, get that roll of packing tape on the table." While Newt went to get the necessary supplies, Damien reminded Leon to place his arms where he had previously instructed him to put them. When Leon hesitated, Damien increased the pressure on the scalpel. "There, that's more like it," he said as Leon cooperated.

Newt brought the extension cords and tape, and with Damien instructing him as to how he wanted it to be done, he secured Leon's wrists to the arms of the wooden chair. He held up an extension cord. "I have one left over. Should I do his feet also?"

"Why, yes, what a splendid idea." While Newt was tying Leon's feet, Damien settled back in his chair and watched. He reached over and wiped the blade on Leon's trousers. "Oh, dear, look what I have done now. How thoughtless of me. I can see by the look on your face that you're alarmed. Don't worry. I know an excellent method of getting blood stains out of cloth. Would you like to know it?"

Leon shook his head, his eyes portraying a mixture of terror and bewilderment.

"Oh, well, Leon, I suppose you must have your own little secret for getting rid of blood stains." Damien took a silk handkerchief out of his pocket, wiped the remaining blood off the scalpel, and gently placed his collector's item back into its case. He waited for Newt to finish securing Leon's feet, taking note that during the whole time Newt had avoided making eye contact with Leon.

"I'm done." Newt backed away from the chair and stood off to one side, still avoiding any eye contact with their victim.

Damien's eyes shifted to his guest. "Newt is such an excellent student, so obedient and resourceful. He would never think of saying no to me even though he may not always approve of my methods." He pointed his finger at the man now strapped to his chair. "You, Leon, on the other hand, have much to learn."

"Wha...what are you going to do to me?" Leon glanced at the scalpel case Damien had placed on the floor between them.

"Oh, I wouldn't have used that...or maybe I would have." Damien shrugged. "I guess we'll never know...for now."

"Look, I've got some savings. I can—"

"It's not money I want!" Damien roared, but quickly changed to a softer, patronizing tone. "You offend me by offering me money. It's like..." He turned to Newt. "What would you say it was like?"

"I don't know. I guess like a bribe."

"Yes, exactly." Damien turned to Leon. "And I have higher standards than that. Don't you know how degrading that is to a sensitive person like me?" He folded his hands on his lap and relaxed in his chair. "Now, Leon, my friend, you know what I have requested. I don't think it's necessary for me to repeat it."

"I told you, I can't do it!" Leon cried. "Believe me, if I could, I would." He looked back and forth between Damien and Newt. His eyes pleaded for sympathy. "It's just too risky to get another body. They're already suspicious of me. I—"

"Enough of your excuses!" Damien folded his arms and glared at his victim.

"But—"

"Enough I said!" Damien screamed. He stood up so abruptly that he knocked over his chair. The sound of it clattering on the cement floor startled Newt, causing him to jump back.

Leon's eyes doubled in size, his breathing came forth in short rapid gasps. He opened his mouth, but no words came forth.

"The only thing I want to hear from you is *Yes, Damien, I will gladly do as you say.* Now, I'll give you some time to think about it." Damien's mouth twisted into a smile as he took a few moments to smooth out a wrinkle in his shirt. "I'm afraid time's up. You see, Leon, unfortunately, impatience is one of my shortcomings." He handed Newt the silk handkerchief. "Stuff this in his mouth."

Leon cried, "Wait, I—"

"Do it now!" he ordered Newt. "I've grown weary of his whining voice."

Even though Leon desperately twisted his head from side to side and tried to keep his mouth clamped shut, Newt managed to force the handkerchief into his mouth. At the instruction of Damien, he also placed tape over his mouth.

"Don't look so alarmed," Damien said over the gagging sounds of Leon. "My handkerchief is clean. I made sure of that. Of course, it has blood on it, but it's yours." He cocked his head as he listened to Leon's muffled cries. "What's that you say? You want to know why I'm doing this. You'll soon find out." He motioned to Newt. "Get my tray table."

Chapter 50

Squirrel strolled into Kass', glanced around, spotted Howie behind the soda fountain and walked up to him just as he was stuffing what looked like a napkin into his pocket. "What's the matter? Can't you afford a handkerchief?"

"What are you doing here?"

"Hey, don't look so stunned." Squirrel plopped on a stool. "I haven't heard from you in a couple of days."

"So?"

"So I'm curious if you've dug up anything on my conniving partner."

"We're still working on the case."

"And so what have you found out?"

"Look. This isn't the time or place to talk." Howie took out a towel and wiped the counter in front of his visitor. "Why don't you come by my office in the morning?"

"What's going on?" Squirrel glanced around. "Are you working on another case?" His nose twitched a couple of times as he sucked air through his teeth. "So that's it, isn't it?"

"That's what?"

"You're working undercover, ain't you?"

"What?"

"Pretty slick if you ask me. That white apron is the perfect disguise." Squirrel leaned over the counter. He glanced around to make sure they were alone. "Your cover is safe with me," he whispered. "I won't blow it."

Howie rolled his eyes. "Thanks, you don't know how much that means to me."

"Don't worry. I'll play along. Just think of me as a customer." Squirrel reached in his pocket, took out a roll of bills, and peeled off a ten spot. "Why don't you whip me up something to satisfy my sweet tooth?"

"Like what?"

"Hmmm." He glanced behind Howie, checking out the various ways his craving might be fulfilled. "How about a chocolate fudge sundae with lots of nuts."

"Okay."

"And give me a pineapple malt to wash it down with."

"A what?"

"A pineapple malt."

"You want a chocolate fudge sundae and a pineapple malt?"

"You got it."

"Suit yourself." Howie shook his head. "It's your stomach."

Squirrel watched as the undercover detective went to work. "Pretty smart cover-up," he said when Howie served him his sundae. "You know, what's cool?"

"No. What?"

"Being a detective."

"It can be at times."

The little guy scooped up a spoonful of nuts dripping with hot fudge, shoved it into his mouth, chewed for a moment, and gulped it down. He smacked his lips and pointed the spoon at Howie. "Can I ask you a question?"

Howie poured the pineapple malt into a tall glass and set it before his customer. "It's not about the case, is it?"

"No, no, no."

"Go ahead, then."

"Do you think I have what it takes to do what you do?"

"You mean to dish up ice cream?"

Squirrel shook his head. He glanced around to make sure no one was in hearing range. "No," he whispered as he leaned toward Howie. "To be a private eye."

Chapter 51

Damien leaned back in his chair and crossed his legs. "Leon, just relax. I'm in no rush. Are you?"

Leon twisted his body and head as much as he could in an effort to see what was on the tray table that Newt had been ordered to get. His eyes bulged with terror. He tried to speak, but only muffled sounds came forth.

"What is that you're saying?" Damien asked. "Leon, I'm afraid that you're just going to have to speak a lot clearer." He cocked his head and raised his eyebrows as though he now understood the garbled sounds coming from his guest. "Oh, so you miss Newt." His tone oozed with sarcasm. "Don't worry. He'll be right back."

Newt hurried back with the tray table and set it along side of Damien. "Anything else?" he asked, still dodging any eye contact with Leon.

"Yes, keep our guest company while I get my...supplies." Damien whistled as he walked to the cabinet and opened it. He took out a small terry cloth towel from the middle shelf. From another shelf he chose a pair of extra-long scissors from amongst several sizes, and from the top shelf, he removed an emerald-tinted glass bottle half full of liquid. He continued to whistle as he walked back, pleased to see the increased terror on Leon's face. He was also delighted to see that Newt had a similar look on his face. He handed the scissors and bottle to Newt and carefully laid out the towel so that it covered the top of the tray. "How does that look?" he asked Newt after he smoothed out the wrinkles on the towel.

"Fi...fine. Wh...why...do you ask?" Newt stammered as though unsure what the correct answer should be.

"Well, I just don't know." Damien stroked his chin and stepped back as though admiring a work of art. "Should I have brought the beige towel instead of this white one?" He turned to Leon. "Which of the two would you recommend?"

"Agggh!"

"What's that you say, Leon? Beige? Hmmm...you think so?" Damien shook his head. "No, I'm afraid that I'll have to disagree. The white one is the one we should have. Isn't that right, Newt?"

"Ye...yes."

Damien took the bottle and scissors from Newt and placed them on the towel, arranging them several times until satisfied. "It's all in the presentation," he explained.

"Wha...what are those things for?" Newt asked.

"You'll see." Damien unbuttoned the cuffs of his shirt and took his time rolling up his sleeves while all the time staring at Leon. He picked up the bottle, unscrewed the cap, and passed the bottle back and forth under Leon's nose.

"Agggh!" Leon jerked his head back.

"Wha...what is that stuff?" Newt asked, backing away and wrinkling his nose as if he had gotten a whiff.

"This?" Damien held up the bottle. "It's a certain chemical that I add to the bleach I use for highlighting hair. It really works wonders." He set the bottle down. "Of course, I'm careful to add just a tiny fraction. One should never, never add more than a few drops." He gave a sideward glance toward Leon, but directed his words to Newt. "It's quite potent."

Newt nodded as if he understood, but Damien knew he had no idea what he was talking about, much less what he had in mind for Leon. The more off balanced he kept Newt, the more control he had over him. He reached over, fingered Leon's hair, and wiped his fingers on the man's shoulder. "Leon, you have such nice thick hair. It's a little oily, however. When did you wash it last?" He moved around Leon's chair, pausing occasionally to do a closer examination of his guest's hair. "You could also use a different hairstyle. Whoever cuts your hair does such an atrocious job. Don't you think so?" he asked Newt.

"Ah...ah...yeah." Newt glanced at the scissors lying on the tray. "Ar...are you going to give him a haircut?"

"Hmmm, I suppose I could, but I have other plans for him this evening." Damien's focus shifted to Leon. "However, Leon, if you would like to make an appointment with me, I would make every effort to accommodate you." He watched with amusement as beads of perspiration rolled down his victim's face. "If I may make a suggestion, however...I think you should seriously consider changing barbers. It is your decision, of course. I do understand that one's hairstyle is such a personal preference."

Another muffled cry.

"What's that you say? That you would like me to style your hair? Oh, my. That is very trusting of you. Newt, isn't that trusting of him?"

"Uh, huh."

"I'm flattered, Leon, I truly am, but I'm afraid that I'll not be able to accommodate you tonight. As I have mentioned..." Damien paused and whispered, "I have other plans for you." He motioned to Newt. "Unbutton his shirt," he commanded in a tone matching the cold look in his eyes.

Leon let out a muffled cry again. He struggled so hard to break free that the chair rocked from side to side, causing it to nearly tip.

Damien's reaction was swift. He grabbed his scalpel and held it to Leon's neck. "You do that again and I'll become very angry," he hissed. "Do you understand?" His breaths came as rapidly as Leon's as he moved the scalpel slowly across Leon's neck, applying only enough pressure to break the skin, allowing a trickle of blood to come forth. "Do...you...understand?" he repeated.

A tear formed in the corner of Leon's eye as he nodded.

"Good, Leon, that pleases me that you do understand. You'll be fine as long as you keep me pleased. And really, you'll find me most agreeable once you get to know me better." Damien wiped the scalpel on Leon's pants, and placed it back in its case. "Now, without any more trouble..." His tone turned threatening. "You will allow Newt to unbutton your shirt."

Newt swallowed hard as he began to unbutton Leon's shirt, fumbling with each button because his own hands shook so much. If he had looked into Leon eyes, he would have seen Leon pleading for him not to be part of this madness.

"Pull his shirt out of his pants so you can unbutton it all the way down," Damien ordered.

Newt quickly did as his boss had instructed and stepped aside.

"That's good." Damien pulled both sides of the shirt back to expose Leon's tee shirt. "A v-neck? That surprises me, Leon. I wouldn't have guessed that of you." He picked up the scissors. "I saved your shirt, but I'm afraid I'm not going to be able to save your tee shirt." In a matter of seconds, Damien cut the tee shirt from the bottom to the top exposing Leon's chest and stomach. "That wasn't so bad, was it?" He set the scissors down and picked up the bottle. "This may sting...no, since you're my guest, I need to be honest...it will burn like a severe sunburn...a very *severe* sunburn."

Leon shook his head, his eyes pleaded for mercy as perspiration flowed down his terror- stricken face. Once again he struggled to break free, but ceased when Damien reminded him about the scalpel.

"I'm going to drip this onto your chest one drop at a time and will continue to do so until I know that you'll never say no to me again." A smug smile appeared on Damien's face. "After we have reached that understanding, I'll have Newt drive you home."

"Wha...what...what if he goes to the cops?"

Damien's eyes shifted to Newt and then back to Leon. "You wouldn't go to the police, would you, now?"

Leon shook his head. His eyes begged for mercy. His cries sounded like the whimpering of a tortured animal.

"I had a feeling you would say that. But for added insurance, consider that I know you have an eight-year-old son, and I know where to find him. Do you see my point?" Damien held the bottle over Leon's chest. "May I suggest that you close your eyes? I wouldn't want to take the risk of having this splattering into them. That would be most unfortunate." He slowly tilted the bottle but stopped. A wicked grin formed on his lips. "Leon, I forgot to tell you. If you listen very carefully when the drops hit your skin, you'll hear a faint sizzling." He tilted the bottle again, allowing several drops to fall onto Leon's chest. In the midst of the muffled screams, Newt fainted.

Chapter 52

During a mid-morning break on Monday, Mary walked into the teacher's lounge. Although a week had gone by since the Sunday Mick had approached her with the subject of them eloping, she was still second-guessing herself about being so adamant on going on with the wedding as planned. She had kept the topic of their conversation to herself, not wanting to even tell her mother for fear of upsetting her. But now, Mary felt as if she needed to share her concerns with someone. She was pleased to see Dianne Lane, one of the music teachers, sitting by herself. In her early forties, Dianne had taken Mary under her wing when Mary first began teaching at the school three years ago. Dianne had become her mentor and confidant, and had graciously accepted Mary's invitation to sing at the wedding.

"Dianne, may I share something with you in confidence?" Mary sat down in a chair next to her.

"Of course." Dianne set her cup of tea aside.

For the next several minutes Mary related the conversation she and Mick had had, her emotions about it, and her apprehension as to whether she had made the right decision to go against Mick's suggestion. Her friend listened without interruption. When Mary finished, she admittedly felt relieved. "Dianne, thank you so much for listening."

"That's quite all right. I know you'd do the same for me."

"So what do you think? Was I wrong to insist on the church wedding?"

"By no means." Dianne reached over and touched Mary's hand. "You made the right decision and I'm sure Mick now realizes that."

Mary breathed a sigh of relief. "You don't know how good that makes me feel to hear you say that. I thought we made the right decision, but I just needed to run it past someone." She took another deep breath. "Weddings can be so stressful, can't they?" For the next ten minutes the two of them talked about how weddings had become more elaborate over the years.

"It must be nearly time for our next class to begin," Mary said, taking note of the other teachers getting up and leaving. She took Dianne's hand and squeezed it. "You're a good friend, and Mick and I are so pleased you will be singing at our wedding."

"I wouldn't miss it for the world." Dianne stood up and straightened her skirt. "Would you like to go out after conferences tonight?" she asked as the two of them walked to the door. "We can have pie and coffee."

"I would love to, but Mick is going to pick me up. There are still a few things that he and I need to talk about. I hope you understand."

"Of course, I do. I can remember what's it like to be getting married. My husband and I have been married now for nearly twenty-three years. Let me tell you, it only gets better as the years go by." Dianne opened the door. "Good luck with your conferences. I hope they go well for you."

Contrary to Dianne's hopes, however, the parent-teacher conferences didn't go well for Mary. Two sets of parents complained that she wasn't spending enough time with their children. One very distraught mother used their entire time together explaining that her son was acting up because she and her husband were going through a nasty divorce. The woman practically gave Mary the whole history of her fifteen-year marriage while sharing intimate details that Mary felt should only have been shared with a counselor or priest. One of the fathers came in with alcohol on his breath, and, as if that wasn't bad enough, had made a pass at her while his wife sat quietly, pretending not to notice. Mary quickly ended that conference by telling the man that her soon-to-be-husband was a detective.

After several meetings with parents that did go quite well, Mary met with a woman who acted as if the whole school district was established for the sole purposes of serving her daughter. After that woman departed, Mary was glad that there was only twenty minutes left for conference visits. Tired to the point of exhaustion, she hoped that the final minutes would go by without anyone showing up. She reached down and got her purse out from her bottom desk drawer. After getting her lipstick and pocket mirror, she was pleased to see that she only needed a touch-up. She frowned, however, when she got a glimpse of her hair. The combination of a humid day and a school building that was too warm had played havoc with her hair. She had just put her purse back when an attractive woman dressed in a stylish pantsuit walked up. The woman looked as if she had just come from the beauty shop. Mary sighed, wishing she had five minutes to run to the teacher's lounge to touch up her hair.

"Hello, I'm Louise Sparks, Bradley's mother."

Mary stood, introduced herself, and asked the woman to sit down. "Is Bradley with you tonight?"

"He's with his father." Louise paused. "I think my son told you that his father and I are divorced."

"Yes, he mentioned that to me." Mary took out Bradley's file. She didn't have to open it to look up his test scores; he had proven to be a model student and very mature for his age. "Bradley's certainly a fine young man and I never have any problems with him. His test scores are consistently high. You must be proud of him."

Louise nodded. "I am."

Mary became self conscious when she noticed Bradley's mother glancing at her hair. "You have to excuse my hair. It's been a very long day," she said, wondering where Louise Sparks had her hair done.

Chapter 53

Howie felt bad about asking Jim Davidson to drop by his office on a Monday evening. It was the detective's night off, but Howie was at a dead end on the Phillips' case. He hoped JD would share any leads the police may have uncovered in the past several days. It was worth a try. Anything would help. He needed to have something to offer his client. Mr. Underwood had called from the funeral home that morning to see if there had been any progress made on the case. "Howard, the family is very anxious to bring this to closure." It was the way he had said *closure* that made Howie feel as if Underwood himself was also getting impatient.

The downstairs entrance door banged shut and the creaking of the stairs gave Howie notice that JD had arrived and was coming up. He drummed his fingers on his desk as he waited for his office door to open. Within moments, Davidson entered. He acknowledged Howie with a nod and walked over to the movie poster. For nearly a minute he stood looking at it before strolling over and taking a seat.

"That's got to be one of my all-time favorite movies," Davidson said. "Bogart was a damn good actor. And that Mary Astor was a classy-looking dame." He stretched out his legs and folded his arms across his chest as he settled back in the chair. "So, what did you call me up here to talk about? And it had better be good because right now I could be lying on the couch watching a ball game and having a cold brew."

Howie cleared his throat. Even though Davidson was a friend and mentor, it wasn't easy to ask for help without feeling as if the veteran police detective might think of him as a failure. "I want to know about any leads you have on those cases."

"Which cases are you talking about?" Davidson asked casually.

"Come on, don't play dumb with me. You know the ones I'm talking about." JD's eyes remained impassive. "Do I have to spell it out for you?" Howie waited, but his friend didn't even so much as twitch an eyebrow. "I'm talking about the bodies of those two young women taken from the funeral homes and then found under the Broadway Bridge."

"Oh, those cases." JD rubbed his chin. "All the leads have gone cold."

"What about the ones you've already checked on?" Howie hoped for any information that might trigger a lead.

"What haven't we checked?" Davidson began to count off using his fingers. "One, we contacted all the funeral homes in the seven county Metro area and conducted interviews with their employees; some of them we interviewed twice. Two, we talked to everyone who works in the cemeteries in the same area, from the grounds' keepers to the grave diggers themselves. And three, we even talked to those who work at the city and county morgues."

"And nothing?"

"That's right. Zippo." Davidson straightened in his chair, shifting his broad shoulders. "I'll share this with you, though, as long as you keep it here. And I'm doing this because I like you." He glanced around the office. "I want you and your partners to keep this little operation going." When he shifted in his chair again, his sport coat opened just enough to reveal the gun in his shoulder holster. "We're going to pull our stakeout off that bridge for one thing; secondly, the chief wants the cases put on the back burner for the time being."

"What? You can't do that!"

Davidson's eyes hardened. "Look, let me give it to you straight up. We all agree that the mutilation of those bodies is sick, and I'd like to get my hands on those who did it just as much as you would, but right now the case just doesn't merit a lot of manpower in the eyes of the chief. We haven't given up on it. We've just shifted our priorities for the time being."

"But—"

"But nothing." JD's tone matched the hard look in his eyes. "We've got our hands full with a double homicide, and the chief is burning our butts to close the case so he can get the mayor and the city council off his neck."

Howie opened his mouth to argue that the families of those young women deserved just as much attention, but Davidson held up his hand to signal that he wasn't finished.

"And then there's this string of neighborhood robberies that haven't been solved yet. With the last one, the creeps beat up an elderly woman. She's still in critical condition. We're working overtime on all this crap."

"How about the fire at Kass' last week? What are you going to do about that?"

Davidson looked tired. He rubbed the corner of his eye. "We've backed off on that."

"Why?" Howie asked, the muscles in his jaw tightening.

"For one thing, there haven't been any more threatening notes, and the chief figures that it's probably some teenage hoodlums who don't have anything better to do."

"You mean you don't have anybody working that case?" Howie said, not restraining his anger.

"I didn't say that!" JD shot back. "The case for the time being has been assigned to one of the junior detectives."

"Who?"

"One of the guys."

"Somebody I know?"

"Yeah."

Howie studied JD's face for a moment. "You're not talking about Herb Manning?"

Davidson nodded.

"Are you crazy?" Howie's head felt like it would explode. "Didn't you tell me that Manning was the most inept detective in your whole department?"

Davidson nodded again.

"And that he was only assigned cases that he couldn't screw up too much?"

The police detective sat impassively, saying nothing.

"Why in hell did it have to be that guy?"

"It was my suggestion."

"What?" Howie fought the impulse to slam his fist on the desk. "Your suggestion? Do you want to explain your reasoning on that?"

"Cool down, will you?" JD said. "Here's the story. The chief came to me and asked if I thought Manning should have that case, or the one involved with the missing bodies of those two young women. I figured that Manning could do less damage on the arson case. I didn't want him sticking his nose in the other case—he would've blown any new leads as soon as we got them. So, it was the lesser of two evils."

Howie closed his eyes and took a deep breath. "I suppose you're right."

"Don't you think I know why you asked me up here?" Davidson said. "I'm not some rookie detective. I had a pretty good idea that you were going to probe me for any new information on those cases. But I also wanted to see how you and your partners were holding up." His eyes softened. "How rough has it been?"

"It hasn't exactly been a cakewalk."

"Any new leads?"

"That depends." Howie folded his hands on the desk and locked eyes with JD. "Are you asking as a cop or as a friend?"

"Does it make a difference?"

"It will in this case."

"As a friend."

Howie kneaded the tightness in his neck. This wasn't exactly turning out the way that he thought it would. Even though JD was a friend, it still wasn't easy confessing that he didn't have much to go on and wasn't even sure what his next step should be. As a friend, JD would be supportive, but what would he think as a cop? That was important, also. Howie took a deep breath and blew it out slowly. "To tell you the truth, I haven't gotten very far either."

"Sorry to hear that," JD said. "But let's face it, with the kind of work we do, measuring our successes and failures can be compared to riding on a roller coaster. One case can be solved within a couple of days, even hours.

The next case...hell, it could take a couple of years." He paused. "And then there are those that are never solved." Weariness crept into his voice. "I've had more than my share of those in my career, and before I retire I know I'll have a few more. That's the way it is."

Even though it hadn't been that long since Howie started the agency, he had quickly learned that the work could be painstakingly slow, and so much depended on luck. Davidson's words made it easier to talk about his own frustrations. "Since that fire at Kass' last week, would you believe that we talked to sixty-seven people, all of them considered to be his friends or close friends?"

"Sixty-seven?" JD let out a low whistle. "That's a hell of a lot."

"You bet it is. And not one of them could think of anyone who would want to harm him." Howie shook his head in frustration. "We didn't get one lousy lead from all that effort. I have no idea where to go next on this."

"Welcome to the real world." When JD smiled, he looked ten years younger. "I told you when you first started out in this business that it's not going to be like what you see in the movies." He gestured toward the poster on the wall behind him. "Even Bogie back there had some bad days, and he was going by a script. We don't have that luxury."

"So, what do I do about Kass? I mean where do I go next?"

"Just keep plugging. Kass doesn't deserve what's been happening to him, but let's hope that the worst is over. At least the chief thinks that could be the case."

"What do you think?"

JD shrugged. "Maybe the chief is right. I don't know."

"And you guys didn't come up with any leads at all?" Howie asked, wanting to make sure he had understood him right.

"Like I told you. Zippo." JD glanced at his wristwatch. "Let's hope that whoever's behind those letters and the fire has gotten tired of his game and has moved on to other things."

"What if the chief is wrong?"

"It won't be the first time."

Howie moved his head from side to side, thankful that his neck muscles had loosened up. "How about those missing bodies? Anything more on them?"

"Not a thing. The leads have gotten ice cold. I've got my ears open, though. If I hear of anything, I'll give you a heads-up." He gave Howie a reassuring look. "I know you guys could handle it better than Manning. Hell, that guy would get lost going to the bathroom at night."

Howie glanced at the clock. It was getting late and he suspected that his friend wanted to get going to watch the ball game. "I've got one more thing to bring up. It won't take but a minute or two to deal with."

"I'll give you three, but no more," JD replied, a hint of a smirk on his face.

"I told you I'm positive that Damien had something to do with those missing bodies."

"You've been dealing with that guy for quite some time, haven't you?"

"Off and on for over a year."

"That's a long time for having that lay in your gut. From what you've told me, he sounds like a psycho."

"We're determined to get him."

"Don't be disappointed when you do."

"What do you mean?"

"It's going to be tough as nails to hang those cases on him." JD leaned forward, his tone turning sober. "Number one, we need proof that he took those bodies. Number two, we have to prove that he's the one who sent that package to Mick's fiancée." He paused as though wanting to make sure Howie was fully absorbing what he was saying. "And lastly, even though you're positive that Damien was there when your partner got conked on the head at the church, there's no evidence. Getting proof for any of this stuff is not always as easy as you think."

"I don't need any proof!" Howie's neck muscles tightened again. His hands curled into fists. "He's behind all of this, all right. And I'm going to get him, with or without your help. You understand?"

JD put up his hands in mock surrender. "Hey, calm down. I'm on your side. I'm simply pointing out that it doesn't matter what the hell you think and how sure you are about his guilt, it has to be proven in a court of law. We have something called the criminal justice system and you're going to need some hard evidence." He settled back into his chair. "The fact of the matter is that whoever took those bodies left no fingerprints and there aren't any witnesses. And it sounds like this guy is too damn smart to confess to anything."

"Don't worry. I'll get proof."

"Good. It'll be one less case for us to bust our butts on." JD's eyes hardened. "But let's say you proved that Damien was behind those things. It's not like he's robbed a bank or committed a murder. Even with the previous charges from your first encounter with him, he'll do some time, but not much."

"I don't care. Even if he's put away for a couple of years, that's two years he'll be off the streets."

Davidson didn't say anything for several moments. "He's really gotten to you, hasn't he?"

Howie stared at JD as the clock continued to tick off the time. "Damien operates by instilling fear into people; he controls them that way. Adam says that he's pure evil."

"Sort of like the devil, huh?"

"You've got it." Howie's head pounded. He needed to take a couple of aspirins as soon as Davidson left. "JD...ah..." He looked away for a moment. "I need a favor."

"Name it."

"Can you come to Mick's wedding a week from this coming Saturday?"

"Yeah, I think so. What's going on with the wedding? Are you expecting some kind of trouble?"

"We think Damien is going to show up. We could handle it, but we're all going to be up front in the wedding party, so it would be hard for us to do anything if he appears. We'd appreciate if you came just in case he does show his face."

"Sure, why not. I'll be glad to." JD offered a half smile. "It'll be worth seeing you all dressed up in a monkey suit."

Chapter 54

Mary closed her class assignment book, placed it in the top right-hand drawer of her desk, and took a few minutes to relax. Five minutes earlier, the school bell had rung ending the last class of the afternoon. Her students had wasted little time; they had scrambled out the door like the school was on fire.

It had been a full day and she was also looking forward to going home. Still tired from last night's parent-teacher's conferences, she needed to get some rest tonight. With the responsibilities of her teaching job and her wedding only two weeks away, she had been busy. Busy? It had been a whirlwind of last minute preparations. She didn't mind, however. She was good at details and her mother gave her lots of excellent advice and assistance. Mick had been helpful, but the details of the wedding had been pretty much left up to her. Besides, her future husband had enough on his mind with teaching full-time while working with Howie and Adam in tracking down that evil man who stole those bodies and sent those gruesome packages. The very thought of Damien knowing where she lived caused her to shiver. She rubbed her arms and made herself concentrate on the papers in front of her. Mick would be picking her up within the hour. It gave her a sense of security and comfort to know that.

The door to the classroom opened and a woman walked in just as Mary was correcting another paper. It only took a moment to recognize that it was Bradley's mother, Louise Sparks. With gorgeous hair as beautiful and stylish as last night at the conference, the woman looked as though she had just stepped out of a movie set.

"Hello, Mrs. Sparks, what brings you here this afternoon?" Mary asked, aware that her own hair probably showed the wear and tear of the day.

"I just dropped in to thank you again for all the help you have given my Bradley so far this year. It means a lot to me."

"Well, your son means a lot to me also." Mary gestured to the chair next to her desk, pleased that Mrs. Sparks took the time to visit her on such a pleasant note. Very seldom did a parent come in to simply express their gratitude; it would be a good way to end the workday. "Would you care to have a seat?"

"Thank you." Mrs. Sparks sat down. "There's hardly a night that goes by when my son doesn't talk about you." She crossed her legs, setting her purse on the floor. "He even talks about your class on the weekend."

"That's nice to hear." Mary felt herself blush. "He's so easy to teach. I wish all of my students were as enthusiastic about learning as your son."

"Bradley certainly likes school more than I ever did. And you've probably guessed by now, you're by far his favorite teacher." Louise looked toward the door as if perhaps her son was standing outside. "But do me a favor and don't tell him that I told you. He'd be too embarrassed. You know how boys are."

"I promise I'll keep it to myself, but I want you to know that is the best compliment a teacher can hear. You have a wonderful son. As I told you last night, I just love having him in class." Mary closed the folder on the exam papers she had been correcting. "Now, is there anything I can do for you?"

"Oh, no. I stopped to bring you something." She picked up her purse and opened it. "It's just a little gift to show you my appreciation."

"Mrs. Sparks, that's not necessary."

"I know, but both Bradley and I wanted to do this. Of all the ideas we came up with, he liked this one the best." Bradley's mother took out a beige-colored, letter-size envelope with burnished-gold trim around its edges. "This is a gift certificate from the salon where I have my hair done. I thought with your wedding coming up, it could be put to good use." She paused for a moment and then, as if to diffuse any reasons Mary might give for not accepting it, quickly added, "It's non-refundable." She snapped her purse shut and handed the envelope to Mary.

Mary glanced at her name written on the envelope in stylized letters, and placed it on her desk. "I don't know what to say...this is so unexpected."

"Bradley and I think you deserve it. I want you to have it not only as a thank-you, but also I really wanted you to have the opportunity of having your hair done by an absolutely fabulous stylist."

"That sounds great, but I know how expensive hairstyling can be." Mary tried to recall how much cash she had in her purse. "I tell you what. Why don't I share the cost? I'd feel much better doing it that way."

"Please don't be concerned about the money. To tell you the truth, it really didn't cost very much." Louise leaned slightly forward and lowered her voice as though sharing a secret. "I was able to purchase the certificate at a very reasonable price, more than half off."

"Really?"

"Yes, the man who does my hair told me that this was a marketing ploy. If you liked how he styles your hair, you'll tell others."

"Well, if my hair turns out half as good as yours, I'd tell a lot of people." Mary picked up the envelope. "Thank you. This is so thoughtful. I've had other gifts of appreciation before, but this is the first time for something like this."

"Oh, I'm so glad. You don't know how happy it makes me to give this to you." Mrs. Sparks paused, bit her lip, and offered a nervous smile. She reminded Mary of a student who was just about to make a confession. "I hope you don't mind, but I told him that he might expect a call from you this week."

"You did?"

"Yes." When she bit her lip again, her eyes asked for understanding. "I only told him that because I so much want him to do your hair. He's just fantastic and I know you'd love him." Her eyes brightened with a smile. "I got him to agree that if you called for an appointment, he'd even find room for you this week. And that's terrific because he's in so much demand." She paused. "I hope I wasn't too presumptuous."

"You weren't and don't worry about it," Mary replied in a tone that was meant to be reassuring. "When you came in for our conference last night I was having a bad hair day..." She moved her hand to the side of her head and lightly patted her hair. "And I'm afraid I'm still having one."

"We all have them."

"I can't imagine you having one, but I do need something done with this hair. I was planning to make an appointment tomorrow so this works out perfectly." Not pleased with how her hair turned out last time, Mary had already asked a couple of the other teachers where they went to have their hair done. She offered Bradley's mother a warm smile. "It's almost like it was meant to happen. I'll look forward to having my hair done by this gentleman. I'll be sure to call for an appointment as soon as I get home."

"That would be great. You don't know how pleased I am that you are going to do this. When you call, be sure to ask for Damon."

"*Day-moan*? It sounds French."

"I know, but he's not...at least, I don't think so." Louise's eyes sparkled and her face took on a radiant glow as she talked about him. "Damon is very sophisticated and has such a charming personality. He's so knowledgeable and can talk with you on any subject you may have an interest in."

"He sounds...intriguing."

"Oh, he is...very much so." Her gaze turned inward for a moment. "And his eyes...how can I describe them? There's a..." She fingered the buttons on her blouse as a hint of a smile formed on her lips. "There's an intensity about them that makes you feel as if...as if he's peering deep into your soul."

Mary had a feeling that Mrs. Sparks just might have a crush on this man. "I'll look forward to meeting him."

"Oh, good." Bradley's mother seemed to breathe a sigh of relief. "I know he's looking forward to meeting you as well."

"He is?"

"Yes, he told me to tell you that he especially likes to work with brides-to-be."

"And why is that?"

"Because he says they are so full of life."

"Really? That's what he said?" Mary glanced at the envelope. "He does sound very interesting," she said, pleased at her good fortune. If she liked Damon's work, she certainly would recommend him to her friends. "By the way, what does he look like? I mean, how will I know him?"

"He's about six feet tall, slender but not skinny. I told you about his eyes. He has long blonde hair that he keeps in a ponytail. You won't have any trouble recognizing him." Mrs. Sparks stood up. "I'm so pleased about this," she said. "Now, you be sure to call him."

After Bradley's mother left, Mary finished grading most of the exams; the others she would take home. She glanced at the clock. Nearly four. Mick would be picking her up in a few minutes. She gathered her stuff together, got her coat, and walked to the door. As soon as she got to the school's main entrance door, she saw Mick waiting in his car. She said good-bye to Larry, the custodian, walked out into a lovely October afternoon, and got into the car.

Mick leaned over and kissed her. "How did school go today?" he asked as he pulled away from the curb.

"Not so bad. The kids were in a learning mode, and I think I got a lot accomplished with them." She gave Mick a knowing look. Both of them took pride in teaching. "And that's not easy to do with my mind on the wedding. It seems like I've got a million things going around and around in my head."

Mick turned the corner onto Fourth Street. "It's hard to believe that in eleven days we'll be married."

Mary nodded. "I know exactly what you mean. And guess what?"

"You've decided to marry someone else," Mick said with a twinkle in his eyes.

"No, silly," Mary replied, playfully poking Mick in the arm. "As a special treat for myself, I'm going to get my hair done this week. I got a gift certificate from the mother of one of my students."

"Hey, that's great." Mick ran his hand through his hair. "You should've gotten one for me," he laughed. "Don't worry. I'm planning on getting a haircut next week so that I don't look so shaggy for the wedding." He slowed the car to a crawl so a little kid could retrieve a ball that had rolled out into the street. After the young boy got his ball, he raced back to the curb. "I've got some good news."

"And what would that be?" Mary asked.

"Howie got our police detective friend, Jim Davidson, to come to the wedding."

"He did?"

"Yes. I asked him to do it just as a little extra precautionary measure."

"I'm glad." Mary put her head on Mick's shoulder. "That makes me feel a lot better knowing that he'll be there."

Chapter 55

After Louise Sparks dropped off the gift certificate to Bradley's teacher, she drove directly to the salon in south Minneapolis. She parked around the corner as Damon had instructed. He had offered the explanation that it was just precautionary so that her car wouldn't be so easily spotted. She didn't understand why he didn't want her parking in front, but if he said she shouldn't, that was good enough for her. She had learned early on in their relationship that she was not to question him on anything.

When she walked into the shop, Damon was just finishing with an attractive older brunette who obviously was enjoying his attention. "Hussy!" Louise hissed, not caring if she was overheard. She watched as the brunette gave him a light kiss on the cheek and whispered something into his ear. As soon as the woman left, she hurried over to him. "What did that bimbo say to you?" she asked.

He stared at her for quite some time, his eyes mocking. "Who are you talking about?" he finally asked in an innocent tone of voice.

She hated it when he played mind games because she never knew if he was serious. It kept her off balance and even though he seemed to enjoy that, she detested it. "You know who I'm talking about." She kept her voice calm so as not to provoke him. "That overweight brunette who just left you. She's old enough to be your mother."

"Oh, her." Damon shifted his eyes toward the front of the store. "That was Mrs. Bigalow. She's such a sweet lady."

Louise glanced at the woman and sneered. "So, what did that sweet lady whisper into your ear?"

"Nothing much."

"I bet." Although Louise felt irritated with his smugness she dare not express it for fear of angering him. He wasn't the type of man you wanted to antagonize. "Come on, tell me," she pleaded, hating the whine in her voice.

A hint of a smirk crossed Damon's lips. "I believe it was something about how she loved the feel of my fingers in her hair."

"Is that so, huh?" Louise eyed the brunette who was now at the counter paying her bill. "Well, if I ever get my fingers in her hair, I'll yank it out by its gray roots." When Mrs. Bigalow glanced in their direction, Louise stuck her tongue out at the woman. A smug smile crossed Louise's lips as the hussy quickly looked away. "I just came from seeing Bradley's teacher," she said.

"Is that so?"

"Yes." She loved doing things that pleased him, only wishing that he would show his appreciation more. "Do you want to hear about it?"

"Of course, but let's go into the back room. It's more private there."

As soon as they were alone in the back, she threw her arms around him, pressed her body against his, and kissed him. "I've missed you," she purred and would have kissed him again if he hadn't moved his head back.

"Not now," he said. "There'll be time for that later."

"Promise?"

"Of course." He slowly but firmly removed her arms from around his neck. "Now tell me what happened."

"I went to the school and gave her the certificate."

"And why did you tell her that you were bringing it?" he asked, using a tone more suited for talking to a child.

Louise hated being talked to like that. It was as if he had to make sure she had enough intelligence to follow his instructions to the letter. She cleared her throat, swallowing her irritation with his superior attitude. "To thank her for how much she has helped Bradley."

"That's good."

"For a minute, though, I wasn't sure that she was going to accept it."

Damon's eyes darkened. "Did you tell her what I told you?"

"Oh, yes. And your idea of it being a promotional for the shop worked like a charm." Louise paused, aware of the intensity of his eyes upon her. She fantasized that he was mentally undressing her. If only she knew what was going on in that brilliant mind of his. She inwardly pouted over not being given the affection she craved. Her charm had always worked with other men, but not with him. She couldn't twist him around her little finger like she had done with the others. Damon exerted a power over her that felt frightening at times, but also excited her. "You think of everything, don't you?" she said.

"Yes, I do," he replied quietly. "Now is there anything else I should know about your visit with her?"

"Not really. Everything worked liked you said it would. She'll probably be calling you later today to set up an appointment for this week." Louise rubbed her fingers up and down his arm. "Honey, I—"

He jerked his arm away from her, his mouth twisting into a sneer as his eyes flashed with intensity.

"I'm sorry," Louise quickly said, forgetting that Damon didn't like to be called by any terms of endearment. She silently rebuked herself for displeasing him. "Do you forgive me?"

"Finish what you were about to say," he replied coolly.

"I was just going to tell you that I spoke so highly of you that she said she was anxious to meet you."

Damon stroked his ponytail. "And I assure you that I'm also looking forward to my meeting with her."

Louise again began rubbing her fingers up and down his arm, hoping he would get the message. "Do I get to see you later this evening?"

"I'm afraid not."

"But we never spend any more time together."

"We will, as soon as this is over. Then I'll give you all the time you need." Damon leaned over and gave her a light kiss on the cheek. "That's only a small down payment." He ran his finger from one side of her neck to the other. "I promise you. More is coming."

"I'll look forward to it," Louise whispered into his ear. She was attracted to him more than any other man she had ever met. Their initial meeting nearly two months ago seemed as if it had been taken right out of some movie script. She had left work one afternoon and when she got to her car, the front right tire was flat. It made her angry because she had purchased the tire the month before. Just as she was opening the trunk to get out the jack, Damon came up and offered his assistance. He was so helpful and charming, and when she asked how she could ever repay him, he had responded, "By having dinner with me this week." Within a couple of weeks they were seeing each other on a regular basis. She had fallen hard for the guy. She remembered the night she told him that she would do *anything* for him. It surprised and disappointed her when he took her offer in a different direction than where she had intended it to go.

"I need a favor from you concerning a certain friend of mine," he had said.

"And who's that?"

"Mick...Mick Brunner."

"You've never mentioned his name to me," Louise said, wishing that he was more open about his past. "Is he an old acquaintance?"

"Yes, you might say that."

Louise knew better than to inquire further. "So what's the favor?"

"Mick's getting married soon and I wish to give him a wedding present, but I want it to be a surprise. His fiancée, Mary Wheeler, is a teacher. I believe she is one of your son's teachers."

"Oh, yes, Bradley adores her." She wondered how he found out that bit of information. "So you know the guy she's marrying? What a small world."

"Yes, isn't it? I thought doing her hair would be a wonderful gift. Only I don't want him to know who's doing it."

"Why?"

"Because I want him to be surprised when he finds out that it was an old friend who did her hair."

"That would be a surprise, wouldn't it?"

"Yes, I think it would." Damon touched her on the arm. "Now listen carefully." He handed her an envelope with Mary Wheeler's name on it. "Here's what I'd like for you to do."

Damien watched Louise walk out. As soon as she went out the door, he wiped off her kiss with the back of his hand and walked over to the sink to wash his hands. The woman's usefulness would soon be over. And if her ex-husband didn't get him another body soon, he would have to get his own. If he needed to do that, then he could perhaps solve both problems at one time. Pleased with himself, he dried his hands and walked back into the main area of the salon. Mrs. Lillian Ganderbuilt, an overweight divorcee in her sixties, was waiting for him.

"Damon, dear, I'm here for my styling." She fluttered her eyelashes at him. "And remember, you promised me when I called that you would make me look *gorgeous*."

"I will, Mrs. Ganderbuilt. I always keep my promises."

Chapter 56

Squirrel never did like Wednesdays; they always turned out lousy and this Wednesday was no exception. He had awakened in a sweat having dreamt that his partner, Newt, had blown all their money in a poker game. It was more of a nightmare, however, than a dream. Newt was the worst poker player that he had ever met, and he should know since he had suckered the guy enough times.

When he had finally crawled out of bed to take his shower, there was no hot water. He called to complain, but the apartment manager had some lame excuse about a water pipe that had busted and would take a couple of hours to fix, maybe longer. Under different circumstances, the cold shower might have felt good, but he was in and out in a flash. His bad luck followed him to breakfast. The toast burned, there was no butter in the frig, and the cream he poured in his coffee had soured overnight. When he left his apartment a half hour later, he discovered that his car had a flat tire. Upon opening the trunk, he swore out loud when he found that the spare was nearly flat and the jack was broken. After having the flat fixed, paying extra to have the service guy come out, he drove to a pool hall on Lake Street and promptly lost two out of three games of eight ball to Shorty Mankowski, a street hoodlum, to whom he had never lost a match before that day. Having dropped a ten spot to Shorty, he decided that the stars were not in his favor and that it was time for an afternoon beer. He drove back to the North Side to commiserate at his favorite hangout, a three-two joint a couple blocks up from the MAC Detective Agency. He ordered a beer and located himself in a back booth, thankful that nobody was playing the jukebox, and he could feel sorry for himself in peace and quiet. He was on his second beer when Sammy, a small-time hustler acquaintance, strolled up to his booth.

"Hey, Squirrel, what's cooking?"

"Not much." He hoped that by the tone of his voice, Sammy would get the message that he wanted to be alone.

"Buy me a beer and I'll keep you company."

"Buzz off. I don't need any."

"Sure you do. You look like you lost your best friend." Sammy slid in the booth, sitting opposite of Squirrel. "Besides, you owe me."

"I owe you?" Squirrel used his pinky fingernail to pick at the gap between his two front teeth. "For what?"

"For last month at the pool hall. You remember that, don't you?"

"That's too long ago."

"Come on, don't give me that line." Sammy shifted in the booth. "Remember when those two guys thought they could hustle you?"

Squirrel's nose twitched. He had walked into the pool hall that day looking for some action when he spotted a couple of guys who thought they were better at pool than they actually were. They were willing to play him for twenty bucks a game. "Get yourself a partner, little man," one of them said. When the jerk had referred to him as *little man* Squirrel had become even more determined to take the sucker's dough. Sammy was shooting at another table by himself and Squirrel had recruited him. The two of them split eighty bucks that day.

"Well, how about that beer?" Sammy asked again. His tongue moved back and forth across his bottom lip.

"Okay, but just one." Squirrel signaled the bartender. "Hey, Charlie, bring another beer over here, will you?"

"How come you look so down in the dumps?" Sammy asked after he received his beer.

"My luck hasn't been so good lately." Squirrel eyed Sammy. If there was ever an easy mark on the North Side, it was the chump sitting across from him. "What do you say we pass some time and play liar's poker for a fin?"

"Are you kidding?" Sammy took a swig from his bottle of beer. He wiped his mouth with the back of his hand. "Do you take me for a sucker or something? Don't you remember that you picked my pocket for a ten spot a couple of weeks ago?"

"So I got lucky."

"Bull! Luck had nothing to do with it." Sammy took another swig of beer. "I had a drink with Jerry the other night. He told me that he also lost big to you in liars' poker." He smirked. "You and your four aces."

"Is that right? I don't remember that."

"You should because you got me with those aces also. Jerry and me figured you're using the same dollar bill all the time." Sammy raised his bottle to Squirrel. "I salute you. You conned me once, but you're sure as hell not doing it again."

Squirrel raised his glass in acceptance of the compliment as he wondered how much Sammy would pay for that bill with the four aces. The bill had served its purpose. Besides, he now had one with five deuces. "You've got me, Sammy. I knew I couldn't pull one over on a smart operator like you."

"I suppose you got Newt on that also."

At the mention of Newt's name, Squirrel's nose wrinkled in disgust. He took a sip of beer but said nothing. The two of them looked on as another customer went up to the jukebox, put some money in, and made his selections.

"How's your partner doing anyway?" Sammy asked, his voice rising above the country western music now blaring from the machine.

"I don't know. I haven't seen him around for a while." Squirrel wasn't about to tell him that his partner skipped with his money. Sammy was a blabbermouth and it wouldn't be long before it was all over the North Side. The last thing he wanted was to have the other street hustlers find out that he had been had. Of course, if he played his cards right, it could work in his favor. "Newt's been out of town."

"Well, he's not now."

"What?" Squirrel set his beer aside and leaned closer. "What do you mean? Have you seen him?"

Sammy pulled out a pack of cigarettes, plucked one out, and lit it. He took a drag, letting the smoke slowly curl from the corner of his mouth. "Yeah, I saw him the other night."

"Where?"

"He was heading into that funeral home up past Penn."

"You mean McNeil's?"

"Yep, that's the one."

"Are you sure it was Newt?"

"Of course, I'm sure. I said hello to the guy." Sammy finished off his beer. "What's going on with him?"

"What do you mean?"

"Well, hell, Squirrel, he was going into a funeral home." Sammy used the palm of his hand to wipe beer he had spilled on the table, and then wiped his hand on his shirt. "Somebody in his family die or something? That sister of his, maybe?"

"Not as far as I know," Squirrel said, almost adding that the odds were three-to-one that he just might strangle his chiseling partner if he ever got his hands around Newt's scrawny little neck.

Sammy ran his tongue over his bottom lip again. He picked up his empty bottle and offered Squirrel a sly smile. "How about buying another?"

For the next twenty minutes, he and Sammy sat drinking. After losing heads-or-tails two out of three times, Sammy bought the final round, drained his bottle, and left. Squirrel remained, sipping another beer and wondering what Newt was up to going into a funeral home. When he finally left the bar, he started towards Howie's office, stopped, and turned to go in the other direction toward McNeil's. He had a feeling that his luck was about to change.

Chapter 57

Adam slammed the book shut and buried his face in his hands. He sat for several minutes before getting up from the kitchen table. He turned off the light and walked into an already darkened living room. After making his way to the window, he stood, gazing at the street below. His mother had gone shopping and he was glad to be alone with his personal demons. He had come home from school an hour earlier after an appointment with Professor Carlson, his advisor at the seminary. For the past forty-five minutes he had been reading, or at least trying to read, the book the professor had recommended.

He had wanted to see Carlson that afternoon. His advisor's only available time, however, was in the early evening. Wednesdays for the white-haired professor of church history were filled with teaching responsibilities and a late afternoon faculty meeting. It was nearly six when Adam had finally met with the man. Adam had been nervous, but anxious to speak of his reservations about becoming a minister. He had hoped the professor would have some insights into his doubts and inner struggles.

His struggles were nothing new; they had been there ever since he entered the seminary last year. With what had happened at the candy factory this summer and his experience with the owner's daughter, he wasn't sure if he would go back to the seminary in the fall. That would be okay with Howie since the guy had no time for anything remotely associated with religion. Mick, however, had encouraged him to continue his studies.

"But why should I?" he had argued, feeling guilty that he had raised his voice. His partner was only trying to be helpful. "It would be just a waste of time."

"Don't talk like that," Mick had replied quietly, seemingly unperturbed by the sharp tone coming from his friend. "Why don't you just take a couple of courses? That way you'll still feel connected while you sort things out."

"I don't feel connected now."

"Look, we all go through struggles."

"Even you?"

"Yeah. Even me."

"Sure. I'll bet."

"Listen. I haven't told anybody this, including Mary," Mick had confessed. "But there were moments during that first year of teaching when I wasn't sure if I was cut out to be a teacher. I came close to quitting."

"That's hard to believe."

"Well, it's true." Mick patted him on the shoulder. "So, just hang in there, buddy. Believe me, I know what it's like to second guess yourself." He offered a reassuring smile. "But I also know that you'll make a good minister."

"I'm not so sure about that." Adam chewed on his lip. "Howie tells me that I have the makings of a good detective if I ever get rid of some of my hang-ups."

"What are you talking about?"

"Come on, quit trying to be nice. You know what I'm talking about."

Several seconds passed before Mick responded. "Okay, I do...but just remember we all have our hang-ups."

Adam brushed aside a shock of hair that had fallen on his forehead. His partners were well aware of his struggle with certain aspects of the work. "Howie says I should forget about being a preacher and come in the agency full time."

"That's our boss for you," Mick said. "You know how he feels about religion. I think he's still angry at God for his mother dying so young." A long minute passed before he continued. "Don't get me wrong. I agree with Howie about you being a good detective, but I think you belong in the pulpit."

"To tell you the truth, Mick...I...I don't know where I belong."

Two days after he had talked with Mick, however, he decided he would take his partner's advice and register for two courses. His conversation with Mick was still on his mind when he had walked into Professor Carlson's office. When Carlson had asked him why he had decided that he wouldn't be coming back to seminary as a full-time student, his only response was that he had some things to work out. He hadn't shared that he also worked as a detective and that he found that fulfilling. It wasn't that he didn't see ministry rewarding as much as it was he hadn't been able to find answers to his nagging questions. As a minister, he could point out the injustices in the world. But as a detective, he could do something concrete about them. "Our clients want justice when they have been wronged," Howie had told him. "And that's what we are here to give them."

"I'm not sure I'm cut out for the ministry," he had told Carlson, who resembled one of the saints portrayed on the stained glass windows in the seminary chapel. "I thought I was, but then all of these questions and doubts come flooding in."

"Don't be alarmed," Carlson had said. "Many students experience that in their spiritual journey. I recall going through that myself."

Adam couldn't imagine Carlson having self doubts since the man came from a family history of ministers. Both his father and grandfather served in the parish and later distinguished themselves by becoming bishops. The man also had three brothers and two sons who were ministers. "So, what helped you get through your doubts?" he asked his professor, hoping that he finally would get some answers.

"I spent a lot of time on my knees." Carlson fingered the well-worn silver cross hanging from a chain around his neck. He inched forward and cleared his throat. His tone was pastoral, not accusatory. "Adam, have you taken your struggles to the Lord in prayer?"

"Yes, sir."

"And?"

Adam shook his head, feeling guilty that his attempt at prayer seemed nothing more than empty words devoid of conviction. "I'm sorry, but...it...it didn't seem to work for me." He looked away, avoiding eye contact with the saint sitting across from him. "I..." He gnawed on his lip again. "I...I must be doing something wrong."

"My son, you shouldn't be so hard on yourself."

"Yeah, that's what people tell me, but...but I'm not so sure they're right."

"Just a minute. I think I have just what you need." Carlson rose, moved to a floor-to-ceiling bookshelf running the full breadth of one of the walls in his office. He ran his fingers across the many volumes on the fifth shelf until he came upon one that looked at least three inches thick. "Ah, here it is." He came back and handed the book to Adam. "Here's something that helped me. Why don't you borrow it for a while? It might be of some help." He smiled. "My grandfather wrote it."

Adam had taken the book home, but it had been of no help. He had barely grasped the abstract theological concepts being put forth. Now, as he stood at the window in his living room, he stared out at the street below, watching people scurrying along the sidewalks. It seemed that at least they knew where they were going in life. He stayed at the window for several more minutes before heading back into the kitchen. He flipped on the light, sat down, opened the book again, and began rereading the first chapter for the third time. He was on the second page when the phone rang. Thankful for the interruption, he set the book aside and walked over to the telephone. "Hello."

"Is this Adam Trexler?" a female voice asked.

"Yes. Who's this?"

"Charlotte Aldrich." She hesitated. "I hope you don't mind me calling you at home, but you said I could if that man showed up again."

"He showed up at the library?"

"Yes."

"When?"

"Earlier this afternoon." Her voice sounded shaky. "He stayed for a couple of hours sitting at that same table by the window. I...I just know he's going to do something to me. I'm so afraid."

"When do you work again?"

"On Friday."

"Does this guy ever show up in the morning?"

"No."

"Okay, then, I'll tell you what I'm going to do. I'll stop by in the afternoon. Don't worry. We'll get to the bottom of this." After reassuring her again not to worry, he hung up and sat back down at the kitchen table. For a long time he stared at the book that Professor Carlson had given him. The book may have had answers, but not to the questions he was asking.

Chapter 58

Mary had been pleasantly surprised when two days earlier she called for her hair appointment and Damon informed her that he would be delighted to fit her in that coming Thursday afternoon.

"That's great, but you see, I'm a teacher," she had explained. "And I wouldn't be able to get there until nearly four."

"Don't be concerned about that," he had replied. He added, "If you don't mind, four-thirty would even be better."

When Thursday came, Mary left school relieved to be finally doing something about her hair. Mick had offered to drive her, but she declined, not wanting to tie him up with having to wait until she was finished. With traffic being fairly heavy, it took her nearly thirty-five minutes to drive across town to south Minneapolis. She parked across from the salon. Getting out of the car she noticed someone in the bay window of the beauty shop observing her. As she walked across the street toward the main entrance, she realized that the person watching her fit the description that Louise Sparks had given her of Damon.

The man with the blonde ponytail opened the door for her. "Please come in," he said, his voice as smooth as the silk shirt he wore. "You must be Mary. I'm Damon."

"Nice to meet you." Mary noted that his eyes were every bit as intense and penetrating as Bradley's mother had described them.

"I've been watching for you."

"I'm not late, am I?"

"By no means. In fact, you're a few minutes early." When Damon extended his hand, Mary did likewise. Instead of shaking her hand, however, he took and kissed the back of it while all the time staring into her eyes. "Welcome to our establishment," he said, holding her hand for several moments before releasing it.

"I'm...I'm pleased to be here," Mary replied, hoping that her face didn't register her shock at her hand being kissed.

"Mrs. Sparks told me all about you."

"She did?"

"Yes and she spoke very highly of you. I've been looking forward to meeting you." His dark eyes scanned her. "You are even lovelier than she described."

"Why...why, thank you." Mary took a moment to regain her composure. No one had ever kissed her hand before, let alone shower her with such glowing compliments in the first thirty seconds of their initial encounter. "Do you greet all your customers at the door like that?" she asked as she glanced around.

"Only the very special ones." Damon's eyebrows rose. No doubt he saw the puzzled look on her face. "I see that you're questioning where everyone else is." He offered a thin smile. "They have all gone home for the day."

"Really?" She glanced around again.

"Oh, yes. On Thursdays we normally close at four." His eyes had a mesmerizing quality to them. "You must be curious then as to why I suggested four-thirty."

"A little."

"The reason is quite simple." His tone oozed with self-confidence as though nothing would be beyond his explanation. "You see, I knew my three o'clock appointment would run late. I didn't want you to have to wait around."

"I appreciate that, but I feel bad that you had to stay later." Mary wondered if another day would be more suitable, but didn't want to suggest it since with the wedding coming up, time wasn't on her side. "I'm sorry if I've caused you any inconvenience."

"Please, there's no need to apologize."

"Are you sure it's all right?"

"Oh, yes. It was my decision to be here and it's certainly my pleasure to have you grace our humble shop." Damon stepped aside and gestured toward the back. "Now, come, let me show you where we'll be. I think you'll find the surroundings to your liking. Most of our customers love the ambiance."

Mary couldn't help but be impressed by the interior. The décor was far and above any of the beauty shops she had ever visited. Whatever money they had saved from not investing in dressing up the outside of the building, they had used for the inside and the furnishings. Walls separated each of the work areas from one another to provide patrons the luxury of being cared for in their own little private rooms. Far from little, however, each space was the size of a small bedroom. "I'm quite impressed," she said, admiring in particular the expensive textured wallpaper with swirl designs.

"Thank you." Damon surveyed the area. "It is a step above most establishments, isn't it?" He led her toward a room in the back, inviting her to sit in a comfortable-looking and quite elegant light-brown, leather-padded swivel chair. On the wall facing her hung a large oval mirror with an engraved burnished-gold scroll design along its edges. The dark-oak workstation sitting below the mirror, and extending from wall to wall, featured an ivory marble top with gold faucets for the two enormous washbasins. Prints of classical paintings hung on the other two walls.

"If you would like, I could play some Bach or Mozart," Damon said. "We have an excellent built-in sound system. Furthermore, if you wish, I could bring in a scented candle or two and light them."

"Thank you, but that's not necessary." She glanced around. "The surroundings already make me feel like a queen."

"And that you are." Damon paused. "You do have lovely auburn hair; it is so soft and naturally curly. And it's just the right length, resting on your shoulders." He tilted his head, examining her hair, lightly touching it. "Do you have a particular style in mind?"

"I'm getting married a week from this Saturday and I thought I would like to try something new, but not radical, if you know what I mean. Mrs. Sparks spoke so highly of you that I think I'll let you decide. If I like it, I'll keep it. If it doesn't suit me, I can always go back to what I had."

"Just place yourself in my hands." Damon turned the chair so that she couldn't see herself in the mirror. He must have noticed the surprised look on her face. "Don't worry. I do this with all my customers. I want you to relax now. Take a couple deep breaths. If you would like, you may even close your eyes." He turned on Mozart, and lit a couple of scented candles. "Think about...about your upcoming wedding and what a glorious day it will be."

Mary nodded. "Okay, that sounds nice. I'll do that."

Damon sighed. "Classical music always brings out the creativity in me."

"Don't get too creative," she said with a smile.

"I won't. I promise." Damon touched her hair again. "You'll just have to trust me," he said softly.

"Well, I've always heard it said if you can't trust your hairdresser, who can you trust?" Mary smiled again. "I ask just one thing, though."

"And what is that?"

"Please don't cut off more than an inch."

"I won't and I assure you, you'll not be disappointed with what I have already decided upon. And don't worry. It will be similar to what you have but more elegant and quite practical." Damon leaned toward her and whispered into her ear. "Thank you for putting your trust in me. You have no idea how pleased that makes me." He touched her on the shoulder. "Now, just sit back and make yourself comfortable."

Mary relaxed and listened to the music as Damon worked on her hair. His gentle hands moved swiftly. Unlike other hairdressers he remained silent, only asking her to tilt her head forward. As he washed and rinsed her hair, his fingers moved slowly, sensuously massaging her scalp. The music was a nice touch and it eased any anxiety that she may have been feeling. The setting and mood was so relaxing that a couple of times she thought she had drifted off. If she did, Damon, like the gentleman he seemed to be, didn't comment.

As he had suggested, her thoughts went to the wedding and how Mick will make such a handsome groom. She smiled to herself as she pictured Howie and Adam in tuxes. As she sat listening to the music, she visualized herself and Mick at the altar. She closed her eyes and mentally went through the vows. *I take thee, Mick, to be my husband...for better, for worse...for richer, for poorer...in sickness and in health...to love and to cherish...until death us do part.* The touch of Damon's hand on her shoulder brought her back to where she was. "Are you almost done?" she asked, guessing that she had been sitting in the chair for more than an hour.

"Just about. A few more touches and I will be." Several minutes later, he slowly turned the chair so she could view herself in the mirror. "Well?" he asked.

"Oh, it's wonderful!" she exclaimed. "I love it!"

"I thought you would."

"I do. You really do have a talent. I never could have guessed that you would have styled it the way you have." She turned her head from side to side as she looked in the mirror. "It's so elegant."

"Thank you." Damon spoke to her image in the mirror. "May I say that it's easy when I have your kind of hair to cut and style."

Mary's cheeks felt warm and she wondered if she was blushing. "You certainly are gracious with your compliments."

"I only give them when they are merited. Your hairstyle is stunning and elegant because it compliments such a beautiful woman as yourself." Damon stepped back and cocked his head. "It has to be one of my finer efforts." He folded his arms across his chest as a pensive look came upon his face. "If only..."

Mary took note of a slight frown that swept over his face. "If only what?" she asked.

"I know this is presumptuous, but may I...no, no I shouldn't."

"What is it?"

"I don't know if I should."

"Please, Damon. Go ahead."

"Could I ask a favor of you?"

"Ah...certainly."

"I sincerely hope that this isn't too bold on my part." Damon clasped his hands in front of him, and took a deep breath. "This coming Saturday, I have entered a hairstyling contest and I was all prepared when I got a phone call from the young lady I was to work on." He reached over and gently brushed her hair with the tips of his fingers. "Just a final touch," he said, smiling and allowing his fingers to linger for a moment. "As I was saying, the woman I was to work on called to inform me that she had come down with a severe case of pneumonia."

"That's terrible."

Damon nodded. "Yes...yes, it is. The poor woman sounded awful on the phone."

"Oh, that's too bad. I hope she'll be okay."

"I'm sure she will be, but the favor I ask is this..." Damon paused. "And I know it is a lot to ask on such short notice, but..." He paused. "I wonder if you would be so kind as to take her place."

"I...I don't know, I—"

"It would only take your morning. I'd pick you up around seven and get you back by noon if not before." Damon waited for a moment. When he continued, he did so with pleading eyes. "I so much want to win that contest. I've waited for such a long time for this opportunity. It'd mean so much to me."

"I...I suppose I could since I'm free that morning, but I just don't know."

"Please, it would be so wonderful if you could. And if you agree, I promise that I'll do your hair at no charge for the wedding."

"Oh, that wouldn't be necessary."

"Yes it would be, and I would insist."

Mary hesitated, but then thought about how hard Damon had worked on her hair and how nice it had turned out. Besides, the extra savings would come in handy for her and Mick's honeymoon. She gave him a warm smile. "Okay, I'll do it."

"Splendid."

"Damon, I must say that you certainly have a persuasive way about you."

"What a nice compliment. Thank you." A hint of a smirk appeared on his face. "And don't worry about eating breakfast before I pick you up. There's a quaint little mom-and-pop family café on the way that serves the best food."

"That's not necessary."

"After what I'm asking you to do for me on such short notice, I couldn't take no for an answer. It's the least I could do at such an early hour of the morning." He paused. "Besides, it will give us an opportunity to get to know each other better."

"I would like that, also," Mary said, curious what was behind those intense eyes. After today, as far as she was concerned, she had found a new hairdresser. "Where is this contest going to be held?"

"It's not far, about an hour away." Damon's mouth twisted into a smile. "I prefer not to tell you because I wish for the location to be a pleasant surprise."

Mary couldn't help but laugh. "First surprising me with the hairstyle and now this. I must say, Damon, you certainly enjoy surprising people, don't you?"

"Yes...yes, I guess I do."

Chapter 59

Friday morning around ten, and Howie had just sat down at his desk after getting himself a fresh cup of coffee when his office door opened and Adam came in. By the troubled look on his partner's face, something was up. Given Adam's mood swings, it could be anything. Maybe he had another sleepless night wrestling with his self-doubts as to whether he should be a minister. The guy lugged around enough doubts to fill a gunnysack. Or, better yet, maybe he finally decided to give up on that God stuff and come down into the real world. Of course, he would have to get rid of his preacher ethics if he was going to make it as a detective. Turning the other cheek and brotherly love weren't ideals too often practiced in this line of work. "Do you want some coffee?" he asked as his partner plopped down in the chair.

"Yeah, I'll have a quick cup."

"Coming right up." Howie went out into the kitchen and poured a cup of coffee. He walked back and handed the cup to Adam. "What's up?" he asked as he sat down at his desk.

"Charlotte Aldrich called me."

"Oh, yeah? What about?"

"That guy showed up at the library again."

"He did, huh?" Howie took a sip of coffee, wondering if this character could be connected with Newt in some way. Or maybe he was just some pervert who had a thing for librarians. "Does she know anything about this guy?"

"Not really." Adam set his cup on the desk.

"Has he ever approached her?"

"No."

"Has he ever followed her home?"

"Not as far as she knows."

"So what's the problem?"

"She feels that all that could change and she's scared."

"Scared? Of what?" Howie asked, thinking that this was just the overactive imagination of a librarian. The woman was probably spending too much time in the mystery section. "Does she think this guy is going to do something?"

"Exactly."

"But she doesn't know what or why or when?"

Adam nodded, the muscles in his jaw tightening, a sure indication that he didn't like the way the conversation was going.

Howie took another sip of coffee. His partner's good intentions to help Charlotte Aldrich could be clouding his reasoning. Good intentions may be okay when you're a preacher, but not when you're a detective. In this business, good intentions could get you killed. "Maybe she's just a little paranoid."

"I don't think so," Adam replied curtly, no doubt resenting his judgment being questioned. "I feel she's in danger."

"Well, then it's good that she called you," Howie said, not wanting to get into it, and hoping the sarcasm he felt wasn't showing up in his voice. If Adam wanted to waste time on this, so be it. His partner had been edgier than usual and maybe this would siphon off some of that negative energy. "So when are you going there?"

"This afternoon once I'm done with class."

"This just may work in our favor," Howie said. "If you can gain her trust, maybe she'll open up a little more about her brother." He picked up his coffee cup to take a sip. "It's about time we got a break in this case."

Adam's eyes darkened. "Look, I'm going because she's scared. If she opens up, fine, but that's not my motive for helping her."

Howie set his cup down and folded his hands on his desk. "But it won't hurt to listen carefully in case she does mention anything concerning her brother, okay?" He waited for a response but none came.

Adam arrived at the library's parking lot around three that afternoon. Of the fifteen or so cars in the lot, he wondered which one, if any, belonged to the man who had been giving Charlotte Aldrich sleepless nights. He locked his car, walked up to the front entrance, and opened the door. He stood aside for a woman and her two young children coming out. "Thank you," the mother said, giving him a grateful look when she noticed him glancing at her children carrying armfuls of books.

Charlotte stood behind the front checkout desk. As soon as she saw him, she motioned him over. "He's here," she whispered.

"Where?"

"He just went into the rest room, but he's sitting at that table near the window," she said, her voice trembling.

"How long has he been here?"

"About an hour."

"Okay, I'll watch for him."

"What should I do?"

"Just act normal and go about your work." Adam walked over to one of the bookshelves and positioned himself where he could see the table through the space between the shelving. He didn't have to wait long. Within a couple of minutes, a short, stocky man with a receding hairline came out of the rest room, walked over and sat down at the table. The man picked up a book and opened it. Although it appeared as if he was reading, he glanced toward the front checkout desk every so often.

Adam didn't have to decide whether to confront him in the library because the man looked at his watch, got up, and headed toward the front door. Once he left, Adam quickly moved from his position. When he saw the bewildered look on Charlotte's face, he stopped at the desk to explain. "Don't worry. I'm just going to have a little talk with him. We'll have the answer soon enough."

Charlotte bit her lip. "Do you think you should do this?"

"You want to know, don't you?"

She nodded.

"I'll be right back." Adam headed for the door. The man was walking toward a late-model white Chevrolet parked in the far corner of the parking lot. Adam quickened his pace. When the man stopped to light a cigarette, he called out to him. "Hey, you! Wait a minute!"

The man turned and looked in Adam's direction. A puzzled look came over his face as he pointed to himself.

"Yeah, you!" Adam yelled. Within moments he was face-to-face with him. "I'd like to have a little talk with you."

"What about?"

The accusation was out of Adam's mouth before he had a chance to think about any possible consequences. "Why are you spying on Charlotte Aldrich?"

"On who?"

"You know who I'm talking about. Charlotte Aldrich, the librarian at the front desk. I saw you watching her."

"Is that so?" The man's mouth curled into a sneer. "Even if I was, it's my business and I don't have to answer to you. Now get the hell out of here." He turned to get into his car.

"Hold on!" Adam placed his hand on the man's shoulder. "You're not going anyplace until I get some answers."

"Get your damn hands off of me!"

"I just want—"Adam was shoved backward, regained his balance, and threw himself at the man, only to be thrown hard against the hood of the car.

"Okay, wise guy, don't you move!" the man yelled as he, in one swift motion, reached into the inside of his coat jacket and pulled out a revolver.

Chapter 60

It didn't take Newt Aldrich very long to realize he had made the wrong decision. In a weak moment, he had gotten hooked up with Damien (or Damon, or whatever the guy wanted to call himself), but now he didn't know how to get out of it.

From the beginning, Damien had enticed him with talk about supernatural powers and how one could draw upon them. He didn't understand everything that the smooth-talking Damien was yakking about, but it sounded cool; something he wanted to try. He went along with the guy. If he could learn more about these powers that Damien boasted of, he would then use them to change his life. Throughout the years, he had always been a follower, but no more. Once he discovered the secret of this stuff, he no longer would have to be dependent upon Squirrel and his nickel-and-dime handouts.

Working with Squirrel over the past several years had provided him with barely enough dough to exist. "Take it easy, will you?" Squirrel always told him. "You'll soon be seeing more money than you've ever dreamt of before." Squirrel had been right in one respect, he did see more money, but none of it was going into his pockets. Even if the dough would've been split fifty-fifty, however, he still didn't feel right about it. It wasn't that he was against gambling or that Squirrel cheated those who bet with them. His partner wasn't a crook, but neither was he an angel, or if he was, his halo needed straightening. Newt wanted a different life, one in which he could be his own man. He wanted to make an honest living and gain respectability. His goal was to move out of the North Side, get himself a nice woman, get married, buy a house, and live the comfortable life in the suburbs.

When by chance he had met Damien in a bar in south Minneapolis and shared a couple of beers with the guy, he was so taken with the man's smarts and blown away by his charm that he had figured this chance meeting to be a life-changing event for himself. And it certainly had been. Within days, he went to the first of several meetings Damien had invited him to attend. The meetings were always late at night in the back room of the beauty salon where Damien worked. He thought the guy owned the place until one night the owner came to the meeting. The owner acted like he was terrified of

Damien. Newt didn't understand why the man was so frightened until later when he himself had experienced Damien's dark side.

Newt would've left Damien's group if it weren't for the fact that he was too scared to do so. After he had handled the stealing of the first of the two bodies, Damien had taken him aside.

"Newton, I've detected a change in your enthusiasm," Damien had said.

"What...what do you mean?"

"You're not thinking of leaving me, are you?"

"Ah...ah, no."

"I hope not." Damien's tone had turned as cold as the look in his eyes. "Because if you ever did, the police would get a packet of evidence."

"Evidence?"

"Yes, the kind that would implicate you and you alone in the stealing of that body. Evidence that would put you away for a very long time."

The thought of spending years in a six-by-eight cell terrified Newt. Ever since he was little and his father had locked him in a dark closet for punishment, he never liked being in closed quarters. When Damien had first asked him questions about his life, it made him feel important that someone actually was interested in him. And so when he was asked to share his deep-seated fears, he did so, thinking he could trust the man. He had come to realize, however, that Damien had had ulterior motives for his questions.

As he thought about the past month, he realized that his troubles all began when he had taken Squirrel's money. Taking the dough had been stupid. Giving the money to Damien had been even more stupid. Damien had persuaded him that he could invest it for him and double his money. Of course, that never happened and he was too scared to ask for the money back. It had been a huge mistake being involved with stealing those bodies. And then the other night when he was ordered to tie Leon Sparks to that chair, he felt sick to his stomach about it. He could barely watch the awful things done to the poor man. No wonder he had fainted, something that Damien chided him for later. He wanted to get away from this madman, but felt like a fly caught in a spider's web.

Now, on a Friday night, Damien had ordered him to come to the funeral home. As he walked unhurriedly toward McNeil's, he wished he had never gone to that bar that fateful afternoon. The thought of everything that had happened since his initial encounter with Damien made him want to puke, and he now yearned for his former life with Squirrel.

Persistence had paid off. For the past couple of evenings Squirrel had stood in the darkened entryway of a shoe repair shop located a half block from the McNeil's Funeral Home. The odds were six-to-two—no, make that eight-to-two, that Newt would probably not show up again. He had to take those odds, though, since this was the only lead he had on his partner. "Well, what do you know," he muttered when his partner walked up to the front entrance. "What is that little weasel up to?" With only a couple of cars in the parking lot, there couldn't have been anything official going on. He looked at his watch—nearly nine-fifteen.

As soon as Newt opened the entrance door and walked in, Squirrel made his move. He wasn't about to take any chances of letting his conniving partner slip away. When he caught up to him, he planned to wring the pipsqueak's neck...after he got his money back, of course.

Squirrel opened the door to the funeral home and found himself walking into what had to be the lobby area. It was more like a parlor of some fancy house; beige couches and matching chairs, oil paintings of peaceful pastoral scenes adorning the walls, floor-standing brass lamps, and a white carpet so plush that it made him feel as if he was walking on clouds. A desk off to the right and facing the entrance door was the only indication that the space also served as a reception area. Music played from undisclosed speakers as the sweet smell of flowers flooded his nostrils.

Newt was nowhere in sight. Squirrel started down one hallway, looked in a room and saw an open casket with a body. The coffin was surrounded by nearly a dozen flower arrangements. He twitched his nose a couple of times and headed in the opposite direction. He hadn't gotten more than halfway down the corridor when he heard voices coming from another room further down the hall. The one voice he recognized was Newt's; the other was that of a woman. Without any hesitation, he stormed into the room.

"Squirrel!" Newt's eyes nearly popped out when he saw his partner. "Wha...what are you doing here?"

"That's supposed to be my question, you little crook!" Squirrel glanced at the lady who looked just as surprised as Newt. He walked up to Newt until they were nearly nose-to-nose. "We need to talk about something you have of mine, or have you forgotten that we're still partners?"

"Listen, I...I can explain."

"Oh, yeah? I bet you can."

"Who is this guy?" the woman asked Newt.

"Ah...he's a...a friend of mine."

Squirrel smirked at the woman while keeping his eye on Newt. "Listen, take a hike, will you?" he told her, gesturing with his thumb. "My *friend* here and I have some unfinished business to discuss."

Adam's mother, Virg, wondered who could be calling her at work. Gladys, the other waitress, had said it was a man's voice, but that it didn't sound like Adam's. "Have you got some guy on the side that I don't know about?" Gladys quipped.

"If I did, I wouldn't tell you," Virg replied. She gestured toward a tall man wearing a jean jacket. The man held up his coffee cup and pointed to it. "Take care of Mel, will you? He needs a refill." She went into the back room, wiped her hands on her apron, and picked up the phone. "Hello."

"Good evening, Virg," the person said, his tone inviting intimacy. "You don't mind me calling you Virg, do you?"

"Go ahead. Everybody else does." She cupped her ear with her free hand to muffle the noise coming from the eating area. "But who's this?"

"It doesn't matter who I am. My name's unimportant." He paused. "You have a son named Adam, don't you?"

"Yeah, why do you ask?"

"He's such a nice young man, isn't he? I'm sure that you're proud of him going to school to become a minister."

Virg felt uneasy. At first, she had thought that the caller was a friend of Adam's but his patronizing tone unnerved her. "Mister, why don't you get to the point? I've got customers waiting."

"Oh, that's right. I forgot that you are a...*waitress*."

When he paused again, she could hear him breathing into the phone. She imagined him sneering, perhaps even mocking her. "I've got to go," she said.

"Before you do, I just thought that you would like to know that you should be concerned about your son."

"What!" Her heart skipped a beat. "Did something happen to him?"

"No, nothing has happened...yet. But I am concerned about his welfare."

Virg reached for a cigarette and padded the empty pocket where she used to keep her pack. She had given up smoking several years before.

"Adam is your only son, isn't he?" Several seconds passed before the caller continued. "I'd feel terrible if something happened to him. Wouldn't you?"

"Who is this?"

"Virg, as I've told you, my name isn't important. I'm just worried about Adam."

"Well, then tell me why."

"Meet me at the corner of Kass' Drugstore at five minutes of ten. I'll explain everything then."

"But—"

"Virg, just trust me. And please don't come early. If you do, I won't meet you and then you'll never know."

"Wait a—" The man hung up before she could finish. She eased the phone back on the receiver and leaned against the wall. Adam hadn't seemed himself lately. Ever since her son was little, he had kept things bottled up. Could this have something to do with his work as a detective? What kind of danger could he be in? The thought of someone harming him frightened her. She thought about trying Adam at home, but he had told her that morning that he would be getting home late. Nevertheless, she did call, letting it ring ten times. She dialed again just in case she had dialed the wrong number. "Where are you?" she cried. She hung up the phone and made the sign of the cross, asking God to watch over her son. Her heart pounded, and she placed her hand over it as if by that very act, she could settle it down. She looked at her watch. Nine-twenty. She took a couple of deep breaths, stood there for a good minute, and went back to work.

"Can you cover for me?" she asked Gladys.

Gladys chuckled. "So, I was right. You do have some man on the side." She winked. "I hope he's cute."

Virg forced a smile. "It's nothing like that. I, ah...just need to pick up something at Kass' in about a half hour. I won't be gone long."

Satisfied that he had sufficiently instilled Adam's mother with a sense of foreboding, Damien headed back to where he had left Newt and Louise. Meeting at the funeral home had been his idea; he liked the feeling of absolute supremacy he got from being around the dead. The owner of the funeral home had initially objected using his establishment for meetings, but had quickly changed his mind. All Damien had to do was to remind the weakling that there were some compromising photographs of him that his wife might be interested in seeing. Damien had taken the pictures over a year ago when the man decided to become involved with Damien's group. Ever since he had taken those photographs, the fool had been at his beck and call.

As Damien walked down the hallway, he heard an unfamiliar voice coming from the room where he had left the others. The idea that there was an unknown person in the area angered him. He stopped short of the doorway, listened for a moment, and peered into the room. A short man with thick, wild-looking hair was frantically waving his hands about as he shouted at Newt. Damien couldn't see his face because the man's back was turned toward the doorway. Louise was standing off to one side. When she saw him at the doorway, he put his finger to his lips. As he stood listening, he realized that it was Newt's partner, Squirrel. The man was trying to convince Newt to leave so they could talk. If Newt went with Squirrel, he might be persuaded to leave the group. Damien couldn't allow that. He glanced around, his eyes settling on an object sitting on an end table. He picked up the brass statue of a horse and moved quietly into the room. He put his finger to his lips again to signal Newt not to give him away. Newt's eyes, however, shifted to him. Just as Squirrel turned to see who was coming, Damien hit him over the head with the statue, sending him hard to the floor.

"What did you do that for?" Newt cried, kneeling down besides the body of his friend. "You've killed him."

"Don't be a fool!" Damien snapped. "I didn't hit him that hard. Now, come, I've made the phone call. We need to go."

"What are you going to do with him?"

Damien's eyes glowed as he offered Newt a twisted smile.

Chapter 61

The phone was ringing as Adam entered his apartment. He flipped on the lights, hurried to the small desk in the corner of the kitchen, tossed his books down, and picked up the phone. Too late. Whoever it was had hung up. He checked the clock. Nine-twenty. It couldn't have been Mick calling because he and Mary had gone out for a late dinner and movie. Howie? Not likely. Howie told him that he was planning to hit the sack early with the hopes of getting a decent night's sleep for a change.

He thought about calling Howie, but didn't want to take the risk of waking him. The man never slept well whenever they were working on a case and all the leads had dried up. Based on having zero leads, the guy probably hadn't gotten a good night's sleep for the past week or so. Tomorrow would be soon enough to tell him about the encounter earlier that day in the parking lot of the library. His partner would be just as surprised as he had been when he learned the identity of the man who had been staking out Newt's sister.

"Okay, let's get at it," he told himself and picked up his books. He moved over and sat down at the kitchen table with the idea of studying for an hour or two. His mother wouldn't be home until well after midnight, having switched to the evening shift at the diner where she worked. That would be to his liking since he would have the apartment to himself. With no interruptions, he could get a head start on the reading assignment for his class on Monday. Not only that, he needed some quiet time to reflect upon where he was at in terms of his own struggles.

The more involved Adam had become with the detective agency, the less relevant becoming a minister seemed to be. He still hated the thought of deceiving people through the undercover work he had done, and he continued to be at odds with Howie about certain aspects of the work. What troubled him most was that he was becoming less trustful of people and he feared he would become jaded. If he was ever to become a minister, he needed to find answers to certain questions such as why would God allow innocent people to suffer at the hands of a man like Damien. As a detective, he could work to put somebody like Damien behind bars. As a minister, though, he wasn't sure what if anything he could do. He inhaled deeply,

195

blew it out slowly, and opened his book. His struggles weren't something that were going to be resolved easily.

He hadn't been reading for more twenty minutes when the phone rang again. Glad for the interruption, he got up and answered it. "Hello."

"Adam, this is Gladys down at the restaurant."

"Hi, Gladys." The woman sounded upset. "What's going on?"

"I hate to call you at this time of night, but I felt I had to."

"Don't worry about it." He could hear customers in the background and the dinging of the pinball machine. "What's wrong?"

"Your mom's acting sort of strange."

"What do you mean?"

"About a half hour ago, she got this phone call and then came and told me that she's got to go to Kass' for something."

"Did she tell you for what?" he asked, wondering if she had gotten one of her migraines.

"No, she said nothing was wrong, but I've worked with her long enough to know that something had upset her. I think it must have been that phone call."

"Is she there? Can I talk to her?"

"She left a couple of minutes ago." Gladys paused. "And Adam..."

"Yeah?"

"She borrowed a cigarette from me."

It had been years since Adam had seen his mother light up a cigarette. She had given up smoking after she had gotten home from attending the funeral of a good friend who had died of lung cancer.

"You won't tell her I told you about the cigarette, will you?" Gladys asked.

"Don't worry, I'll keep that between you and me," he reassured her. "Anything else?"

"Yeah, I kidded her about meeting some guy, but she brushed me off." Gladys lowered her voice as if she thought that customers could be listening. "But I really think she's meeting somebody."

"Thanks." As soon as Adam hung up, he rushed out the door, flew down the stairs, and out the front entrance onto the sidewalk. He looked down the street toward Kass' and saw his mother approaching the corner across the street from the drugstore. He slipped into an entryway and watched, feeling guilty about spying on his mother. Everything seemed normal until she started to cross the street over to the drugstore. Tires screeched as a dark-colored Buick flew past her and turned the corner.

"No!" Adam ran toward his mother as she lay on the street next to the curb. He couldn't tell if she had jumped back or if the car had struck her. "Mom, don't try to get up!" he yelled. "I'm coming!"

His mother, however, picked herself up and brushed off the front of her uniform. When she saw him running toward her, she stepped back onto the curb.

By the time Adam reached her, the Buick, having turned onto Broadway, was now nearly a block away. "Are you okay?" he asked his mother.

"I think so," she said, her face drained of color. She rubbed her left arm as if it hurt. "That idiot nearly ran me over."

"Did you get a look at the driver?"

"Not really." She reached out and hugged him. Her eyes glistened with tears. "How about you? Are you okay?"

He gave her a questioning look. "Me? You're the one who almost got run over."

"I just want to know that everything is all right with you," she said, her voice quivering. "Is it?"

"Yeah, but you need to tell me what this is all about."

"I will, but let's go back to the restaurant. We can talk there."

"Are you sure you shouldn't go home?"

"No, I'm all right." She bit her lip and her tone turned apologetic. "Don't be angry, but I really could use a cigarette."

From the front seat, Newt turned and glanced back through the rear window of the Buick to see if anyone was after them. Louise Sparks, sitting in the backseat, offered him an anxious smile. She appeared shook up by the experience.

"Yo...you sure scared that woman," he said to Damien who was driving.

"Yes...I did, didn't I?" Damien eased up on the gas.

"I thought for sure you...you were going to run her over." Newt's mouth felt dry. He needed a beer. "It was lucky that you missed her."

"Luck had nothing to do with it," Damien replied curtly. "I intentionally avoided her."

"You...you did?"

"Of course. I wanted to send a message to a friend of mine that I haven't had the pleasure of seeing for a while. Now, no more questions." He looked over at Newt. "Don't you know that I have to keep my mind on my driving? You wouldn't want us to get into an accident, would you?"

Newt settled back in the seat and stared out the window, wishing he were back with Squirrel, and angry with himself for ever getting mixed up with such a madman. He stole a sideways glance at Damien, praying that the man didn't have the power to read minds. He also offered a prayer for Squirrel.

Chapter 62

Squirrel's head throbbed. The last time his head had felt this bad was the morning after an all-night party with some of his friends. Then it was only one jackhammer at work; this time, the entire construction crew showed up. It even hurt to open his eyes. He blinked a couple of times, but it was too dark to see anything. It took him a moment to realize that he was lying on his back. When he tried to get up, he banged his head and nearly knocked himself out. Still groggy, he felt around. At first, he thought the space was closing in on him until he realized that he was in some kind of wooden crate. As his mind cleared, he recalled that he had been talking to Newt when he turned to see what had caught his partner's eye. That's when it happened. Whamo! Some guy clunked him on the noggin. It happened so fast that he only caught a glimpse of his attacker. Some creep with a blonde ponytail. That jerk would pay as soon as he got out of wherever they had locked him up. He pushed on the crate's lid but it wouldn't budge.

"Let me out of here!" he yelled. "I'm suffocating!" He laid his head back down. It was only when he became aware that his head was resting on what felt like a satin pillow that he realized that he was in a crate all right—a body crate! "Let me out of here!" he yelled again, pounding on the wooden lid with his fists, and trying to control his panic.

"Who's…who's in there?"

Squirrel breathed a sigh of relief. "Let me out, will you?" he hollered. "I'm locked in this thing!"

"You're not dead, are you?"

"What!" Squirrel's panic gave away to anger. "Of course, I'm not dead! Now, get me out of here!"

"My friends always told me that some mighty strange things happen in funeral homes and I…I believe them now."

"Who am I talking to, anyway?"

"Clarence T. Johnson. I'm the night janitor."

Squirrel felt like screaming at the idiot, but controlled his tone so as not to drive the man away. "Well, nice to meet you, Clarence T. Johnson, but could you *please* let me out of here before I run out of air?"

"What are you doing in there if…if you're not dead?"

"What do you think I'm doing, taking a nap or something?" Squirrel vowed to wring the guy's neck if he ever let him out. "Look, let me explain." He paused to take in a breath. "Somebody knocked me over the head and put me in this thing."

"Are you sure you're not dead?"

Squirrel clinched his teeth. "I'm talking, ain't I?"

"Yeah."

"Well, dead men don't talk. So, just open it, will you?" He waited, listening for any movement. Either Clarence T. was too petrified to move or he just decided to quit his night janitor's job right then and there. The image of the man sneaking out and leaving him locked in the casket unnerved him.

"Clarence! Are you still there?" Squirrel was about to plead his case once more when he heard a lever move on the side of the casket and the lid began to slowly lift up. Not willing to wait, he pushed up so hard that the lid flew open. Squirrel bolted up, adjusted his eyes to the light and sucked in fresh air. A movement to his right caught his eye. Clarence T. was slowly backing away; his face was as pale as a cue ball, his eyes were bulging, and his mouth was wide open. Before he could assure the guy that there was nothing to be afraid of, Clarence T. Johnson fainted.

"Serves you right," Squirrel muttered as he climbed out of the casket and took off, not caring if Newt and his friends were still there. He wasn't about to spend one more second in that funeral home. Rushing out the front door into the night air, he knew exactly where he was going and who he needed to see.

Whoever was pounding at the office door was persistent and loud enough to wake Howie from a sound sleep. He reluctantly peeled back the covers and sat on the edge of his bed. The pounding continued. "I'm coming," he mumbled as he felt about for the switch on the lamp next to his bed. Once his eyes adjusted to the light, he stood up, pulled on a pair of pants and tee shirt, and stumbled barefoot through the corridor into his office, only stopping to switch on the floor lamp. He glanced at the clock. Twelve-fifteen. The pounding on the door continued. "I'm coming, I'm coming. Hold your horses," he muttered. No sooner had he unlocked the door than the door flew open, knocking him backwards as Squirrel rushed in.

"I'm glad you're here!" Squirrel cried, his nose twitching at twice its usual speed. He immediately went to the window and peeked out at the street below.

"Where else would I be at this time of night?" Howie closed the door, but not before looking down the stairs to see if anybody had been chasing his midnight visitor. "Squirrel, don't you realize that it's past midnight?"

"I know, but I had to see you." The little guy glanced out the window again.

"This better be good because I was sound asleep." Howie massaged his shoulder where the door had slammed into him. "So what's going on?" he asked, brushing the sleep out of his eyes. "You look like you've seen a ghost or something."

"I saw him."

"You saw who?"

"My partner."

"You mean Newt?"

"Yeah. I was talking to him when some guy clobbered me on the head." Squirrel's eyes widened. "I woke up in a casket." He began pacing back and forth as words flew out of his mouth. "I nearly suffocated in that body crate. You can't breathe in there! I wouldn't have lasted another hour." He stopped and stared at Howie. "Have you ever been in one?"

Howie shook his head.

"Well, good, because I felt like I just rolled the dice and got boxcars. I would've given you ten-to-one odds that I was going to croak. It was just lucky that Clarence T. got me out, but—"

"Wait a minute, who's Clarence?"

"The night janitor. He fainted when he saw me." Squirrel's nose stopped twitching, but then he thrust his hand into his pants pocket and began jingling coins. "I got out of that place as fast as I could." He pulled out a handful of change and began counting it. "Oh, man!"

"What?"

"I'm short four bits." Squirrel scrunched up his nose and began sucking air through his teeth. "It must be in that casket."

"Do you want to go back and get it?" Howie quipped.

"Are you kidding?" Squirrel said, his eyes nearly popping out. "No way am I going back there. I was lucky to get out. You're the first person I thought of. I ran all the way here. I—"

"Slow down, will you?" Howie pleaded. He gestured to the chairs by his desk. "Why don't you sit down? I'll make a pot of coffee and you can tell me the whole story."

"Have you got anything stronger than coffee?"

"I've got some bourbon," Howie blurted out without thinking.

"I could use a shot."

Howie went back into the kitchen. He got the bottle of bourbon he had hidden in the breadbox. After he had a shot, he poured his friend a third of a glass. As soon as he came back into the office with the bourbon, Squirrel slammed it down and asked for more.

"I don't think so. I need you to think straight." Howie paused. "Now, how about some coffee to settle your nerves?"

The little guy looked disappointed, but accepted the offer.

Once the coffee was done, it took Squirrel four cups and the better part of an hour to tell his story as Howie wrote down the essential details in his notepad. Besides the four cups of coffee, Newt's partner also consumed a lunchmeat sandwich, a half bag of potato chips, and five crackers with cheese. "I always get hungry when I'm stressed," he mumbled, his cheeks bulging with two chocolate chip cookies. "It calms me down."

Howie took a sip of coffee, his second cup. "Now, you say that this guy who hit you was blonde and had a ponytail?"

"Yeah, that's right."

"And you've never seen him before tonight?"

"Right again." Squirrel pounded his fist on Howie's desk. "That creep will live to regret that he's crossed paths with me."

Howie checked the clock. Nearly one-thirty. He leaned back in his chair and yawned. "Look, I don't have any more questions. Let's call it a wrap for now. I'm so tired that I can't even think straight."

Squirrel twitched his nose. "How about letting me use your couch tonight?"

"What?"

"The couch. Can I sack out here tonight?"

Howie wasn't too keen on the idea, but was too tired to say no. Besides he felt sorry for the guy. "Suit yourself. I'll get you a pillow and a blanket." When he came back, his houseguest was sitting on the couch, testing its cushions.

"It's not very firm," Squirrel said.

"Here you go." Howie tossed him the blanket and pillow, and started back toward his bedroom.

"Hey, Howie?"

"What now?"

"What's for breakfast?"

Chapter 63

Howie had had a terrible night. Squirrel had awakened him on three different occasions. The first time was around two. The little guy had knocked on his bedroom door and asked if he could have another blanket, claiming the office area was cold. He then came knocking on his door an hour later.

"Now what?" Howie had mumbled. He had tossed and turned from the last intrusion on his attempt to sleep. "What do you want?" he yelled.

The door cracked open and Squirrel peeked in. "Do you have an extra toothbrush?"

"A what?"

"Toothbrush. I always like to brush in the morning when I get up."

"Oh, geez." Howie buried his face in his pillow for a moment. "Get out of here and let me get some sleep."

"What about the—"

"Just use your fingers."

"My what?"

"Your fingers, Squirrel. Your fingers!"

"But—"

"Good night, Squirrel!" Howie turned over, giving his back to his houseguest. "And shut the door."

The third interruption of Howie's attempt at sleeping occurred when Squirrel used the bathroom a half hour later. The man gargled so loud and long that Howie came close to storming into the bathroom and informing the guy that he was being evicted right there and then. Too tired to get up, however, he simply put a pillow over his head. At ten after six that Saturday morning, he awoke to another knock at his door.

"What time did you say breakfast was?" Squirrel asked with a toothy grin, and looking well rested.

Howie groaned. "Just give me a minute or two to wake up, will you?"

"Sure enough, take your time. I can wait." Squirrel folded his arms and leaned against the doorframe.

As Howie lay there, gradually drifting back to sleep, the stillness was punctuated by what sounded like air being released in short intervals from a balloon. He opened his eyes to the sight of Squirrel digging the wax out of his ear while sucking air through his teeth. Howie let out a puff of air. "Okay, let me get dressed and splash some water on my face, and then I'll make your breakfast." He shot Squirrel a sarcastic glance. "I mean, if that's okay with you."

"No problem."

Howie lay there, waiting for Squirrel to leave. A good minute went by. "I'm a big boy now, Squirrel. I can dress myself."

"What? Oh. Sure. I'll wait in the kitchen."

After fixing Squirrel four eggs, two helpings of bacon, a double order of toast, and three cups of coffee, they adjourned to the office to go over again what happened at the funeral home the night before. Squirrel had nothing new to add, but chattered incessantly about how exciting he thought detective work could be.

"Man, now I know why you have that poster of Bogart," Squirrel said. "Ten-to-one it's because you've always wanted to be just like him, right?"

Howie took a sip of coffee and settled back in his chair.

"Bogie was my kind of guy." Squirrel reached into his shirt pocket, dug around, plucked out a toothpick, and began picking at his front teeth. Once he finished cleaning his teeth, he moved the toothpick to the corner of his mouth, letting it loosely hang like Bogie would let a cigarette hang from his mouth. "Hey, Howie?"

"Yeah?"

"Do you think I have what it takes to become a gumshoe like you?"

"A what?"

"A gumshoe. You know, a private eye." Squirrel's eyes danced with excitement. "What do you think?"

"I think I need a couple of aspirins."

"Come on now. Be serious. Do you think I could cut it as a detective?"

"I don't know. Maybe."

"Thanks! I think so, too." Squirrel moved the toothpick from one side of his mouth to the other side and back again. He leaned back in the chair, puffed out his chest, and crossed his arms. "Yeah, I could handle it," he said. "Tagging along with you and your partners, I bet I could nail down this business in no time at all."

Howie was thankful when the phone rang. He grabbed it on the first ring. "MAC Detective Agency."

"It's Adam. I didn't wake you, did I?"

"Oh, no." Howie looked over at his houseguest. "I got up with the birds." He almost added *and the squirrels.*

"Listen, I need to stop up for a minute. Is that okay?"

"Sure, I'm not going anyplace. See you in a little while." Howie hung up and glanced at the clock, feeling depressed that it was only seven-thirty on a Saturday morning.

"Who was that?" Squirrel slipped the toothpick into his shirt pocket.

"Adam."

"Is he coming over?"

"Yep."

"Must be important, huh?"

Howie nodded. Whatever Adam had to tell him, it sounded urgent. Ten minutes later his partner walked into the office.

"What's he doing here?" Adam asked, pointing to Squirrel lounging in the chair that Mick usually sat in.

"It's a long story, but here's the short version." Howie summarized what had happened at the funeral home, including the description of the woman Squirrel had seen with Newt. "From her description, it had to be Louise Sparks."

"Really?" Adam settled in the chair next to Squirrel. "That certainly puts a new twist on the case, doesn't it?"

Howie agreed. "Don't ask me what the connection is, but we're going to find out."

"Who was the guy?"

"We don't know, but Squirrel said he was blonde and had a ponytail."

"He had a what!"

"Ponytail," Squirrel said. "Some guys like to wear their hair that way. It's when you grow your hair long and—"

"Yeah, I know what you're talking about." Adam turned to Howie. "Somebody tried to run down my mother last night."

"That's terrible!" Squirrel exclaimed. "I know your mom; she's a good person. Why would anyone want to do that to her?"

"Does she have any idea who it was?" Howie asked.

"No, but the driver had a ponytail."

"What!" Squirrel jumped up from his chair. "It's got to be the same creep who tried to crack my head open." He slammed his fist into his palm. His beady eyes grew dark, his face turned crimson, and his nose began twitching. "That no good crumb-bum!" He placed his hands on the desk and leaned toward Howie. "I tell you, bums like that give Broadway a bad name. That guy should be tracked down and taught a lesson. Picking on poor defenseless women..." He glanced back at Adam. "Sorry, no offense to your mom, but there are times when us men have to take matters into our own hands." He straightened up, folded his arms, and stuck out what little chest he had. "Squirrel is at your service. I'm ready to give you all the help I can in tracking this street scum down. What do you want me to do, boss?"

"You can sit down and quit calling me boss." Squirrel's ranting was giving Howie a headache. After the wannabe detective sat down, Howie turned his attention to Adam. "Is she sure about that ponytail?"

"That's probably the only thing she's sure of."

Howie made a notation in his notepad. "Anything else?"

"Yeah, it's..." Adam gave a sideways glance at Squirrel.

"Don't worry about him. He's okay."

Squirrel slapped his hands and rubbed them together like he had just drawn to an inside straight. "Thanks. I'm already feeling like part of the team."

"Not quite," Howie said. "Just keep what you hear to yourself or else we're dropping your case."

"You wouldn't, would you?"

"Like a hot potato. Now, just sit back and be a good boy." Howie turned back to Adam. "Okay, go ahead."

"I found out who was spying on Charlotte Aldrich."

Squirrel's mouth dropped open. "You did! Hot diggity-dog!" His eyes narrowed as he wrinkled his nose. "It wasn't the guy with the ponytail, was it? Five-to-one that creep is after my dough."

Howie shot Squirrel a stern look. "If you don't keep a lid on it, the odds of you staying here won't be much to your liking. Do I make myself clear?"

Squirrel opened his mouth as if to reply, but stopped and clamped his lips together. He brought his hand to his mouth, made a twisting motion as though turning a key to lock his lips, and placed the invisible key on the desk. He offered a sly grin and folded his arms as he settled back into his chair.

"Go ahead," Howie said, nodding for his partner to continue.

"The guy's a cop, a detective."

"He's what?" Squirrel shot forward in his chair. "Don't tell me now that the cops are after my dough, too? I bet—" He stopped in mid sentence after one glance at Howie's furrowed brow. He offered a sheepish smile, took the invisible key off the desk and ceremoniously locked his lips for a second time. Glancing at the two detectives, he tossed the key behind him and folded his arms again.

Howie flipped a page in his notepad. As infuriating as Squirrel could be, the guy's quirky personality continued to grow on him. "What's this detective's name?"

"Herb Manning."

"Oh, no. Not him." Howie tossed his pen on the desk and closed his notepad. For sure now, he had to take a couple of aspirins. Maybe even slam down a shot of bourbon after Adam and Squirrel left.

"What's the matter?" Adam asked. "Do you know him?"

"Not personally, but JD does. And according to him, Manning is the worst screw-up in the whole department." Howie shook his head in disgust. "He's a loser from the word go."

Squirrel scooted to the edge of his chair, raised his hand and waved it furiously while whimpering like a puppy.

"What is it now?" Howie asked.

Squirrel pointed to his own lips and made a motion as though unlocking them.

"Go ahead."

After Squirrel unlocked his mouth with a key snatched out of the air, he smacked his lips together as though they needed limbering up. "I know this Manning. He's run me in a couple of times, but had nothing on me. Davidson's right—the guy's a jerk-off. If Manning's watching Newt's sister, it's either because he doesn't have any other leads or he's goofing off and just killing time. I'd lay you twenty-to-one on that."

"No bets, but I think you might be right," Howie said. "Did you tell Charlotte who he was?" he asked Adam.

"Yeah, even though Manning told me not to. He said that if I broke his cover, he would run me in for obstruction of justice."

"What a joke!" Squirrel said. "The only obstruction of justice is Manning, himself."

Howie cocked his head as the downstairs entrance door slammed and the stairs began to creak and groan.

"Who's that?" Squirrel asked.

"Sounds like Mick," Howie said.

When Mick came in, his eyes registered surprise upon seeing Squirrel. He looked at Howie, but only received a shrug as a reply.

"Come join us," Squirrel announced.

Mick walked over and stood by the window. Howie filled him in on what had happened to Adam's mother and let Squirrel share his experience at the funeral home. "I have a bad feeling about this guy with the ponytail," Mick said.

"What do you mean?" Howie had noticed Mick rubbing his chest at the mention of Squirrel's ordeal of being locked in a casket.

"I don't know, but this guy sure sounds like Damien."

"Who's Damien?" Squirrel glanced around at Howie and his partners.

Mick cracked his knuckles. "I'm going to call Mary to see if she's okay." He moved to the desk, picked up and dialed the phone. Only the ticking of the wall clock broke the silence as everyone waited. "Hi, this is Mick. Is Mary there?" Even though he flashed Howie a worried look, he kept his tone conversational. "When did she leave?" Howie and Adam exchanged glances as Mick's face revealed a growing anxiety. "Do you know who she went with?" The muscles in his jaw visibly tightened. "No, there's no problem. I'll talk to her later. Thanks." He hung up the phone and stared at Howie.

"What's going on?" Howie asked.

"Her mother said that a man picked her up forty-five minutes ago to take her to some hairdressing contest. Apparently he's using her as a model."

Howie opened his notepad to a blank page. "You didn't know about that?"

"No. Her mother said that Mary didn't want to tell me because it was supposed to be a surprise. But get this, the guy who came to get her was blonde, had a ponytail, and his name was French sounding. When I asked her what it was, she said, 'Damon'."

"Damon?" Howie leaned back in his chair for a second. "Are you thinking what I'm thinking?"

"You bet I am!" Mick said. "It's got to be Damien." He curled his hand into a fist. "What are we going to do?"

"Who's Damien?" Squirrel asked again.

Adam shot Mick a worried look. "Where did he take her?"

"That's the problem. Her mother said that Mary didn't tell her. She only said that she would be back by noon."

"Let's figure this out," Howie said. "How did Mary and this Damon character get connected in the first place?"

"Let's see…let me think." Mick looked toward the window. "I remember now. Mary told me that she got a gift certificate to have her hair done. It was given to her by the mother of one of her students."

"Do you know who it was?" Adam asked.

"No, but I'm betting her mother might know." Mick picked up the phone and dialed. He massaged the back of his neck as he waited. "Hi, it's Mick again. I'm wondering if Mary mentioned who she got that beauty shop certificate from…say that again?" His eyebrows knitted together. "No, there's no problem. I was wondering because Mary and I talked about getting her a little gift in return."

"Ask her if Mary told her where she was going," Howie whispered.

Mick nodded. "Did she say where this contest was going to be? Oh. Well, thanks anyway." He hung up the phone. "Her mother doesn't know, but Mary told her that she got the certificate from Louise Sparks."

"Leon's ex-wife?" Adam said.

"Who's Leon?" Squirrel asked.

Howie turned to Mick. "Isn't it odd that Mary never mentioned to her mother where she was going?"

"Mary did tell her that they were going to stop and have breakfast at some family-style restaurant, but the man wanted the destination to be a surprise."

"I'm ready to help," Squirrel declared as he jumped up. "Just tell me what you want me to do."

"You're not doing anything," Howie said. He motioned to Adam. "Can you stay here with Squirrel?" he asked. "Just in case we get a call."

"Sure, but what are you guys going to do?"

Howie glanced at Mick. "We're going to pay Louise Sparks an early morning visit."

Chapter 64

Howie and Mick arrived at Louise Spark's place shortly before eight-fifteen. Louise answered the door wearing a ruby-red, terry cloth bathrobe and gold slippers. Even at that early hour of the morning, with no makeup, she looked terrific.

"What do you want?" she asked Mick while shooting Howie an unfriendly glance.

"To talk to you," Mick said. "This is my partner, Howie Cummins. Can we—?"

"I have nothing to say."

"We just have a few questions."

"I said I have nothing to say." Louise tried to shut the door, but Howie pushed his way in, surprised that his partner hadn't done so.

"You have no right coming in here!" Louise cried as she backed into her living room. "Get out!" She moved to an end table where her telephone sat. "If you don't leave right now, I'm calling the police."

Howie walked over, picked up the phone, and handed it to her. "Go ahead and call. I want you to."

"He's serious," Mick warned.

"That's right, lady, I am. And when they get here, they'd be interested in knowing why you were at McNeil's Funeral Home last night. And then there's the matter of some missing bodies. I know they'd have a few questions for you about that."

Her eyes shifted between the two detectives. Several moments passed before she spoke. "I don't know what you're talking about."

"Why don't you have me make that call for you?" Howie reached for the phone, but she stepped back, holding the phone away from him.

"Okay, I was at the funeral home." The defiance in her eyes faded. "But I was with a friend who needed to make some arrangements."

"Arrangements?"

"Yes, for...ah...his grandmother who died."

"Is that right?" Howie smirked. "Well, your friend's grandmother should have taught him better manners."

A look of puzzlement swept over her face. She still had the phone in her hand, but gave no indication that she would make good on her threat to call the police.

"Go ahead and call them," Howie taunted. "And when the cops come you can tell them all about how your grieving friend conked a guy over the head."

"And locked him in a casket," Mick added.

"He nearly suffocated," Howie said. "That makes you an accessory to attempted murder."

Louise's eyes widened. It took her a moment to regain her composure. "That man attacked me and…and my friend had to subdue him." Her beauty faded a bit when she frowned. "I was so upset that I left immediately." She hesitated, but put the phone back on the receiver. "I have no idea what happened afterwards."

"Look, don't play around with us," Howie said. "Where's Damien?"

"Damien?" For the first time since they had arrived, Louise's eyes reflected that she didn't know what they were talking about. "Who's he?"

"You know him by Damon," Mick said.

"But it's the same person," Howie added. "He's six feet and on the lean side. He used to have short, black hair, but now it's long and blonde, and tied in a ponytail."

"And he's a smooth talker," Mick said. "His eyes can bore a hole right through you."

"So don't play dumb with us," Howie said. "We know that you know him."

Louise chewed on her thumbnail. "What if I do?"

"Look, Mary's my fiancée," Mick said, his eyes pleading. "You gave her a gift certificate to have her hair done by this Damon."

"So what if I did?"

"He picked her up earlier this morning to go someplace, and I want to know where he took her."

"I have no idea, and even if I did, I wouldn't tell you." Her defiant tone reappeared. "I know Damon and he's a good person." Her eyes flashed with indignation. "He's kind and gentle."

Howie laughed. "Give me a break, lady. That guy doesn't know the meaning of kindness."

A young boy walked into the room, a piece of toast in his hands. He stopped and stared at the two men.

"Hi, Bradley," Mick said. "Remember me?"

The kid glanced at his mother before replying. "You're the detective," he replied quietly.

"That's right." Mick pointed to Howie. "He's a detective, also. We're partners."

"Is my mother in trouble?"

"No," Howie said. "We're just having a little talk with her."

Louise took a step toward her son. "Bradley, go back to the kitchen and finish your breakfast."

CHARLES TINDELL

"Just a minute." Mick walked over to Bradley, knelt down on one knee, and put his hand on the boy's shoulder. "We need your help."

"Leave him alone!" Louise cried. "He doesn't know anything."

Howie moved closer to Louise. He lowered his voice. "I suggest you not say anything more or else I'm calling my friend at the police department and have him come over. There's enough evidence to pull you in for questioning." He hoped she wouldn't call his bluff. "Now you wouldn't want your son to see his mother led away in handcuffs, would you?" After a moment, he signaled Mick to go ahead. Bradley's mother had taken the bait.

"Bradley, I'm looking for someone who's very special to me." Mick kept his tone gentle. "Has a man with a blonde ponytail ever been here?"

The boy nodded.

Louise tried to inch forward, but Howie took hold of her arm. "Trust me," he whispered. "You wouldn't look good in handcuffs."

Mick positioned himself so as to block direct eye contact between Bradley and his mother. "This man took my friend some place," he said to the boy. "Would you know where he could have taken her?"

"What do you mean?"

"Did he ever talk about places he liked to visit...like parks or lakes or anything like that?"

Howie opened his mouth, but closed it. For now, he would leave it up to his partner whether to mention cemeteries. Mick was trying to be gentle with the kid. That was the teacher in him, but this wasn't a classroom. Too much was at stake. If Mick didn't get some quick answers, Howie was prepared to get rough with Louise.

Bradley peeked around Mick to look at his mother.

"Son, it's important," Mick said, getting Bradley's attention. "This man is going to hurt her."

"I overheard him talking about this one place."

"What place?"

"It's where people climb rocks."

"They climb rocks?"

Bradley nodded. "It's by some water, but I forget the name of the place."

"There are cliffs on part of the Mississippi River. Could it be there?"

"No."

"Minnehaha Falls then?"

"I don't think so."

"How about Taylors Falls?" Howie asked.

Bradley's eyes widened. "Yeah, that's it."

Mick and Howie rushed out the door. They weren't sure what Damien's plans were, but Taylors Falls was a scenic place high above the Mississippi River on the Wisconsin border. For years, people had gone there to walk trails, spend time admiring the many different rock formations, and climb the cliffs. After several accidents and one death over the period of a couple of years, however, certain areas were declared to be too dangerous and had been roped off. If someone fell from one of the cliffs into the river, unless

210

they were an excellent swimmer, they would almost certainly be sucked under by the powerful undercurrents. Mick had once told his partners that although Mary had lived her entire life in Minnesota, the land of ten thousand lakes, she had never learned to swim. At the time, they had all joked about it.

Chapter 65

Damien and Mary spent over an hour talking while having breakfast. He hadn't planned to spend as much time at the café as they had, but he had found Mick's fiancée intriguing and wanted to learn as much about her as she would permit. Knowing the personal history of someone always made the *game* more interesting. He had questioned her about her childhood, believing that a person's inner being was so often revealed in the stories they remembered from their formative years. "I'm so pleased that we shared this time together," he said, holding the door open for her as they left the café.

"Damon, I hope I didn't bore you too much."

"On the contrary, I thoroughly enjoyed the conversation. Our time together gave me a chance to know you better. And I must say that you're quite the woman." He noted the hint of a blush on her cheeks. "Your future husband...ah, what was his name again?"

"Mick."

"Well, Mick is indeed very fortunate."

"Thank you, and thank you again for breakfast."

"It was my pleasure. And I do want to hear more about your wedding." Damien walked her to the passenger side of the car. "On the way back you can tell me all about it."

Mary waited while her breakfast companion got his car keys out. "I also was most impressed by your life and the things you have done."

"Yes, I guess I've been involved with a few things, haven't I?" Damien smiled inwardly at how easily she believed the life history he had fabricated. She had been especially impressed when he shared his experience serving as an assistant to a priest. It had been only a small lie; the priest was a priestess, and she had served him. He unlocked the passenger side and opened the car door for her. "Allow me," he said as he helped her inside.

"Thank you. You are such a gentleman."

He held the door open and leaned toward her. "I wonder what Mick would say?"

"About what?"

"About his lovely future bride being helped into a car by a man who had just spent an hour learning about her past?"

"You're not worried that he might be jealous, are you?" Mary asked, seemingly amused by the concern in his voice.

"Perhaps. After all, I wouldn't want him to be upset with me."

"You don't have to worry about Mick. He's not the jealous type. And I'm sure he would be very happy to meet you some time."

"Really? I would like meeting him also." Damien closed the door. He walked around to the driver's side. He would send a sympathy card to Mick afterwards. That would be a nice touch. Of course, he would sign it. The thought of Mick opening the card and seeing his signature brought a twisted smile to his face.

"You're cracking your knuckles again," Howie said as he and Mick traveled north on Highway 95 toward Taylors Falls.

"Sorry, I can't help it. I'm just..." Mick turned away for a moment. "We have to find her. We just have to."

"We will." Howie stepped on the gas. Traffic had been light, and they had been able to make good time.

"How much of a head start do you figure they have on us?" Mick asked.

"What time did her mother say they left?"

"Seven."

Howie glanced at his watch. "Okay, they left at seven and we didn't get started on the road until after eight-thirty."

"Oh, man. That's a big lead."

"Weren't they going to stop for breakfast?"

"That's what her mother told me."

"Good. We'll pick up some time there." Howie pulled out and passed a truck, narrowly getting back into his lane before an oncoming car flew by, its driver giving him an angry gesture. He glanced at his partner. "Let's hope they took their time eating."

"I'll never forgive myself if anything happens to Mary." Mick stared out his window. His hands, curled into fists, waited on his lap like coiled springs. "I don't even want to think of what that monster might do to her."

Howie pushed the speedometer past seventy-five. Damien's twisted mind was capable of anything. The cliffs overhanging the river at Taylors Falls flashed through Howie's mind. When he and his two partners were in high school, they had climbed those cliffs. They nearly killed themselves when they had foolishly dared each other to inch across the wall of a cliff overhanging the river with only a six-inch ledge for footing. Taylors Falls, known for its spectacular scenery, could prove deadly if one didn't heed the warning signs. Damien had taken Mary there for only one reason. He glanced over at his partner, wondering if he was thinking the same.

"How are we going to know where he's taken her when we get there?" Mick began kneading the fist of his right hand. "We don't even know if it's the Minnesota or the Wisconsin side."

"My bet's on the Minnesota side, so we'll try that first."

"But what if it's not?"

Howie offered his friend a reassuring smile. "Don't worry, we'll find them in time," he said, trying to sound more optimistic than he felt.

Damien made a deliberate show of checking his wristwatch as they approached the main stretch of highway leading into Taylors Falls. "We're going to be too early."

Mary looked at her watch. "I thought you said that we needed to be there by nine."

"If I did, I apologize. We don't need to be there that early."

"We don't?"

"No. The doors won't open for another forty-five minutes." His passenger gave him a dubious look, but he had expected such a reaction. "I'm sorry for this mix-up," he said, intentionally sounding exasperated. "But I've been so nervous about this contest that my mind isn't working right. I feel so foolish."

"Don't feel foolish. This happens to everyone."

"You forgive me then?" Damien asked, offering her his most charming smile.

"Certainly."

"Thank you. You're so kind. Your fiancé…what was his name again?"

"Mick."

"Yes, of course. Mick is so fortunate to have you." Damien drove for several more miles. "I've got an idea," he said.

Mary glanced at him, but said nothing.

"Why don't we stop at the park in Taylors Falls and I'll take some photographs of you?" He noted the skeptical look she gave him. "Sorry. I'm not making sense, am I? Let me explain. These photographs would be the before-and-after kind. It would only take but a few minutes to take some now, and then we could take some after the contest. Once I finish with your hair, I'll take the pictures right at the shop. The place has stunning floral wallpaper; it would make a perfect backdrop." Pleased with his web of deceit, he continued spinning it. "If they turn out, and there's no reason they wouldn't, they could be used at the salon. And I know just the place to display them. What do you think?"

"I…I don't know what to say."

"Just say that you'll do it."

Mary remained silent, staring at the road ahead.

"It would be a wonderful promotional at the salon," Damien said. "My boss would be so pleased. And it would be a feather in my hat."

She gave him a sympathetic smile. "Okay, Damon, you've persuaded me."

"Fabulous."

"But there's one condition."

"And what is that?"

"That I have the final say on the pictures. I wouldn't want photographs of me being displayed that I felt were unflattering."

"You needn't worry. The camera will love you," Damien replied. "You have my word, though, that you'll have final approval. I wouldn't have it any other way."

"Thank you. I appreciate that."

"Good. There's a parking area on the right side of the highway just as we get into town. We'll leave the car there and walk the trails until we find the right setting for a picture." He glanced over at her. "Have you ever been to the park at Taylors Falls before?"

"A long time ago. Aren't there rock formations there?"

"Oh, yes, there are some very interesting ones." Damien slapped the steering wheel. "Now that I think about it, there is this one formation that would prove to be an excellent setting for the photograph."

"I hope it isn't too close to the river."

"Why is that?"

"Damon, I feel embarrassed to tell you this."

"Please. I won't tell anyone. You can trust me."

Mary took a deep breath. "I have a fear of water."

"Oh, no." He looked at her with shock. "And why would that be?"

"I can't swim."

"Really?" Her revelation pleased him, making the game even more exciting. "Well, neither can I." Damien loved how he could lie so easily. "But you needn't worry. It's very safe and not anywhere near the river."

"How close is it?"

"Some thirty to forty feet away." The river was forty feet away all right—forty feet straight down. "It's a perfect spot. You can sit while I take your picture."

"I don't have to climb the rock, do I?" Mary asked. "I'm a little scared of heights."

"No, no. The rock is shaped like a chair. You just sit in it." He glanced at his victim. "Are you familiar with it by any chance?"

"I don't think so. I was only about six or seven years old when my parents took me to Taylors Falls."

"Did you enjoy it?"

"Not really. I was terrified of the river below the cliffs. I remember seeing the different rock formations, but I don't recall any that resembled a chair."

Damien slowed the car for the turnoff into the parking lot. He toyed with the idea of telling her that the rock formation was known as The Devil's Chair, but that would be his surprise.

Chapter 66

At a few minutes after nine, Damien pulled into the parking lot at Taylors Falls, pleased to see that there were only two other cars. A couple months ago, he had made a special trip to this spot, seeking out and talking to the park ranger.

"Hello, sir. I'm wondering if you could tell me when would be the best time to come here before the snow flies and not run into a lot of people."

The ranger, a short man with a walrus mustache and a weathered face took off his cap and scratched the back of his head. "I would say toward the end of October," he had said as he put his cap back on. "Once the weather begins to cool and school has been in full swing, the crowds thin out. During the week is best."

"How about on the weekend?" Damien had asked, knowing that he couldn't get Mary to come during the week because of her teaching duties.

"If you're thinking the weekend, the morning is usually pretty good. Toward afternoon, you'll see more people. But if you come in the morning, just be aware that there are no park officials here until ten so you're on your own." The ranger pointed in the direction of the cliffs. "And be sure to stay along the pathways and don't do anything foolish; those cliffs can be mighty dangerous."

"Is that so?"

"You bet your bottom dollar it's so." The ranger stroked his mustache. "Why, just last week, some fool started climbing up one of the cliffs. He fell and broke his leg. If he would've been climbing on the river side, he would've fallen into the river and swept under by the current."

"Thank you for the warning. I'll keep that in mind."

Damien recalled the ranger's warning as he parked in the corner of the lot away from the other two cars. He turned off the ignition. Whoever belonged to those other cars would be of no concern; they wouldn't be in the area he would be taking Mary. After all, didn't the ranger say that would be foolish? He smiled at his passenger. "This is a splendid setting for the photograph."

"It seems so deserted," Mary noted, a hint of uncertainty in her voice.

"Oh, just a few minutes. What I have in mind shouldn't take very long."

Damien opened the door, got out, walked over to the passenger's side, and opened the door for Mary. "There's a slight chill in the air, but other than that, it's a perfect morning. You may want to bring your sweater, though."

"I hope the pictures turn out," Mary said as she got out and slipped on her sweater. "I'd like to give one to my fiancé as a wedding gift."

"That's a splendid idea. I hadn't thought of that." A photograph of Mary's body floating face down in the river excited him. He could send several copies to Mick and his partners, perhaps with even a greeting attached to it. Of course, the one he would send to Howie would be enclosed in another card with the picture of the grinning cat peering into a doghouse. "And I think I can guarantee that Mick will long remember the photograph."

Mary got a puzzled look on her face. "You talk as if you really know him. Are you sure that the two of you have never met?"

"Believe me, as much as I would have liked to, I've never had the pleasure of meeting him. But I believe you did talk about him quite a bit when I was doing your hair earlier this week." Damien could tell that she was unsure about what he was claiming. "Don't you remember? You were telling me about the wedding."

"I remember talking about the wedding, but I don't recall talking about Mick." Mary smiled. "I guess I have too many things on my mind."

"Oh, yes, I'm sure you do. A bride has to be aware of so many details." *And my dear, so do I. For example, shall I slit your throat from left to right or right to left before I toss you into the river? Or should I just push you in and watch the currents suck you under?* "Shall we go?"

"Aren't you forgetting something?"

"And what is that?"

"Your camera."

"Oh, of course. I'd forget my head if it wasn't attached. It's in the backseat." Damien opened the car door and got the camera. "Okay, I'm all set."

"Which way do we go?"

He pointed to a pathway leading off to the right. "We'll take that trail. If I'm not mistaken, that should lead us to some rather interesting rock formations." As they walked the path inclining toward the cliffs, he explained that he chose this outdoor setting because it complimented her natural beauty. The rocky path continued to gradually slope toward the cliffs. After trudging for several minutes, he pointed to a lightly trodden path off to their right. "Let's go that way."

Mary stopped, looked worriedly at the direction he had suggested, and pointed to a posted sign. "That sign says *Danger! Do not go beyond this point.* I don't think that we should go up there."

"Don't worry. I've been up there many times. Trust me, it's very safe."

Mary shook her head. "I really don't want to go up there."

"But I insist." Damien took hold of her arm.

"What are you doing?"

"You're coming with me!"

"Stop it!" she cried. "You're hurting me, let go!"

"Not until we're up there." His tone turned as chilly as the air. "There's a rock formation called the Devil's Chair that I would like for you to see."

"I'm not going." Mary struggled to break free.

"And I insist you are." She screamed when he slapped her across the face. He moved behind her and put his arm around her neck; with his other hand he gripped her jaw. "My dear, if you scream again, I'll snap your neck." He twisted her head back toward him until she winced in pain. "And I assure you that I am quite capable of doing that," he hissed, pleased to see the terror in her eyes. "I have—"

"Mary!" The yell came from the direction of the parking lot.

Damien didn't recognize the voice until he noted Mary's eyes. It had to be Mick. "I'm afraid that we'll have to finish this some other time," he whispered and then backhanded her, knocking her to the ground.

Chapter 67

Howie and Mick rushed in the direction of Mary's scream. Several agonizing minutes elapsed before they reached the general location and another couple of minutes passed before they finally spotted her lying behind some bushes.

"Mary!" Mick cried. He ran to her, knelt down, and cradled her in his arms. "Are you all right?" he asked again and again.

"Oh, Mick." Tears welled in her eyes. "It was awful, just terrible." She buried her face in his chest.

"Don't worry. You're safe now." He stroked her head, his eyes glistening. "He can't hurt you anymore."

"He tried to take me up to the cliffs. When I refused to go with him, he hit me." She touched her bruised cheek and brushed away tears. "He knew I was afraid of water. That I can't swim. That I'm scared of heights. That I—"

"Just calm down, Mary. Breathe easy." Mick continued to stroke her hair.

"He was going to…" Her body trembled.

Mick looked at Howie with eyes now glaring with rage.

Howie scanned the area. Damien could be watching them at this very moment. "Do you know which way he went?" he asked Mary.

"No, when he knocked me down…" She winced as though having a flashback. She covered her face with her hands before wiping away more tears. "I crawled over here to get away from him. I didn't see him leave. Maybe I should've—"

"You did what you needed to do. How badly are you hurt?"

She touched the side of her face. "My jaw is sore and I'm sure I'll have some bruising, but I think I'm all right." She leaned her head against Mick, clutching his arm. More tears came. "I was afraid he was going to hit me again. He was like a madman."

"That no good son-of-a…" Mick's voice shook with rage. His nostrils flared. "So help me, Howie, I'll kill the—"

"Take it easy." Howie placed his hand on Mick's shoulder. "What kind of car did he drive?" he asked Mary.

"A blue Buick," she replied, sounding calmer now. "It's parked in the corner of the lot."

"You stay with her," Howie told Mick.

"Where are you going?"

"If I know Damien, he's probably circled around us." Howie took off running. As he got near the parking lot, he heard a car engine roar to life. By the time he got to the edge of the lot, he saw the blue Buick heading for the exit leading onto the highway. He ran for another ten yards but stopped. The car had turned left onto the highway, heading back toward the Cities. He swore silently at not being able to get a clear reading of the license plate.

Damien glanced in the rearview mirror as he drove out of the parking lot. Howie stood in the middle of the lot, shaking his fist at him. "Well, my friend, you've won this round, but the next one shall be mine." He turned on the radio. Classical music would help calm the fury within him. Although the fools had disrupted his plans, he had already formulated what his next move would be. Howie Cummings and his partners would live to regret that they had ever crossed paths with him. And Mary? She hadn't seen the last of him either.

Howie kicked at the gravel as the Buick disappeared from sight. Without another moment's hesitation, he dashed to his car. "Damn it!" he cried. The right front tire had been slashed. He looked toward the highway, swore again, and headed back to where he had left the others. He hadn't gotten halfway back when Mick and Mary came walking toward him.

"Did he get away?" Mick looked past Howie toward the parking lot.

"Yeah. The creep slashed my tire so I couldn't give chase."

"We've got to get that guy!" Mick said, his eyes burning with rage.

"We will, Mick. We will." Howie noted how exhausted Mary looked. "I tell you what. We'll get the tire changed, and then get Mary home."

On the ride back to the city, the three of them rode in the front seat. Mary recounted the circumstances leading up to how she had met Damien, or Damon as he had called himself. She gave Howie the name and the address of the salon. Even though Damien had a good thirty-minute head start, Howie hoped that maybe he was unlucky enough to have had a breakdown along the way. Or better yet, a fatal accident.

"I don't know how I could've been so naive," Mary said.

"Don't be so hard on yourself," Howie said. "He's good at misleading people."

"Including us," Mick added.

Howie gripped the steering wheel tighter. Although his partner was right about them also being deceived by Damien, he didn't want to admit it.

"I'm just thankful that we got there in time." Mick took hold of Mary's hand. Outwardly, he appeared to have settled a bit, but a smoldering anger could still be seen in his eyes.

Mary leaned her head against Mick's shoulder, intertwining her arm with his.

Howie sensed that it would be better if Mick stayed with her. She needed his support. Besides, his partner needed to cool off. Howie didn't need someone coming with him whose emotions were as raw as Mick's were right now. "I'll drop the two of you off at Mary's place. Okay?"

"Why don't you take me to my parents' house," Mary said. "It's closer."

"Are your parents home?" Mick asked.

"No, but it feels safer there. Will you stay with me for a while?"

"Of course." Mick turned to Howie. "What are you going to do after you drop us off?"

"I'm going to make a quick stop at the office and get Adam." His partner would come in handy in case he ran into a problem. Although Howie was tough for his size, he didn't think he could take Damien on his own. "And then Adam and I are going to pay a visit to that salon."

"You better hurry," Mary said. "It closes at noon on Saturdays."

"What time is it?"

Mick checked his watch. "Ten-thirty."

The speedometer moved past seventy-five as Howie pressed the accelerator nearly to the floor. If traffic continued to be in his favor, he could drop off Mick and Mary, get Adam at the office, and still get to the salon just before closing time.

"Do you think he'll be there?" Mary asked.

"I doubt it, but maybe we can find out where he lives, and if we do, we're going to pay him a little visit."

"Call me if you find out where he lives," Mick said. "I'll go with you."

"No, you stay with Mary."

"But I owe that guy."

"Don't worry. You'll get your payback."

With Howie pushing past the speed limit, the drive back to the Twin Cities didn't take long. After dropping his passengers off, assuring Mick that he would call him if anything of importance developed, he drove straight to the office. His partner was sitting in a chair reading a magazine when he stormed in. "Come on Adam, we're going."

Adam tossed the magazine on the desk and headed toward the door. "What's up? Did you find Mary?"

"Yeah."

"How is she?"

"She's had a rough time, but she's okay." Howie and his partner raced down the stairs. "Mick's with her at her parents' home. I told him to stay with her."

"Where are we going?"

"To find Damien. I'll tell you the whole story on the way." Howie had noticed the rumpled blanket on the couch before shutting his office door. "What happen to Squirrel?" he asked as he and his partner hurried toward his car.

"He got tired of waiting."

221

Mary fixed a cup of tea for herself and Mick, brought the tray into the living room, and sat next to him on the couch. "I don't think I should tell my parents what happened. It would upset them too much."

"What are you going to say about your face?" Mick asked. The makeup she had applied partially concealed the bruising.

"I don't know, but I'll think of something before they get home. I may not even see them tonight."

"How come?"

"They're visiting with some old friends from high school. Mother told me that they wouldn't be home until late. I'll just go to bed early, and in the morning I'll..." She paused. "What's wrong, Mick?" She set her teacup down on the coffee table.

"What do you mean?"

"I've known you long enough to know when your mind isn't completely on the conversation. Something is troubling you. What is it?"

"Nothing."

"Is it what happened today?"

Mick took her hand. "I was really scared knowing that Damien had you."

"But I'm here with you now. That's all that counts."

"Yes, but that guy's still out there. You don't know Damien like we do. He's the type who never gives up. Once he starts something, he's determined to finish it." He stroked her hand. "I know that we've talked about this, but..."

Mary cocked her head. "You're not thinking about eloping again, are you? I thought we already decided against that."

"I know we did." Mick's eyes met hers. "I was thinking that it might be better if we got married in a private ceremony with just Howie and Adam as witnesses."

"What?" Mary looked at him as though he had just called off the wedding.

"Just hear me out," Mick said. "Your parents could be there, and given the circumstances, they would understand."

A determined look settled in Mary's eyes. "Mick Brunner, with all the plans we have been making for this past year, no. We're going through with it as planned. It's too late to cancel. What about all the people who received invitations? And then there is the reception hall."

"I know. I considered all of that."

"Listen, didn't you tell me that Howie's detective friend was planning to be there?"

"Yes, but—"

"But nothing." Mary gripped his hand. "We just can't let this man control our lives. If he does that, then he wins. Mick, don't you understand?" she pleaded. "For the rest of our lives we would have to live with the knowledge that we never had our wedding the way we wanted it because of that man. Is that something you want? I certainly don't."

Mick sighed. "I know that you're right. I just don't want anything to happen to spoil our wedding."

"How can anything happen with you, Howie, and Adam there, and nearly two hundred guests?" She offered him a reassuring smile. "I'll be safer there than I would be in my own house."

Chapter 68

Howie and Adam arrived at the House of Beauty Salon in Edina, parked their car, and moved quickly to the front entrance just as a middle-aged woman with reddish-tinted hair was locking it. She stood on the other side of the glass door eyeing them suspiciously.

"We're closed," she said, pointing to the *Closed* sign in the window. "Come back on Monday. We'll be open at ten."

"We need to talk to you now about one of your employees!" Howie shouted, gesturing to her to unlock the door.

"Come back Monday." The woman turned to walk away.

"Lady, we're detectives!" Howie yelled as he pounded on the glass so furiously that the woman rushed back to the door.

"Stop that!" she cried. "You're going to break the glass." She eyed the two of them. "Who did you say you were?"

"We're detectives. I'm Howie Cummins, and this is my partner, Adam Trexler. We're working with the police." He noted but ignored the recriminating look from his partner concerning the lie he just told. "We need to talk to you about one of your employees." When the woman still hesitated, he added, "It concerns a murder case."

Her eyes doubled in size as she put her hand to her breast. "Oh, dear me. Just...just a minute." She fumbled with the lock.

"What are you talking about, murder case?" Adam whispered as the woman unlocked the door.

"Hey, she's letting us in, isn't she?" As soon as she opened the door, he stepped in with Adam following him.

"Who got murdered?" the woman asked, her chest heaving up and down. Her eyes flickered with excitement.

"Sorry, I can't reveal that." Howie noticed a young blonde woman in the back of the shop. "Where's Damon. Is he here?"

"He hasn't been here all morning," the woman said. Her eyes grew even larger and her mouth dropped open as if she just realized the implication. "He's not involved with it, is he? He can't be—he's such a nice man."

"We just want to question him about a few things." Howie wondered just how many others Damien had fooled. "Do you know where he lives?"

"No."

"You must have his address someplace. How about personnel or payroll records?"

She shook her head. "We're not that big of a shop to have personnel records. And as far as payroll, Damon always insisted on being paid in cash."

"And he's always paid in cash?"

"Oh, yes. I accommodate him because he's very good at what he does." Her chest swelled with pride. "He brings in a lot of repeat customers."

"You wouldn't by chance have a last name for him?" It was a long shot, but Howie figured with a last name, he might be listed in the phone book.

"No, I only know him by Damon. Perhaps, Mr. Weisand might know. He's the one who says it's okay to pay him in cash."

"Who's Mr. Weisand?" Adam asked.

"He's the owner. Mr. Weisand is very accommodating to Damon. If anybody has the information you're asking for about Damon, he would."

Howie glanced toward the back of the store, wondering if the owner had his office there. "Is Mr. Weisand here?"

"No, he left earlier. It's only Vicki and me."

"Who's she?"

"She works here in the salon." The woman gestured toward the blonde woman in the back. "That's Vicki back there. She's cleaning up her work area."

Adam spoke up. "How about her? Might she know where he lives?"

"Oh, I don't...wait a minute, now that I think about it...Vicki just might be able to help. She gave Damon a ride home a couple of months ago. I guess his car was being repaired or something like that."

"We need to talk to her," Howie said.

"I'll go get her."

"This may be the break we've been looking for," Adam whispered.

"Yeah, let's hope that Damien's finally slipped up."

Howie and Adam arrived at Damien's apartment building within twenty minutes after they finished talking with Vicki. She had given Damien a ride home one night, and most importantly, remembered the address since his place was only a few blocks from one of her girlfriends.

"This is the place," Howie said as he parked the car in the parking area of a large apartment complex.

"Do you think he's home?"

"We'll soon find out." Howie and his partner got out of the car, hurried to the main entrance, and stepped into the entryway.

"Do you see his name?" Howie scanned the several rows of mail slots.

"Not yet...wait! I found it."

"Well, what do you know...no last name, just Damon." Howie stared at the black call button next to Damien's apartment number. "He won't answer his buzzer."

"So what are we going to do?"

"Just wait. Somebody will come along. If not, I'll ring the manager's apartment." In less than a minute the entrance door opened and three teenagers, two girls and a boy, came in. When the young girls looked at them oddly after they followed them in, Howie explained with a smile, "I forgot my key."

Once Howie and Adam got in, they took the stairs to the third floor and quickly found Damien's apartment.

"What do you think we should do?" Adam whispered as they stood to one side of the door, not wanting to be spotted by anyone who might look through the apartment's peephole.

Howie took a stick of gum from his pocket. After unwrapping it, he popped it into his mouth and chewed it for several moments. He took the wad of gum out, stuck it over the peephole, and knocked on the door. "I'll disguise my voice and tell him that the manager sent me up to warn him of a possible gas leak."

"Do you think he'll fall for that?"

"Have you got a better idea?" Howie waited and knocked again.

"Maybe he didn't come home," Adam said.

"In that case, we'll just invite ourselves in."

"How?"

"Just watch." Howie pulled out a billfold-size, black leather case and opened it.

"What are those things?"

"Our way in. These are lock picks."

Adam chewed his lip as he glanced up and down the hallway. "Where did you get them?"

"It doesn't matter where I got them." When Howie took hold of the doorknob and turned it, however, the door opened. "I guess I'll have to save these for another time." He slipped the case back into his pocket. After entering and quietly closing the door behind them, the two of them found themselves walking into a living room.

"Do you hear anything?" Howie whispered.

Adam shook his head, but pointed to an envelope taped to an oval-shaped wall mirror above a lamp to the right of them. "Look at that."

Howie moved quickly to the mirror and read the printing on the legal-size envelope. *To the amateur sleuths of the mac detective agency.* He took down the envelope and tore it open.

Welcome to my humble abode. Please make yourselves at home. Sorry, I couldn't be here to meet you. There's a bottle of white wine in the refrigerator. Feel free to pour yourselves a glass.
D
P.S.
Tell Mick that I sincerely enjoyed having breakfast with his fiancée. Mary is such a delightful woman, and is quite an interesting person. I feel I have gotten to know her quite well.

Chapter 69

Nearly a week had passed and there had been no breaks in the case; the whereabouts of Damien had remained a mystery. Howie and his partners had divided their time staking out Damien's apartment building as well as his place of work. In addition, Howie talked to Arthur Weisand, the owner of the salon, but the man was of no help. "If you hear from him, give me a call," Howie had told him, feeling that Damien had the poor guy too scared to cooperate. With growing frustration, he had even enlisted Squirrel's help, asking the reformed street hustler now turned hopeful detective if he would be willing to stakeout Louise Sparks' place. "It'll help us while giving you some practical experience," he told the little guy. Squirrel jumped at the chance. He, however, had also struck out reporting that the dame barely left her house and had no visitors.

"Is detective work always this dull?" Squirrel had asked when he reported the results of his first assignment to Howie.

"It's not any different than police work."

"What do you mean?"

"Ninety-five percent of the time, the work is routine and boring."

"You don't say?" Squirrel wrinkled his nose and began sucking air through his teeth. He scratched the side of his head as he appeared to be pondering what he had just been told. "And what about the other five percent?"

"Sheer panic."

"Really!" His eyes lit up. "That's what I'm looking for, man." He slapped his hands together. "So, when do we get to that?"

"Don't be so anxious. It will come."

On Wednesday Howie had asked Adam to come up to his office that Friday morning to talk with him and JD about Mick's wedding the following day. The two days had passed slowly and now with the three of them together, Howie quickly got to the reason for their meeting. "What are we going to do if Damien shows his face tomorrow?"

"Have you got any ideas?" Adam asked Howie.

"Not anything solid. JD and I were talking about it just before you came." Davidson had arrived ten minutes before Adam. "We both agree

227

that there's not much we can do except to be on the alert."

Adam turned to JD. "Are you going to bring some of your men along?"

"That's not in the cards."

"What?" Adam's face darkened. "Why not?"

"The department is already busting its ass on other cases and we're shorthanded as it is," JD said. "The chief wouldn't see this as high priority. If I brought this to him, he'd be quick to tell me where to shove it."

"JD's doing it on his own time," Howie interjected, taking note of the argumentative look on Adam's face. If his partner could have his way, the entire North Side police department would be at the wedding. "Between all of us, we should have it covered. Even Squirrel volunteered to help. And Damien should be pretty easy to spot with that ponytail."

"If he still has it," JD said.

"What do you mean?" Adam asked.

"If I was him, I'd cut it off and dye my hair."

"He can change his hair color and style all he wants," Adam said. "But we have dealt with this guy enough to recognize him by his eyes and that smug smirk of his."

"So, what are you going to do if you spot him when you're up there at the altar?" JD asked. "You're sure as hell not going to give chase, and he knows that."

"I tell you what," Howie said, afraid that Adam would react to JD's casual tone by assuming that the detective wasn't taking this whole thing seriously enough. From his experience with the veteran police detective, however, JD's casual approach was just a cover for his own intensity. "While we're up front, Adam and I will keep our eyes open for him. If we see Damien, we'll signal you."

"Oh, yeah? And just how are you going to do that?"

"We'll...ah..." Howie remembered the terrible cold JD had the last time he was there. "We'll rub our nose."

"You'll what?"

"We'll rub our noses," Howie said. "It's an innocent gesture—nobody's going to pay any attention to it. If we do it with our left hand, it means Damien's sitting somewhere in the left-hand part of the church. That's simple enough, isn't it?"

JD folded his arms and remained silent as he studied Howie. "My left or your left?" he finally asked, a hint of a smile appearing on his face.

"Your left. And if we do it with our right hand, he's on the right-hand side. Is that clear enough?"

JD settled back in his chair. "It couldn't be any clearer." A flicker of amusement flashed across his face. "And if this works out, I'll share it with my peers down at the squad bay. Hell, maybe I'll even ask the chief to make it part of our S.O.P."

"Okay, wise guy. Have you got a better suggestion?" Howie asked, not appreciating JD's sarcasm.

"Naw, I like this one. It's new and refreshing."

Howie eyed Adam. "Why don't you tell him what happened at the library the other day?"

Adam turned toward JD. "I ran into one of your detectives."

"Is that right?" A cool curiosity replaced the twinkle in his eyes. "Who was it?"

"A guy by the name of Manning. He was doing undercover work at the library watching Charlotte Aldrich." They had told JD about Newt's sister without going into details.

"Manning? Are you sure?"

"Sure, I'm sure. He told me his name and showed me his badge."

"When did you say this was?"

"Last Friday."

"What's wrong, JD?" Howie asked.

"Hang on." JD waved Howie off and focused his attention on Adam. "Describe this guy for me."

"Short and stocky, has dark thinning hair, and a gruff sounding voice."

JD's eyes shifted to Howie and then back to Adam. "I don't know who you're describing, but that sure as hell wasn't Manning."

"What!" Howie exclaimed as he also took note of Adam's startled expression. "What do you mean it wasn't Manning?"

"Because Manning twisted his ankle a month ago chasing a petty thief down some back alley. He's been shuffling papers at the office for the last three weeks making the most of his injury. And I should know because I have had to put up with his pissing and moaning every day." The corners of JD's mouth turned up ever so slightly. "Besides, Manning is as thin as a rail, nearly bald, and has a voice that sounds like a canary being squashed to hell. Whoever this joker was, it wasn't Manning."

"But he showed me a badge."

"Did you get a good look at it?"

"I thought I did."

JD kept his tone casual. "Did you ask to see some ID?"

Adam shook his head.

"What are you thinking?" Howie asked JD.

"That it was somebody posing as a cop." The detective shifted in his chair. "Some guys get turned on doing that kind of thing. Maybe it was some pervert who got his kicks watching her."

"Oh, man. What did I do?" Adam buried his face in his hands. "How could I have been so stupid?"

"Don't worry, you couldn't have known," Howie said. It had been a dumb mistake, one that made them appear as amateurs, but he didn't want to say that to Adam in front of JD.

Adam glanced at his watch. "I'm going to run over to the library to talk to her. I've got time before the rehearsal."

"Do you think he might show up again?" Howie asked

"I don't know, but if he does, he's not going to get away so easy this time." Adam headed for the door. "I'll see you later."

"Don't be too hard on him," Howie said after Adam left. "He's a good guy. This is going to bother him that he got suckered."

JD shrugged. "Hell, I know how it feels to get suckered. It's happened to me more than a couple of times."

Howie picked up his coffee cup. "Do you want some coffee?" he asked as he stood up. "I'm going to get a refill."

"I'll pass."

"I can put a shot of bourbon in it."

The detective's eyes narrowed. He gave Howie a troubled look. "Since when did you start drinking?"

"Don't worry. I only take it when I've got a headache."

"And how often do you get headaches?"

"I'll be right back." Howie walked out into the kitchen, filled his cup three-quarters full of coffee and topped it off with bourbon. "Are you sure you don't want any?" he asked as he came back into the office.

"Yeah. I'm sure." JD waited for Howie to sit down. "Can I give you a word of advice?"

"About what?"

"Your headache remedy."

"What about it?"

"It doesn't work. Trust me. I speak from experience."

Howie took a sip of his spiked coffee. "Well, it works for me."

"So that's the way you want to play it?"

"Yeah." Howie had heard rumors about JD's drinking and how it almost cost him his badge in the first years on the job. "Don't worry, I can handle it."

JD broke eye contact for a moment. "Okay. It's confession time."

"What are you talking about?"

"I've told you that I've been suckered from time to time." JD folded his arms across his chest. "How about you?"

"How about me what?"

"Now, you're playing around with me." JD's eyes turned cement gray. "Come on. Confess up. Have you ever been suckered?"

"Me? Never." Howie took a sip of his headache remedy, thinking that it needed a little more bourbon.

Chapter 70

It took Adam less than a half hour to drive to the library. After parking and locking his car, he hurried to the entrance. He had a number of questions and hoped that Charlotte would provide some answers. An older woman with gray hair and reading glasses, however, was behind the checkout counter. He glanced around, but Charlotte was nowhere in sight. The woman at the checkout desk was just waving good-bye to two teenagers as he approached.

"Pardon me, ma'am." He waited for her to turn his way. "I'm looking for Charlotte Aldrich. Is she on break now?"

"No, she's not here today."

"Wasn't she scheduled to work?"

The woman moved a stack of books to one side. "Yes, but she didn't come in."

"She's not sick, is she?" The woman gave him an inquiring look. "I'm a friend of hers," he explained.

"I see." She peered over her glasses, looking at him as though wondering how close of a friend he was to Charlotte. "Well, we don't know if she's sick."

"What do you mean?"

"She didn't call in."

"Has she ever done that before? Not called in?"

"Oh, no. That's very unusual for her." She took off her glasses and set them on the counter. "You say that you're a good friend of hers?"

Adam nodded.

"Well, then, I have to tell you that in all the time I've known her, she's been very reliable and has never missed a day of work. Perhaps you should check on her."

"Thanks, I will." Adam turned and walked out to his car, praying that the man who had posed as Manning hadn't gotten to her. Whatever was going on in the life of Charlotte Aldrich, however, he couldn't do anything about it now. Mick's wedding rehearsal was in a couple of hours. He would check on her as soon as he could after the wedding tomorrow.

"This is the church where Mick and his lovely bride will be getting married tomorrow," Damien said as he and Newt slowly drove by the gothic-style cathedral. It was the third time that they had encircled the block. Newt had balked at going to the church with him, pleading that it was too risky.

"What if we're seen?" Newt had asked, his voice quivering.

"You're coming with me." Damien started toward the car. He hadn't bothered to look back to see if Newt had followed. The fool wouldn't dare refuse his command. Yes, there was the risk of being seen, but he loved living on the edge. He had even considered parking the car and walking into the building to observe the rehearsal from the back of the church.

Damien now slowed the car for an older couple crossing the street. The woman nodded her appreciation and he returned her nod with a smile. He glanced over at Newt, amused at how his helper had scrunched down in the passenger seat each time they drove by the entrance of the church. "Is our *package* ready?"

"You mean..."

"Yes, of course. What else?"

"But how are—"

"Is...it...ready?"

Newt swallowed hard. "Ye...yes."

"Splendid. We'll pick it up tonight." Damien glanced at the church in the rearview mirror as they drove away. "I think it will prove to be a very unique wedding gift—one of a kind." He smirked. "Don't you agree?" The horrified look on Newt's face amused him.

Chapter 71

Charlie, one of the ushers for the wedding, came rushing into the room where Howie and Adam were giving Mick a last minute check over. In a few minutes Mick would go to be with the priest. Rehearsal had gone without incident and the day of the wedding had finally come.

"What's going on, Charlie?" Howie asked.

"I just spotted some guy with a blonde ponytail sitting in the church."

"Where?" Howie had instructed the ushers to let him know if they spotted any man with a ponytail.

"He's sitting on the right-hand side about halfway down."

"Let's go," Mick said.

Although the ceremony was to begin in ten minutes, Howie along with Mick and Adam rushed to the doors leading into the sanctuary. The church, with a seating capacity of nearly three hundred, was filled.

"Do you see him?" Adam asked Howie.

"Yeah, I can see the back of his head."

"Is it him?"

"I can't be sure, but we're not going to take any chances."

"Wait a minute." Mick grabbed Howie's arm. "That isn't Damien."

"What?" Howie gave his partner a puzzled look. "Who is it then?"

"Stan."

"Who's that?"

"He's a cousin of mine," Mick said, a note of relief in his voice. "I haven't seen him in a couple of years. When his wife called to tell me that they were coming, she said that Stan was going through a mid-life crisis. The ponytail must be part of it."

"Okay," Howie said, disappointed that it wasn't Damien. He glanced at his watch. "Mick, you better hook up with the priest. We'll meet you up front. Don't worry, everything will be fine."

A few minutes after Mick left, the bridesmaids found Howie and Adam. Several more minutes passed and the processional began. Although the ceremony seemed to be moving fine with no sign of Damien, Howie felt edgy. The priest had just begun the wedding vows when Howie felt a nudge on his arm.

"Anything?" Adam whispered.

CHARLES TINDELL

"No, but keep watching," Howie replied. A quick, stern look from Father Duval told him that he, like Adam, needed to keep his voice down. "Okay," he whispered, giving the priest a sheepish smile. He had informed Father Duval of the circumstances without going into any specific details. The priest had given them his blessings, but also reminded them that the service was being recorded. He also made it clear that he would keep an eye out as well. "There's not going to be any shenanigans going on in my church," he vowed.

Mick was just finishing his vows when Howie caught a glimpse of Damien in the back of the church, sitting in the last pew. He quickly looked for JD, spotted him, and tried to signal him. At the moment, however, his police friend wasn't looking at the wedding party; he was also checking the crowd. *Come on, JD, look to your left, the last pew on the end.* He next spotted Squirrel, but the little twerp looked like he was hustling some pretty young woman sitting next to him. Howie nudged Adam and was about to whisper that he spotted Damien when he heard his name being called by Father Duval.

"What?" Howie said, and then heard a smattering of snickering from the congregation.

"The rings, Howard, may I please have the rings?"

"Oh, yes, Father, just a minute."

Father Duval addressed the congregation. "Ladies and gentleman, I have been a priest for over thirty years and this is the first wedding I've had where the best man seems to be more nervous than the groom." This time the snickering turned into laughter.

Howie fumbled for the rings in his right-hand coat pocket, got them out, and handed them to the priest. As soon as Father Duval took the rings, Howie shot a glance toward the last pew. Damien was gone.

"What an absolutely wonderful day for a wedding," Damien said as he met Newt on the front steps of the church. He looked at the nearly cloudless sky and took a deep breath. "The air is so crisp and invigorating."

"Don't you think we should be going?" Newt asked, glancing around. "Somebody might spot us."

Damien took another deep breath and started down the steps. Everything was working out as he had planned—better than he had planned. He and Newt had brought the *wedding gift* late last night. He had entered the unlocked main entrance to the church, telling Newt that he would meet him at the back entrance. It took him only a few minutes to navigate through the church and locate the back door. "Wasn't that thoughtful of the priest?" he now asked Newt.

"I'm not sure what you mean."

"That the good Father keeps the front doors open for any lost souls that may need spiritual guidance."

"If you say so."

Damien and Newt had hid the gift well. He was certain that it would go undetected. The next day, after morning confessions were over and the priest had gone back to the rectory, they had returned to find their gift a more appropriate location. Newt had been so scared of being caught that he nearly fainted. For Damien, however, the experience only enhanced his feeling of omnipotence.

Now, as Damien walked toward where Newt had parked the limo, he enjoyed the warmth of the sunshine upon his face. "Yes, it is a beautiful day for a wedding."

"He's here," Howie whispered out of the corner of his mouth to Adam just as Father Duval was pronouncing Mick and Mary to be husband and wife.

"Let us pray," the priest announced, looking directly at Howie.

Howie bowed his head, but didn't close his eyes. He fought the urge to turn around and scan the sanctuary.

"What did you say?" Mick whispered to Howie after Duval finished his prayer.

"Damien's here."

"What!" Mick glanced over the congregation. "Where?"

"He was in the back row. He's not there now, but I saw him."

"Are you sure?"

"Oh, yeah."

Father Duval gave Howie a quizzical look and beckoned him closer as he switched off the microphone clipped to his robe. "Do you mind telling me what is going on?" he asked as Howie, Adam, and the bride and groom stepped forward for a conference. A murmur swept over the congregation.

"Father, the man I told you about is here," Howie said. "He's dangerous and we need to find him and fast."

"What do you suggest I do?"

Howie glanced at Mick and Mary. "Finish the service, and then Adam and I will skip the receiving line and go looking for him."

"Not without me," Mick said, his tone determined. He turned to Mary. "I'm sorry, but I have to do this."

Mary gave a worried look to Howie and Adam as though pleading with them to take care of her new husband. She turned to Mick and whispered, "I understand that you need to go with them. Just be careful, please."

"That settles it." Howie tapped Mick on the chest to make sure he heard what he was about to say. "You wait for us before you go running off by yourself, do you hear?" He turned to Mary. "Make sure this new husband of yours stays with you in the narthex until Adam and I get back there."

"In that case," Father Duval said, "since the three of you are going to be taking off immediately, I'll announce that the receiving line will take place at the wedding hall instead of right after the service."

"Thanks, Father," Mick said.

"You're not going to say anything about why, are you?" Howie asked, worried that it would be too big of a tip-off.

"Don't be concerned about that, my son. I'll think of a reason by the time we're finished up here." An impish grin appeared on Duval's face. "Just because I'm wearing this collar doesn't mean I can't tell a little fib once in a while if it's for a good cause." His eyes looked upward. "Forgive me, Lord." He crossed himself and said, "Now go ahead and get back to your positions, and just act normal."

Howie nudged Mick. "Just remember, wait for us," he whispered.

Once everyone was in their place, Father Duval turned his microphone back on and addressed the congregation. "I wish to announce that the bride and groom have decided to have the receiving line at the reception hall instead of in the narthex immediately following the service as printed in the bulletin. The reason for this..." He paused, looked at Howie and winked. "The reason is because our best man is feeling a wee bit under the weather." When he smiled, his eyes twinkled. "As I have said, this is one wedding where the strain is harder on the best man than it is on the bride and groom." After the laughter died down, he continued. "He assures me, however, that he is able to last until the service is over. Isn't that right, Howard?"

Howie nodded.

"Good. So let us continue."

Howie kept looking over the congregation, waiting for the service to end. When his and JD's eyes met, Howie mouthed *he's here*. JD got the message and quickly got up and left. Howie wondered what Squirrel was doing when he noticed him pointing at his own nose. It was only when Squirrel started to rub his nose in an exaggerated fashioned that he realized that he was reminding Howie not to forget to signal if he spotted Damien.

"You may kiss your bride," Father Duval announced.

After the kiss, Mick and Mary paused briefly at the altar, and started down the aisle, the two of them setting a speed record rushing out of the sanctuary. Right after them, nearly on their heels, were Howie and the maid of honor, and then Adam and the bridesmaid. When Howie got to the narthex, he apologized to the startled maid of honor for rushing her, and to the priest. "Father, it might be good if you took Mary to the privacy of your study while we search the area."

"That is an excellent suggestion, Howard. I'll do just that."

"And will you stay with her, Father?" Mick asked.

"Certainly."

"Thank you." Mick breathed a sigh of relief. "I appreciate that."

"You're welcome, my son. Now, you just catch that man and may the Lord have mercy on his soul."

"Father?"

"Yes, Adam?"

"That man doesn't have a soul."

Chapter 72

After Father Duval and Mary reached the safety of his study, he made sure he locked the door behind him. "You're a brave woman," he said removing his cassock and hanging it on a hanger in his closet.

"Thank you, but I don't feel brave."

"Why do you say that?"

"Because, Father, here I am hiding on my wedding day." She fought back tears, determined not to cry. "It's Mick who's brave. It can't be easy for him after…"

"After what?"

She looked away for a moment. "After what that man did to him."

"And what would that have been?" Father Duval asked in a tone that he no doubt used in the confessional.

She had known Father Duval all her life. He had helped her family out a number of times and had even been a guest for dinner at her parents' home on several occasions. Still, she felt reluctant. "I don't know if I should say anything."

"My dear, confession is good for the soul."

Mary set her wedding bouquet on the desk. "If I tell you, do you promise not to say anything to Mick? It would upset him if he knew I told you."

Father Duval offered a sympathetic smile. "Mary, my dear, you're talking to a priest. I'll just pretend that we're in the confessional booth. Whatever you say to me, I can assure you that I will never divulge." He moved over, leaned against the desk, and folded his arms. "Please, go ahead and tell me. It will do you good."

As soon as Mary and Father Duval left, Howie mapped out a plan of action. "Adam, you check out the parlor where the receiving line was going to be held. Damien may just be there waiting for his opportunity."

"I'll go with him," JD said.

"What should I do?" Squirrel asked, his eyes dancing with excitement.

"You stay with me and Mick." Howie didn't want Squirrel to get into a situation that he couldn't handle. Nor did he want to run the risk of the little

237

guy getting hurt. Squirrel didn't know Damien as well as they did. "We'll start with some of the classrooms down the two hallways; he could be in one of them. We'll check the east hallway first. After we're done with the classrooms, we'll go down to the basement."

Squirrel glanced toward the stairway leading to the lower level. "You mean he could be down there?" He began moving in that direction.

Howie grabbed Squirrel by the arm. "Hold on. I told you to stay with us. He could be anywhere, so be alert and keep your eyes open."

"And if we spot him, then what?" Mick asked.

"Just let me at him," Squirrel said, scrunching up his face to show that he was ready for a fight. "I'll clean his clock for conking me over the head and sticking me in that casket." He slapped his hands together and vigorously rubbed them back and forth. "Just let me at that sucker. He's going to be sorry that he ever met me."

"My word!" Father Duval exclaimed once Mary finished recounting Mick's experience with Damien that night in the cemetery nearly a year ago. "What a horrible thing to go through!"

"I know. Mick still has nightmares about it."

"Oh, the poor lad. Who wouldn't have nightmares after that experience?" The priest crossed himself and kissed the silver cross suspended by a chain hung around his neck. "It just reaffirms my belief in the existence of evil in this world."

"And Damien is surely evil," Mary said. "I can—" She jumped when the knock at the door came. She looked to Father Duval for direction.

"Don't worry, I'll handle it," Father Duval whispered. He put his finger to his lips and motioned for her to move to the side of the room where she couldn't be seen if the door was opened. Once she was situated, he went to the door, paused, looked back at her, and gave her a reassuring smile. "Who is it?" he asked.

"Oh, Father, it's me, Mrs. Amundson." The woman's high-pitched voice sounded as though she was on the verge of hysteria. "You need to come, quick!"

"Why? What's wrong?"

"An elderly man just fell on the steps." The lady sounded like she was about to cry. "The poor man may have broken his hip! He's asking for you, and Father, he's claiming that he was pushed."

"Go ahead," Mary said. "I'll be safe here."

"Are you sure?"

"Yes, don't worry. I'll keep the door locked."

The screams and commotion sent alarms off in Howie as he, Mick, and Squirrel rushed out into the hallway after having finished checking out the first classroom.

"Man, what's all that screaming about?" Squirrel asked.

"I don't know, but it's coming from the narthex area," Mick said.

"Let's go!" Howie took off. When he and his friends got to the narthex, a crowd was milling about the open entrance doors into the sanctuary. Both Adam and JD were already pushing their way through the crowd. Howie quickly joined them with Squirrel right behind him. When they broke through, Howie discovered the reason for the commotion. An older woman lay on the floor near the confessional booth in the back of the sanctuary, her face pasty gray. Another woman, younger, knelt beside the older woman and fanned her with one of the wedding programs.

"What happened here?" Adam asked a man sitting in the last pew whose face had been drained of color.

"She fainted when she saw..." He swallowed hard and pointed to the confessional booth. "She just wanted to see what one looked like inside."

Howie and his friends went to the confessional and opened the door.

"Whoa!" Squirrel stumbled backwards, his eyes doubling in size.

"Oh, my gosh!" Adam cried.

Both Howie and Mick stood speechless at the sight.

"Get those people back!" JD commanded two men standing by the entrance to the sanctuary, gawking at the sight. "And shut those damn doors!" The police detective pointed to a heavy-set man in his forties. "You! Call the police and make it fast." He turned his attention back to the waxen corpse of an elderly woman propped up against the corner of the confessional. Pinned to her pink sweater was a note addressed to Mick.

Sorry, my friend, but this was the best wedding gift I could get on such short notice. Hope you like it because it can't be exchanged. D

P.S.

Sorry, but I can't stay for the reception; I have other plans.

"Mary!" Mick cried and pushed through the crowd before heading in the direction of Father Duval's study.

At first, Mary had thought the knock at the door was Father Duval returning. "Who is it?" she asked, wanting to make sure.

"It's the limo driver, ma'am. Your husband asked me to come get you. He would like for you to meet him in the limo."

Mary opened the door. The young man dressed in a dark suit, white shirt and black bow tie, and wearing a black cap, gave her a friendly smile. "Congratulations." He presented her a bottle of champagne. "Our compliments to you on your wedding day."

"Thank you." Mary took the champagne and glanced down the corridor leading to the narthex area. The corridor went the full length of the building and then turned sharply to the right; even though it made another turn to the left, the corridor acted as an echo chamber. "Do you know what that commotion is all about?"

"Some pregnant woman fainted," the young man said. "I guess it was just too warm for her in the church with all the people."

"Is she going to be okay?" Mary looked in the direction.

"Don't worry. Her husband said that she'd be okay." He cleared his throat. "Speaking of husbands, if you would come this way, your husband is waiting."

"Why aren't we going out the front way?"

"Because Mick—your husband told me I could call him by his first name—he wanted you to know that it would be safer by avoiding the crowds. He said that you would know what he meant by that. Do you?"

"Yes," Mary said, nodding.

The young man showed her to the rear door leading out to a small parking area for church staff. The black limo was waiting, engine running, its tinted windows providing privacy for her and Mick. "Allow me," the limo driver said as he opened the door to the backseat for her.

Mary went to get in and then froze. "You!" she cried.

"Hello, Mary."

She attempted to back out, but Damien grabbed and pulled her in as the limo driver shoved her from behind. The driver slammed the door. Within moments, he raced to the driver's door, opened it, got in, and sped away.

Chapter 73

Howie and his two partners, with Squirrel trailing behind them, ran down the tiled corridor toward Father Duval's study, the sounds of their footsteps echoing throughout the long hallway. JD had stayed where they had found the body, explaining that he needed to secure the scene and wait for the police.

"The door's open!" Mick cried as he and the others approached the partially opened door leading to Duval's office. Their fears were realized as soon as they barged into the room.

"Where is she?" Squirrel asked.

"He's got her. I just know it." Mick's voice shook with rage. "We've got to find them."

"We will," Howie said, feeling that Damien had already gotten away.

Adam moved to the door and peered down the hallway. "They probably went out the back door."

"Where's that?" Howie asked as he and the others joined him out in the corridor.

"It's down the hallway and to the left. It leads to where Father Duval parks his car."

"Let's go!" Squirrel started in that direction.

Howie grabbed the would-be detective by the arm. "You stay here and keep an eye out." With Squirrel vowing that he would stomp Damien if he should meet up with him, Howie and his partners dashed down the hallway, flew down a short flight of stairs, and pushed through the back door to the outside. The only sign of activity were kids playing in the backyard of one of the houses across the alley.

"Let's go back," Mick said. "They must still be in the church."

"Wait a minute." Howie pointed in the direction of the houses across the alley. An elderly man sat on the back porch looking at them. "Let's go talk to that guy."

"Do you think he could've seen something?" Adam asked.

"Maybe. It's a cinch that Damien didn't get away by going out the front." Howie turned to Mick. "They're not in the church anymore. Damien's too smart for that."

If the sight of three young men rushing toward him frightened the old gentleman on the porch, he didn't show it. He just kept rocking in his rocking chair and puffing on a pipe.

"Mighty peculiar wedding you're having," the old man said as the three detectives came up to the porch.

"We looking for the bride," Mick said. "Have you seen her?"

"By those fancy duds you're wearing, you must be the groom." The man took a deep puff, blew out curls of white smoke, and chuckled. "What's the matter? You lose your bride already?"

"Have you—"

"In my day and age that was called a Shivaree. Do you know what that is?"

"No sir." Howie waved Mick off.

"Well, son, let me tell—"

"Look!" Howie said. "We don't have time to hear your story. Did you see the bride?"

"I've been sitting on this porch for nearly fifty years watching weddings. Yours is the most peculiar."

"Just tell us what you saw!" Mick said.

"Don't get snappy with me young man," the man shot back, pointing the stem of his pipe at Mick. "You're on my property and I don't take a liking to people getting huffy with me. No siree."

Adam stepped forward, tapping Mick on the arm as a signal to back away. He offered a warm smile to the man and spoke in a gentle tone. "I apologize for my friends, but we just want to know if you saw the bride come out of the back door of the church."

"Why didn't you ask that in the first place?" He tapped the bowl of his pipe on the weathered palm of his hand and blew away the ashes. "I sure did. Thought it was mighty odd her coming out the back like that."

"Was she alone?"

"Nope." The old guy waved at some children walking by.

"Who was with her?'

"The driver."

"Driver?"

"Yep."

Howie took hold of Mick's arm when he started to move forward. "Let Adam handle this," he whispered.

"So she got into a car?" Adam asked.

"Yep. One of those long black fancy ones." He took out a small pocketknife, opened it, and using the knife's blade, began digging in the bowl of the pipe. "Mighty strange thing about it, though."

"What do you mean?"

"Well, the poor thing acted as if she didn't want to get in. By the looks of it from here..." The old man leaned forward in his chair. "Now you got to understand that my eyesight ain't as good as it use to be, but it sure looked like to these old eyes that the driver either shoved her in or somebody in that fancy car pulled her in." He reached in his flannel shirt pocket and pulled out a pouch of tobacco. "Mighty peculiar wedding if you ask me!" he yelled at the three young men who had already turned and were rushing back to the church.

"I wouldn't try to get out," Damien warned. Mary sat across from him in the back of the limo. "We are traveling around sixty miles per hour right now and I'm afraid your pretty white wedding dress would get soiled and torn if you decided to leave." He glanced out the window. "And even if we have to slow down, you won't be able to get out because the doors are locked and the controls are with me."

"Why are you doing this?"

"Does wearing white mean that you're still a virgin?" When no reply came, Damien reached down to the floor and retrieved the bottle of champagne that Mary had dropped when she was pulled into the limo. He held the bottle in front of her. "Would you care for some? I brought glasses." He read the label on the bottle. "Hmmm, it's not the best, but it's adequate."

"You're insane!"

Damien leaned back, popped the cork, and poured himself a glass of champagne. "I believe it would be proper for me to offer a toast to you and your husband. What shall it be now?" Silence filled the car. He raised his glass. "May you have a wonderful life together...as long as it lasts." He took a sip. "Or is this one better? May you have a wonderful life together until...hmmm, now how do the wedding vows go?" After another sip, he continued. "Oh, yes, I remember now...until death...us do part."

Chapter 74

"Nobody came this way," Squirrel reported as Howie and his partners got back to where they had left him in front of Father Duval's study. "How about you guys? Did you have any luck?"

"What are we going to do now?" Mick asked Howie.

"I don't know yet. Let me think this through."

"I guess you guys didn't find her, huh?"

"Come on, Howie," Mick pleaded. "What are we going to do?"

"Just give me a second, will you? I'm thinking." Howie massaged the back of his neck.

"Did you guys look in the basement?"

Adam gently touched Mick on the arm. "Don't worry. We'll get her back."

"Damien must have her, huh?"

Howie tried to figure out what their next step should be. He needed to come up with a plan of action and fast.

Squirrel tugged at Howie's arm. "Damien got her? Is that right?"

"Yeah, yeah, he's got her."

"Why that lousy no good creep!" Squirrel slammed his fist into his palm. "I'm going to cream that guy when I meet up with him."

"We can't waste any more time here," Mick said, his tone panicky.

"That guy's going to be mash potatoes when I'm done with him," Squirrel announced.

"We've got to go after them," Mick pleaded with Howie. "And now!"

"I agree with Mick," Adam said.

"Okay, but where did he take her?" Howie asked, hoping his tone didn't reveal his own frustration. "To hop in the car and race off is fine, but in what direction? We need to think this through." He looked at Mick. "I know that every second counts, but if we go off half cocked…" The look of dread on Mick's face indicated that the dilemma of their situation had sunk in.

"Could he have taken her back to the beauty shop?" Adam asked.

"I don't think so." Howie could have used a shot of bourbon to ease his anxiety about not coming up with any quick answers. "He knows that his cover there has been blown."

"How about the funeral home?" Squirrel piped in. When no one responded, he yanked on Howie's sleeve.

"What?"

"The funeral home?" Squirrel said, looking pleased that he now was being listened to.

"What are you talking about?"

"Maybe he took her to the funeral home. You know. The one where he conked me over the head and stuffed me in that wooden box."

"He wouldn't go there during the daytime," Adam said. "Not in a limo with a woman wearing a wedding dress."

"Yeah, I guess you're right," Squirrel said, sounding like his horse had just finished last in the race. "I didn't think of that." He touched the top of his head where Damien had hit him. "When I meet up with that creep again, I'm going to finish what he started."

Mick shot a look at Squirrel. "What did you say?"

"That I'm finishing what he started."

Mick turned to his partners. "That might be it!"

"What are you talking about?" Howie asked.

"I think I know where he may have taken her."

"Where?"

"Taylors Falls."

"Are you sure?" Adam asked.

"No, but Damien promised Mary that they'd go back and see the sights together some time, and you know Damien."

"I see what you're getting at," Howie said. It was a risk, but one they had to take. Standing around and talking wasn't helping Mary. And he hadn't come up with any other plan of action. "Come on, let's get to my car." The three of them started down the hallway toward the front entrance.

"Wait for me!" Squirrel yelled. "I helped, didn't I?" he asked as soon as he caught up to them, following on their heels. "What was it I said that gave you the clue, huh?"

"How long do you think it'll take to get there from here?" Mick asked Howie.

"I don't know. Maybe forty, forty-five minutes."

"Come on, guys. How did I give you the clue?"

Adam looked back at Squirrel. "You said that you wanted to finish what Damien started with you."

"How's that a clue?"

"Damien thinks he can always finish what he sets out to do."

Squirrel trotted to keep pace with Howie and his partners. "I get it now. He's taking her there to finish what he started. Right?"

"That's right," Adam replied.

Squirrel's eyes lit up. "So that's how detective thinking works." His nose began twitching. "I'm getting good at this stuff."

When they got to the front of the church Howie quickly explained to JD what was going on and where they were going.

"I'd go with you, but I've got to stay here to secure this scene," JD said.

"I'll go," Squirrel piped up.

"Not this time." Howie motioned for him to stay put.

"But I want to help."

"You stay and help JD." Howie ran to join his partners who were already heading out the front door of the church. The three of them scrambled down the steps and ran toward the church's parking lot. Within moments, they hopped in Howie's car and took off.

"How much of a head start do you figure they have?" Adam asked from the backseat of the car.

"Not more than fifteen minutes," Howie replied, hoping they could make up the time before Damien finished what he had started out to do.

Chapter 75

"Where are you taking me?" Mary demanded, still determined not to show any sign of fear to her abductor.

Damien gazed out the window at the passing farmland before turning to her. A smirk formed on his face as he studied her. "Are you quite positive that you wouldn't like a glass of champagne? After what you have been through, I'm sure you could use a drink by now."

"You're not going to get away with this."

"I'm not?" Damien put his hand to his chest as though he had been wounded by her remark. "Why, Mary, I'm surprised at you for making such an unfounded statement. You wouldn't allow one of your students to get away with something like that, would you?" He folded his arms and settled back into his seat. A smug look came over him. "It appears to me that I've already gotten away with it. Don't you agree?" He reached over and touched her knee, laughing when she jerked away. "After all, I have you, don't I?" he asked, his tone mocking.

"Not for long. Mick will find me."

"He will?"

"Yes, he will," Mary said, her tone defiant.

"You know, you're quite lovely when you're angry. Has anyone ever told you that?" Damien waited for a response but none came. "As far as your husband finding you, I have my...Mary, I just realized something." He waited for a moment. "Aren't you curious to know?"

"Not in the least."

"I'll share with you anyway." His eyes bore into her. "Am I the first to refer to Mick as your husband?"

Mary glared at him but said nothing.

"I'll ignore your rudeness for now." Damien sneered. "I have my doubts about your wonderful husband finding you." A thin smile formed on his lips. "At least he won't find you for a while and when he does..."

Mary looked out the window to get a sense of where she was being taken. As soon as they turned onto Highway 95, a sense of dread came upon her. "We're going back to Taylors Falls, aren't we?"

"You're quite observant."

"Why Taylors Falls?"

"Oh, Mary, don't be so naïve. We have some unfinished business there." He looked out the window at a herd of cows grazing in a pasture. "So why don't you sit back, relax, and enjoy the scenery? We'll be there shortly."

Mick looked in vain for any sign of the limo up ahead in the Saturday afternoon traffic. "Pass that truck!" he ordered Howie. "We've been following it too long! We've got to make up some time."

"Take it easy, will you? I'll pass it the first chance I get." Howie had been pushing the accelerator ever since they got onto the main highway. Only once did he slow down to below the speed limit; that was when a highway patrol car had turned onto the road ahead of them. For a moment, he had thought about flagging the officer down, explaining the situation and asking for assistance, but he thought it would take too much time. He was relieved when five minutes later the police car turned off onto a county road.

"I sure hope I'm right on this," Mick said, sounding like he was beginning to second-guess himself.

"Don't be too hard on yourself," Adam said. "Taylors Falls would've been my first guess as well." He leaned forward and gave Mick a reassuring pat on his shoulder. "Don't worry, we'll get Mary back."

"But what if he took her someplace else?"

Howie glanced over at Mick. The poor guy had been cracking his knuckles for the past ten minutes. "She's got to be there," he said, trying to sound optimistic. He just hoped that if she was there, they would make it in time.

The buzzing of the intercom startled Mary. She watched as Damien opened up a compartment on his passenger door and took out a phone.

"Yes, I understand," Damien said. "No, there may be cars there." He glanced at Mary and smiled. "We'll go to the other one. It's the first turn to the right after the park." He placed the phone back in its compartment and closed the panel door. "That was our driver. Would you like to know what he was inquiring about?"

Mary glowered at him, determined not to allow Damien to get her involved in any of his sick mind games. She turned and looked out the window.

"You're being rude again, Mary. After all, it's your wedding day and I was good enough to show up as your guest." Damien sneered. When he continued, his voice had an ominous edge to it. "Even though you offended me, I'm going to be nice and tell you anyway." He leaned toward her. "Instead of going to the main parking lot where we were before, there's another parking area that very few people know about. We can park there and not be seen from the road. Won't that be cozy?"

Mary shut her eyes, not wanting Damien to see her fear.

Chapter 76

Although Squirrel felt important helping Detective Davidson, he had wanted to go with Howie and the others. When he reported to Davidson, the police detective gave him a hard, cold look, but didn't say anything.

Squirrel shifted from one foot to the other and back again. "Come on, Detective," he finally said. "Let me help."

Davidson eyed him for several more seconds. "Okay, but just as a favor to Howie. And just make damn sure you don't screw this up." He pointed toward the confessional booth where the woman's body still sat. "I'm going to be over there doing some stuff." He tapped Squirrel on the chest. "You stay here and keep the curious onlookers away." He tapped the little guy's chest again, but this time, harder. "Do you understand?"

"Sure. Anything you say."

"And keep your mouth shut."

Squirrel almost pulled out his invisible key to show the detective that he would lock his lips, but nodded instead, knowing from experience, that cops didn't have much of a sense of humor except amongst themselves.

Davidson walked away, only glancing back once.

As Squirrel now stood there trying to look official, he took notice of an older, rather stout woman entering the narthex area. She paused, looked at him, and started moving in his direction. Although he flashed her a smile, he wondered what the old bag wanted.

"Are you one of the detectives?" she asked him, coming so close that she nearly overwhelmed him by her perfume.

Squirrel glanced behind him toward the confessional. He was in luck. Davidson's back was to them. "Yeah. Yeah, I'm a detective. Have you got a problem, lady?"

"What! Me? Of course not." She sounded offended that anyone would even think a woman such as she would have a problem. "I'm merely inquiring about what happened to the others."

"Others?" Squirrel wrinkled his nose. "What others?"

"The other detectives."

"Oh, those guys." When he sucked air between his teeth, the woman moved back a step. "They took off after I told them where they could find the missing bride."

Her eyes enlarged to twice their size. "You gave them the clue? Really?" Squirrel nodded. "Yeah, but that's between you and me." He gestured with his thumb toward the front entrance door. "Move on lady, we need to keep this area clear. There's detective kind of stuff going on right now."

"I hope they catch whoever did this terrible thing."

"You can bet that diamond necklace you're wearing on it." Squirrel looked back toward Davidson. He lowered his voice. "I'll tell you what..." His nose began twitching. "I'll give you eight-to-five odds that we'll catch the creep before the sun sets."

The woman looked at him as though her girdle had just shrunk two sizes. "How dare you even mention gambling in the House of God?" She made the sign of the cross, threw out her chest at him, and huffed away.

"Loser!" Squirrel muttered under his breath. No sooner had the woman walked away when Father Duval came into the narthex, spotted him, and approached. Squirrel gulped, wondering if Duval had heard what he had muttered.

"My son, thank you for helping out here."

"Sure thing, Father." He paused. "It's okay me calling you, Father, isn't it? Me not being a Catholic."

"Of course it's okay."

"Thanks." Squirrel pointed to the confessional. "I suppose you're going to have to exercise that thing." He wondered why Duval gave him such an inquisitive look. "You know what I'm talking about, Father, don't you? When you guys put on your fancy duds and squirt some of that holy water on it to chase the evil spirits away."

Father Duval smiled. "Oh, yes, I'm sure we'll have to do that." He cleared his throat. "And what kind of work are you in?"

"Me? Ah, I deal...ah, with financial speculation."

"Hmmm." Father Duval fingered a button on his coat. "So does that mean you handle other peoples' money?"

Squirrel's eyebrows shot up. "Yeah...yeah, I never thought of it that way." He glanced around, wanting to make sure no one was within hearing range. "Let me tell you though, Father, it's a tough way to make a living."

"I imagine it is."

"Hey, thanks for understanding. You're all right for a priest."

Duval's eyes continued to smile. "I'm glad you feel that way."

"You know, Father..." He paused. Davidson still had his back toward them. Squirrel nevertheless spoke in hushed tones. "I've been thinking about changing my line of work."

"Really?" Duval's eyebrows rose slightly. "And what would you like to be doing?"

Squirrel moved so close to Duval that he could smell his after shave lotion. He didn't think priests were allowed to wear stuff like that, but he wouldn't rat on the guy. "Father, can you keep something to yourself?" he asked, not wanting to take any chances that Duval would mention it to

Davidson.

"Keeping secrets is part of what I do."

"Is that right? Cool." Squirrel's nose twitched several times. He raised his right hand, blew on his fingernails, and made a show of buffing them on the lapel of his sport coat. "I'm thinking about becoming a detective."

"Is that right? Well, I'm sure it must be a noble profession."

"You think so, Father?"

"Oh, yes."

Squirrel glanced around again. "How about blessing me, then? Can you do that?"

"Of course."

"Father?"

"Yes."

"Before you do me up, I need to confess something."

"That's not necessary."

"I don't know about that." Squirrel dug in his ear with his pinky finger. "After I tell you, you might change your mind."

"I doubt that, but go ahead, my son. I'm listening."

"Father, I hope you don't hold this against me, but I hate fish."

Chapter 77

The limo turned off the highway onto a dirt road flanked by evergreens. When the black sleek car finally came to a stop, Mary felt isolated. Trees and bushes shielded the car from the highway. Without drawing attention to herself, she slowly slipped off her high heel shoes, knowing that she wouldn't be able to run very far in them. She tried to see the highway through the trees, but couldn't. The highway couldn't be that far away, however; she could hear the sounds of cars going by. Her plan was to make it to the highway. If she could do that, she might have a chance.

Howie kept his foot on the gas pedal. He had seen a sign indicating that they still had fifteen miles to go until they reached Taylors Falls. He shot a sideward glance at Mick. His partner had been quiet for the past twenty minutes. "How are you doing, Mick?"

"Not good. What if she's not there? What if..." He turned away and stared out the window.

"Hang in there, Mick," Adam said. "I've been praying that we find her."

"Thanks, I appreciate that."

Howie hoped Mick wouldn't ask if he had been praying also. If he did, he would have to lie. Praying can be left to Adam. For now, he would concentrate on his driving.

"Isn't this just a splendid spot?" Damien asked. "It's so private and...out of the way. Nobody will bother us here." His eyes flickered with excitement at the thought of having Mick's new bride in his possession. He stared at his prize for several moments before letting his gaze drift down to her shoeless feet. He smiled knowingly at her pathetic attempt to outwit him. "Would you care for a glass of champagne before we go?" He glanced at her feet again.

"No, I..." To Damien's amusement, her eyes flickered as she hesitated. "Yes, I think I'll need one."

"So you've changed your mind. How very nice." Damien got a wine glass, filled it half full, handed it to her, and refilled his glass. Her feeble attempt to buy time amused him. "Before you take a sip, allow me to make another toast to your happiness."

Chapter 78

"Hang on!" Howie yelled while negotiating a sharp curve. He almost lost control when the car fishtailed. Out of the corner of his eye, he saw Mick grab the dashboard.

"Take it easy, will you!" Adam shouted from the backseat. "You almost lost it that time!"

"But I didn't!" Howie's heart pounded. He checked the rearview mirror. Adam's teeth were clinched and his hair tousled, but he appeared okay.

"How much longer?" Mick asked.

"Another ten minutes."

"Damien better not have..." Mick pounded his fist into the palm of his hand. "So help me, God, if he's hurt her, I'll..."

"Don't worry, we'll get there in time," Howie said, trying to sound reassuring, but not feeling it himself.

Damien lifted his champagne glass toward Mary. "Here's my toast. Are you ready?"

Mary sat unmoving. She remained silent, hoping that he would see the loathing she had for him.

"Here's to you and Mick." Damien raised his glass to his lips. "May the two of you always be blessed with fond memories of this, your wedding day." He took a sip. "And may you always have a warm spot in your heart for me." He wiped the corner of his eye as though wiping a tear away. "Pardon me, Mary, but at times I'm even touched by my own words."

"You're sick!"

Damien moved his glass toward hers and waited. He showed no sign that her remark had upset him. "My dear, in order to validate the toast, we need to clink our glasses together. I believe that's the tradition."

Mary kept her glass in her lap, holding it with both hands. Her eyes met his, but she refused to raise her glass.

"What's wrong? Didn't you like my toast?"

Although she felt like throwing the champagne in his face, she refrained, knowing that she needed to buy as much time as possible. "My stomach's upset. If I drink this now, I'll get sick."

"Oh, I'm so sorry to hear that," Damien said, his tone mocking. "What a terrible thing to happen on your wedding day." He leaned forward. "Is there anything I can do to help?"

"No. I just need some time."

"And then you'll toast with me?"

Mary nodded, knowing that she would never do it.

"And how long do you suggest that we wait?"

"Fifteen, twenty minutes, and then I should be fine."

Damien settled back and crossed his legs. He took a sip and slowly moved his finger around and around the edge of his glass as he studied her. Several moments passed before he spoke. "My poor Mary, I can understand having a nervous stomach on one's wedding day, I really can. After all, such a day can generate a lot of tension. Making sure everyone gets the right flower, and the ushers needing last minute instructions." He cupped his chin with his hand, tapping his forefinger on the side of his cheek as he looked upward. "Hmmm, now, let's see, what did I forget?" His eyes locked onto hers and he grinned. "And oh, yes, let's not forget attending to *unexpected* guests." He raised his glass to his lips. "Here's to unexpected guests." He gulped down the rest of his drink. "I'm afraid we can't wait any longer. Drink up, now."

She raised the glass, but let it slip from her hand. The glass fell on her wedding dress, spilling its contents, and bounced onto the floor.

Damien glared at the glass and then at her. "That was clumsy." The look in his eyes could only be described as diabolical. "Shall I pour you another glass?"

"No." She put her hand to her mouth. "I think I'm going to get sick. Just give me a minute," she said, and looked away.

"I'll tell you what I'll do. I'll grant you that minute, but that's all." He sat quietly, looking at his wristwatch.

Mary stared out the window. She needed to get to the highway. Her only hope was to flag down a passing car.

"Time's up," Damien announced, cutting short the minute to less than fifteen seconds. "Now, please don't try my patience any longer with your pathetic attempts at stalling for time." His tone turned menacing. "It doesn't matter how long you stall, Mick isn't coming to get you. Do you know why?"

Mary glared at him.

"He won't come because the poor man has no idea where you are. He only knows that you are with me." Damien chuckled. "Excuse me. I don't mean to snicker, but it just occurred to me what a comforting thought it must be for Mick knowing that his new bride is in my possession." His eyes drifted down to her feet. "Aren't you going to wear your shoes?"

"My shoes?" Mary tried to swallow but her mouth was too dry. "They hurt my feet. I'm not going to wear them."

"I see." Damien stroked his chin. "I've heard high heels can do that." Without taking his eyes off of her, he set his empty glass on the floor and reached into his jacket pocket. He pulled out what looked like a black eyeglass case, opened it, and took out a knife with a pearl handle. "Do you know what this is?" he asked.

She remained silent.

"It's a scalpel." Damien held it up and turned it so she could view it. "I've had this for quite some time. It's my prize possession. I used it in my previous work." He paused. "I once worked in a funeral home. Did you know that?"

Mary put her hand to her chest to calm her pounding heart. She needed to get away from this madman. Once outside, she would somehow distract him and make a run for it. "Yes, I knew that," she finally said.

"How did you...that's right, I forgot. Mick must have told you." Damien chuckled again. "Your husband is quite familiar with this scalpel. I'm sure then that he's also told you how razor sharp it is...or perhaps he showed you the evidence of what it can do." He leaned forward, holding the scalpel in front of him, the blade toward her. "If I were you, I wouldn't try to run away when I open the door."

"I wasn't think—"

"First of all, even if you're not wearing shoes, you're still not going to get very far in that dress; and secondly, when I catch you...and I would catch you..." He caressed her cheek with the scalpel's blade. "I think you know what would happen," he whispered.

Chapter 79

Howie's car flew into the nearly empty parking lot. He slammed on the breaks and skidded to a stop in a cloud of dust and gravel. A half dozen cars were parked in the lot, but no limo.

"How about that campground we passed back on the highway?" Howie asked. "Maybe they turned in there."

Adam leaned forward from the backseat. "I looked as we drove past. The place was deserted."

"Oh man, guys, I blew it!" Mick pounded the dashboard with his fist. His nostrils flared. The veins in his neck grew taut.

"Hold on, Mick," Adam said. "Maybe the limo was here."

"What do you mean?"

"Let's suppose that Damien told the driver to park it someplace else, out of sight," Adam said. "If he brought Mary here, he wouldn't want the limo parked in the lot."

"That's right," Mick said, a note of hope in his voice. "It would draw too much attention, wouldn't it?"

"I don't know about this." Howie didn't place much credence in Adam's theory, but for Mick's sake didn't want to extinguish what little hope they had of finding Mary. Besides, he had no plan B. "There's only one way to find out if it's been here." He put the car in gear and headed toward a maroon 1961 Chevy parked at the far end of the lot. "There's somebody in that car," he said. "Let's hope they saw something."

The occupants of the Chevy turned out to be a teenage boy and girl. As soon as Howie pulled up to the vehicle, Mick jumped out. Howie and Adam soon followed. The wide-eyed teenagers immediately locked their car doors.

Howie rapped on the driver's side window. "We're detectives," he said as the kid fumbled with his car key, attempting to insert it into the ignition. "We just want to ask you a couple of questions." The boy inserted his key, but didn't start the engine. "Roll down the window, would you please?"

The two young people glanced at each other, both looking as though they had been caught cheating on a test. The boy slowly shifted his head toward Howie. "Are you really detectives?" he asked.

"That's right, kid." Howie took out one of his business cards and held it to the window.

The boy read the card and then had the girl read it. After she finished reading it, she whispered something into his ear. He nodded and turned his attention back to Howie. "Our parents didn't send you, did they?"

"You don't have to worry about that." Howie waited while the boy rolled down his window. He noticed that the girl had turned away to button the top couple of buttons of her blouse. "Look, we just want to know if you've seen a black limo in this parking lot."

"A limo? No. Why?"

"How long have you been here?" Mick asked.

The boy's face reddened. "A little over an hour. We...ah...were talking about a science project at school."

Adam stepped to the window. "If you didn't see a limo, did you spot a bride in a wedding dress?"

"No." The boy's face turned into a question mark. "Say, what kind of weird case are you guys working on anyway?"

"I don't have time to go into that now, kid." Howie glanced around. "Do you know if there are any other parking areas around here where somebody can park and have access to those cliffs above the river?"

"Not really." The boy scratched the fuzz on his chin. "There's the campground down the highway, but that would be too far away."

Howie closed his eyes, his head felt like it was going to explode. He could only imagine what Mick must be feeling by now.

"I know where there's another parking area," the girl said.

"Where?" Howie asked.

"Turn left out of the parking lot. I think you go about a third of a mile or so, and then turn left again onto a dirt road."

"Where does that road go?"

"It winds back quite a ways to a grassy area that some people use for picnics."

"And you can park back there?"

"Yes, and you won't be seen from the highway." She looked at the boy who was staring at her with his mouth wide open. "I've never been back there," she explained to him. "Suzie Peterson told me about it. Freddie Becker took her there last month."

"Is it close to the cliffs?" Mick asked.

"Oh, yes," the girl said, but quickly added while at the same time giving a sideward glance toward her companion. "That's what Suzie told me."

"Let's go!" Howie said to his partners. They jumped in Howie's car and peeled out, leaving the kid to figure out just how true his girl had been to him.

Damien opened the limo door, got out, stretched, and inhaled deeply. "Oh, Mary, you must join me. It's gorgeous out here for late October. May I help you?" He extended his hand. When she sat unmoving, he frowned. "Don't make me have to drag you out of there. I wouldn't like that and I guarantee you, neither would you." He brandished his scalpel, slowly waving it back and forth. "I don't think the place Mick rented this limo from would be too pleased if it came back with..." He looked at the scalpel and offered her a half smile. "With stains on the seats...do you understand what I'm saying?"

Mary stepped out, but without taking his hand. She looked around. The area appeared deserted. The chirping of sparrows caught her attention as a squirrel jumped from one branch to another. A few lingering leaves floated down from the trees like miniature parachutes. At another time, in different circumstances, she and Mick would love coming here and having a picnic. "Why are you doing this?"

"It's quite simple," Damien said. "Your husband and his two friends disrupted my life a year ago. I just wish to return the favor."

"I hope you burn in hell."

"Why Mary...what a terrible thing to say." Damien chuckled. "That's a side of you that I didn't know." He continued to smirk as he waited for the limo driver to join them.

"What do you want me to do?" the driver asked, not making eye contact with Mary.

"Stay here," Damien said. "The new bride and I are going for a little walk to see some scenery. I won't be gone long."

Chapter 80

"There it is!" Mick cried, pointing to the left side of the highway where a dirt roadway disappeared amongst the trees and bushes. "She's here. I just know it."

Howie took his foot off the gas and gently pressed the brake.

"Why are you slowing down?" Adam asked.

"Because if the limo is here, we don't want to go charging in there like gangbusters. I'd like to take them by surprise." Howie hoped there was no other way out. The thought of a car chase with Mary at risk wasn't a scenario he wanted.

"He'd better not have harmed her," Mick said, his hand already on the door latch.

Howie turned left onto the dirt road and drove slowly for thirty yards before bringing the car to a stop. He turned off the ignition. "We'll get out here and walk the rest of the way."

The three detectives slipped out of the car, quietly shutting the doors, and started up the dirt road. They hadn't gone more than thirty feet when they came around a bend and spotted the limo some forty yards away.

"Let's go!" Mick started past Howie.

"Hold on!" Howie pointed to the limo driver standing next to a tree along the side of the dirt road. They watched as the man took a drag off a cigarette, flipped it into the bushes, and got into the driver's side of the car.

Adam touched Howie on the arm. "What are we going to do?"

"I'm not sure yet. Let's get closer."

"We don't have much further to go," Damien said as he and Mary moved along a grass-trodden pathway ascending to the cliffs above the river. He walked behind her, prodding her with the point of the scalpel whenever she slowed down.

Each time he had jabbed her, she bit her lip, determined not to give him the satisfaction of hearing her cry out in pain. She felt the warm dampness of blood on the nape of her neck.

"It's unfortunate that your wedding dress is getting so...*soiled*," Damien said. "I hope Mick knows how to get blood stains out. Do you think he

259

does?" When she didn't reply, he jabbed her again. Again, she made no reply. "Mary, I'm quite impressed. I thought for sure you would beg for me to stop. Others have."

Mary looked ahead toward the cliffs. The sound of swift running water indicated that they were getting closer to the river.

"Move a little faster, Mary," Damien ordered. "I have other things planned for the day."

"It's hard walking in this dress."

"Take it off, then," Damien said, laughing in a wicked tone.

Up ahead, the path turned to the right. To the left there appeared to be a sharp decline of five or six feet. She decided that she would make her move there.

Howie and his partners had silently crept up to the limo and now were kneeling behind bushes not more than ten feet away from the driver's side door. Besides their own breathing, the only other sounds were the chattering of a squirrel in a tree and the faint roar of the river in the distance.

"Do you think she's in there?" Adam whispered to Howie.

"I can't tell with those darkened windows, but I don't think so."

"That limo driver must know where they are," Adam said, the tension in his voice increasing.

"I agree," Howie said. "But if we don't take him by surprise, he's going to warn Damien by laying on the horn." He turned to Mick. "Have you got any ideas?"

"Yeah." Mick stormed out of the bushes like a bull charging a red cape, rushed to the limo's door, yanked it open, and pulled the surprised driver out. "Where's Damien?" he said as he slammed the guy against the hood. Before the man could reply, a woman screamed in the distance. Mick looked toward the cliffs. "Mary!" he yelled and took off running.

Chapter 81

Mary's plan almost worked. When they reached the bend in the trail, she pretended as though she tripped, and fell to the ground. Damien offered his hand. As he helped her up, she tried to pull him off balance hoping that he would tumble into the gully, but he held his ground.

"You fool!" he roared. He slapped her several times and yanked her arm behind her back so hard that she screamed in pain.

Howie and Adam ran, following Mick, as their partner headed toward the sound of Mary's scream. In less than a minute, all of them caught sight of Mary and Damien. Mary and her abductor were not more than thirty yards away. He had her by the arm, dragging her toward the top of the cliff.

"Let her go!" Mick yelled as he picked up his pace.

Mary managed to break free from Damien's grip. He went after her, grabbed her, but she pulled away again. Instead of pursuing her, he headed toward the top of the cliff. She ran stumbling toward Mick and the others.

"Are you all right?" Mick asked as he ran to Mary and embraced her. Howie and Adam soon joined them.

"You're safe now," Howie said.

"He's a madman!" Mary cried. "He...he..." Tears streamed from her eyes.

Mick used his handkerchief to wipe the blood off the back of her neck.

"You stay with her," Howie said. "We'll go after him." By the time Howie and Adam got to the ridge, Damien was sitting calmly, legs crossed, in a chair-shaped rock formation on the other side of a sheer wall of rock. The only approach to him was a six-inch-wide ledge that jutted out over the river. He looked at them, smiled, and waved as if greeting old friends.

"Welcome!" Damien shouted. His voice could barely be heard over the rushing water of the river below.

"The game's over!" Howie yelled back.

"It is?"

"You're damn right!"

Damien sneered. "Come and get me, then." He pointed to the narrow ledge. "Are you brave enough, Howie?"

261

"Don't do it!" Adam took hold of Howie's arm. "He's baiting you. I'll go for the police. He's not going anyplace."

Howie jerked free of Adam's grip. "I'm going after him."

"I'm going with you, then."

The two detectives began to inch their way across the ledge as Damien sat watching, looking amused.

"Be careful," Damien taunted. "Don't fall into the nasty river."

"Don't look down...don't look down..." Howie kept repeating the litany to himself while keeping focused on Damien. Although he and his partners had known each other for years, he had never told them about his fear of heights. He swallowed hard as he inched forward. Beads of perspiration formed on his forehead. The cliff wall, clammy to the touch, had few places to grip. Sweat now ran down his face mingling with the mist rising from the churning water below. He wondered how his partner was doing when his foot slipped and he nearly fell.

"Are you okay?" Adam yelled.

Howie's heart beat against his chest. He pressed the side of his face against the wall and closed his eyes. His head pounded in rhythm with his heart.

"Are you all right, Howie?" his partner asked, sounding as though he was close enough to touch him.

"Yeah...I'm okay," he finally managed to say, hoping that his voice didn't reveal the panic he felt. He tried to swallow but the lump in his throat blocked any attempt.

"What's the matter, Howie?" Damien called out. "Are you stuck?"

He focused on Damien. The Evil One, as Adam once called him, sat smirking, enjoying the scene as though he could be watching a Saturday matinee thriller. "Don't look down, don't look down..." he kept whispering as he started inching his way across again.

After several long anxious minutes, they reached the other side and rested, each taking deep breaths. The rock formation Damien sat on was still another seven feet up. They would have to climb it and wrestle him down.

"What now?" Adam asked as he and Howie kept an eye on Damien.

Before Howie could reply to his partner's question, Damien spoke up. "That was very exciting. I didn't think you two would make it. I'm impressed."

"Give it up, Damien. It's over," Howie said.

"I don't think so. Not today." Damien stood up, waved, and leaped into the raging black waters below.

Chapter 82

"So nothing has turned up yet, huh?" Howie shifted the phone to the other ear. "That's too bad." He took his notepad from his shirt pocket, flipped it open, and set it on the desk. "Just a minute, JD." He opened his desk drawer and began rummaging for a pen, wanting to make some notations while he still had his detective friend on the phone. "Hang on for another sec, will you? I want to jot down what you just told me." After trying a couple of pens that didn't work, he settled for a pencil that needed sharpening. As he wrote down the information he heard Davidson yell to somebody named Duraski to get him a cup of coffee.

JD's voice came back over the phone once he had placed his coffee order. "Hey, Cummins, are you about done?"

"Just finished." Howie checked his notes. "Now, you'll call me if you hear anything else?"

"Oh, sure. Why not? I don't have anything else to do with my time."

"Come on, JD, don't be like that." Howie drummed the pencil on his notepad. "Besides, you owe me."

"Like hell I do. I don't owe you a damn thing and you know that." When Davidson mumbled thanks, Howie figured he must have gotten his coffee. "But since I like you," JD continued, "I'll call if anything important comes up."

"Thanks, I appreciate that."

"See you around, Howie."

"Wait, JD. Don't hang up."

"Now what?"

"Just one more thing." Howie glanced at Mick. His partner had informed him that he had postponed his honeymoon trip for a few days with the hopes of Damien's body being found before they left. Howie turned his attention back to JD. "Any problem with me getting in touch with the coroner's office?"

"What do you want to do that for?"

"Just to check in case they have anything."

JD was silent for a moment. "What the hell. Go ahead. And you can drop my name if they give you any trouble. Talk to Stan if he's around. He knows me best."

"Thanks. I'll do that." Howie flipped to a new page in his notepad. "By any chance, would you have the phone number handy?"

"You sure don't ask for much, do you?" JD let out a deep sigh. "Okay. Hang on. Let me dig it up for you."

Howie cradled the phone between his chin and shoulder as he took the information. Out of the corner of his eye he noticed Mick leaning forward in his chair, listening intently to the conversation. Mick would be disappointed, however, since the news coming from JD wouldn't be to his liking.

"Now be damn sure and tell your partners about this," JD said. "I don't want them calling me and tying up my phone. I'm still working two robberies and a murder case."

"Hey, don't worry. I'll tell them right now. They're here in my office."

"They are, huh." JD paused as though he had taken a sip of coffee. "How's Mick doing?"

"He's doing okay." Howie made eye contact with Mick. "He and Mary are leaving on their honeymoon on Thursday."

"That's good. He needs to get away." Howie heard somebody in the background call Davidson's name. "I got to go," JD said.

"What did he say?" Mick asked as soon as Howie hung up the phone.

"That they haven't found Damien's body yet." Adam took the news without expression, but Mick's jaw muscles tightened.

"Are they still dragging the river?" Adam asked.

"Yeah. At least for another couple of days."

"Finding his body would be the best wedding present Mary and I could have," Mick said.

Adam turned to his partner. "You don't really mean that, do you?" he asked, his tone reflecting the shocked expression on his face.

"You better believe I do." Mick's voice turned as hard as the look in his eyes. "It would be better for everybody if the guy drowned. We'd be done with him once and for all."

Howie agreed with Mick. It was obvious by Adam's facial expression, however, that he was uncomfortable with such a strong expression of revenge. In Adam's view of the world, the bad guys would get their due punishment in the afterlife. That wasn't good enough for Howie, though. Guys like Damien shouldn't have to wait.

"What happens after a couple of days?" Mick asked. "They're not just going to give up, are they?"

"There's not much else they can do." Howie felt sorry for Mick. The whole experience had transformed his personality into one that was so out of character for him. His partner, usually easy-going and talkative, had been irritable and sullen for the past several days. Mary had even called and expressed her concern, asking Howie and Adam to do what they could to help Mick move past this. Howie had assured her that they would do everything they could to support her new husband. "Don't worry," he had told her. "If I know Mick, he'll come around."

Mick shifted uneasily in his chair. "Why can't they continue the search until they find him?"

"They figure that the currents could carry Damien's body a long ways, maybe many miles," Howie explained. "They'll keep checking bends in the river and other spots where the body might get snagged on something. Other than that, they just have to wait until it surfaces."

"And when will that be?"

"Nobody knows for sure. JD says that with many of these cases, the body is most often discovered by the general public. It could be somebody out taking a cruise on the river, or kids looking for an out-of-the-way spot to have their beer bust." Howie put his pencil aside and closed his notepad. "But even saying that, it doesn't mean it's going to happen soon. It could be today, or next week, or even next spring."

"That's just great." Mick formed his right hand into a fist and ground it into his palm.

Adam reached over and touched Mick on the shoulder. "Nobody could have survived that current. We saw him go under and he never surfaced."

"I hope you're right because as far as I'm concerned, the river can take his body all the way to New Orleans and flush it into the ocean."

"Come on, Mick," Adam said, having winced at his partner's remark. "You don't really mean that."

"With all my heart."

Howie spoke up. "Adam?"

Adam stared at Mick for a moment longer before turning to Howie. "What?"

"Do we know anything more on the whereabouts of Newt's sister?"

Although Adam appeared as though he wanted to say more to Mick, he turned his attention to Howie. "I've been checking with the library, but nothing so far on Charlotte. Her boss, a Mr. Fillmore, tells me that this isn't at all like her."

"Has he notified the cops?" Howie asked.

"He did, but Fillmore said that although the police were sympathetic, they couldn't do anything about it until there's evidence of foul play. When he pressed them, they sent a detective over to talk to her neighbors."

"And what did he find out?"

"He was told the same thing that I was told. All the neighbors think that Charlotte left for a vacation."

"That's crazy," Mick said. "Nobody would go on vacation without informing their boss. It sounds phony to me."

"I agree," Adam said. "Fillmore told me he made the same argument."

"And what did the cops say?" Howie asked.

"What they usually say in these situations: if they investigated every report of an employee not showing up for work, they'd have no time for anything else." Adam shrugged. "So all we know now is that she's disappeared just like her brother."

Howie drummed his fingers on his desk as he tried to figure out if there was a connection between the two disappearances. Maybe Charlotte found out something and had to be silenced. Or maybe Newt and his sister were splitting Squirrel's dough. Anything was possible. "I wonder if that guy who posed as a detective had something to do with it."

"I've been wondering that myself," Adam said. "Has JD come up with any leads on him?"

"No, but he hasn't had much time to spend on it." Howie had asked JD if he would make a few inquiries amongst his peers. He had, but none of his fellow detectives knew of anyone going around posing as a detective. "With all the cops and the real detectives in this city, someone would hear about a phony like that," JD had pointed out.

"Did you check with Leon's ex-wife?" Mick asked Howie.

"I did, but she's not saying anything more. She's threatening to get a lawyer if I don't quit bothering her. The last time I called her, she hung up on me."

"Did you tell the cops about her involvement?"

"Yeah, but they told me that since she hasn't done anything they weren't prepared to bring her in for questioning."

"But she knows Damien," Mick pointed out.

"Sure, she knows him, but there's no evidence of her being involved with those missing bodies." Howie felt as frustrated as Mick sounded. "As far as that is concerned, there's no evidence that directly links Damien to those bodies either."

"But we know he did it!" Mick cried.

"Yeah, the three of us know that," Howie said, trying to reason with Mick. "But the cops want hard evidence and we don't have that." He understood and identified with his partner's irritation. From their very first contact with Damien, the guy had always managed to stay just beyond their reach. "We need to get a break on this case."

The downstairs entrance door slammed shut. "There's someone coming up the stairs," Adam said. "Maybe this will be that break."

Howie leaned forward, cocked his ear toward his office door, and listened to the stairs creaking. He tried to figure out who it could be by the sounds of the footsteps, but he was too tired to spend the energy speculating.

Within moments the door opened and Squirrel came bouncing in. "Hi, you guys! What's cooking?" He stopped at the poster of Bogart, scrutinized it for a moment, and straightened the frame. He stepped back and eyed the poster once more. Apparently pleased with it now, he gave Howie thumbs-up.

"What do you want?" Howie asked, wondering if Squirrel needed glasses. The poster appeared more crooked than before.

Squirrel walked over by the window and leaned against the wall. "Have they found that Damien character yet?"

Howie took a few minutes to share what he had been told by JD, taking note that Squirrel kept glancing at Mick.

"So, is that it?" Squirrel asked.

"That's about where we stand," Howie said. "As of now, unless we hear differently, we're assuming he's drowned."

"It would serve the jerk right if he became fish food," Squirrel said. "It would be nice, though, to have his sorry butt as proof."

"That's what I've been saying," Mick said. He directed his remarks to Howie. "Without the body, we can't be sure he's dead."

Squirrel's nose twitched. "I'll give you some odds."

"Odds?" Howie gave the little guy a puzzled look. "What are you talking about?"

"Simple." Squirrel blew on his fingernails and buffed them on the sleeve of his jacket. "I'll lay you five-to-three that I can predict within two days—forty-eight hours—of when his body will be found."

"Nothing doing," Howie said.

"What's wrong with that?" Squirrel acted as though he had just been accused of playing with a pack of cards with six aces. A sly smile crossed his face. "Oh, I know your game. You want better odds, don't you? Okay, that's cool. I can do that." He scratched his chin. "Okay, I got it. Because I like you guys, how about if I give you six-to-two?"

Howie shook his head.

"Okay. How about this? Seven-to-three that I can tell you within three days of when they'll find his body." His eyes grew large. "What do you say to that?"

"Let's talk about your partner." Howie wondered if there was anything Squirrel wouldn't give odds on. "Have you heard anything from him?"

Squirrel put up his hands in mock defense. "Hey, I can take a hint. If you don't want to bet, just say so."

"Just tell us about Newt."

"There's not much to tell, but I'd give you four-to-one that the bum skipped town with the cash. He's probably sunning himself on one of those beaches in Florida, surrounded by gorgeous babes." Squirrel wrinkled up his nose. "I hope he's having a good time with my dough while he can because I'm going to wring his neck if I ever catch up with him."

"Why don't you follow up on Newt's sister," Howie said to Adam. "Maybe you could find out who her friends are and talk to them. One of them might know something."

"What's going on with her?" Squirrel asked.

"She's missing," Howie said.

"What do you mean, missing?"

Adam spoke up. "She hasn't been at work all week and the neighbors haven't seen her."

"Oh, man!" Squirrel slapped himself on the forehead. "Five-to-one she's skipped town with her brother." He moaned. "Now, I got two people spending all my hard-earned dough, and it's going twice as fast."

"I don't think so," Adam said, sounding irritated. "She's not that type."

"I tell you what," Squirrel shot back. "I'll give you five-to-one that—"

"Good-bye," Howie said.

"Where are you going?" Squirrel asked.

"It's not me who's going."

After Squirrel was shown out the door, Howie came back and sat down at his desk. He noted that Mick sat staring toward the window. "What's on your mind?" he asked his partner.

"I don't know. It's just that…"

"That what?"

"That I just know Damien's still alive."

Chapter 83

When the phone rang Saturday morning, Adam hoped that it would be Howie calling to tell him that Damien's body had been recovered. Although it had only been a week since their nemesis had leaped into the river at Taylors Falls, it seemed longer than that, much longer. It was the waiting that was getting on his nerves as well as his partner's. He picked up the phone on the third ring. "Hello."

"I need to talk to you."

The female voice sounded familiar. It took a moment for him to realize who it could be. "Is this Charlotte?"

"Yes, you haven't forgotten about me, have you?"

"Of course not." Adam sat down, stunned that Charlotte Aldrich, Newt's sister, would be calling him after all this time. "Where have you been?"

"I can't go into that now."

"Why?"

"Please, you'll have to trust me on this." She lowered her voice. "I'm not at liberty to talk freely right now. I'm at a friend's house. Can you meet me tonight?"

"Sure." Whatever was going on with her, she sounded scared. "Where?"

"At Como Park, by the polar bear exhibit. Do you know where that is?"

"Yeah. What time?"

"At nine."

"Nine? Don't they lock the gates earlier than that?"

"Yes, but if you park down the street across from the Conservatory—that's where they have all those tropical plants..."

"I know the place."

"Well, park on that street and then come back past the Conservatory to the entrance to the zoo. The gate will be left unlocked."

"How are you going to arrange that?"

"I have a friend who works at the zoo. She's agreed to unlock the gate to repay a favor I once did for her. We need to be careful, though. She's afraid."

"Afraid? Afraid of what?"

"That she'll get in trouble for allowing us in. We need to be careful not to

269

be seen. She doesn't want to lose her job."

"Why don't you just come up to Howie's office? I'll—"

"No, I can't. I won't." For a moment, it sounded like she would hang up. "Please trust me on this," she pleaded. "I used to go to the zoo as a child. It's the only place where I'd feel safe right now. Once we're inside the grounds, we'll be by ourselves."

"Okay, I'll be there at nine."

"Thank you so much."

"What's this all about anyway?"

"It's about my brother, Newton."

"What about him?"

Several moments passed before she spoke. "I have information that you and your partners will find very interesting."

"What sort of information?"

"It concerns…" She lowered her voice to a whisper. "Sorry, but I have to go. Please come and come alone."

"Wait, I—" Adam sat unmoving, listening to the dial tone before hanging up. Whatever was going on, Charlotte Aldrich sounded terrified. He picked up the phone and dialed Howie's number.

"MAC Detective Agency."

"Howie, this is Adam. I just got a call from Charlotte Aldrich."

"Is that so?"

Adam heard his partner open his desk drawer and rummage through it, probably getting a pen to take notes.

"Did she tell you where she's been for the past couple of weeks?" Howie asked.

"No, but we're going to meet tonight. Maybe I'll get some answers then."

"Where are you meeting her?"

"Como Park at the polar bear exhibit. At nine."

"What! Why there?"

"That's where she wanted to meet."

"I'll go with you."

"No. She told me to come alone."

"I don't know about that." Howie paused. "I don't like it. It doesn't sound right to me. Why would she want you to come alone?"

"Because she's scared and she only trusts me." He told Howie about Charlotte's friend unlocking the gate for them. "Her friend is concerned that even with Charlotte and myself being there it could draw too much attention. Besides, if the two of us show up, I've got a feeling it might spook Charlotte."

"Did she tell you why she wanted to meet?"

"Yeah, she's got information on her brother for us. I have a feeling that she's going to tell me where we can locate him."

"Good. Squirrel will be glad to hear that. Just be careful."

"Don't worry. I will be."

"And call me as soon as you get back."

"Sure."

At eight-thirty that evening, Howie decided that he didn't want to wait for Adam's phone call. He would go to Como Park and see for himself what was going on. He trusted Adam's ability to handle the situation, but felt uneasy about the meeting and wanted to provide backup. He would have liked to have Mick with him on this, but his partner had left for his honeymoon several days earlier. "Maybe they'll be able to get their minds off of the past couple of weeks," he had told Adam, but not really believing it himself. The newly married couple would be back in three or four days and he hoped by then he would be able to greet them with the news that Damien's body had finally been found. He had just slipped on his coat when the office door opened and Squirrel came jaunting in.

"You look like you're going out," Squirrel said, his nose twitching. "What have you got cooking, a hot date or something?"

"I have a possible lead on your partner."

"On Newt? You do? Hot diggety!" Squirrel slapped his hands together and rubbed them back and forth. "So where is the bum?"

"I don't know, but I hope to find out."

"Let me go with you."

"I don't—"

"Come on, Howie. I won't cause any trouble." Squirrel's face lit up. "You might need an extra pair of eyes."

Howie checked his coat pocket to make sure he had his car keys as he considered Squirrel's offer. "Okay, but you have to follow my orders."

"Will do, boss."

"I'll fill you in on the way."

"Great."

"And don't call me boss." Howie checked the time. If he stepped on it and didn't get pulled over for speeding, they would have a good chance of making it by nine. He knew Adam would be punctual, but hoped Charlotte wouldn't be.

Chapter 84

Adam took a right onto the road across from the Como Park Conservatory and brought his car to a stop nearly a block away. He hoped that his dark maroon Ford parked in the shadows, away from streetlights, wouldn't draw attention. He got out and headed back up the road. Within a few minutes he moved quickly past the Conservatory and headed toward the gate Charlotte had mentioned.

The roar of a lion startled him before he realized that it was coming from inside the zoo's main building where they housed the large cats. For the most part, he had always visited the zoo in the daytime. Those few times he had come in the evening, he had gone with friends. During visiting hours, there were always crowds of people around. Now, at night, however, with nothing but shadows and the sounds of animals, it proved unnerving.

He reached the gate and found it unlocked just as Charlotte had said it would be. The gate squeaked as he opened it. He held his breath as though the very act of breathing might give him away. During the normal comings and goings of the day, the noise from the gate would have been lost amidst the clamor of the people, but now it seemed that even the beasts grew silent as they waited to see who was entering their domain. He scanned the area, but saw no one. Very slowly he pushed on the gate until it opened enough for him to slip through. After closing the gate, he cut behind the main zoo building and took the service drive toward the polar bear exhibit avoiding moving past the bird sanctuary and monkey island. The last thing he wanted was birds and monkeys screeching the alarm that an intruder had entered the area.

He glanced at his watch: five minutes of nine. Quickening his pace, he only stopped once when he thought he saw something move in the shadows. Up ahead he could see the figure of a person, a woman. It had to be Charlotte. She stood at the railing gazing at the polar bear exhibit. When she heard him approaching, she turned toward him and waited; her face gave no hint of what she was feeling as he walked up to her.

"Nice to see you," Adam said. He looked at the two large polar bears in their man-made, open-air habitat. One of the large beasts slipped into their swimming pool as the other one lay lounging. The beast that had been relaxing lifted his head, looked in their direction, and sniffed the air.

"I'm so relieved that you came."

"I told you I would."

Charlotte gestured to the bears. "Don't you wish you could be like them and lie around your very own pool every day and not have a care in the world?"

"I don't know about that," Adam replied, surprised at how relaxed she sounded compared to that morning on the telephone. "I don't think I'd like people watching my every move," he said, deciding that maybe small talk was her way of keeping her nerves calm. "I'd want my privacy."

"Oh, so would I." Charlotte gestured to the cave-like entrance going into the granite wall behind the bears. "See that? They can go into their den when they want to be alone. My friend said that when the zoo constructed this exhibit, they wanted to make it look as natural as possible for the bears. I think it's great, though, that they can roam free in their space without being caged up."

"Well, as long as they stay over there." Adam was thankful for the fifteen-foot-wide, twenty-foot-deep chasm separating zoo visitors from the bears. "You sure picked an unusual place to want to meet."

"She didn't pick it, I did."

Chapter 85

Adam swung around and came face to face with Damien. "You?" He made a move toward Damien, but stopped when he saw the revolver pointed at his chest.

"Do you like it?" Damien asked as he glanced at the weapon he held. "It's my new play toy and it's aimed right at your heart." He smiled at Charlotte. "You've played your part quite well, my dear."

Charlotte brushed past Adam, taking her place by Damien's side.

"You set me up," Adam said.

"And you fell for it." Charlotte moved closer to Damien. "You were right. He went for it just like you said he would."

"She's quite the little actress, isn't she?" Damien said. "I happened to be with her when she called you this morning. She was so good that even I was convinced that she was terrified of something." He motioned with the gun. "Come, let's take a little walk."

Adam didn't move. "Where are we going?"

"Where there's a little more privacy and we can have a better view of these magnificent creatures." He gestured toward the bears. The one that had been in the pool had climbed out and lay next to the other one. "Aren't they a splendid example of raw power? Ursus maritimus is their proper name. Do you know what that means?"

"No, but I'm sure you'll tell me."

"Certainly, it will be my pleasure." A twisted smile appeared on Damien's face. "Ursus maritimus is Latin for sea bear." His right eyebrow rose slightly. "Don't they teach Latin at the seminary?" He paused but his student didn't reply. "You don't seem to be very talkative tonight, Adam. Perhaps this fact will interest you." His tone turned ominous. "Did you know that polar bears are direct descendants of the grizzly?"

"I know that you're a descendant from something that slithers in the dust."

Damien glared at Adam. "You certainly do have a sharp tongue. That's not very appropriate for one who is planning to become a man of the cloth. You'll have to learn some bedside manners." He gestured with the gun. "I think it's time to take that walk."

"Why don't you lead? I'll follow you."

"That's very good. I do hope you keep up your sense of humor, Adam. It will make for a more pleasant evening." Damien motioned to Charlotte. "You know where we're going. Lead the way. Our detective friend will follow you, and I shall be right behind him." He cocked the revolver. "And Adam, don't try anything foolish."

Charlotte led them on the walkway skirting the bear's habitat on the right. When they got to the backside of the exhibit, the ground sloped up to the exhibit's back wall. They moved up the slope. A six-foot, iron rod fence set back several feet from the top of the back wall stretched from one end of the wall to the other. The sign on the partially opened fence's gate read *Warning. Do Not Enter.*

"When did you have him open it?" Charlotte asked.

"That was done earlier." Damien nudged Adam with the revolver. "One of my associates is quite handy at picking padlocks," he said as Charlotte swung open the gate. "Having the gate unlocked is much better than trying to climb over the fence. Don't you agree, Adam?"

The three of them went through the open gate and moved toward the edge of the back granite wall. Adam looked at the bears lounging some twenty feet below. "So are we here to see the sights?"

"Do you know that the polar bear is the largest land predator living today?" Damien asked. "And that they have pointed teeth in the front of their mouths for catching and tearing prey?"

Adam glanced around. If he could catch Damien and Charlotte off guard, he would make a dash for it.

"They're not white in the true sense of the word," Damien continued, obviously enjoying himself. "Their hair is actually transparent." He paused, watching Adam, no doubt hoping to see signs of terror. "Their hair has a hollow core which scatters visible light. It makes their fur appear white. And the—"

"I'm not impressed." Adam locked eyes with Damien. "You didn't bring me here to lecture about polar bears. And if you did, you're boring me."

"Adam, you are so impatient." Damien sighed. "I always thought that furthering one's knowledge was good for the soul."

"That leaves you out then since you don't have a soul."

Damien's mouth twisted into a sneer. "I'll ignore that remark."

"So what are we going to do, now?" Adam asked casually, trying to keep the fear out of his voice.

"It's not what *we,* but what *you* are going to do." Damien peered over the edge at the bears relaxing by the pool. "I'm afraid that you're going to have a little accident. People will say that you were foolish to come here and that you got too close to the edge."

"You're out of your mind if you think I'm going to go along with that." Adam pointed to the gun in Damien's hand. "Go ahead and shoot. Somebody will hear it and call the cops."

Damien smirked. "Adam, you and your partners are so predictable. I anticipated that you would raise that argument." He uncocked the gun and handed it to Charlotte. "She'll shoot you if she thinks you're going to try anything."

"Lady, I give you this," Adam said. "You had me fooled." Anger enveloped him. Anger at Charlotte. Anger at Damien. Anger at himself for being so easily fooled. "How did you ever get hooked up with this guy?"

Charlotte looked to Damien as though seeking permission to reply. After he nodded, she turned to Adam. "We met over a year ago at a gathering. His way at looking at the world intrigued me." She smiled at Damien. "He's very intelligent. Did you know that he planned this whole thing, even the phony detective at the library?"

"Who was that guy, anyway?" Adam berated himself again for being duped.

"His name is Eddie, and he owes his allegiance to Damien."

Adam's eyes shifted to Damien. "So you're up to old tricks again, huh?"

"Yes, and I have one more trick to show you. Take off your coat."

"And if I don't?"

"Then I suppose I'll have to have her shoot you."

"Can I, Damien? Can I?" Charlotte's eyes grew large as she cocked the revolver.

Chapter 86

"I thought you said Adam was meeting her by the polar bears," Squirrel said. "I don't see anybody there."

"Keep your voice down," Howie cautioned. For the past ten minutes he and Squirrel had moved amongst the trees that lined the edge of the service road. They were now nearly directly across from the polar bear exhibit. "He has to be around here someplace. Let's move a little closer."

"I still don't—hey, who's that up there?" Squirrel pointed to the back wall above the bear's enclosure. "Isn't that Adam?"

"Yeah, it looks like him, but who are those—" Howie recognized the ponytail.

"That's Damien, isn't it?"

Howie nodded.

"And that must be Newt's sister," Squirrel said. "What's that she's— Holy cow! It looks like she's pointing a gun at Adam. What's going on?"

"I don't know."

"What are we going to do?"

"Hang on. I'm thinking."

"Are you going to use your rod?"

"What?"

"Your gun. Are you going to use it?"

"Squirrel, I've told you that I don't carry one."

"Maybe you—"

"Look, we've got to get around in back of that exhibit."

"Then what?"

"Then we'll have to distract them in some way so that Adam can make a break for it." Howie's temple pounded as his mind raced. "Whatever we do, it's got to be good."

Squirrel's nose began twitching. "This is a zoo, right?"

"Yeah. Why?"

"And there are wild animals here, right?"

"What are you getting at?"

"I've got an idea."

Howie gave the little guy a skeptical look.

"Trust me, boss," Squirrel said. "Ten-to-one this will work." He took off his jacket and began unbuttoning his shirt as he explained his plan.

Chapter 87

Charlotte's eyes flickered with excitement as she pointed the revolver at Adam. Damien stood next to her, smugly grinning at her intended victim.

"Hold on," Adam said, needing time to formulate a plan. The crazed look on Charlotte's face told him that she wouldn't hesitate to pull the trigger. Obviously, the quiet librarian yearned for something more than cataloguing books. "I'll take my coat off."

"That's more like it," Damien said.

"Tell her to uncock that thing before it goes off." Adam would take his jacket off and fling it at her, hoping that the momentary distraction would give him a chance to make a break. With any luck, he could make it to the gate before she fired. He also counted that she wasn't a good shot; at least, he hoped that was the case. He locked eyes with Damien. "Tell her to do it. I'm not taking my coat off until she does."

She looked to Damien for instruction.

"Do as he says."

"But—"

"Do it!"

Charlotte glared at Adam as she slowly uncocked the revolver.

"It's your turn now, Adam, to live up to your part of the bargain." Damien moved a step closer. "Off with the jacket."

As Adam slipped off his jacket, Damien lunged at him with what looked like a knife. Too late to deflect the thrust, the steel blade penetrated the upper part of his chest near his right shoulder. He cried in pain as Damien pushed him back while twisting the knife before pulling it out. He staggered back a couple of feet, but then, instinctively, rushed his attacker.

"You fool!" Damien cried as he slammed his fist into Adam's wound.

Adam moaned. He stumbled backwards and slumped to his knees, his chest and shoulder exploding with searing agony.

Charlotte's eyes flickered with excitement. "I didn't know you were going to stab him."

"Nor did he," Damien calmly replied. He picked up Adam's coat and used it to wipe the blood off his hands and the knife.

"Damn you..." Adam's chest felt as though a thousand nerve endings had come into contact with white-hot irons; his breath came in short spurts, his vision momentarily blurred, beads of sweat broke out on his brow. He placed his hand where he had been stabbed. Warm, wet blood oozed onto his fingers.

"Do you need help getting up, Adam?" Damien asked, his tone, mocking. "Let me help you." He extended his hand.

"Get away from me!" Adam knocked Damien's hand aside, and struggled to his feet. He blinked several times to clear his vision and took a shaky step toward Damien.

"You think you're brave, but you're still a fool," Damien chided as Adam took another step toward him. "When will you ever learn?" He thrust the knife into Adam's right thigh, pulling it out in an upward motion.

Adam screamed in agony and sank to his knees. He struggled to stay upright, but fell over on his side.

"I warned you," Damien said as he squatted beside his victim. "We're going to let you bleed for a while."

"Then what?" Charlotte asked in a voice filled with anticipation.

"And then I have a little surprise for him."

Before Damien stabbed Adam the second time, Howie and Squirrel had quickly circled around to the back of the polar bear exhibit and crept up the incline to the gate at the fence. While Howie positioned himself at the partially open gate, Squirrel moved toward the far end of the fence and began climbing it.

Howie swore under his breath when Damien stabbed his partner in the leg. He almost rushed in, but with Charlotte and Damien facing in his direction, he knew that he wouldn't make it five feet before being spotted. Once spotted, he would find himself in the same predicament as Adam. His only hope was that Squirrel's plan would distract Charlotte and Damien long enough so that he could cover the distance between them and surprise the two of them. Once he wrestled the gun from Charlotte, he would have the upper hand. He didn't like guns and had never fired one, but he was ready to use one now. If it appeared as though Damien was about to stab his partner again, however, he would have no choice but to rush them and take his chances.

"Why are you with him?" Adam asked Charlotte, getting the words out in spite of his labored breathing. He fought against passing out.

"And why not with me?" Damien said, sounding offended. "You should know that I have excellent character references." He knelt to examined Adam's shoulder and leg. "My, my, your clothes are soaked in blood." He offered Charlotte a knowing smile. "In another minute or two we'll be ready for tonight's finale."

"What are you planning?" Charlotte asked, her voice as shaky as her hand holding the gun. "Are you going to kill him?"

"Me? Of course not. Our friend here is going to have an accident of almost...shall we say of biblical proportion." Damien turned to Adam. "I suspect you're familiar with the story of Daniel and the lion's den, aren't you?" When no reply came, he continued. "I couldn't arrange that, but will a polar bear's den be sufficient?"

Charlotte gasped. "With him bleeding, they'll tear him apart."

"Yes, I believe they will." Damien took hold of Adam's leg and began dragging him to the edge.

In spite of his injuries, Adam kicked Damien in the knee causing him to fall to the ground.

"How dare you!" Damien roared. He quickly got to his feet and stomped Adam in the chest several times. "If he does that again, shoot him!"

Charlotte nodded. "I will. I—"

The ear-piercing cry of a wild animal shattered the night air. Both Damien and Charlotte turned to look. A naked, ape-like man stood not more than thirty feet away, jumping up and down. The ape-man grunted and screeched while beating on his chest. Charlotte screamed as the beast came rushing at them.

Squirrel's appearance even took Howie by surprise. In the dark, the little guy had enough chest and body hair that he could be mistaken for an ape. Squirrel had told him that the odds were five-to-one, maybe even six-to-one that they would think some kind of wild beast had escaped. Howie had been skeptical, but nevertheless went along.

Now, as Charlotte and Damien had their backs turned to Howie, he broke his cover and ran toward them. Within seconds, he slammed into Charlotte, jarring the gun out of her hands and knocking her to the ground. She screamed as the ape-man came upon her.

Damien went for the gun, but Howie leaped on him. The two of them rolled on the ground wrestling for possession of the weapon. They rolled to the edge, teetered there for a moment, and plunged into the darkness below.

Chapter 88

Howie couldn't be sure how long he had lain there. His arm was broken. He was sure of that. And maybe his left leg as well. When he tried to move, he winced in agony, clenching his teeth so he wouldn't cry out. His rib cage ached with every breath. To take a deep breath proved impossible. With labored effort, and only after several tries, he managed to sit up. Even though the night was cool, perspiration ran down his brow.

It took several moments for Howie to recall what had happened. Charlotte had screamed. While Squirrel kept Charlotte occupied, he and Damien had struggled. He remembered grabbing Damien's wrist to prevent him from using his knife. They had rolled over the edge and plunged into the darkness below. The thought of his adversary heightened his foreboding, and he deliberately pushed his pain aside. When he checked his surroundings, however, he quickly forgot about Damien.

Two massive mountains of white fur with coal-black eyes stared at Howie from twenty feet away. Both bears were on all fours. With heads lowered, they swayed back and forth. Their heavy breathing came in menacing snorts. The beasts were obviously not pleased with sharing their domain with a two-legged creature.

Howie realized his options were limited. He couldn't run if he had wanted to, and even if he were able, there was no place to run. The closest wall was at least ten feet away. He could, though, hobble to the wall and try to scale its jagged surface.

Movement near the back wall grabbed Howie's attention. He glanced back and forth between the two creatures he could see and the area from where he now heard noise accompanying the movement. The sounds were human…shoes shuffling on cement. Within moments, Damien staggered out from the shadows.

"You're mine now!" Damien cried as he moved toward Howie. His right arm hung limp, but his left hand held the knife.

"Stay there," Howie said, trying to keep his voice calm. The swaying of the bears had become more pronounced.

Damien ignored the warning. He kept coming until he was between Howie and the bears. Either he wasn't aware of the danger behind him or he didn't care.

Howie watched in horror as the larger of the two beasts took a step forward, snarled, and then charged. "Look out behind you!" Howie yelled.

Just as Damien turned, the beast was upon him, knocking him to the ground. Howie watched as Damien tried to ward off his attacker, striking out with the knife. His screams filled the night, answered only by the restless roar of the large cats.

Chapter 89

When Adam first heard the screams, he thought it was Howie. Ignoring his own pain, he dragged himself to the edge and looked down at a horrific scene. Some poor soul was screaming as a snarling bear clawed at him. Over to the right, some ten feet away, another person sat in an upright position. Adam recognized the other person as his partner.

"Howie, are you okay?" Adam yelled.

"Do something! That bear's going to kill him."

Adam wiped the sweat from his eyes and looked around, his mind racing. He was near panic until he saw the revolver. "Get me the gun!" he yelled at Squirrel.

Squirrel picked up the weapon and rushed over to Adam. After handing the gun to the detective, he peeked over the edge at the events unfolding.

Adam aimed the gun to the right of the bear and pulled the trigger. The gunshot sounded like a cannon being shot off. The bullet ricocheted off the cement floor sending pieces of cement flying and startling the bear. Adam fired twice more. This time both bears retreated to the safety of their den.

"I'm going to check on Damien," Howie yelled. "Keep that gun handy in case those bears come back."

Adam nodded, but felt too weak even to hold the gun. He handed it to Squirrel. "If I pass out, you're going to have to use that. Okay?"

"Sure thing."

"Where's Charlotte?"

"She's still out cold." The woman fainted when Squirrel came running at her.

"Just keep an eye on her, will you?"

"You've got it," Squirrel said, shivering in the cool night air. He and Adam watched as Howie crawled over to Damien.

"Is he still alive?" Squirrel yelled.

"He's breathing, but his face is half torn off."

Chapter 90

"How's the arm doing?" Adam asked as he gently lowered himself into one of the leather chairs across from Howie's desk.

"It's itching," Howie complained.

"That means it's healing."

"Good, because it's driving me nuts." The cast on Howie's arm had been on two weeks now. The doctor informed him that morning that the cast could be on for another couple of weeks, if not longer. In addition to a broken arm, his right leg had been badly bruised; even though it was healing, his mobility had been severely curtailed. Going up and down the stairs to and from his apartment continued to be a challenge. Driving was out of the question. If it hadn't been for Squirrel, he wouldn't have been able to go anyplace. Squirrel's driving, however, left something to be desired. Besides his erratic behind-the-wheel behavior, he was constantly chattering and seldom paid attention to traffic lights. After going through yet another red light, Howie had visions of his whole body being put in a cast; the odds of being involved in an accident increased every time he got in the car with Squirrel.

"Doc, you've got to write me a note saying it's okay for me to drive," Howie had pleaded that morning.

"I can't do that. You've just got to be patient," the doctor said. "You're lucky that you only broke your arm out of that fall and not your leg also. What did you land on, anyway?"

"I'm not sure, but I think it could have been the other guy."

The doctor was even more amazed that Damien not only survived the fall, but also even managed to get up and walk. "That other fellow must have been in remarkable physical shape. What were his injuries?"

"He had compound fractures on both his left arm and leg, and suffered a severe concussion," Howie replied, not saying anything about what the bear had done to Damien's face.

After Howie finished at the doctor's office, he had Squirrel drive him back to his office. Now, several hours later, he and Adam waited in the office for Mick to join them. "How are you doing?" he asked Adam.

"Okay. I'll have scars on both my chest and leg, but other than that, the doctor says that the healing is going well." Adam had been released from the hospital last week. The doctor had told him that he was fortunate that the stab wounds didn't sever any arteries. "How about you? What did the doctor tell you this morning?"

"That I'm progressing, but that I might have some problems with arthritis when I get older."

Adam offered Howie a knowing smile. "Talk about getting older, I feel like I've aged twenty years with this case."

"I know what you mean." Howie took a sip of his bourbon-laced coffee, rationalizing that the bourbon helped the pain. "I guess we were lucky."

"Not as lucky as Damien. Is he still in the hospital?"

"He's out, but he has to go back for checkups." JD had told Howie that Damien would have a pretty ugly scar running from his right eye to the lower part of his jaw, and possibly could lose the sight of his right eye. Howie had no sympathy for Damien, secretly wishing that the bears had finished the guy off.

"How long is he going to prison for?" Adam asked

"Hopefully ten to fifteen years, depending upon how slick his lawyer is."

"That guy should be locked up for good."

"I know." Howie took another sip of coffee. "At least he's going to be off the street for a while."

"How about Charlotte?"

"She's not going to do any jail time at all."

"Why not?"

"Because there's just not enough evidence against her."

The downstairs entrance door slammed and the wooden stairs creaked with someone running up them. Very shortly, the office door flew open and Squirrel bounced in.

"Hi, guys." Squirrel stopped at the movie poster, straightened it, gave a nod to Bogart, and waltzed over and plopped down in the chair next to Adam.

"Did Newt ever show up?" Howie asked.

"No, but I don't care."

"What do you mean? Doesn't he have all your money?"

"It doesn't matter. I've turned over a new leaf." The little guy stuck out his chest. "You're looking at a new Squirrel. I've decided to make a change in my life and make an honest living."

"That's very commendable," Adam said, having told Howie how thankful he was for what Squirrel had done for them at Como Park. "Have you thought about what you want to do?"

"Yeah." Squirrel's eyes lit up as he rubbed his hands together like he was ready for action. "I want to become a detective just like you guys." His nose began twitching. "What do you think?"

Before Howie could reply, the phone rang. "MAC Detective Agency," he answered, still amused at Squirrel's announcement. "Oh, hi, JD. How are— what?" JD's words hit him like a bolt of lightning. "How in hell did that

286

happened?" he shouted. The muscles in his stomach twisted into knots. "Damn!" he cried and then slammed the phone on the receiver.

"What's wrong?" Adam asked.

"Damien's escaped."

"What? How?"

"JD doesn't know the details. It happened at the hospital this morning." Howie felt the pressure mounting in his temples. "Damn it!" he cried as he slammed his fist on the desk. The pounding in his head increased. He looked toward the window, stared at the outside world for several seconds, and leaned back in his chair and shut his eyes. He needed a drink.

Charles Tindell's writing career began one hot July day in 1995 while sitting in a canoe in the Boundary Waters Canoe Area in northern Minnesota. His first book *Seeing Beyond the Wrinkles* is the recipient of the National Mature Media's coveted GOLD AWARD designating it among "The Best in Educational Material for Older Adults." His second book *The Enduring Human Spirit* is the recipient of the National Mature Media's Silver Award, symbolizing that the work is among the best of the best.

He and his wife, Carol, have three sons, four grandchildren, and two cats. Oil painting, ventriloquism, baking bread, canoeing, jigsaw puzzles, collecting hour glasses, and writing are among his interests. He serves as a volunteer police chaplain for his community. He also has had the privilege of speaking around the country on the subjects *Spirituality and Aging* as well as *The Courage to Be.*

This Angel's Halo is Crooked is his third mystery in the MAC Detective Agency Mysteries featuring Howie Cummins and his partners, Adam Trexler and Mick Brunner. His first two mysteries are *This Angel Has No Wings* and *This Angel Doesn't Like Chocolate.* He is currently working on his fourth mystery in the series, *This Angel isn't Funny.*

4615512

Made in the USA
Charleston, SC
19 February 2010